Something to Talk About

Also by Dakota Cassidy

Talk Dirty to Me

Look for Dakota Cassidy's next novel
Talking After Midnight
available soon from Harlequin MIRA

Dakota Cassidy

Something to Talk About

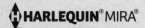

ISBN-13: 978-0-7783-1627-5

SOMETHING TO TALK ABOUT

For questions and comments about the quality of this book, please contact us at CustomerService@Harlequin.com.

Printed in U.S.A.

™ www.Harlequin.com

To my amazing sister-in-law, Laura.
Without the peace and quiet of your beautiful
mountaintop, and the bedroom that overlooks it, this
book would have never been done.
Thank you, thank you for the respite,
the peace of mind while we house-hunted.

For my BFF, Renee George,
honestly, is there anyone else
who could talk me down in the middle of
shipping my son off to college, downsizing
my house, writing five books in a year, and moving
across country, like you can? Methinks not. :)
You're an amazing friend, and I treasure you so.

And my youngest son, Cameron,
my well-adjusted, funny, super smart,
way more mature than I'll ever be college kid.
I miss you, son. I miss your chubby cheeks as an
infant. Your haughty glare of disdain as a tween.
Your grunts hello as a young adult. Your amazing
conversations just before you left for college
to take the world on. You are, and will always be,
one of the brightest moments of my life.
To say I'm simply proud of you will never, ever be enough.

One

"Hellooo," Emmaline Amos growled comically slow into her cell phone. "This is Mistress Taboo. Are you worrrthy?" The infamous line her best friend Dixie Davis had perfected during her three-month stint as a phone-sex operator bounced off the walls in the offices of Call Girls Inc., sounding ridiculous coming from her lips.

As a follow-up, Em looked in her best friend Dixie's direction, and attempted to mimic her famous sultry gaze. Or what their group of mutual friends had all officially dubbed the "Dixie Smolder."

The smolder was a combination pack—one part come-hither glance, one part dreamy half wink of her eyes. When Dixie did it, all the men fell at her feet in a big pile of redneck limbs and puddles of drool.

When Em tried it on for size like she had tonight during girls' night out—it was as though she'd invented the unsexy.

From behind her reception desk, Nella Carter, Call

Girls' new operator in charge of assigning calls, began to giggle until she had to hold her stomach and cover her mouth.

When she caught her breath, she pointed at Dixie. "You," she snorted, "were Mistress Taboo, boss? I still get calls for her. Seriously, *you?*"

Dixie rolled her eyes at the mention of her former phone-sex operator nom de plume. "Em's had too much wine. I absolutely never, ever sounded or looked like that," she protested, sipping her glass of wine with a giggle, knowing full well she had.

Em reached for the bottle of wine between them on Nella's desk and nodded her head, the giddy buzz in her brain making her mouth work overtime. "You did, too. You sounded just like that, all sexified and naughty."

"Then we can all thank heaven Mistress Taboo is officially retired from phone-sex operatin' and instead became the owner of Call Girls, 'cuz that was plain painful to my ears." Dixie mocked a shudder.

Em poured herself another glass of wine, the fluid sloshing in time with her liquid-filled stomach. "Do not deny the win that encompasses Mistress Taboo, Dixie Davis. Just look what that very naughty name, and winning this crazy phone-sex contest Landon thought up for you and Caine, got you."

Nella adjusted her headset, her hazel eyes wide with surprise. "You won Call Girls? In a contest?"

Em slapped her hand on the desk. "You bet she did. Not only did she win a multimillion-dollar phone-sex company, but she won a house the size of Atlanta, with that camel you pass by every day in the backyard, no less. She got Sanjeev, the personal assistant from heaven above. The whole shebang, lock, stock and flyswatters posing as floggers. To boot, she also found her way back to the arms of your other boss, Caine Donovan, a man so divine, angels weep with longin' for him." She waved a wobbly hand around the lush guesthouse office where Call Girls was headquartered and grinned. "And she talked me into running it all as general manager. This wasn't just a win, it was an epic win."

Dixie grinned. "Who better to keep us all in line when Cat and Flynn ran off and got married and are now preparin' for their first child than you, Em? If you could keep me and Caine on the righteous path, you could keep Satan himself honest."

Nella gave her lush surroundings a fresh eye. "So Call Girls Inc. belonged to Landon Wells, right? The one everybody's either callin' richer than God or crazier than a bedbug?"

"Uh-huh. Rest his soul. And now it belongs to Dixie here." Even two months later, Em still hadn't quite digested the situation.

Nella frowned. "I don't get it. How do you win a phone-sex company?"

"You have the most amazing best friend ever, who even on his deathbed, knew what was good for you. Landon was both Dixie's and Caine's best friend. Dixie and Caine were engaged ten years ago, but they had a fallin'-out to beat the likes of World War Three, broke up and left town."

Dixie shook her head of red curls with a giggle.

"Your general manager exaggerates. It was not like World War Three."

But Em disagreed. "Hah! Lest you forget the fire and rain… Anyway, Landon, in all his wisdom and hilarious sense of humor, knew they belonged together. So when Dixie and Caine came back for his funeral, he left this very company to them in his will—with one stipulation. They had to become phone-sex operators and work the phones. Whoever collected the most calls at the end of two months won the company."

Nella suddenly grinned. "So that's what all the talk about the Phone-sex Hunger Games is? I hear the rumblin's in town all the time about you and Caine and how you two got back together. I ignored the bad and focused on how romantic it was under such a crazy set of circumstances."

Yeah. Em sighed and nodded at Nella. "The most romantic set of circumstances ever. Friends like Landon don't come along often. He loved these two so much, he meddled from the afterlife."

Dixie's smile was misty-eyed and blissful at the same time. "I'll always wish Landon was here to see it—see us finally together. Maybe walk me down that aisle now that Caine's proposed. And see you and I such good friends after a long spell of resentment." She patted Em's hand, tipping the glass she held upright to keep more liquid from sloshing out.

"Oh, I heard all about you and Em from that Essie Guthrie. My, she can talk," Nella confided.

Em waved a finger. "Never you mind what that Essie

tells you. She'd just as soon Call Girls was banished from Plum Orchard for good."

The Mags, Plum Orchard's generations-old society of women of prominence, had really given running Call Girls out on a rail their best efforts. They'd made all sorts of pleas to the mayor and the county—even the state of Georgia, and in the process, they'd attempted to make everyone's life associated with Call Girls miserable.

Landon had done his homework when he'd moved the company here, and so far they'd been lucky, but Em still worried those bunch of gossipmongers might come up with a way to shut them down.

Dixie wrinkled her nose. "Just you forget about those awful Mags, Em, and let's focus on the good stuff. Like how I also got LaDawn, Marybell and Cat as the best employees and friends a girl could ask for. For that, I'll always be grateful. So a toast to Landon?" She raised her wineglass toward the ceiling in silent salute to her best friend.

"Hear! Hear!" Em cheered. Though her sigh, hot on the heels of her good spirits, was forlorn and wistful.

Nella leaned forward on her desk, folding her hands. "If you don't mind me askin', how did you become involved in all this, Em?"

"I don't mind at all. I worked for Landon's lawyer, Hank Cotton, at the time. So I spent his last days with him, doing all sorts of things he needed taken care of, and that's when he asked me to oversee Dixie and Caine if they decided to stick around and accept the terms of his will. He said it was time Dixie made an ally here in Plum Orchard. I thought it was the throes of death talkin', knowin' how Dixie and I didn't get along in school, but how could I say no to a man I'd come to love and respect in the course of our dealin's? He was dyin'. I'd rather have died myself than say no to him."

Dixie rubbed Em's arm. "But he left her a letter to open once things settled down with Caine and I to explain everything, didn't he, Em?"

Now Em's smile was wistful. "He did, and once I read it, it all made sense. But to think, he'd appoint prim and proper Emmaline Amos, once Dixie Davis's biggest target in high school, the mediator of her phone-sex contest… Well, everybody thought it was just crazy. They still talk about it now, almost three months later."

They talked because she was the most unlikely suspect. Who'd believe good-girl Em knew much of anything about sex?

They talked plenty about how scandalous it was that an actual phone-sex company was housed in the middle of their quaint little town, and how horrible Dixie was for talking dirty.

They talked. That's what Plum Orchard did, and though Em loved her small town and almost everyone in it, faults and all, they'd forgotten the core of what Landon had intended with all those machinations.

The purpose, the driving force behind Landon making Dixie and Caine play his game—the reason he'd gone to such great lengths to see his two best friends happy, had been lost in the mire of gossip Dixie's return had created.

Love. Landon's love for his friends, their love for

each other—one that even after almost a decade, hadn't died.

The kind of love Em found herself feeling a pang of yearning for as of late. One that lasted—one that filled her soul. One that didn't want to divorce her because he wanted to cross-dress and become Miss Trixie LeMieux and he'd been too ashamed to tell her...

She cupped her chin in her hands and sighed again, listening with fondness to the music of the chirping phones from the back offices, where the on-duty operators took their calls from clients. They'd hired four more operators since she'd taken over as GM. Business was good, even if her jump back into the dating pool wasn't.

She was certain she wasn't destined for the kind of love Dixie and Caine had fought so hard for. You only bore witness to something like that once in a lifetime, and if what Clifton said about her was true, she was too conservative and prissy to ever find that kind of passion.

But she had her new job here. She didn't care what the people of Plum Orchard said about it, either. Working for Call Girls made her happy—gave her purpose. "Look how far we've come, huh?"

Dixie grinned, twisting a long strand of her red hair around her index finger in dreamy satisfaction and sighed. "I can't even believe what's come to pass in the past few months since I've been back from Chicago, Nella. For both of us. Did you know, not four months ago, Em was in the middle of divorcin' that cheater Clifton, I was up to my britches in debt, Caine and I were at each other's throats trying to beat each other at phone sexin', and everyone here in good ole Plum Orchard,

Georgia, still hated me because of my mean-girl high school days—Caine included. So much has changed," she marveled.

Em's smile was wry. It was true. But Dixie still wasn't very popular. She'd tried hard to put to rest her wrongful ways since she'd returned, but some just couldn't let go of the past. She popped her lips with a smack of a reminder. "Well, not everything's changed."

Dixie flapped a dismissive hand at the implication Em made in reference to her archnemesis. "Thank you for reminding me Louella Palmer still sniffs the air when I walk by as though I've been dipped in cow dung."

No one wished Dixie more ill than Louella. Dixie's old high school rival still held her responsible for allegedly stealing Caine Donovan out from under her nose.

For the past few months since she'd become such close friends with Dixie, Louella and her fellow group members, the esteemed Magnolias, had outright shunned Em for forgiving Dixie and her jaded Plum Orchard past.

A burp threatened to escape Em's lips. She swallowed the acidic bite back with a wince before saying, "I just want you to know your enemies. I can't have Louella sneakin' up behind you when you're not lookin'. Remindin' you of the people that wish you ill is my duty as your person."

Dixie cocked her head, her pretty blue eyes playful. "This person thinks your person's had too much to drink tonight. I know your theory is Jesus drank wine, and that's supposed to make it okay to indulge—and usually, I'd roll with it. But *He* didn't go out on girls' night with you tonight—and I'm pretty sure *He* never had a hangover. So, it's my duty as *your* person to tell you, you might suffer one come mornin'."

But Em wouldn't hear of hangovers and Jesus. She'd spent two minutes too long thinking about disapproval and Plum Orchard when there were other things to attend. Like learning to smolder—it was what brought all the boys to your yard, or so she'd heard.

She focused on watching her reflection in her phone as she tried once more to perfect this thing Dixie did with her eyes while men lined up for her.

It would be nice to have just one man stand in a grocery line, even if it was just next to her. Like the man she'd shared the longest, most breathtaking stare with in the square the night her life had almost fallen apart. The night when she'd accused Dixie of something so deplorable, she still couldn't breathe from the horror.

She'd overheard the man's name was Jax, but in her mind, when she daydreamed about him, he didn't have a name. To use his name was too intimate—too personal. Attaching his name to her fantasies was akin to writing him personalized love letters. Once you knew a person's first name, next you were inquiring about their well-being, and that always led to personal details you were better off not knowing. Fantasies didn't have morning breath or scratch their unmentionables.

So the man on that night in the square was simply *him*.

And she hadn't seen him in well over two months.

Em "smoldered" again at Dixie, putting her back into

it and rolling her shoulders, pretending she was seducing *him*. "How's this?"

Dixie patted Em's hand, wrinkling her nose. "When you smolder at me, do it like you're thinkin' about doin' the do, not like you're squinting because the sun's in your eyes, honey. More Marilyn Monroe, less like you have bug guts in your eye," she teased lovingly, pulling Em to her office and waving back at Nella to carry on with her calls.

Em gave her a pouty expression, plunking her phone down on Dixie's desk with a sigh. "I guess you'll just have to stay the Smolder Queen, Dixie. I try and try. Practiced all week for girls' night tonight, but I just can't seem to look anything other than a darn fool. Just ask that poor man at the bar who thought I used those drops you get at the ophthalmologist to dilate my eyes." She batted her eyelashes for effect, only to have them stick together from the extra mascara she'd applied.

She was officially a girls' night out failure. Maybe everyone saw what Clifton saw, and trying to change that perception of her was a waste of time.

Dixie brushed Em's hair from her face with a chuckle of sympathy, her slender fingers gentle, her blue eyes warm. "If there's one thing I've learned in the business of smoldering, it's all about the subtle at first. Stop trying so hard to be someone you're not. You're beautiful and funny and sweet all on your own. You don't need the smolder or anything other than just *you* to do the talkin'. Turn down the volume on the sexy, Em."

"Way down," LaDawn Jenkins, fellow employee, friend and the best fetish-related phone-sex operator

Call Girls had, advised, strolling inside from the guest-house pool area.

Marybell Lymen, another operator and friend, followed behind, handing an open bottle of wine to LaDawn, who slugged back the liquid straight from the bottle.

Catherine Butler-McGrady, now retired after handing her Call Girls GM position over to Em, nodded her agreement, letting Marybell help her perch awkwardly on the end of a purple velvet chaise.

She rubbed her small swollen belly with a content smile. "You're plenty sexy without the smolder, Em. Flynn said so just the other day. He said, 'The longer that sad sack Clifton's gone, the prettier Em seems to get.'"

Em snorted. "He did not." She was not.

"Did, too," both LaDawn and Marybell said, dropping into the chairs on the other side of Dixie's large, white oak desk.

"And it's true," LaDawn confirmed. "You're much less stuffy since divorcin' Mr. Shady, honey."

She wrinkled her nose at her friends. "Flynn doesn't count. He's my cousin, for gravy's sake, and I might not be as stuffy, but I'm definitely not any sexier."

Marybell and LaDawn oozed sexy, and they certainly weren't afraid of the opposite sex. If she could just have an ounce of whatever it was they had that made talking to anyone other than old and deaf Coon Rider easier...

Cat waved a hand and scoffed. "You are, too. You're sweet-sexy. Makes all the boys want to know what's goin' on under all that prim and proper. Peel away your layers and such."

Em threw her hands up, frustrated with the lack of interest she stirred in the male population. "You make me sound like an onion. And where were all those boys who like onions at, I ask you? I can tell you this, they sure weren't out tonight."

Cat sighed. "Oh, honey, they just weren't the right men. Nobody said dippin' your toes back into the dating pool would be easy."

LaDawn bobbed her head. "Peelin' onions isn't for the faint of heart, Miss Em. When the right one comes along, he'll peel you raw."

Em's cheeks went hot. "Why is it so easy for you to say things like that and when I try, I sound like a bad actress in one of those dirty movies?"

Marybell threw her head back and laughed. "Because, silly, we do this for a living. We're paid to entice men. We know all the tricks of the trade."

She eyed the women who'd become some of her closest friends these past few months. "So teach me." There. She'd said it. Maybe if she took a few lessons in flirting from the experts, she wouldn't look like such a darn fool come next girls' night.

Dixie's eyes went wide with surprise. "You mean like teach you to talk dirty to men?"

Em smiled and nodded. Since she'd left her job as Hank Cotton's legal secretary after Dixie offered to make her general manager of Call Girls, she'd spent a lot of time listening to LaDawn, Marybell and the other operators talk about all manner of "making the business" as Dixie called it—and she was sometimes horrified.

But most times, especially lately, she was intrigued by the things men wanted the operators to talk about.

Each day, while she monitored call stats and reports and kept the office running smoothly, she overheard conversations that made her blush the color of her mother's red velvet cake. Yet, they also left her insatiably curious.

Maybe it had to do with what Dixie had called her molting process. She was shedding her old married life skin for a new single one, and hearing all the sex talk all day long left her secretly wanting to explore some of those things.

It was an about-face almost no one would understand. Maybe not even Dixie. Em was everyone's good girl, well mannered, almost decorous to a fault—and dull as dirt. No one would believe the thoughts Emmaline Amos was having as of late.

She found her dull was slowly chipping away to reveal a shinier Em. Though she definitely didn't feel very shiny after her failures tonight. Not even with the added shine of her semisexy new dress and the jellylike cutlets she'd stuffed in her bra to see if having larger breasts would keep her from repelling men like mosquito spray.

So Em nodded her head again—more sure than ever her alcohol-dipped brain was sending her a subliminal message that she was on the right track. "You heard me. I want to talk dirty. Bring it on."

Her friends frowned at her as though she'd just told

them she wanted to have relations out in the middle of the square on the steps of the gazebo.

Em dunked her fingers into the top of her lower-than-usual cut dress and pulled out one of the offensive gel breasts, slapping it on the desk with disgust at their wide-eyed surprise. "Stop lookin' like I just confessed to a murder. Why does everyone think I'm such a priss?"

LaDawn scooped up the gel breast and shook it like a raw chicken breast, making it jiggle. "Because you are?"

With alcohol came fearlessness. "I am not. I quote the Lord, yes. But that's only because Jesus analogies are all I have to make comparisons to real life. My mama was a true Southern Baptist, and it just so happens Bible verses are what stuck. So while I might be conservative on the outside, I don't buy into it all the way you think I do. I like sex. I like it *a lot*."

LaDawn reached out and patted her hand, her tone a little condescending, a little amused. "Good for you, honey. You still shouldn't be playin' with the big girls."

"Em, talking dirty to some stranger on the phone isn't like practicing to flirt with a man in real life," Dixie reminded her. "I'm not sure how you're connecting the dots here."

"She connected them with wine." LaDawn barked a laugh at her own joke.

Which only infuriated Em further. She raised a finger and swished it around. "Let me tell you a thing or two, Miss LaDawn, I could do it! I hear you naughty Nancys take calls all day long—I've learned some things from you.... I'm not sayin' I want to talk to the

men LaDawn considers herself 'companionators' to—
that might be rushin' things, what with the latex and
flogging, but maybe something tamer. Who knows,
maybe it'll help me get better at talkin' up the opposite
sex—free me from the chains that bind or something."

Or something. Anything to loosen her up and help
her forget there were days when she felt like she was
nothing but a stale loaf of day-old bread. There were
days when Clifton's words, even after almost a year,
still stung. *"How was I supposed to know, someone like
you, conservative and nigh on prissy, would entertain
the idea I liked to wear women's clothes?"*

Conservative and prissy.

She wanted to be a new Em. Open to owning her
sexuality and leaving the buttoned-up perception of
her behind.

Marybell snickered, swirling her glass of Pinot.
"Very dramatic, Em, this freein' of your sexuality. Next
you'll want to read the *Kama Sutra* cover to cover and
pose nude for *Playboy*." Marybell chuckled. "Taking
calls isn't like flirting in real life. We openly have sex
using our words—we don't just suggest it. Don't con-
fuse the two, pretty lady."

"Girl, you are somethin' else when you an' libation join hands in holy alcohol, ain't you?" LaDawn
squawked, slapping her hand on her thigh. "Two glasses
of Chardonnay and all of a sudden you're Em the Emas-
culator."

Em felt the office chair she was sitting in wobble. Or
was she wobbling? She couldn't be sure. She giggled on

a hiccup, one that jolted her so hard, she fell into Dixie, who stroked her hair with a soothing palm.

She took a deep breath and waved a finger at LaDawn's lithe form in a "fooled you, didn't I?" fashion. "It wasn't Chardonnay, FYI. I had four drinks at the bar. The ones with the orange swirly stuff and the pretty umbrellas in them. *Four*." Take that, conservatism.

"Four?" LaDawn and Marybell chirped their surprise in unison.

"Okay, who was on Em duty while I was off two-steppin', *LaDawn?*" Marybell asked, casting a glance of aspersion LaDawn's way.

LaDawn popped her heavily lined lips, brushing her platinum hair off her shoulder with a scoff. "Oh, no. I told you I was gonna take second shift. That means before 11:00 p.m. you were babysitting."

Marybell shook her head, the pointy spikes of her red-and-green Mohawk beginning to sag after a long girls' night out. "Nope. Dixie was supposed to take eight to ten. I was ten till 12:00 a.m. We let Cat take the night off, seeing as she can't keep her eyes open for more than twenty minutes at a time."

Cat, now sprawled across the chaise, snored to prove their point.

All eyes went to Dixie, who shot them a sheepish grin, full of dimples and sunshine.

LaDawn grabbed the bottle of Chardonnay and poured her and Dixie another glass to share while Marybell dug a blanket out to cover Cat, tucking the edges under her chin. "You were textin' with that confounded dreamboat of yours again, weren't you? It's not girls' night if you're textin' with your man, Dixie. Then it's girls' night and *Caine,*" she admonished with a stern tone, but a smile she couldn't hide crept across her lips.

Dixie wrinkled her nose. "But he's so cute when he texts me," she defended her schoolgirl behavior.

"If you can't spend twenty minutes without contact with one Mr. Caine Donovan, you can't be a girl out on a girls' night. Then you're just pathetic and maybe should be textin' someone about obsession therapy," LaDawn teased, poking Dixie's arm with a glittery, purple nail. "So I'm callin' it now, next time we all give up our cell phones at the beginning of the night so we don't lose track of Em and her newfound love of spirits. Because look what happens when we do that. Four drinks and she gets to thinkin' she should be learnin' the tricks of the trade instead of just running the place." She leaned forward and ruffled Em's mussed hair with a chuckle.

Em stuck her tongue out at LaDawn.

LaDawn popped her lips at Dixie, ignoring Em. "While you're off moonin' over that man, it doesn't mean Em doesn't need lookin' out for. She's new to the single scene. Especially in a place called Cooters where every horn dog from here to Johnsonville goes to ladies' night 'cuz the drafts are only a dollar. If someone doesn't watch her, they'll eat our innocent Em alive. You dropped the ball, Dixie Davis. Next time, you have to pull your shift and take my shift, too."

Em gave her friends a sour face, tucking her hair behind her ears. "I'm plenty of adult sittin' right here, I'll have you know. I don't need a babysitter, and I'm not so innocent. And if I want to have four drinks, I will. Maybe I'll have five," she said defiantly.

She deserved five. It had been a long two months since the finalization of her divorce. Seven total if you counted the time since she'd found out Clifton was an infidel who wanted to wear women's clothing and live in Atlanta as Trixie LeMieux.

Most of the pain of that discovery had passed. That Clifton hadn't even given her the chance to understand that part of him still stung. She'd always prided herself on being open to new things, despite the fact that she was born and raised in a town stuck somewhere in the 1950s.

Cross-dressing hadn't ever entered her mind when she'd been thinking about what the word *open* meant, but who's to say she wouldn't have adjusted? Clifton just never gave her the chance to say one way or the other. He'd just left.

And now, here she was, single at thirty-six with an eight-year-old and a five-year-old to raise with little help from her ex-husband. His embarrassment after an incident in town, where his secret was publicly and cruelly revealed by none other than Louella Palmer, had kept him from coming to see the boys as often as they needed seeing by their daddy.

Dixie stretched her arms upward with a yawn of her perfectly glossed, pink lips. "Fine. Next girls' night out, I'll take two shifts. Now, what do you say we get you home, Em?"

Em shook her off, reaching for more wine. She could drink as much wine as she liked, her internal rebel coaxed. "Stop appeasin' me, Dixie. I'm a grown woman, and I don't want to go home to my lonely, empty house right now. Gareth and Clifton Junior are spendin' the weekend at Mama's, so I'm a free bird. Just like Lynyrd Skynyrd says."

Dixie gave her a pointed look—one you'd give a willful preschooler. "You know what they say about idle hands and the devil."

"As Satan's closest confidante, I'm sure you've heard all the gossip," Em shot back, squeezing her friend's arm with a giggle.

When they'd been forced into the race for the phone-sex contest Landon set forth with Em as mediator, leaving them in each other's company more often than not, she'd used Dixie's former cruelties full force as a way to continually poke her with what she now lovingly referred to as a "gentle Em reminder." Nowadays, since they'd become so close, she did it with love, but she still did it.

"I thought we were past my mean girl and well into forgiveness. Will you ever run out of nails for my coffin?" Dixie inquired with gooey sweetness.

"Lucky Judson's Hardware store has aisles' and aisles' worth. How's never suit you?" Em shot back with a lopsided grin.

LaDawn burst out laughing, the sound rich and deep. She flicked a purple-painted nail at Em. "Phew! You are all 'bout your sass these days, aren't you, Miss Emmaline? Every time I turn around you're assertin' yourself in one way or another. You're all breathin' fire at us at the drop of a hat lately."

Marybell nodded, reaching into a bag of Cheetos Dixie had produced from her deep desk drawer. "Oh, yes, ma'am, she is. If you look at her cross-eyed, flames come right out of her cute little mouth," she said on a giggle, tweaking Em's lower lip.

It was true. She'd become a little testy in this quest to show anyone within earshot she was no longer Emmaline Without A Spine. Some would even say she'd gone overboard. Nonetheless, she protested. "Bah! They do not."

Dixie popped a Cheeto in her mouth, licking her fingers. "Do so. If I simply say the word *no,* even if it's when you're askin' me if I'd like another glass of sweet tea, you jump right down my throat. You're always barking orders at us like we wouldn't listen to you if you didn't holler them with that stern teacher voice you've adopted. Reminds me of old Mrs. Beauchamp. Remember her from third grade?"

Marybell nodded her agreement, her eyes, heavy with dark makeup, playful. "Next thing you know, she'll show up with a ruler and crack our hands to get her point across."

Em rolled her eyes at them. Admittedly, as of late, she had a case of the "I will be heard" syndrome. The one where everything she said had to be full throttle or she was convinced she wouldn't be taken seriously. It would just take some time to find her balance. Toning her stern teacher's voice down would probably be a good place to start.

"Uh-huh," LaDawn confirmed, patting Marybell on the back. "You know what, I take back my protestin' from earlier. Some days, the way you've been orderin' us all around, maybe we should just let you take all the calls and we'll all go shop for shoes, seein' as you seem to know how to do it better."

That sudden need to prove herself, the one she'd just reminded herself was on the warpath, the one that was completely unwarranted and absolutely unnecessary, reared its badly mannered head—again. "I bet I could answer your calls—all of 'em." She rolled her neck in the "wanna go 'round?" way LaDawn did. "I know all the dirty words because I hear Miss LaDawn here say them like she's recitin' her prayers before bedtime, all day long."

Em's defensive answer sparked the competitive streak in LaDawn. She sat upright and pointed to the wine bottle. "You just stop talkin' crazy from over there and have another glass of wine. You would faint dead if you had to pretend to spank some man with my special spatula and scream, 'You dirty, dirty boy!' You know it, and so does everyone else sittin' here."

Dixie held up a hand, leaning forward and putting it between the two women with a look of admonishment. "Girls, how quickly we forget I've banned all forms of competition. Em, you stop riling the caged beast, and both of you play nicely with each other."

"You only banned them because you can't resist them, Dixie," Em taunted, knowing full well she was again poking her friend for her former habit of turning everything from pie eating to merely breathing into a death match.

Dixie narrowed her eyes in Em's direction, her husky voice raspy when she said, "You're baiting me, Em."

Em nodded, throwing her a smug smile, though it was full of love. "If I had a worm, I'd dangle it in your face."

"I still say you couldn't do it," LaDawn coaxed with a sly grin, twisting her hair and tying it up with a rubber band she always kept around her slender wrist. "You couldn't even answer one phone call and say the *P* word without callin' out forgiveness from on high. We'll all be home and in our beds in no time flat before you get 'round to it. I'd bet next week's girls' night drinks on it."

Dixie held up a finger, her eyes flashing warning signals at LaDawn. "In Em's condition, she'll end up meeting some crazy killer for chicken and waffles at Madge's. Stop goading her, LaDawn."

"Oh, really?" Em challenged, using her hands to push off the desk's top and stick her face in LaDawn's. She balanced herself on her waist, teetering. "You're on, Latex Lady!"

Dropping back to her chair, she picked up the phone on Dixie's desk and rang Nella.

"Nella? It's Emmaline. Next caller who doesn't know his foot from the *P* word, send them to me on Dixie's line, please." She hung up the phone with a triumphant drop of the receiver, almost hearing poor Nella's jaw drop all the way from the other end of the guesthouse.

"Right here, right now, I'm callin' it. This is a mistake, Em. You've had a little too much to drink, and tomorrow, you'll regret it," Marybell said with confidence, fighting a grin. LaDawn cackled, crossing her arms. "So what's your name for the naughty gonna be, Em? I think Not Gonna Happen's already been taken."

Dixie and Marybell erupted in a fit of laughter, followed shortly thereafter by LaDawn.

Oh, they could laugh all they wanted. She'd thought about it long and hard. All while LaDawn ordered her clients around in dominatrix fashion and during request after youthful voice request for Marybell. She'd even thought about it tonight at Cooters, and she didn't have to think too hard. At least not with four swirly drinks in her stomach and her sense of reason fully affected.

She narrowed her gaze at every one of her friends, sputtering and snorting at the very idea Emmaline Amos could say the *P* word. Maybe she might even use the—gasp—*C* word. "Well, won't you all be sorry when that phone rings and I answer to the tune of Em 'n' M?"

"Like the rapper or the candy?" Dixie squeaked out between gasps of air tucked between bursts of laughter. She covered her mouth with her hand to keep from disturbing the operators in the back rooms.

She eyed Dixie with a defiant glare, surely fueled by her alcohol consumption. "It might not be as mysterious or sexy as Mistress Taboo or as sticky sweet as Candy Caine was, your Mr. Smexy's old operator name, but it's cute, just like me." Cute and adorable and like someone's worn stuffed animal. Ugh.

LaDawn was the first to buckle. She hopped up from her chair, coming around the desk to give Em a tight squeeze from behind, her lilting voice clear in Em's ear, the sweet scent of her lavender body spray in her nose.

"We were just teasin' you, Em. We know you're a force to be reckoned with, and we wouldn't have ya any other way. So no phone calls for you. You're just not made outta the same cloth as the rest of us dirty girls. You're fine silk and we're just a polyester blend."

The jarring ring of Dixie's office phone created a shrill silence between them—reaction suspended for a mere second before all three women were scrambling to grab the phone to keep it from Em. Chairs scraped against the tile floor, desk organizers fell to the floor with pen-filled thuds.

But Em was quicker, and when all was said and done, and she was high on regret for ever taking LaDawn's bait, she'd pat herself on the back for just how quick she'd been on the draw being as tipsy as she was.

She snatched at it, holding the receiver up like she'd just won the coveted Swarovski tiara at their local Miss Cherokee Rose Pageant. Triumph streaked her eyes before she growled, "This is Em 'n' M. Would you like some candy?" Her eyes opened wide at her brilliance. Associating her name with the pleasure of the famous candy. Hah! Innocent Em couldn't make the dirty, huh? She'd show them.

"You have candy? My daddy loves candy. Maybe he'd like you, too." A voice so pure, so full of spun sugar and innocence, filled her ear.

Leave it to her to get the one call, out of all the hundreds of calls Call Girls received in a night, from a child.

The universe was obviously conspiring against her and her sexy.

Two

LaDawn pressed the speaker button, the little girl's voice ringing throughout the office as though on angels' wings. "So do you have candy? My daddy needs a girlfriend, and I like candy. My uncle said it would make him nicer, the girlfriend, but maybe not the candy. I tried giving him candy, but that didn't make him nicer." There was a definitive determination to her charming voice—a voice that to Em's experienced ears sounded right around six or seven.

Mercy.

No one moved. Everyone froze in their respective spots as three pairs of eyes, full of panic, watched Em.

How had a child managed to get past Nella-Nator? She was like a SWAT team when it came to manning the phones against children violating Call Girls' strict, over-eighteen policy.

"Hello? Miss Em 'n' M?"

In a flurry of hands, Dixie and Marybell motioned

for her to hang up while LaDawn slid her forefinger across her throat, signaling she should cut the child off.

But Em knew what to do. She had two children of her own, and this one obviously needed to be heard. She cleared her throat, holding up a hand to her friends. "I'm here, and I think you have the wrong number, sugar snap."

A pout she virtually heard pulsed in Em's ear. "You mean you don't have girlfriends there where you are? My daddy needs a girlfriend. At lunch when they were cuttin' up my grilled cheese sandwich in triangles, I heard my uncle Tag say so to my uncle Gage. They said he needs a girlfriend. I asked them where you get a girlfriend and they said the girlfriend store. I see on the paper my daddy has on his desk that you live in a place called Call Girls. Is that a store where we can buy my daddy a girlfriend? Like Toys 'R' Us?"

Em sat down on the chair and smiled into the phone. The child's sweet voice, so heartbreakingly clear with desire for her father's happiness, clenched her heart with a vise grip. The leap she'd made with the words *call girls* wasn't just adorable, it was smart.

"No, sunshine," she said gently. "You can't buy girlfriends here. And you know what? I think your daddy should do the shoppin', don't you? He knows what he likes best. Now, I bet it's about bedtime, right? Long past, if I'm readin' my clock correctly. You need to scoot off to bed now—all the pretty girls need their pretty sleeps. Can you do that for Miss Em?"

There was a sniffle from the other end of the line, and the muffle of possibly her hand, as though she'd cupped the phone to her mouth to keep her voice hushed. "Are you sure you don't have any girlfriends there? I know it would make my daddy happy. He hates to cook. He makes all those grumble noises and sighs when it's suppertime."

Em's heart melted bit by gooey-filled bit at this angelic voice and the genuine request she made, one that in a child's mind, probably should be as simple as shopping for a girlfriend. "I'm sure we don't have girlfriends here, sugarplum. Now, off you go to bed like all good little girls do and sleep the sleep of the sweet—"

"Who the hell is this?" a megamasculine voice hissed into the phone, clearly enraged.

Em straightened her spine, her eyes wide. Oh, mercy, the poor child had been caught. Em was just about to explain that when Angry Man bellowed into her ear again, *"Who the hell are you?"*

Sucking her cheeks in and giving her invisible caller the stern-teacher tone, she responded with crisp coolness, "This is Emmaline Amos, general manager of Call Girls—"

"How dare you allow a little girl of six—she's six, do you hear me—talk to one of your operators?" he growled. "Don't you have some kind of security that prevents this sort of thing from happening? What kind of business are you running there?"

Em's tipsy state flew away on wings of outrage. How dare he accuse Call Girls of lax security? Clearly there'd been some mistake, but the quick decision to shoot him down for being so incredibly rude outweighed the notion he might someday be a future client she needed to reassure.

She clamped a hand on her hip. "Excuse me, sir—we're running a very reputable business with plenty of security, I'll thank you kindly to remember! Your little girl found our phone number on, according to her, *your desk*. So, in the future, when you take it upon yourself to seek solace with a woman who is not your intended or otherwise, I highly recommend you don't leave such things lyin' about in a place an innocent child of *six* can find!" Em slammed down the phone with a huff, infuriated their above-standards security measures had been called into question.

As she fought for breath, so incensed she wanted to hurl every item off Dixie's desk and slam it against the wall, Dixie, Marybell and LaDawn all stood, still rooted to their spots in quiet mode, waiting, watching.

Cat stirred, eliciting a small snore.

Em's lips thinned, her fingers clutching the back of her chair, her knuckles white from the effort. "I will not have our security questioned by some man who can't keep track of his adorable little girl and her penchant for girlfriend shopping. Will not!"

LaDawn was the first to approach her, though it was hesitant. "I'm afraid a' you, sugarlove."

Marybell nodded numbly and raised her hand, her bangle bracelets jingling and sliding into place at the bend in her forearm. "Me…too."

Dixie's mouth was slightly open, her brow creased. "Wow. You were on fire. See what we mean about the fire breathing?"

If there was one thing Em had in her life besides her boys, it was her job. One she took incredibly seriously. "I take great pride in making sure everything runs smoothly here at Call Girls—especially the phones. How dare he outright declare we would have allowed something like that!"

LaDawn came up behind her and massaged her shoulders with nimble hands, breathing a sigh of a giggle. "Okay, Rocky. It's over now, and you set him right. Why don't you grab your chicken breasts? I think it's time we all head on home and get a good night's rest. You fought the good fight. You should take a break between matches."

As her wits gathered, Em couldn't help but replay the sweet voice in her head, wanting a girlfriend for her daddy so he wouldn't be so cranky. There had been a hint of sadness, the wish to make everything better for her father that in a six-year-old's mind meant snuggles and kisses and a girlfriend you bought at the girlfriend store.

The spike of anger she'd rolled with when she'd spoken to that arrogant jackass of a man dissipated in a puff, leaving her with a combination adrenaline/alcohol-related pounder of a headache, and a sad ache in her heart that a sweet little girl wanted her father to have a girlfriend.

This was what she got for thinking she was ever going to be capable of simulating sexual acts with LaDawn's special spatula and a chair.

Oh, libation, what have you done?

* * *

The hard drop of a hammer on metal had Em gritting her teeth and wincing with pain. No more girls' night—not ever. At least not when it factored in swirly orange drinks accompanied by chicken cutlet breasts.

Making her way toward Lucky Judson's Hardware store, she stopped on the curb, unable to properly appreciate the cooler weather with early winter in full swing. Usually, it made her happy to finally be able to wear sweaters and boots. Today, it grated on her hangover and bit at her sinuses, forcing her to tighten the belt around her thigh-length coat to keep the sharp wind from clawing at her silky blouse.

Typically, the square, sitting directly in the center of Plum Orchard, surrounded by the local establishments and quaint row of Victorian houses where the local doctor, lawyer and dentist were housed, made Em smile.

It was always busy and humming with the people she'd grown up with all her life. Today, she'd rather not see any of those people, for surely they'd see her red eyes and sallow skin and label her with a big, fat letter *H* for shamefully hungover.

Her hangover reminded her of that innocent, sweet voice dipped in angels' wings on the phone last night. There was something, something the mother in her had picked up on that told her the little girl had sensed a need in her father—loneliness maybe? Children had an uncanny knack for picking up emotions, leading them to act on their simplistic views of the world just to make the boo-boo better.

Not thirty feet from Lucky's, the scent of freshly

brewed coffee rose, making Em's alcohol-weakened stomach lurch, taking her mind off the little girl momentarily. Or was her stomach lurching at the sight of the Magnolias, lying in wait, all phony smiles as they sat at the new café, hoping to make her their first pounce of the day?

The Magnolias, or Mags as everyone around town called them, were the backbone of all town social events, and what everyone perceived as the cream of Plum Orchard society. The chosen ones with rich families, and what was considered the proper connections.

Em always secretly compared them to henchwomen due to the fact that getting into the Magnolias was as difficult, and probably as bloody, as joining the mob. Unless, of course, you entered by birthright. She'd never been a Magnolia, but Dixie had once been the leader of their pack. They were exclusive, snobbish and plain old mean if anyone dared cross them.

When Dixie had come back to town—a changed woman—she'd crossed the Mags, and they were never going to let Em forget that even though she wasn't allowed access to their exclusive club, she'd betrayed them simply by accepting Dixie.

Squaring her shoulders for the barb they'd certainly shoot at her, Em forced herself to make her feet move past Louella Palmer and her gang of Magnolia-scented thugs, each sipping on fancy coffee with whipped cream and sprinkles.

Louella, beautiful and blonde, pristine in a winter-white cowl neck dress and deep burgundy knit shrug, coupled with knee-high, brown leather boots, wiggled her fingers at Em. "Hi, Em! How's tricks—I mean, Trixie?" Lesta-Sue Arnold and Annabelle Pruitt giggled on cue like all good gang members do when their head gangster tugged on their puppet strings.

If there were ever a day, today would be the one, when slugging Louella Palmer right in her perky nose was highest on her bucket list. Her reference to Em's ex-husband, Clifton, and his cross-dresser name, Trixie, had everyone in town turning around.

Always look your demons square in the eye, Emmaline Amos—then lift your chin and show 'em all your secrets. You get there before they do, there's nothing they can touch if you've already touched it.

Sage advice from Dixie the ex-demon.

Em lifted her chin, securing her dark sunglasses on her nose to fight the effects of the glaring sun and the stares of everyone around them, waiting to see if she would react.

She chanted in her mind, *Be Dixie. Be one with the Dixie.* "Oh, he's right fine, Louella. How's that rhinoplasty you've got scheduled comin' along?" she called back, stopping just feet from the white steel table they'd gathered 'round like it was a cauldron and they were witches, mixing a brew.

She smiled with innocence at the group, eyeing each one of them, then setting her sights on Louella, still recovering from her crack about the bump she currently had on her nose, courtesy of tanglin' with Dixie. "Silly me. How insensitive to make mention of it when it's clear you still haven't even made the appointment."

Em didn't wait to see their faces. Pivoting on her

heel, she breezed off, catching the low cackle of Dixie's future mother-in-law, Jo-Lynne Donovan, from the corner of the café. Jo-Lynne flashed her a quick thumbs-up and a warm smile before returning to her steaming coffee, making Em instantly regret her unkind comment.

Just because Louella Palmer had come precariously close to ruining her life in Plum Orchard, had turned her children into the subject of cruel jokes at school, was no reason for her to take pleasure in cheers from the crowd. That would make her as bad, if not worse, than Louella Palmer.

But she shot a conspiratorial smile back at Jo-Lynne anyway; because today, Louella's gruesome was something she just couldn't cotton on top of her minihangover.

Head down to fight the yellow beast of the sun in the sky, Em went straight for the hardware store's door, stopping just shy of entering when she sensed a presence, a large, warm, almost-imposing presence.

Her eyes flew upward, locking gazes with an intense pair of light brown eyes surrounded by a thick fringe of lashes. The sun glazed them for a moment, turning them a deep, glimmering whiskey.

It was *him*.

Her cheeks went hot.

The *him* she'd spent far too many hours daydreaming about since they'd first made eye contact over two months ago. Him laughing, his perfectly straight white teeth flashing when he smiled at her. Him, gruff and darkly beautiful, his thickly roped arms wrapped around her waist, securing her to his side.

Him when he leaned in low and took her mouth, letting his tongue rasp along hers and kissing her like her lips were the very reason he breathed.

And yes, even him naked, with every corded muscle that made up his smooth planes and rigid lines hovering above her, hard against her belly, her legs tight around his waist as he thrust into...

Her heart stopped pumping, the unquenchable heat in her veins threatening to set her limbs on fire.

His square jaw was almost too square, too hard and unforgiving until it shifted when his lips turned up in a smile of inquiry, leaving Em holding her breath.

Apparently, "him" didn't recognize her. Disappointment flared in the pit of her belly. To be fair, her hair was a little longer now, and she did have dark sunglasses and a hat on.

Somehow, in her daydreams, when they saw each other again, he would've known her if he was blind.

Em's stomach clenched and released then contracted into a tight fist again when he cocked his dark head in the direction of the interior of the hardware store as if to say, "Ladies first." He patiently held the door, his squared fingers covered in Band-Aids, scratches and hangnails.

The cool breeze blew another swift gust, carrying with it his scent, crisp and clean—like Irish Spring and fresh creek water. The way he smelled made perfect sense to Em. A man like him, hard and raw, sinful from head to toe, didn't need expensive cologne as a final touch to his rough perfection.

Em's heart finally struck up the band again, and

began to boom in time with her head. Her fingers clutched the strap of the purse slung over her shoulder. Words, as they always did with a man, especially this man, failed her.

A bump from behind jolted her forward, making her aware she was staring. "Gawking, honey," Dixie whispered in her ear. "Stop gawking and say, 'hello, divine man. Need a screw for your screwdriver?'"

Em did everything she could to keep from gasping at Dixie's suggestive words, nudging her in the ribs before sending the man a cool smile and whisking past him into the hardware store, Dixie in tow.

She headed straight for the farthest aisle from the door, almost running into Nanette Pruitt and Essie Guthrie without even acknowledging them, refusing to stop until she was as far away from that man as possible.

Dixie's ankle boots clacked behind Em, skidding to a halt when she rounded the corner and hid behind a pallet of two-by-fours.

Em grabbed Dixie by her arm and pulled her close, scrunching her eyes shut. All that rapid forward motion left her stomach sketchy at best.

Dixie fought to catch her own breath in a harsh wheeze, before asking, "Why did we just run all the way across Lucky's like we were runnin' from a band of Magnolias with lit torches?"

The stomp of work boots as Lucky's employees loaded and unloaded pallets of heavy wood made her wince, but it was the stench of turpentine and furniture polish that was almost her undoing. She took a gulp of air, thanking whoever was in charge of the universe the moment passed.

Dixie smoothed Em's hair off her shoulder, giving it a gentle tug. "One more time. Why did we run all the way to the back of the store when what you need is in the front?"

"Because that's him!" Em wheezed back, pressing her fingers to her queasy stomach and tugging her knit beret farther down her forehead.

Dixie snickered, unwrapping the turquoise scarf from her neck. "I know it's him, Em. I remember. I was in the square that night when the two of you all but consummated your mad lust just lookin' at each other. If you'd stared at each other much longer? Total combustion. Poof." She gestured an explosion with her fingers and a grin full of mischief.

Em groaned out her misery in both ailment and bad memory. One of the worst nights of her life had included the best ten seconds of her life. One long searing gaze over picnic blankets and children's heads was really all it had been. Yet, there had been more bad that night than good.

"Didn't you once say you heard Louella call him Jax? What a gorgeous name. You'd better make haste before Annabelle Pruitt lures him to her house for her special fudge candy pops. Or the seal-the-deal cherry crumb pie," Dixie teased.

But Em was back in the square—locked in the memory of all the horrible stares, the gasps of shock when Clifton's secret was revealed. "I don't want to think about that night ever again, Dixie."

Dixie scoffed, lifting Em's sunglasses to gaze directly into her eyes. "Stop clinging to a bad memory, Em. It's over. Everyone knows Clifton cross-dresses now. So what? If anyone should hate the memory of that night, it should be me. Or have you forgotten you thought *I* was the one who'd gossiped about Clifton's secret to someone and that 'someone' told Louella, who accidentally on purpose included the picture of him at the Founders' Day slide show all dressed up in his Trixie LeMieux gown?"

Em's lips thinned, snapping her back to reality and the sounds of a busy Saturday at Lucky's. "We're not far from the nail aisle, Miss Dixie. Do you want to buy some to seal my coffin all right and proper?"

Dixie snorted a chuckle, scanning the surrounding area and lowering her voice. "Hah! I'll just borrow some of yours."

Oh. That night. She'd said so many unforgivable things to Dixie, it left her with an actual physical pain when she remembered them. "I've apologized for that night. Over and over, might I remind you?"

Dixie's smile was full of warmth and sympathy. "Which is sort of my point, silly. You don't need to apologize anymore because it's *over,* Em, long ago. And might I remind you, just before all those bad memories happened, you made a good one, too. A really, hot, longingly, deliciously good one. One that involves that enormous man dipped in delicious all the way up to his eyeballs. Whose name is Jax, in case you needed remindin'."

Fear and humiliation rooted her to the spot, refusing

to allow her to move an inch. Her thighs ached from sitting on her haunches, but she'd rather sit on them all day than have that man recognize her.

"So, are you going to go see if you can recapture that magical moment in the square—or are your eyes too bloodshot?"

"I'm not reliving anything. He saw everything that night. *Everything,* Dixie."

All on a big screen. Clifton, larger than life, dressed better than Em would ever be capable of dressing herself. He'd heard, too, she was sure.

Who hadn't heard her call Dixie a sorry excuse for a human being that night? Remembering those awful, ugly words, words Dixie had long ago forgiven her for, still made her feel sick with shame.

The frosty white icing on the cake? She'd run smack into him upon fleeing the square that evening, tears soaking her cheeks, her nylons ripped from tripping over a child's bike in her mad dash to get away from the prying eyes of everyone attending the Founders' Day celebration.

Em hadn't seen him since that night when just before she'd humiliated herself in front of all of Plum Orchard, they'd shared a moment when their eyes met—a brief few seconds still suspended in her mind, and probably much bigger than it had truly been.

What was he doing back here anyway? He couldn't have been here for the past two months. There was no way you could hide someone the size of him in Plum Orchard—droves of the town's single women lining up outside wherever he rested his gorgeous, dark head wasn't something you'd likely miss.

Sure as the day was long, a fresh man even remotely passable didn't stand a chance in a place where a new face didn't go unnoticed and the single women outnumbered the single men five to one.

Dixie sighed, finally sliding to sit entirely on the floor, crossing her legs. "Who cares what *Jax* saw? He probably doesn't even remember anything but that across the crowded square thing you two were doing with your eyes. I saw him look at you, Em. That cancels everything else out. Why didn't you just say hello to him out there to begin with? You can't ever do lascivious things to his incredible body if you don't at least say hello. Well, hold that thought. I guess technically, you could, but I think that classifies you in a category unbefitting a lady."

Em slid down next to Dixie, letting her head rest against the ends of the wood with a weak sigh. "Stop being plum crazy. A man like that isn't ever going to let a woman like me do anything to his incredible body."

"Why the heck not?"

"Spoken like a woman who's never doubted her incredibleness." And why would Dixie doubt how gorgeous she was? She exuded confidence and this raw sexuality that oozed from her pores.

"Leave me out of this, and stop making excuses. So tell me again why a man like that wouldn't let a woman like you have her way with him?"

"Because he's just *too* much incredible. Incredible men look for incredible women." At least, that's the experience she'd had since they'd begun girls' night. A man like that wouldn't be interested in her. He'd want a woman who was dynamic, worldly and far more interesting than a woman who'd rather stay at home and bake apple pies while she sipped grape Kool-Aid from a wineglass, fancying herself a real academic because she read mystery novels by the dozen.

She was simple, in taste and in her way of life. He looked like he should drive an Aston Martin and call some elderly woman Miss Moneypenny. He might appear big and gruff, but there was a primal elegance to it—a Daniel Craig air about him that left her knees weak.

Dixie rose, holding out her hand to Em, who took it, moaning when the motion of merely rising unsettled her precarious stomach. "The not-hungover Dixie is going to tell hungover Em to stop being so maudlin and more important, stop talking about yourself like you're not just as incredible. Because that's just plain not true. Now," she said, tucking her gloves inside the pockets of her sweater, "why are you here again? I forgot in light of the hunky man."

"Tile. I need to pick out some new tile for my bathroom. But first, I need you to take a peek around that corner and be sure he's gone. Please." She pointed over her shoulder.

Please let him be gone, please let him be gone.

Dixie poked her head around the tall steel shelves, housing smaller cuts of wood. She gave Em the thumbs-up, holding out her arm to her.

Em hooked arms with Dixie, forcing her shaky legs

to keep up. "I warned you you were headed for a hangover, didn't I?"

"You bein' the expert, and all," she remarked dryly, using all her energy to focus on picking new ceramic tile for her bathroom. Since Clifton left, she found herself itching to change the things he'd once loved but she'd hated about their small house. Seeing as she was good with a band saw—or almost any saw—and Dixie had afforded her a generous paycheck, she could do it.

Dixie grinned. "Hangovers and a little sleepin' around were my specialties. Don't take from my résumé, Em. It messes with my street cred, lessening the value of all my hard work all those years. It hurts."

Em giggled. "Stop chattering. It makes my head swim."

Dixie rested her arm high on a rack holding row after row of colorful tile. "That's because you're hungover. A swimming head's a sure sign."

"Hush, and help me pick out some new tile, would you, please? I don't want to waste a Saturday doing nothing while the boys are away."

"Are you really going to tackle this project alone? It's a lot of work. Why won't you just let me pay someone to do it for you?" Dixie's face had skeptical all over it.

"It's called Em's big, fat pride. If I let someone do it, I won't have done it myself. There's a certain sense of self-satisfaction in remodeling an entire house all on your own. It's not like I don't know my way around a wet saw, Dixie. I mean, I did spend the first months of my divorce watching nothing but the DIY channel and YouTube. It gives me something to do while the boys are off at Mama's, or when Clifton finally gets around to bringing them to Atlanta for his visitation. It's clean, hard work—and it's good for the soul. But also because I don't want these busybodies to start talkin' and saying I'm just your person because of all that money you have now. So let's be clear." She raised her voice a decibel so there'd be no mistake about whether Emmaline Amos took handouts. "I don't love you for your mountains of money."

Dixie held up a blue ceramic square with a yellow sunflower on it for Em's inspection. "Then why do you love me, Em?"

Em shook her head when she peeked at the tile by lifting her dark glasses. No sunflowers. "I love you because lovin' you is like havin' an in with the devil's head playmate. I'm always guaranteed an invite to the exorcism."

Her phone buzzed against her hip, cutting Dixie off. She dragged it out of her pocket, frowning when she saw it was Nella, Call Girls' receptionist.

Em held the phone up to Dixie so she could see who was calling. "My work never ends, does it? Sure, let's give Em a job, you said. Let's give her a juicy paycheck to match, you said. Let's give her a title like general manager to match her big paycheck. I should have known there'd be Saturday strings attached with you in charge, Dixie," she joked, scrolling her phone's screen. "Nella?"

"Let me start right out by apologizing." She rushed her words together, her voice riddled with anxiety. "I confused my lines again, and crossed wires, or pressed the wrong button, or whatever it is you do when you do it wrong—I did it. I'm so sorry, Em! I'm still learnin' the phones. I would never want to do anything to jeopardize the good fortune that's come my way since you hired me."

Em smiled into the phone, full of sympathy for Nella. She'd hired Nella three weeks ago on a recommendation from her cousin Flynn. She didn't know the details about what initially brought Nella to Plum Orchard, and she made it her business not to ask why she always looked so sad when she thought no one was looking.

She only knew Nella's circumstances had left her jobless, and she kept to herself, but her sweet face, enormous round green eyes and cute pixie haircut were a total contradiction to the way she handled parsing out good calls from bad like a two-hundred-and-fifty-pound linebacker. "Nella? It's okay. Everyone makes mistakes. You're new. It happens."

Nella groaned into Em's ear, a vibrating buzz like a dentist's drill to her sensitive head. "I promise you, it won't happen again. I heard all that yelling, and I just knew I had to apologize for causin' trouble, but I couldn't find you to do it by the time I had a free moment."

That's because by that time, she'd been flat out on her big bed, clothes still on, snoring and drooling. "Nella, please don't fret a second longer. Everything's fine. You made a simple mistake, and I took care of it. That poor little girl shouldn't have had access to a number…" She trailed off when she caught sight of Dixie, jumping up and down, waving her arms.

Em furrowed her brow, cocking her head in question while Dixie danced around. "She said she found it on her daddy's desk! I was horrified, and this poor, sweet angel—"

"It was damn well you," a voice as deep and booming as a canyon accused, creating a hush in the chatter of gossipy conversation all around her from the patrons of Lucky's.

Em whipped around just in time to see Dixie stood behind him. She threw her hands up in the air in obvious defeat, shooting Em a digusted roll of her eyes.

It was him. The him.

But he wasn't looking down at her with the look of her two-month-old daydreams. The look that said he'd gobble her up whole and no one in the world compared to her.

No.

This him was glaring at her—lording over her as though she was personally responsible for the Civil War and global warming.

His thick, squared finger rose, pointing directly at her. "It was *you* on the phone last night with my daughter."

Three

Em's eyes slid upward, scanning the length of *him*. This wasn't her him. Her him wouldn't have been the angry father from the phone last night. He also wouldn't be an angry father with a phone number for a place like Call Girls.

She was certainly open to many things since she'd begun working for Call Girls—she would never judge a client, or at least she tried her best not to. But a man she'd turned into a knight in shining armor by virtue of one long glance, calling women for sex who were complete strangers?

"Nella?" She fought the squeak in her voice. "I'll call you back." Em slid the phone off and dropped it back into her pocket, taking in a deep breath before confronting him.

Arms crossed over his big chest, encased in a black sweatshirt with a plaid flannel jacket over it, he flared his nostrils. "*You* spoke to my daughter on the phone last night. I'd know your voice anywhere after you read me the first-grade teacher 'how dare you' riot act."

Dixie was about to rush to her aid. Em knew it just by the sound of her heels clacking with a swift pitter-patter across the hardware store's floor and the narrowing of her eyes. The angry narrow, not to be confused with the smolder narrow.

Em held up a hand to ward off Dixie, who came to stand at her side nonetheless. When it came to looking out for Call Girls, nothing could fluster her. Not even *him.*

She cleared her throat and adopted a businesslike tone. "I think we got off on the wrong foot last night. First, let me introduce myself—or reintroduce myself. I'm Emmaline Amos, general manager for Call Girls Inc." She held out her hand.

He stared at it, his once-promising lips now a hard line.

Em straightened, sucking in her cheeks. Hoping to avoid a spectacle everyone in town would talk about until she made the next spectacle of herself. "Maybe we should discuss this outside?"

His face grew harder, if that was possible. "The hell. I'm fine with discussing it right here. Mind telling me how a six-year-old managed to get through to one of your operators?"

Em's eyebrow rose. She bristled at the implication she was anything less than acutely aware of everything that went on at Call Girls. "Mind telling me how your *six*-year-old got her hands on a number like ours? She did say it was on *your* desk."

He ran a hand over his jaw, already littered with stubble, or maybe it had remained littered with stubble because he hadn't shaved.

His face, formerly known as hard and angry, went suddenly boggled and tame. He scratched his head. "Come to think of it, I have no idea how she got her hands on the number. I sent her straight to bed, and I didn't have time to talk with her about it this morning. She made me tea, which distracted me because she's dang cute when she makes me her special tea. That's how I left her—having tea."

Which would imply there was someone else looking after his little girl if he'd left her at the house, and still didn't explain why he had a number for Call Girls. She struggled with how deeply that disappointed her and gave him her "aha" look, hoping her glare would reach him from behind her sunglasses.

It was the glare she gave her boys when they held the answer to their own question. "Then your number-one priority right now is to go focus on bein' a better parent, and ask her. You obviously missed the chapter on putting things in high places where small children can't reach them," she condescended.

He grinned—suddenly, inexplicably. And it was magical. "I obviously did."

Just like that, he wasn't angry or yelling anymore. He was like Texas weather. Stormin' and ragin' one minute, sunny and blue-skied the next.

"So you—" he leaned in toward her and whispered "—manage a phone-sex company?"

Now that his accusatory tone and mad face were

gone, Em's words suddenly were, too. She swallowed hard, tongue-tied. When he said the words *phone sex,* her heart stopped again. It was husky and raspy like he'd taken a swig of whiskey and it had left him hoarse. His deep timbre vibrated up along her spine with soft fingers.

She understood exactly what he'd said, but somehow, his words had turned into the man of her daydreams asking her to have sex with him. Which couldn't be right.

Her cheeks flushed.

Dixie pinched her arm and smiled at Em with encouragement. "She does manage a phone-sex company, and she's amazing."

Em nodded because it seemed like the right thing to do, not because she considered herself amazing. "I do."

Now his eyebrow rose, dark and questioning. He made the shape of a phone with his fingers. "So, do you, you know, talk to…people—callers?" He seemed fascinated by the idea that he might have encountered a real live phone-sex operator out and about in the wilds of Plum Orchard, Georgia.

Em knew he was waiting for an answer, but she was mesmerized by the sharp planes of his face, the deep grooves on either side of his mouth, his dark hair, shaggy and curling around the collar of his jacket. And the pink barrette, dangling from a strand of it just behind her ear.

Her heart melted like cold ice cream on a hot July day. A man with a pink barrette in his hair was exactly the man of her daydreams.

"So do you?" he repeated, his eyes intense.

Did she?

"No!" Dixie was quick to answer in her stead. "No. Em doesn't talk to our clients, do you, Em?" She rubbed Em's back to prompt her. "But she does talk. I promise. She's just tired. It's been a busy week doing all that managing."

The world morphed back into shape again, bringing with it the crisp colors of the stacks of ceramic tile, people milling in and out of the aisles, and Dixie, pinching her again, even harder. "Yes!" She forced her lips to move, watching the barrette he was so completely unaware of, bobble. "I do talk, but I can't right now. I have to go. So I hope you'll excuse us."

He stuck out his hand, preventing her from leaving. "Before you go, Jax Hawthorne. My apologies. I'm a little overprotective when it comes to my daughter. I really don't know how she got her hands on a number like yours. Not that your number is bad or anything. Just, well, you know."

Jax Hawthorne. She'd once mentioned to Dixie, his first name sounded like something out of a romance novel. His last name cinched the deal.

Em hesitated. Touching his hand, that rough, wide, callused hand, the one she'd wondered what it would be like to have touch every inch of her, was probably a bad idea. It would leave an imprint on her skin—one she was afraid she wouldn't be able to stop thinking about.

But her upbringing and good manners insisted she take it. Em dropped her hand into his, squeezing hard to assert herself in yet another way to prove to the world she was capable—independent. *Because stern teacher's voices and extrafirm handshakes are sure signs of empowerment, Emmaline.*

"Anyway," he said, dragging her back to reality by dropping her hand. "My apologies for reacting without investigating first. Have a nice Saturday, ladies."

Just as he was about to turn his broad back to walk away, the pink barrette slipped from his hair, dropping to the ground at Em's feet with a tinny clink.

She lifted her glasses to set them atop her head as she knelt and scooped it up at the exact moment he knelt to retrieve it, their heads almost touching.

And their eyes met, too—again—in another one of those stares. Long, short, intense, soft. Em couldn't decide which adjective to lend it. She cleared her tight throat, holding up the barrette. "You dropped this."

If Jax recognized her without her glasses, he didn't show it.

He grinned again. "My daughter's."

She melted again.

"She likes pink?"

"She said it's my color. For dress up, I mean," he corrected, grumbly and deep.

Em smiled at him. "I agree."

"Then it's settled. Pink forever."

"Pink rules."

"Just like my daughter."

More melting. "Tell her Miss Em said hello, won't you?"

"I will." He took the barrette from her fingers, their skin touching then not, doing hot, delicious things to places on her body that shouldn't be hotly delicious from just touching fingers. He dropped it in the pocket of his flannel jacket.

"Have a nice afternoon, Mr. Hawthorne." Em swung upward, thankful for Dixie, who grabbed her by the arm to steady her, murmuring a goodbye to Jax and ushering her out of the hardware store.

Outside, the cold air struck her cheeks, cooling their heat, but assaulting her headache with prickly pinches.

Dixie fanned herself, tugging at the collar of her sweater and lifting her chin to let the air hit it.

So it wasn't just her. Em fanned herself, too. "It was like Hades in there. Someone needs to tell Lucky to turn down the heat in that store. It felt like August."

"No, someone needs to tell the two of you to turn down the heat. You and Jax *Hawthorne,* that is." She smiled, tucking her purse under her arm with that look of confidence on her face.

Em peeked back over her shoulder at the hardware store and made a warning noise at Dixie. "You hush."

"I surely will not. It's the truth. Jax Hawthorne is hot. As your person, it's my duty to tell you, he's hot for you."

Jax Hawthorne. A flutter of nerves made Em shiver. Just the notion he might find her equally attractive after all that fantasizing about him wasn't acceptable. She'd only end up disappointed when the fantasy ended. "He's hot for my backside on a silver platter because of his little girl callin' up a sex line. Nothing more."

Dixie shook her head no with an impish grin. "Tell

me that the next time the two of you spontaneously combust with one little glance."

Em shuffled her feet, giving in to Dixie's theory just a little. Jax's face at the mention of his daughter left her heart fluttering like it had hummingbird wings. "Did you hear him talk about his little girl? He wears barrettes in his hair for his daughter when they play dress up." How endearing and in tune to his daughter's needs for a man so big and rough. More melting ensued.

Dixie giggled, lilting and girlish. "I saw. I heard. I conclude. Hot man, hot for you, who loves his little girl so much he'll let her dress him up, grows hotter."

Em let just one schoolgirl sigh escape her lips— allowed herself just a second or two to believe a man like Jax Hawthorne could find her attractive. But then the cold wind, growing colder by the minute, blasted her in the face and she winced. "It doesn't matter. He said he left his little girl at home. He surely didn't leave her alone. That must mean there's a Mrs. Hawthorne." Less melting, more gut-gnawing disappointment.

Dixie wiggled her finger in Em's direction. "Would his daughter be lookin' for a girlfriend for her father if there was a Mrs. Hawthorne? And if there is, he owes her an apology, 'cuz he's been cheatin' on her with his eyes. Now, come with me. I'll have Sanjeev fix you up some hair of the dog and we'll take care of that hangover. Then we'll talk more about the cues a man gives a woman when he's hot for her and almost certainly unmarried."

Em began a slow stroll alongside her when doubt

set in. "He didn't even remember me." *Jax Hawthorne,* that is.

"That's because you had your sunglasses on. He couldn't see those eyes he all but made the business with in the square that night."

"I took them off, and anyway, shouldn't he have known me just by my scent…or something?"

"Only if he's a vampire, or is that werewolf?"

"Let's not talk about him anymore. I need hangover relief STAT." Em popped open the doors of her Jeep.

"Him's name is Jax Hawthorne. I know you're turning his name over and over in your mind. And we can avoid the subject of him all you like because that's what you do when you're flustered. But we'll have to address this eventually, because I heard a little something while you were giving him hell. So, guess who's movin' to Plum Orchard permanently?" Dixie hopped in the car with a grin and shut the door.

Em's stomach nose-dived while her heart fought for a way out of the captivity of her chest. Permanently? How, in the name of the good man above, would she survive his sexual napalm living in a community as small as Plum Orchard?

Jax shoulder bumped Caine Donovan, his longtime friend and old college roommate, before dropping down on a stool at the breakfast bar. "This—" he craned his neck to indicate the enormity of what Caine called the Big House "—is some shit. That guy that used to come visit you all the time in college left you all of this? Your best friend, right?"

Caine smiled, his grin easy as he leaned forward on the breakfast bar and sipped his beer. "Yep. Landon Wells, and yes, again. Technically, he left it to my fiancée, Dixie, but I scored big because I'm smart enough to marry her. He also left us something else. Something that's gonna blow your head off. It's one of the reasons I called you when I heard you were moving into your aunt's place. You need something to do with your time since you sold the business. Your brothers told me you're a total shithead lately."

Jax was still reeling after meeting one Emmaline Amos up close and in person. The woman he'd seen across the town square when he'd been here two months ago, signing the papers to take possession of his aunt's house.

When she'd run from the square that night and straight into him after seeing a picture of what he'd heard through Plum Orchard's gossipy grapevine was her husband dressed in drag, her vulnerability, her raw humiliation, had touched a nerve.

Soft and sweet, her dark hair falling over her shoulders like silk, she'd caught his attention then and stuck like glue to his mind's eye since.

Today, when she'd used that tone with him, under the guise of some good old-fashioned Southern decorum, it did something funny to his chest. It was like telling him to go straight to hell while she smiled that cute smile.

She was hot and sweet, and she'd tried pretty hard to maintain her composure, leading Jax to believe she remembered him from that night, too.

"Jax?" Caine nudged him across the marble countertop.

"Sorry. Got a lot on my mind. So what's gonna blow my head off? Like this palace isn't enough? You have a camel, man. There's a camel in the backyard." He still couldn't believe it.

Caine chuckled. "That's Toe, by the way. You'll need to know that when you come work for us. He actually likes people—especially people who need a swift kick in the ass."

He didn't want to do anything but renovate his aunt's house and hang out with his daughter, Maizy. Jax stiffened, cracking his scratched knuckles. "I don't need a job, Caine. Since I sold the company, I've just been catching my breath."

"And driving Gage and Tag crazy," Caine said, but this time, he wasn't grinning or coaxing or doing any of the things everyone did to try to get him motivated to get off his ass.

The mention of his two younger brothers, who were also part of the "get off your ass or at least get laid" brigade, made him chuckle. "Speaking of asses, they don't know theirs from their elbows."

Caine hitched his jaw in the direction of Jax's hands. "Well, neither do you, if the Band-Aids on your fingers are any indication."

Both of his brothers were skilled carpenters; both had offered to come and renovate their aunt Jesslyn's house. Because they'd declared parts of it were unsafe, and the last thing those two knuckleheads wanted was anything to happen to Maizy. They loved Maizy as much as he did.

So, because he had nothing but time on his hands, he'd been trying to help with the renovations. Or making shit worse, as Tag said. He and their sister, Harper, were the brains of the family, Tag and Gage, the brawn, Gage always said.

Except there was no more Harper—she was dead. He clenched his fist and shoved that memory to the farthest region of his mind. "So why don't you tell me why you're plying me with beer, pal. What's with all the secrecy?"

Caine shoved a bowl of tortilla chips at Jax. "Didn't you get the message I left you? I called the house phone and left a message with Gage when I couldn't get you on your cell."

He smiled—because even when Maizy ruined something of his "on accident" she was still damn adorable. "Maizy spilled apple juice all over the damn thing—it crapped out. What message?"

"The one about Call Girls. I left the number."

"Call Girls?" It hit him all at once. That's how Maizy had gotten her hands on a phone number that, according to her, belonged to a store where you could "buy girlfriends." His always-in-a-rush brother must have taken down the most minimal of information and left it on his desk, hoping Jax's psychic abilities would link Caine to Call Girls.

Oh, shit. He'd fucked up and the stern teacher's voice Emmaline Amos had lambasted him with hadn't been without warrant.

"Yeah. Call Girls' is the phone-sex company Dixie and I own. Someday, I'll tell you how that crazy shit went down. Until then, that's what this is about. I need someone to write some encryption software for security purposes. We want to tighten things up and branch out while we do. You're the biggest tech geek I know. When I heard you were moving to Plum Orchard, you were the first person I thought of."

"Maybe I'm not connecting the dots. Call Girls is a phone-sex company you own? Here in Plum Orchard? How the hell did you make that happen? I only visited during the summers, but people aren't exactly progressive here. Not progressive enough to have a phone-sex company."

Caine grinned. "Money talks in the PO. Landon made a lot of money. The town, and all he offered it with all that money, made up for their disapproval. He made sure of that before he left this place. So whaddya say? I'll hook you up with your own office over at Call Girls, which is in the guesthouse, by the way—this way you can get out from under Tag's and Gage's feet while they fix that beast up, and it'll give you something to do while Maizy's in school."

"I don't need a job." He needed his sister—alive. Since she'd been killed almost two years ago, he couldn't keep his head in the software development game. Every time he thought he might go back to work, the memory of Harper, the other half of his geeky brain, kept his fingers as far away from a computer as he could get.

She'd been his sounding board, his right-hand man,

or woman, as she'd often reminded him, and he couldn't seem to focus on the intense kind of details government security contracts required.

Caine clapped him on the back. "Well, this job needs you. If you can create software for the Defense Department, you damn well can do it for something as rinky-dink as a phone-sex company. It won't use up a lot of your brainpower, and you won't be moping around, ruining perfectly good pieces of two-by-fours by measuring them wrong. I'll give you your own office and everything. C'mon… You can even eavesdrop on the girls' phone calls," he joked with a wink.

"I don't need an office to develop software. I can do it from home." That he was even considering Caine's offer shocked him.

"Nope. You don't need an office, but I'm gonna give you one anyway because you need to get the hell out from under Gage's and Tag's feet before they hack off your fingers. And then you won't be developing anything, will you?"

Jax sat silently.

"Look, bro, if not for yourself, do it for Maizy. I bet she'd really like a playroom that has a roof," Caine said, ribbing the state of his aunt's dilapidated house.

"Caine? Honey?" a familiar voice called from the large entryway, echoing off the marble tiles. "Know where Sanjeev is? I need him to mix up one of his hangover specialties."

Caine held out a hand to the woman who'd been with Emmaline in Lucky's, a woman who looked at him like his old college buddy had invented high-heel shoes.

Pulling her to him, he gave her a long kiss that almost made Jax uncomfortable.

So he chose to take that moment to think. Caine was only trying to do what everyone had been trying to do since Harper died. Get him back out into the world— where crazy assholes roamed free and killed your sister.

He wasn't sure he was ready for that. He had no motivation in him to do anything that was productive or useful, and everyone knew it.

It was at that undecided moment—while he searched for this motivation everyone seemed so eager to instill in him, when Emmaline Amos walked into the big kitchen, her hand squeezing her temples while she looked down at her feet—that he forgot everything.

Caine let go of Dixie, circling her waist with a loose grip. "Dixie, Em? I want you to meet my old college roommate, Jax Hawthorne. His aunt Jessalyn owned that big Victorian over by the creek. He used to spend his summers here. You remember her, right?"

Em's steps stuttered then stopped altogether.

And there it was again—their stare. The one that connected them in a way Jax tasted on his tongue, felt in his freakin' marrow.

A weird shift of his gut, his emotions all tangled up in it, happened again. This time stronger than the last.

Jax caught Caine and Dixie sending each other some secret signal only lovers shared. Dixie was probably trying to warn Caine that he and Emmaline had already been introduced, but like the man he was—the man they both were, Caine totally missed the signal.

When Em didn't respond, Caine said, "Em, this is Jax. Jax, Em's our GM at Call Girls."

Yep. She sure was.

Enough said. He was in before he even understood why.

Oh, and hello there, motivation.

Four

Em virtually ran past Jax's newly appointed office, hoping to avoid eye contact. She'd done it for a week. If she worked hard, stayed focused, was aware of her surroundings, she could keep right on doing it for as long as she was forced to work alongside Jax Hawthorne.

Picking up the pace, she moved with quick feet, willing herself not to run and appear rude. She nearly twisted her ankle taking the sharp corner while aiming straight for safe haven—aka Marybell's office.

"Emmaline?"

Em stopped dead, her right heel catching on the carpet, forcing her to grab at the small crushed-velvet chair with the enormous fern on it to keep her balance. She swatted at the leaves and willed her voice to come off easy. "Yes?"

"Can I see you for a minute?"

Em frowned. Will it really only be a minute? Much longer and she'd probably melt into a puddle of lusty goo. In fact, since Jax had taken up residence at Call

Girls a week ago, her record for staving off puddles of lusty goo when he was in the vicinity was eighty-eight point three seconds. A whole two minutes could pose a troublesome challenge.

He stuck his dark head out the doorway to locate her in the hall, filling up the space with his muscle-y chest and wide shoulders.

Em had to swallow back a sigh when she allowed herself a quick peek of the fitted, indigo shirt he wore, which hugged his pecs and tapered into his lean waist. The color of it made his eyes look like a dark, raging sea. Her eyes continued to travel, drawn to his thighs, thick and hard and making an uncomfortable heat pool between her legs.

Jax smiled at her, all white-toothed and luscious lips. "Em?"

She held up the screwdriver as though it was her magic wand—a wand that would ward off his penchant for turning her into lusty goo. "Sorry. Sometimes I have a one-track mind. I was off to fix the doorjamb in Marybell's office. How can I help you?"

His eyes, thickly fringed with dark lashes, crinkled at the corners. "So you're handy?"

Randy? Yes. Yes, she was. Wait. Handy. *Are you handy, Emmaline Amos?* She looked down at her traitorous magic screwdriver without meeting his eyes, hiding her gulp. "I'm very handy."

"Like big-power-tools handy? Or just screw-in-a-lightbulb handy?"

Was that a little admiration she heard in his voice?

When she finally let Jax's gaze take hold of hers, she was actually able to smile with more ease. Safe subject.

If they were talking about power tools, confidence took over where schoolgirl puddles of lusty goo left off. She knew a band saw. "I really am. I can handle almost anything but a lathe. I just can't seem to master the fine art of sculpting the leg of a table without turning it into a toothpick."

Jax folded his arms across his chest and smiled his appreciation. "I have no clue what a lathe is, but I bet it's an impressive piece of machinery. My brothers would love you. They're both contractors, very handy guys. They're helping me renovate my aunt Jessalyn's house. Me? I'm useless when it comes to anything with a bit or a blade." Jax held up his bandaged hands to show her the proof.

Forget his lack of expertise with power tools. He had brothers? There were more men running around the PO looking like him—all sorts of rough around the edges and dirty-hot?

It must be some sort of conspiracy. Just when she was beginning to feel something other than apathetic about the other gender, the universe decided to simply throw rough, yet beautifully hewn men at her for sport. How thoughtful.

Though she'd bet neither of his brothers matched the silent, almost-caged prowess Jax emanated. He was so many things: sleek, rough, unkempt but totally in control. Yet, he moved with such grace while his muscles bunched and flexed. Contradictions aplenty.

Still, no way it was legal to have another two just like him in Plum Orchard all at once.

Em inched a little closer to him. Just close enough to behave as though she wasn't on high lusty-goo alert, but far enough away that she couldn't quite smell his cologne. Which changed the game entirely.

If his presence weren't already hard enough on her dirty, dirty libido, his cologne would surely trump all varieties of goo. She'd gotten a lingering whiff of him when he'd left Call Girls for the night and she'd had to drop some reports on his desk. Clean and fresh. Like Tide and sunshine.

Jax's step closer roused her from her thoughts. "Em?"

"Your brothers, right. How nice of them to offer their services. So they're here, too? That must be so comforting for your little girl—bein' in a strange, new town and all. Having your wife and your brothers around must have made the move much easier on her." Fishing. She was going fishing. Throwing her line into the pool of unanswered Jax questions, waiting to see what her hook snared.

For a week, she'd refused to ask Caine or any of the girls if they knew what Jax's relationship status was because of the razzing she knew she'd get from them. Maybe he was just separated from Maizy's mother? Maybe it was his turn for visitation, and Maizy was just here temporarily?

She'd wondered all sorts of things about Jax, thought up every scenario imaginable.

Then she had to talk herself out of wondering. Her wonder was treading on the personal information she'd sworn not to wonder about. Yet had wondered about endlessly all week long.

Complications—she was gifted at creating them for herself.

"I don't have a wife. Just some brothers. Two, to be precise. Gage and Tag."

Relief flooded her veins when his voice cut into her thoughts. Jax didn't have a wife. So, her lusty goo wasn't breaking any girl codes. Phew. "A single dad, huh?"

"Yep. You're a single parent, too, right?"

Her cheeks flamed hot and red. She gripped the screwdriver harder in some bizarre effort to force the magic Jax-Away-A-Nator juice into oozing from its metal tip. Had he inquired about her personal status? Things like that didn't come up in general conversation unless you made it a point to bring them up.

"I am. Two boys. Clifton Junior, and Gareth. Eight and five."

"We have a lot in common then. Bet your boys don't call phone-sex lines, do they?"

Her laughter tinkled from her throat without consulting her. It slipped with ease from her loose lips. "I'm sorry I was so harsh and judgmental with you. It's not easy to parent with two people, let alone one. Especially if they're precocious and as smart as your little girl, but I'm about as overprotective about Call Girls as I am about my boys. I work hard to maintain our integrity—so you caught me off guard, and I got a little high on my horse." And tipsy—he'd caught her very tipsy.

He held up a hand with a wrinkled Band-Aid across

the broad back of it. "No. You were right. Maizy, that's my daughter's name, shouldn't have had access to a number like that. My brother took a message from Caine for me. He just didn't take the *entire* message, and he left it right on my desk where she could find it. She's pretty smart, and very curious. She's a handful to keep track of—but when she gets an idea in her little head, there's no telling her otherwise."

Em nodded with a grin of single-parent solidarity. "Oh, I know all about stubborn little mules, dead set in their ways. I have one of my own." A picture of Clifton Junior found its way to the surface of her mind's eye.

A picture of him happy and giggling—the picture of him before his father had left without warning, and before he thought it was his responsibility to be the man in the Amos household. Her heart tightened in her chest. She'd give anything to have that little boy back again.

"You're such a dirty, dirty boy, Lionel!" the new day-shift operator, Simone, squealed in exaggerated delight from the office across from Jax's. "If you keep this kind of behavior up, you know what's gonna happen to me, don't you, mama's nasty little boy? You'll make me scream for you to—"

Em coughed loudly, reacting without thinking before Jax had the chance to hear another word of Simone's phone call. She forgot that touching the chest she'd dreamed of for two months would be the end of her. She forgot that her palms would ache to touch more of him. She just wanted to drown out listening to a phone call like Simone's while standing right next to him.

Since she'd begun working at Call Girls, most of the

naughty rolled right off her back, became background noise she heard it so much. But listening to it with Jax was akin to acting out the *Kama Sutra* page by page.

Placing her palms on his chest, she fought the swift rush of heat all those muscles created, battled the weakness in her knees, and gave him a shove into his office. "Let's talk in your office," she all but shouted to cover Simone's next request of her client.

Their limbs tangled up, tripping and stuttering until they ended up pushed against the wall, Jax holding her firmly to keep them from falling.

But he didn't let her go. He kept his hands sprawled over her hips, letting them rest along the rounded swells like they belonged there. He laughed, his minty breath washing over her face, his eyes amused. "The girls told me you could be pushy. Who knew?"

Somewhere. Her next breath was somewhere in her diaphragm, afraid to come out for fear her exhalation would press her tighter to Jax's length. She took a step back, still clinging to the screwdriver for all she was worth. "I am not pushy. Don't you listen to those women. They tell tales out of school. Next they'll have you thinkin' I'm some sort of ogre."

"Ogres have warts." He tilted her chin up with his Band-Aid–wrapped forefinger, examining her face. His eyes went smoky when he grinned. "No warts."

Em's breathing hitched in her throat when he placed a thumb just beneath her lower lip. "Not a one."

"Definitely not," he agreed, still keeping his hands loosely on her hips, still wreaking havoc with her forbidden bits. "So things get a little racy around here, huh?"

Em hid her gulp and shrugged her shoulders to fake nonchalance. Like she was a sexpert. "That? I'm so used to it, it's like hearin' someone report the morning news."

Jax laughed, sort of low, which did squishy, unidentifiable things to her belly. "Can't say I ever remember hearing Katie Couric use those words to describe the war in Iraq," he quipped.

"That was probably Bryant's fault, always tryin' to keep a good woman down." She giggled a little then silently reprimanded herself for behaving like an inexperienced schoolgirl.

While not off the mark, that wasn't the impression she wanted to give. She was Emmaline Amos, general manager of Call Girls Inc. In charge of a multimillion-dollar corporation. In. Charge.

Jax cleared his throat, still staring down at her. "Anyway, that question…" he muttered.

She snorted when she remembered there'd been a reason Jax had asked her into his office. *And it's probably a sexless question, Nympho Nancy.* Then she covered her mouth when she realized she'd snorted, flustered and red all over again.

This was a perfect example of why she and small talk with devastatingly gorgeous men were twains that would never comfortably meet. "Oh, my apologies! I forgot all about the reason you asked me in here. What can I do for you?" *Or do to you?*

"I forget the reason I asked you in here, too. But I

have a better reason for you to be in my office that's just as compelling."

She totally backed away from the heat of his big body and the intoxicating scent of man, finally finding her footing. Em placed a hand at her throat in a familiar, soothing gesture. "Yes?"

"First, Maizy and I had a talk about her using the phone without permission—a long one."

Instantly, her concern was with that sweet voice that had struck a chord in Em's heart. "I hope you weren't angry with her. I don't know if she told you the nature of her call, but it was out of concern for you."

Jax's expression went from soft to softer at the mention of his daughter, his granite jaw relaxing, his eyes flashing pride. "She did, and we talked it all out. But you made quite an impression on my girl. She said you were so nice to her and your voice was pretty in her ear. In fact, she wondered about you again today."

Em's heart sped up, pushing against her chest. She lost track of how many times she'd tried to form a picture in her mind of what Jax's little girl would look like—what precious face the voice was attached to. "She was really very sweet, and exceptionally polite. You should be very proud of her manners."

"I am, and she's a great kid—which is why I wondered if I could ask you a favor."

Em didn't hesitate. "Oh, of course."

"I know we don't know each other, but you struck such a chord with her, and she's feeling a little displaced since we left Atlanta. I don't know many women here in Plum Orchard, and I really need a woman's touch."

Love slave. He was going to ask her to be his love slave. Yippee!

Wait. That had zip to do with Maizy.

He leaned back against the wall, letting his long legs stretch out in front of him. "Seeing as you're admittedly handy with power tools, I'm betting you're just as good at picking out colors for a little girls' room. We're almost done with the renovation in Maizy's room, and I want to surprise her with something that will make her happy." He held up his hands in a sort of helpless gesture, his smile lopsided.

This smile, different from his half grin, changed his whole face from ruggedly sculpted to playful and adorable. "What can I say? I'm a guy with guy tastes. Whatever I pick out will unequivocally suck. I can just picture her wrinkling her cute little nose at me in that, 'oh, you're so stupid, Dad' way, if I'm left to my own devices. But I need help picking colors for the walls—girl things, you know?"

He needed an interior decorator? That didn't sound like love slave at all. But her heart did that twitchy-melty thing again. He really loved his little girl. No one could fault him for that. Em smiled at him.

How could she say no when it would make that enchanted voice on the phone from the other night happy? She agreed without even thinking. "Of course. I'd be happy to help you pick colors."

"Furniture, too, maybe? She's been bunking with me while my brothers Tag and Gage finish up her room, but she's grumbled about my stinky feet on more than one occasion. It's time she has her own space like all little girls should."

Em laughed even while she couldn't imagine a single inch of Jax was stinky. "Sure—just say the word."

She couldn't read what was in his eyes because she was afraid to read wrong, but they looked lighter. "Tomorrow night? Are you free? I'd like to get her situated as soon as possible. I'll buy you dinner for your trouble."

Giddy. Oh, that wave of giddy at the mere thought of sharing a meal with Jax hit her hard. She pictured him biting into a juicy hamburger, his white teeth sinking into…

This would never do.

Shoulders squared, Em reminded herself his request was about Maizy. She was proud of the way she waved him off as she inched around his enormous frame to head back out into the hall. "Dinner's not necessary, Jax. Really. I'm happy to help with anything that will make such a charming little girl smile. And tomorrow night's fine. I'll ask Aunt Dixie and the girls to babysit."

"Well, you have to eat, right? I definitely have to eat. I won't get out of here much before the dinner hour anyway."

How would she ever eat with Jax across a table from her when she almost couldn't breathe around him? But she found herself agreeing. "Okay. Tomorrow after work. See you then."

"Thanks, Emmaline. Maizy and I appreciate it."

"Anytime," she managed, like spending an evening with him was going to be effortless and breezy. She even squeezed out another smile before she made one more clumsy break for Marybell's office.

Rounding that hazardous corner again, she slipped inside Marybell's office, shut the door, and leaned back against it, still clinging to her magic screwdriver.

It's just dinner and some paint, Em. Breathe.

But it was dinner and some paint with him. Him.

The him.

The effects of Jax, after spending only ten minutes in his presence, left her body tingly and hot all over. Breathless, shaky and dizzy, too.

What would an entire evening and a meal bring?

An Em bonfire?

"You're going where?"

"To dinner with a gorgeous woman." Jax smiled to himself. His off-the-cuff request of Em had been genius. Since he'd met her at Caine's a week ago, and agreed to take the freelance work, he couldn't think of anything else but seeing Em again.

Not good. He didn't want that. He didn't want all the sticky, mostly messy end result of a relationship. Especially with a woman who had as many battle scars as she had. He'd been to a war once, and he'd just barely gotten out alive.

Though, she'd been damned elusive this week, seemed their paths almost never crossed while he'd set himself up in the office Caine and Dixie had appointed him. So when the opportunity finally presented itself today, and she was so close it was all he could do not to haul her up against him just to see what it felt like to have all that soft, feminine woman against him, he'd done the next best thing.

Asked her to help him pick paint colors while he silently berated himself for even opening the door just a crack to being around her more than at the office.

Dumb ass.

But everything, from the swell of her hips in her tight-fitting, yet somehow modest skirt, to the slope of her breasts, perfectly shaped beneath the black, figure-hugging sweater she wore, made his damn mouth water.

The small pearl buttons, running from the edge of her sweater right up to just under her chin, had him spending the time after she left fantasizing about how fast he could pluck them open and reveal what was beneath.

The scent she wore, pears, sunshine—a combination that, when recalled, made him wonder if every inch of her smelled like that.

And her lips. Jesus. Her lips. Soft, plump, red, just begging to have his mouth on them, nipping them, and it took more restraint than he'd like to admit to keep himself in his office while she stood so close to him he could see her pupils dilating.

Stir her cute Southern drawl into the pot and the way she drew out his name a little longer than everyone else, and he couldn't stop himself from thinking about her.

Tag poked his head over his brother's shoulder, his eyes finding Jax's in the crooked bathroom mirror. "Wait. You have a real date? With a real woman? Or one of the blow-up variety?"

Jax smoothed some aftershave over his jaw and

grinned at his brother's reflection. One that wasn't as haunted or pained these days. "Like you'd know the difference? And it's not a date."

Tag punched him in the shoulder and smiled, his eyes lighter than Jax had seen them in a long time. "So who's this gorgeous woman?"

"Emmaline Amos." Just saying her name made his gut tighten, bringing to mind those red, red lips of hers. *Double shit.*

"The one with the ex-husband who wears women's clothes?"

Jax's jaw stiffened, his grin fading. He'd never forget the pain on Em's face the night he'd first seen her in the square after her husband's secret was revealed at the Founders' Day gathering.

Raw and so damn palpable. Raw enough that even without knowing anything about her, he'd wanted to beat the shit out of the person responsible for making her cry. "You heard, then?"

Tag nodded, leaning his arm against the chipped pink-and-gray ceramic tile on the wall. "Who hasn't? This town sees everything, man. *Everything.* They talk the hell out of it, too. Especially those women who're part of that gladiola club—or whatever they call it."

Jax chuckled. "I think it's Magnolias, and I've met Louella and her crew. Interesting bunch." Somehow, in all the summers he'd spent at his aunt's, he'd managed to overhear bits and pieces of the gossip that seemed to fuel such a small community, and the Magnolias were almost always at the center of it. Or if Aunt Jess's words were right, they were the cause of it.

Tag's broad shoulders rolled. "I don't know. It's some damned flower or another. You can't go into that diner without hearing something about someone." He put a hand on Jax's shoulder, his eyes searching his older brother's.

Tag knew how and when to look for signs something was up with Jax when no one else did. "So what's so special about Emmaline Amos that she made you decide to crawl out from under your rock after not a single date since the Stone Age?"

Jax shifted his eyes first, focusing on rinsing the sink. He didn't have an answer to what drew him to Em. He was just drawn—sucked in—total immersion. That was more than he could claim about a woman in a long time. "Not a date," he repeated.

"Jax's coming out from under his rock?" Gage asked, pushing his way into the crowded bathroom just like he'd always done since he was ten. "Good. Means you can do the dishes."

Tag slapped his little brother on the back. "Yep. So that means we're on dish duty tonight, bro, and Maizy duty, too. Big brother's got a date." He cackled the words like they were joke-worthy.

But it wasn't a joke. He hadn't dated in a few years. And he wasn't dating tonight.

Gage whistled and grinned, his face lighting up. "A date? Nuh-uh. Who'd date you, you ugly schlub?"

"Not a date," Jax repeated.

"Emmaline Amos," Tag replied, adopting his impression of a feminine voice, complete with a bat of his eyelashes and a twirl of his finger around a lock of his shaggy hair.

Gage's eyes opened wide. "No shit! The one that works at the phone-sex company with Caine?"

Jax's eyes narrowed in Gage's direction. "Get your mind out of the gutter, Gage. She's the GM. She doesn't answer the calls."

Gage flicked his fingers at Jax's reflection. "Oh, stop getting your back up. Still, workin' in a place like that—" he wiggled his dark eyebrows "—I bet she knows a thing or two."

Tag slapped him on the back of the head. "Shut up, Gage. This is the first time our wee boy's been out in as long as you've been sexually active. Leave him the hell alone." Tag's eyes sought Jax's again with the "If you need to talk…" signal before he said, "I'm happy for you, man. Glad to see you're getting out. New town—new life. Clean slate, right?"

Jax and Tag had a clear understanding of clean slates. Both of them wanted one—both of them were going about finding them in their own ways.

Maizy, the final piece to their nonconformist, but totally a work-in-loving-progress puzzle, dipped between pairs of legs to latch on to Jax's thigh. "You're going out, Daddy?"

He looked down at his daughter; her bright auburn hair and freckles so much like her mother's, so unlike the Hawthorne's dark looks, and his chest tightened with that unconditional love her dark, chocolate-brown eyes summoned. "I am, kidlet." He scooped her up in his arms, dropping a kiss on her freckled nose. "You got a problem with that?"

She captured both sides of his face and rubbed their noses together. "Only if you're going out for ice cream. Then I'd be madder than a hornet."

Jax hitched his jaw, making a comically confused face. "A hornet? Where'd you learn that, Maizy-do?"

She roped her arms around his neck, resting her cheek on his. "Uncle Gage says it all the time. He said it's better for me 'n the *S* word."

Jax rolled his eyes at Gage. "A sight better, I'd say. So, you gonna eat all your dinner like a good girl for Uncle Tag while I'm gone?"

"If he promises not to burn the fish sticks again." Her honesty always made him laugh. They were all shitty cooks. Him probably being the shittiest. On the best of nights, they only managed to eke out a barely passable meal for Maizy. It included all the approved food groups suitable for a six-year-old.

It just wasn't always edible—at least not the outside of it. Sometimes, if you picked your way to the middle of a chicken breast, there was a silver lining. But what Maizy lacked in their culinary finesse, they more than made up for with love. No one would ever mess with Maizy Hawthorne as long as her uncles and father were around.

"Note to self—Daddy needs to watch the Food Network more." He'd made a vow—once they settled into this rundown house so full of all the potential Gage and Tag kept talking about, he'd learn to cook. For Maizy.

Because everything was for her, and that's how it was going to stay.

"Hey!" Tag teased, tugging on a tightly coiled ringlet of his niece's hair. "They were blackened fish sticks, thank you very much, Ms. Food Critic. Cajun style. I was trying to broaden your food horizons."

Maizy shook her head full of curls and wrinkled her nose with her trademark display of disapproval at Tag. "Uncle Gage said that was a fib. It was really just burned. It was yucky."

Gage scooped her out of Jax's arms and swung her around his back so she could hold tight to his neck piggyback style. "It sure was yucky. Probably the biggest fib Uncle Tag ever told you, too. It was right up there with, 'Look, Maizy-do—this big ole gooey mess tastes just like Chicken McNuggets if you close your eyes and pretend. Give it a chance.'"

Maizy giggled, squeezing Gage's neck. "That was so gross. So if Daddy won't be here, will you be my unicorn tonight, Uncle Gage?"

Gage reached upward and ruffled her hair with a smile. "I'll always be your unicorn."

The phone interrupted Maizy's giggling as Gage galloped out of the bathroom with her. "I'll get it. You finish prettying up for your daaate," Tag drawled with a laugh.

One last glance in the mirror, and Jax sucked in a deep breath, bracing his hands on either side of the pink, shell-shaped sink. Damn. He was nervous. When was the last time he could lay claim to that emotion? Especially when it concerned a woman whom he absolutely wasn't dating?

He rolled his head from side to side to loosen his muscles, tight with anticipation.

Tag's scruffy head was back in his line of vision. "Uh, Jax?"

"Yep?"

"Someone's on the phone for you."

His ears picked up something in Tag's voice—something almost urgent, maybe even ominous. No one ever called them. No one who stirred up the kind of warning Tag's voice held anyway. "Who is it?"

Tag's throat worked, his Adam's apple sliding up and down. His lips fell into a thin line as he jammed his hands into the pockets of his worn jeans.

A strange chill rolled along his spine. A warning chill. "Who the hell is it, Tag?"

"Reece. It's Reece."

The floor fell away from Jax's feet in a tidal wave of his blood pounding in his ears and his heart dropping to his feet. Well, that explained why Tag's voice sounded alarms in Jax's head.

Fuck. Fuck, no.

Five

The front door to Em's small ranch blew open with a gust of winter wind, Dixie's beautiful face in the middle of it. "Well, hello, fine sir! Might I interest you in a cheeseburger and some fries with your aunt Dixie and the girls? Like a real dinner date?" Dixie swung Gareth up into her arms, nuzzling his neck with her nose until he was in a fit of giggles.

The moment Dixie walked through Em's front door, Gareth launched himself at her. Dixie, Caine, Sanjeev and the girls had become as important to Em and her children as any family member.

Her mother didn't like it, and no one in town did either for that matter. But she no longer cared what other people didn't like. She didn't care that the women in town mocked her parenting for letting the boys be around the women of Call Girls. Their "I can't believe she'd allow young, impressionable boys in the presence of *those* women" snide comments rolled right off her like water off a duck's back.

At least *those* women were honest. They might talk dirty, but they didn't talk behind your back.

Over the months, during the hardest transition of their lives, Dixie and the girls were always there for her and her sons.

While she'd picked up the pieces of her life, while she'd driven Clifton to his counselor, while she'd learned how to be single—they'd been there, too. Helping her through meltdowns, passing her tissues and teaching her how to be a part of a group of women who accepted her for who she was. That was more than she could say for her judgmental mother and the Mags.

"Stop, Aunt Dixie!" Gareth cried between bouts of laughter as Dixie kicked the door shut with her foot. "I have somefin' to tell you 'bout school. It's 'portant!"

Em held her breath. Please, don't let it be another incident where one of his classmates poked fun at him about his father's cross-dressing.

Dixie's eyes twinkled down at Em's youngest son. "Did you find a new sweetheart? You better not be courtin' someone new," she teased, walking her fingers up his chubby arm until he squealed. "I'm your only girl, buddy. You'd do well to remember that."

Gareth instantly let his head fall to Dixie's shoulder to signify his loyalty, snuggling against it and wrapping his legs around her slim waist. "No, silly. I got an A on my alphabet test."

Em let air into her lungs, sending up a silent prayer it had been a torture-free day for Gareth. That, on top of a phone call from her mother, Clora, reminding her the boys lacked proper discipline because she didn't make them tuck their shirts in, would have been too much.

"You are the smartest boy ever!" Dixie punctuated her words with kisses. "Now, you scoot—go get handsome for Miss Dixie. I can't have you goin' out on the town with me if your hands look like they've been rootin' around a pig farm. Tell that good-lookin' brother of yours, Clifton, to kick it into overdrive, too!" She let Gareth down with a plunk and a pat on his behind, shooing him upstairs. "Are MB and LaDawn here yet?"

Em sighed with a nod, watching Gareth run upstairs to get his pouty brother. "Upstairs charmin' Clifton Junior. You're all so good with them. I wish Clifton would talk to me like he does to y'all. What is it with you and the opposite sex, Miss Dixie Davis? Honest, it's like anyone with a man-garden falls ripe from the tree when you're within range."

"What is it about *you* and a man, Miss Emmaline?" Dixie closed the front door, putting her hands behind her back and strolling over to Em with a smile on her lips.

Em's eyes fell to the floor, her fingers tangling up in a shaky knot. "Oh, hush. It's not like that. We're just picking out colors and some furniture for Maizy's room."

It wasn't like that. It really wasn't like that because she wouldn't let it be like that even if Jax wanted it to be like that. Which, surely, he didn't.

As she'd carefully applied makeup in preparation for tonight, she'd decided to get control of her wandering thoughts and behave like an adult. She was going to put her fantasies about Jax on a shelf where they belonged.

He was a coworker she was helping out because she had a skill he lacked by virtue of being the opposite gender. Single parents needed to stick together and support each other. Rah-rah.

Besides, her life was in such upheaval with the boys and the constant trouble they were having at school with everyone teasing them about their father, she didn't need another complication in it. Men were complicated.

All she wanted was freedom right now, some room to breathe after holding her breath for so long she didn't even know it was happening.

But wasn't it you just a few days ago who was thinking about dabbling in the friends with benefits section of the relationship aisle? Yes. That had been her, but was it the real her?

Was she capable of having sex with no lingering emotional ties? Was she willing to find out? Was she the kind of woman who could take a lover in the afternoon and discard him for another the next day?

Now that a man had taken an interest in her—even if it was only about color palettes and canopy beds, a gorgeous man she'd logged hours daydreaming about, she was all tail between her chicken legs. One more reason to maintain a careful distance.

Just a few nights ago, she'd been ready to learn the finer points of talking dirty so she could nab a man and quell this raging desire to explore her lack of sexual experience. Tonight, she was throwing salt all over her libido's fire.

Dixie ran a hand over the red knit beret Em wore and fluffed the scarf around her neck. "Helping a man pick out colors for his daughter's room is very personal in nature, leading me to believe Jax wouldn't just ask anyone."

"He said I'm the only woman he knows in town. That's why he asked me, troublemaker."

Dixie's arched eyebrow rose, skeptical. "He knows me…."

"Maybe he's seen Landon's guest bathroom?" she teased. The horrors she'd corrected with Dixie's bad eye for color since she'd moved into the big house were too numerous to mention.

Dixie rolled her eyes. "I'm tellin' you, Em, it looked like taupe. Who knew taupe had so many undertones?"

"I did. I knew, and if you'd asked me, I woulda told you so."

"Point is, Jax asked you because he likes you. He's clearly interested in you. Why is that so hard to believe?"

"Because big, rugged, beautiful men like Jax Hawthorne don't like girls like Em, right?" Marybell quipped, making her way down the stairs, Clifton's jacket in hand. "That's plain nonsense, and you know it. I don't know how you see you, but you trust me when I tell you, we don't see you in the same light. And by the way, he knows me, too. We've had some very nice chats in the break room at Call Girls. Not only is he so hot I think I burned myself on just his fingertips when he passed me the ketchup, but he's funny, too. So funny. And can that man eat. Finished a whole pizza all by himself on pizza night. Which means his other appetites are probably just as big." She fanned herself with a chuckle.

Em blushed more at the stab of jealousy she felt over the ease with which Marybell must have conversed with Jax than the implication his *appetite* was as big as he was. Why was it so hard for her to loosen up and just be Em?

Maybe because lately she wondered if simply being Em wasn't enough. It hadn't been enough for Clifton.

"So why didn't he ask me to help choose colors for Maizy's surprise bedroom reveal? If we go by your standards, he knows me better than y'all." Marybell pondered, settling into a puffy beige chair by the window seat Em had created late one long DIY marathon night.

"Or me?" LaDawn called from the kitchen where she was gathering wet wipes for Gareth. She sauntered out into Em's small living room, dropping the bag on the couch. "I had a nice cup o' coffee with your heart's desire just the other day, and he sure wasn't askin' me to be his companionator in color coordination. Know why? Because he doesn't like me or us the way he likes you. I've seen the way he's been lookin' at you, Em. Like he'd sop you up with a biscuit." She waved a finger at her, tucking the wet wipes into her oversize purse. "I know men. He likes what he sees when he sees you."

"Clifton liked what he saw, too. Now he's off liking something else he's seen." Sometimes, the insecurity she fought so hard to overcome, overcame, and it blurted out of her mouth, weak and whiny. Which was why she probably overcompensated at work. To show she was strong. Tougher 'n nails.

Dixie pulled Em's hand into hers. "Oh, honey, you can't base everything that happens from here on out on your experiences with Clifton. He didn't trust you enough to tell you his struggles. That has nothing to do with how perfect or imperfect you are. That's a Clifton problem."

Pulling her purse over her shoulder, she shook her head. She'd told herself that over and over. It wasn't her, it was him. But what was it about the woman he'd left her for that had inspired his confessions? What had she had that Em didn't?

She didn't love Clifton anymore. Of that she was sure. In hindsight, she realized they'd been drifting apart long before his big revelation. Yet, she'd lost most of her respect for him when he'd all but abandoned the boys just because he wanted to wear dresses. He didn't have the courage to tell them the truth. Instead, he'd left the truth tellin' to Em. While Clifton went off and enjoyed his new life, she dealt with the day-to-day fallout.

"It doesn't matter anyway. I'm not interested in getting involved with anyone so soon after Clifton. I have too much upheaval in my life right now. The boys, the dog, the house, Clifton, my mother. I think I need to figure out who Em is and what she wants before I go figurin' out another man. Who wants to do all that work anyway? Men are work."

Marybell's head tilted to the right, her lip ring catching the soft rays of the new, overhead track lighting Em had just installed. "Nobody encourages that more than we do. You should definitely find out who Em is. While you're there, could you also find out if she's going to be the stern teacher all the time or if this is just transitional while you assert your newfound independence. Just so we're forewarned."

LaDawn's lips pursed as she pulled on her faux fur vest. "So all that talk about makin' the business is off the table for you now Em 'n' M? We don't have to worry you're gonna look for lust on Craigslist? Because we worry, you know. You're not yourself these days, and I won't have you makin' a rash decision, or bein' talked into something you don't want to really do."

Who was herself? She'd decided that was the quest she was on. To find out who she was.

Em giggled, reaching out to hug LaDawn. She dropped a wet kiss on her friend's cheek, warmed by her concern. "No Craigslist. No one-night stands. Thanks for taking the boys tonight, girls. Promise I won't be late."

Dixie popped her front door open, blowing her a kiss. "Now, if the situation takes a turn, and you change your mind and decide you wanna make some business your business, you call us. We'll keep the boys." She winked, giving her the famous sexy smolder.

Em rolled her eyes back at Dixie, digging for her keys in her purse. "There will be no makin' anything but decisions about color palettes and whether I'll have a big plate of fries with my hamburger, so never you mind with your lewd suggestions. Now, give the boys a kiss for me, and have a great time."

* * *

Intentions and hell. There was something about a road and the paving thereof. Em just couldn't put the two thoughts together well enough to clearly summon the metaphor.

All while she and Jax pored over paint swatches at Lucky's, while they'd strolled the aisles of antiques stores and furniture departments in Johnsonville, while they'd tested mattresses, while they'd had a glass of wine and a bowlful of creamy pasta, Em had tried to remember the metaphor.

It applied to good intentions—none of which she had after spending the evening with Jax. There wasn't a pure thought in her head. Not when he'd sat beside her on the pillow-top mattress and his thigh had brushed against hers, creating a shiver of awareness so intense, she'd bitten the inside of her cheek to bring it under control.

Not when she'd sunk so low into one of the mattresses they were testing, he'd offered his hand to pull her up, and she'd ended up falling into him, resisting the insane urge to rest her cheek on his stubbled jaw.

Not when he'd placed his hand at the small of her back to usher her through the restaurant. Or when he'd offered her a forkful of his meatball so she could have a taste.

Touchy.

Jax had been touchy. Not in a "How many hands do you have, you octopus?" way. In the best possible way. The way that set her skin to a delicious slow burn, made her feel sexy, desirable, like a woman.

Every last indecent thought she could cram into her

head was swimming right beside her raw nerve endings. She'd never met a man who'd left her so edgy with awareness, who did things to her insides with just a glance.

Now, as they sat under a secluded tree in his driveway, bare of its leaves, while the creek babbled in her ears, and Jax filled up her Jeep with his everything, her nerves were at their white-flag stage. It wasn't like he could help filling up her Jeep—he was an enormous man, enormous men filled things up. But it wasn't just his body filling up the space. It was him—his scent— his aura—him.

The glow of the dashboard lights made his hard jaw harder, the thick gleam of his hair soft and blurry around the edges.

"You're good fun, Em. Thanks for coming with me tonight. I had a really good time."

"Anything for Maizy."

Jax leaned over the armrest between them and smiled—this was the devastatingly charming smile he'd bestowed upon her more than once tonight. Sexy and secretive with a hint of some flirt. "Was it really just for Maizy? I'd like to think it had a little something to do with all the charm I radiate."

More flirting. He was teasing her, and the more he teased her, the stiffer she became. The more tightly strung she became, the more likely she was to say something stupendously stupid.

Em shifted in her seat, begging her body to move away when all it wanted to do was sprawl out on top of Jax's. "I'm always happy to help out a coworker."

He found her hand, running his finger over the outline of her red nail with a light touch. "Speaking of, how long have you worked for Call Girls?"

Work. She could talk work, if he would just stop rubbing sensual circles along her fingers. Em cleared her throat. "Just a few months as GM. I worked for our local lawyer, Hank Cotton, as his legal secretary before that. Dixie hired me when Cat retired to have a baby."

He nodded his head, letting it roll to the headrest. His throat, long, strong, was exposed, every tendon, each muscle making her breathing hitch. "Right. I remember Caine saying you were a mediator when there was some contest for ownership of the company between him and Dixie. Caine said the two of them had to start their own phone-sex lines and win clients, right?"

"The phone-sex games. That's what the girls and I call it."

"Hah!" He barked the laugh. "Caine had to talk dirty to *men?* Can't wait to tell the guys at our college reunion."

Em's head bobbed at the memory, her grin wide. "Actually, it was women he claimed he was doin' the talkin' to. He was so sure he'd win he bet Dixie he could take the harder road. We all thought he was gonna smoke her with all those celebrity voices he does, especially Sean Connery, but come to find out, he never talked to a single woman. Not one. He had some college friend hack the system to make it look like he was getting a bunch of calls."

Jax winced, ducking his dark head playfully. "Confession time. That was me."

"It was *you?* Well, it all makes sense now. You bein' a software developer."

"Well, not me, but I'm guilty by association. I was in a bad place when he called me and asked me to help, so I referred him to a buddy of mine. I feel stupid for not making the connection. Swear it was all on the up-and-up, though. Caine just said he was doing something to win back the woman he thought he wanted to spend the rest of his life with. I didn't pry."

A bad place was all she garnered from his confession. "So you know the rest of the story, then?" Somehow in her excitement over retelling the tale, she'd moved closer to him, let her fingers curl into his.

Jax brought his fingers to his chin and rubbed them against the accumulation of dark stubble. "There's more?"

"All that time we thought he was locked away in his office, building his clientele, he was really devisin' a plan to win Dixie back. He was calling her line and pretending to be someone else entirely so he could get to know the newly changed, not so mean girl anymore Dixie."

Jax whistled. "Wait. Dixie was a mean girl? Dixie Davis?"

She grinned, her eyes skimming his. It was so much easier to talk Dixie. "The meanest. Anyway, that's how Caine reacquainted himself with her."

Jax grumbled his approval. "Smooth. Very smooth. Gotta give it to Caine, he knows what he wants. Must have been something to see."

"I can verify, as their court-appointed mediator, it

was a sight to see. The two of them always trying to one-up each other. But it all worked out in the end, and they're happy now."

"Bet there was no funny stuff while they were on your watch. You can be pretty forceful."

Her cheeks grew hot. She was a bag of hot air. All bluster, no substance. It was all just a show so people wouldn't feel sorry for poor, divorced-by-her-cheating-husband Em. "The girls call it my stern teacher's voice."

"I never had a teacher that looked like you."

"I'm convinced there was funny stuff from the two of those devils, and I just wasn't clever enough to find them out. But make no mistake, Dixie and Caine were a handful."

"And now they're in love and getting married. It's good to see Caine so happy."

"Dixie, too. Life's funny, isn't it?"

"And Landon was responsible for all of that?"

"Did you know Landon?"

"Only met him a few times when he came to see Caine back in college. Nice guy. Bought us all a steak dinner and tickets to the Falcons game."

"Landon was one of the most amazing human beings I've ever known. Kind, loyal—"

"And a little eccentric, if I remember right."

Em laughed with the fond memories Landon had left in his wake. "Yes. He was all that and more. Some people say he was crazy. But I choose to believe he was crazy about love, and life, and when he knew his was ending, he decided to ensure Dixie's and Caine's futures. So he threw them together in the one way he knew they'd never be able to resist just so they could find each other again. It's probably the most romantic gesture I've ever witnessed. How many people do you have in your life that would go to such extremes, from the grave no less, to do something like that for you?"

"He sounds like he was something else."

Em's eyes grew watery remembering Landon. "I spent some time with him…in the end before he passed, taking care of things for him, getting Dixie here for the reading of his will. I can't ever seem to put into words his kind of generosity. How…how *hard* he loved everyone in his life. I didn't know him much growing up—he was two years older than me and always with Dixie and Caine—but it didn't take long for me to recognize, Landon knew his heart. He knew how to love people, and he knew how to show it."

Jax sat still, his eyes on her face, his fingers moving over her arm.

Too intense. Too intimate. Way to frighten the man while you're just bein' you. She drew her hand back, embarrassed by her obsession with a romantic tale. "Sorry. I'm just a silly romantic who loves a happy ending. Sometimes I get carried away."

Jax pulled it back into his grasp and held it there. "Personally, I think it's attractive on you. Especially the way your eyes light up when you talk about it. It sounds like you grew to love him as much as everyone else seemed to. There's nothing wrong with that."

His approval was so warm in her ears, so unlike Clifton's disapproval when she found a cause she wanted to support, or became too loud in her defense of something, that was so intense she had to change the subject.

"You have a beautiful house," she said, craning her neck to get the full view of the old farmhouse with a wraparound front porch that went on for days. It needed work. The paint was peeling, the windows were sagging, the trees and shrubs were overgrown and out of control, but Em didn't see that. She saw the possibilities.

His chuckle was thick when he leaned over and gently shifted her chin to point her in the direction of the full view of the house. "Are you kidding? Do you see what I see? It's a dump. It doesn't need a renovation, it needs a bomb squad."

Em shrugged and smiled, lost in her mind's revival of Jax's home. "Well, you see what you see, and I'll see what I see. What I see is beyond that, and this amazin' house has tremendous possibilities. It could be a real showstopper. Add in the gorgeous location, the creek and the two acres of land, and it could be a divine place to hang your hat. That porch for instance, can't you just see it in the summer? Close your eyes and picture ivy climbin' up the trellis at each end. Hanging plants all along the porch full of petunias and trailing geraniums. Potted plants lining those wide steps in the fall in a riot of colorful mums and big fat pumpkins carved for Halloween. Maybe a vegetable garden over there where that patch of dead grass and leftover bricks are. Antique white rocking chairs to sit on with a glass of sweet tea while you listen to the creek. It could be magnificent—just breathtaking. And think about how much Maizy would love a swing right over there in that big oak." She pointed to it with her finger, closing her eyes and exhaling to stop her rambling.

When she opened them, Jax's eyes were crinkling up into another smile, an indulgent one. "You know, when you describe it, I can almost see it. You really like the DIY thing, don't you?"

Realizing her enthusiasm had taken over again, probably making her sound rabid, Em toned it down. She lowered her voice a notch when she said, "I do. I love taking nothing and making it something. I love fixing what others think is unsalvageable. And I like knowing I did it myself."

"Where does that come from?"

"What?"

"The need to say you did it yourself?"

Em pulled back. "Did that come out like someone was stopping me from doin' what I like? I'm sorry. I didn't mean to imply that it was anything more than me stopping myself. But nowadays, I just have a lot of...free time."

His eyes pierced hers, blue and intense as he drew her back toward him, his hand strong on her arm, his face so close to hers she could see the twitch in his hard jaw. "You mean since your divorce?"

A hard knot had formed in her throat, one she had to fight the words around to get them out of her mouth.

She lifted her shoulders in a "maybe" shrug. "I guess." Once the boys were in bed, it was just her and a long, lonely night. She'd decided early on, she could fill those nights with regret and sorrow, or she could fill them with projects and self-improvement.

"Em?"

"Yes?"

"I'm going to do something right now. Something that might piss you off. But I'm gonna do it anyway. Because it's driving me damn crazy. *You're* driving me crazy."

Em flinched. Just when you thought your small talk skills had hit a new low, you aimed lower. "I'm talking too much, right? Boring you to death with my enthusiasm over something that obviously doesn't interest you." Her heart drove against her chest; embarrassment flooded her cheeks. *Good heavens, Em. Will you never learn babbling's not high on a man's list of endearing qualities?*

Jax's breath was on her face, warm, coming in quick bursts, his hard features outlined by the blue glow of the dashboard lights. "Not even close. You're enthusiasm interests me—makes me want to grab a hammer and start pounding nails. Chew some wood up with my teeth, maybe. Something we both know, and the evidence shows—" he held up his bandaged hand "—I just shouldn't be allowed to do. That aside, everything about you interests me. And that's why I'm going to do it. Too soon or not be damned."

The words he spoke didn't quite sink in. She didn't understand where he was going. She only knew, their lips were so close she was slightly intoxicated by the heady heat between them. "Do…do what?"

"This," Jax muttered, gravelly, sexy-low as he cupped her neck and pulled her as close as he could with the barrier of the bulky armrest in their way.

Em froze—stilled until her muscles ached from the tension.

He wasn't going to…

Her?

Why would he want to do that with her?

Six

"Kiss you. I'm going to kiss you, Emmaline Amos, and I think I might do it without your permission if you keep holding things up. Interested in knowing why?"

Jax's chest constricted when she clammed up. This was the adorably freaked-out Em. He'd had glimpses of this Em all through mattress shopping and right into dinner.

Every time he'd touched her, even just brushed against her, she couldn't decide whether to enjoy it or run away from it. "Okay, then, I'll tell you. Because your mouth is driving me crazy."

Her eyes were so wide—so full of disbelief, he almost laughed. Had no one ever told her how damn hot her lips were? Well, he'd just be the first.

Snap out of it, man. This is not the road that leads to no dating. You have other things to worry about—like Reece. But Em was like kryptonite, and forcing Reece from his mind was easy when he looked at Em's lips.

She winced, her beautiful features lining with disgust. "You mean my mouth is big, don't you? You want to shut me up because I talk too much? I do that sometimes. I forget myself. I'm sorry."

Her apology made him chuckle. Whoever had given Em the impression her enthusiasm, her ability to draw you into what brought her happiness, was annoying, made him want to beat the shit out of them.

Cupping her jaw, he said, "No. I mean your hot mouth is driving me crazy—words and all. I don't care what's coming out of them."

Letting his tongue finally caress the soft flesh of her lower lip, his gut tightened on impact when he glided over the silky surface, tasting, testing.

Christ.

She stiffened beneath his hand, so he eased his grip, caressing the back of her neck, stroking the soft skin until she relaxed. "Is that okay, Em? If I kiss you?"

"Why would you want to kiss someone like me?"

She said it like those lips weren't amazingly kissable. Fuck. Who'd messed with her head like that? Jax nibbled on the corner of her mouth, smiling against it when she shuddered then leaned into him. Just a little, but enough to signal her body language was adjusting to his touch. "The question here is, who wouldn't want to kiss you? I can't imagine watching your mouth move and not wanting to kiss you."

And then she was softer, her shoulders relaxing in a downward slope. Though her eyes strayed everywhere but his face. "Look at me, Em." He tried to keep the demand soft, but it was using up what little self-control he had.

Em was just as attracted to him as he was to her. Whatever was holding her back, it wasn't lack of sparks. He might have been out of the game for a while, but he knew chemistry. "I'm going to kiss you. Question is, do I have your permission or are you going to pretend you don't really want me to? Because I won't, if you don't want me to. Your move," he coaxed with a grin.

Her lashes lowered to brush her cheeks, thick and full. They were like the fourth or fifth thing on his list of what he liked about her. Right behind the demure but sexy as hell clothes she wore, and her waist. He liked that, too. The way it pinched sharply inward before it sloped into the curve of her hip—hips that swished with an enticing rhythm—and made him smile.

"So, that kiss?"

Jax didn't wait long after Em gave a slight nod. Pulling her head to his, he inhaled her sigh, breathed in her scent, traced the outline of her lips with his tongue before putting his mouth on hers.

He didn't move. He just wanted to feel them against his own. Memorize them, taste them. Hot rushes of blood coursed through his veins when Em let him take the lead with a tremble and the surrender of her mouth.

Just this connection, this contact, and Jax was on fire. He had to hold back, control the need he'd been fighting with all night or he was going to scare her off.

But when he felt Em melt into him, reach for more of him by scrunching either side of his jacket in her fists, sigh again into his mouth, that damn predatory streak welled up in his chest. Made him grip the steering wheel with one hand to keep himself in check.

He slanted his mouth over hers, letting his tongue glide into the heat held behind the object of his fixation.

When Em's fingers clenched his hair, Jax gave up on restraint with a growl and instead focused on getting her closer. His fingers went to the armrest between them, lifting it up, grunting his pleasure when Em helped him, her fingers gripping his forearm.

Then he was pulling her willing body to his, adjusting the setting on his seat, positioning her to straddle his lap.

Em's arms went around his neck, her lips never leaving his, her soft tongue sliding along his in hot passes designed to make him harder than a rock. With leverage on her side, she wedged herself into his lap, her long legs draping on either side of his hips.

His hands found the small of her back through her winter sweater with the ruffles that framed her face, gliding over the swell of her hip, all the while, his hard-on driving at the seam of his jeans.

"We're in a car," she husked out between hungry pulls on his lips.

He silenced her with more hungry drawing, suckling the soft flesh of her bottom lip until she let one of those heady moans escape from her throat, gritty and breathless.

Em pulled away enough to allow words to flow more freely from her mouth. *"A car..."*

He knew this wasn't Emmaline's bag—getting raunchy in a car in someone's driveway. Just by observing her all this week, he knew.

Emmaline Amos was a lady. At all costs, the perception of her reputation should remain sterling. And he was fucking that all up with his dirty thoughts. He saw the war she was having in her mind with her body. It was in the way she tried to stop kissing him by pulling back, filling the void between their lips with words, only to seek his mouth again.

He brushed her crooked red beret away from her eyebrow. "It's a Jeep. But that's just me being picky."

Again, she dipped her head back down, her liquid eyes glazed with moonlight and doubt. "This is crazy." More protests, more driving him insane with the press of her breasts against his chest, enhancing that insanity when she inhaled with a ragged breath.

"Jeeps? I think Jeeps are conservative. Crazy would be a Smart Car." Jax draped his hand over the top of her hip, using the heel of his hand to keep himself from latching on to her ass and grinding against her.

But Em did the grinding for him. Hard, pressed together grinding.

His cock scraped against the seam of his jeans in a painful pulsing response to her pussy, just a slip of a dress and a pair of panties away.

She used the heels of her hands to lever herself upward a little, her chest rising and falling. "Not Jeeps. Making out in a car."

Jax put his hands around her wrists and caressed the width of them. "A Jeep."

She gathered handfuls of his jacket, leaning her forehead against his, huffing out sharp breaths, sinking deeper into him. "Is there really a difference?"

Jax lifted his hips and hissed his appreciation. "Is it

because we're not in the confines of some dark room where I wouldn't be able to see your lips do that thing where they tremble just before you plant them on mine?"

More evasive eyeballing before pretty Em whispered, "Ye...yes."

"Then I'm glad we're in a Jeep. Because I wanna see. As much as you'll let me."

If glowing in the dark were humanly possible, Em achieved it by flushing red. So Em wasn't used to having someone lavish her with the proper attention a woman like her deserved? He'd be happy to be the first.

Knock it off, Hawthorne. Last you said, this wasn't a date—now you want to reassure her she's sexy? What next?

"You want me to show you how much I wanna see it?" His fingers stopped roaming over her hip. If she said no, he was going to have a helluva night alone in the shower—but he wanted to earn her trust—not scare the shit out of her.

Earning her trust isn't how you "don't" date, buddy. You say thanks for dinner, see you at the office. Not how can I make you feel more secure while I rip your clothes off?

He ignored the flash of red flags and tugged on her lips with his mouth. "You okay?"

She was shy again. Torn. Pulling away, leaning in. "Yes," she exhaled the word, blowing it across his mouth with her warm breath—shivering.

Jax didn't hold much back this time, splaying his hand over her back and crushing her against him until she made a soft sound. Her curves seeped into his like caramel over an ice-cream sundae, sticky sweet and hot.

He let his hand travel along her spine, smiling when she reacted to his touch by tightening her muscles in rigid increments.

He dropped the seat and slid it back, giving Em full access to spread out on top of him. Her surprised gasp when their bodies met lengthwise filled Jax's ears as he began to peel her sweater off her shoulder.

The Lord will punish your wanton ways, Emmaline. Ladies do not fornicate in cars.

Jeep. It's a Jeep, Mother.

You say tomato, I say no fornicating in anything with wheels. This will be frowned upon.

Em was too stupid drunk with hot need to care what her mother or anyone else would think. When was the last time that had happened?

Never. She'd never been so totally unaware of everything around her when she was making love. She'd never been swept up. She'd never been so carried away the only thing she did hear was the throb of her pulse. Feel the throb of a man beneath her.

Jax shrugged her sweater from her shoulder, tugging at the end of the sleeve to pull it off her arm while her mother's voice became a distant buzz, clearly masked by her shrieking hormones.

Each touch of Jax's hands, each slip of his tongue into her mouth stoked the dormant part of her that wanted to forget propriety—forget she didn't do things like this. Not once in her life had she even made out in a car, let alone allowed a man to slide his hand along her bare thigh until…

Her gasp echoed in the small space.

"You like that there," Jax murmured, but he wasn't really asking. He was only echoing what her body was screaming at his.

Yes. She loved the caress of his touch along the backs of her thighs, thought maybe it was what she'd always been living for and was now, after all this time, forced to openly admit it.

Fingers, long and thick, glided over her skin, teasing, pushing, easing away, kneading. Over and over until he skimmed the outline of her panties where her hip met thigh.

Em tensed, mewled a small sound she'd never heard come from her mouth before, but Jax muffled it with his lips.

Mercy, his mouth. Soft and hard in the same breath. Commanding, domineering, gentle with just a hint of the taste of the beer he'd had at dinner. More adjectives than her mind could parse—or even cared to.

His fingers slowed, her frustration mounted. She clung to his jacket in fistfuls of leather, afraid to let her hands touch anything else on his body, anything that would encourage him to continue. Yet, wanting—wanting to climb inside him—devour him.

The ripple of his abs beneath her when he reached over with his free hand and turned the key in the ignition to the off position elicited another gasp from her.

Everything about his body screamed in control, powerful. From nowhere, she wondered what a man like Jax would be like out of control. What he'd be like if she did to him what he was doing to her.

Her shiver brought his free arm back around her again, allowing her to burrow closer, bury her nose in his neck. His scent left her weak—it was man and fallen Georgia leaves and some more man and it left heat whooshing through her veins.

Jax tilted her chin up, stroked the flesh of her lower lip, capturing it with his teeth, a new sensation to her, unfamiliar and sexy—a tweak of pain soothed with the rasp of his tongue.

Her manners were all but forgotten—her everything was all but forgotten when Jax wiggled a finger inside the edge of her panties, letting it rest there so she could adjust to the feel of him.

It wasn't a long adjustment period before Em could no longer stand the wait. She wasn't prim and proper Emmaline tonight. Tonight she was possessed by some demon—some part of her that was going to take what she wanted no matter the gossip that would surely ensue. No matter the cost to her stellar reputation.

Her hips became someone else's when she rolled against the hard length of his finger, coaxing Jax, daring him to hurry up and touch her.

Touch her now.

Jax smiled beneath her lips, a slight tilt upward of arrogance maybe, before he stroked downward, spreading her wide, using another finger to tease her, torment the tight bud at her core until her heart tried to push its way out of her chest.

Pricks of fire teased her belly, turning into flames,

licking at her, forcing her to push against Jax's fingers, whimper against his delicious mouth when he did the one last thing she knew would send her over an edge. An edge she was unfamiliar with—unsure of, but one Em dared to teeter on anyway.

His finger slid into her with hot, wet ease—so easily, she gasped, shuddered, saw stars, brilliant splashes of light. She didn't know what else to do but cling to him, relish his big hands on her, moan when he used his other hand to push up her dress and find her breast.

Jax cupped it, thumbed it through the material of her bra until that agonizing slow burn was stealing bits of her sanity, pushing its way along her veins, screaming to find relief.

He drove deeper, stroking, thrusting in long pulls, while his musky scent filled her nose. All of her senses were on board Train Jax, every single one engaged in ways she hadn't known existed.

Suddenly, it was too much—too soon—too everything. Her brain said retreat. It was dangerous to want anything this much—to want *anyone* this much. But her body said "eff your brain, Emmaline Amos" and fell into the dark cauldron of her boiling hormones.

When she fell, it was hard. She rode Jax's hand, heard his grunt of satisfaction at her slippery descent, pressed so deeply into him, surely the seat would crash through the floorboards of her Jeep.

Everything, his hard thighs under her, his wide chest making her feel small and delicate, his thick fingers thrusting into her, became a heady aphrodisiac. The last roll of her hips, the last bit of air she was able to suck in before she came was a blur.

There was nothing but the sharply sweet victory of total completion when each nerve in her body hummed and the rush of her pulse roared in her ears.

She knew she screamed. Buried her face in Jax's yummy-smelling neck until she made the snap decision to pretend she did things like this all the time.

Em's fingers fumbled to reach between them so Jax would know this wasn't just about her despite how she'd just behaved.

"I don't think you're ready for that just yet," he grumbled in her ear. He wrapped his hand around her wrist and brought it up under his chin, rubbing her skin against the stubble.

"Because you're too much man for little ole me to handle?" The words growled from her throat, sounding sated and still not like her voice at all.

His laughter vibrated in her chest, rumbly and sexy. "Hah! I doubt there's much you can't handle. I meant emotionally."

She used the heels of her hands on his shoulders to lever herself upward. "Now you're my emotional compass?"

He smiled, sort of rakish and smug. "You were worried about making out in a car, Em."

Fair. "But I did it."

"Total chore?"

She rolled her eyes with exaggeration, tucking her chin into her shoulder in a sudden bid to pull off the Dixie flirt. "Ugh. Horrendous. Couldn't you tell?"

Cupping the back of her head, Jax pulled her tighter to him. "I'm saying this all wrong."

"You're not winning any wordsmith awards."

"What if I said *I* wasn't ready?"

What if? Or what if you're just a gentleman? One of those nearly extinct beings that takes pity on a woman and her deprived libido, but wants nothing in return. "Right. Because I'm far more woman than a man like you can handle."

"That might not be far off the mark. And some truth here, it's been a long time for me. But what I meant was, I have no condoms, and seeing as you don't make it a habit to make out in cars—"

"Jeeps."

"Jeeps. I figured you wouldn't have any on hand, either."

Smart and Dreamy McSteamy. Did his perfection know no bounds? "You're noble and wise."

Now he growled, tightening his hold on her, the rigid line of his cock burning between her thighs. "Make no mistake, if I'd had that condom, I can't promise you wouldn't be naked with me buried inside you right now. All night long if I could manage it in such cramped quarters. I'm hornier than I think I've ever been for any woman, Emmaline Amos."

Gulping. She was suddenly speechless and gulping. No one had ever used words like that with her before. They made her shaky—uncomfortable, but the good kind of uncomfortable.

Jax read her body language with ease. "No one's ever said that to you before, have they?"

Everything became too much again. Too big, too loud, too honest. She began to pull away as reality set in.

But Jax wasn't letting her off so easy; he drew her back in by flattening his palm on her butt. "Jesus. Okay then, I'll be the first. You're damn hot, damn irresistible, too."

"I don't know if *irresistible* is the right word. But I can tell you I'm not myself." No. She sure wasn't. One minute she was shy and all worship-y like he was some sex god, the next she was lusty and flirty like she was the sex goddess.

Jax's eyes teased, but his words were direct. He curled a finger under her chin and nipped the corner of her mouth. "You want to run away and hide, don't you?"

Yes. No. Yes. She couldn't think when his mouth was near hers. "And never see you again."

"That's going to prove difficult, seeing as we work in the same office."

She began grasping at straws, pulling away, straightening, putting back on her Em-face. "It's only temporary. You're not a permanent employee."

"Neener, neener, neener."

"What?"

"I'm making fun of your playground move. You know, pull my hair and run away?"

Em winced, her shoulders sagging. "Childish, right?"

He shrugged, his muscles rippling beneath her hands. "Defense mechanism. Totally understand. You feel exposed, vulnerable."

Which reminded her… "I think I have to go home."

"I think you're going to overthink this when you get home."

You bet she was. She was going to think so hard they'd see the smoke clear over in Johnsonville. "I think you're right."

"Damn. That means we're going to be awkward at the office, doesn't it? Avoid each other in the halls—suck in our stomachs so we don't brush against each other when we're in the kitchen?"

"*You* have to suck in your stomach? Preposterous."

"Reactive. You know, make yourself small to avoid contact. So, is that where we're headed?"

"Count on it."

"I don't like it."

"I don't think I can help it."

"Try."

"Why?"

"Because I like you, and I don't want you to feel uncomfortable."

"I really have to go home."

"Not until you promise not to be awkward at work."

"We just had almost sex. Awkward is a given."

"Not if you try. Don't make me take your keys from you until you promise you'll at least try not to be awkward."

"Promise."

He clucked his tongue and shook his head, but his eyes teased hers. "Lies."

"Guilty."

A sharp rap of knuckles on the Jeep's window sent her into a heart-thumping panic. Em scrambled to push her dress down, horrified at the mere thought they'd been caught fooling around in a car.

Jeep, Emmaline. You said Jeep.

Yes, Mama. My Jeep. Tack on I'm messin' around with a man I hardly know and every nosy crony in Plum Orchard'll be sewin' up scarlet letters to paste on my chest in no time.

Her mother's words in her head made her move faster. She cracked her head on the ceiling just as Jax was smoothing her sweater back up over her shoulder and making a stern face at the shadowy figure outside the car.

His hand instantly went to the back of her head to protect her from crushing in her skull. "My brother Tag," he offered. If he was at all embarrassed at being caught in this state, he was a good poker player.

A face a lot like Jax's, but rougher, even harder angled, grinned into the window while moonlight poured over her indecency through her sunroof.

Perfect.

Still facing the wrong way, she crawled across the seat just as Jax turned the key and hit the button for the automatic window. He poked his head out while Em yanked at her dress, caught on the edge of the middle console.

There was a loud tear, solidifying the nightmare her good sense had become. Embarrassment stained her cheeks with a hot whoosh, but her reactive cringe was what almost drove them over the edge.

In her hot dose of humiliation, she stepped on the

gas, revving the engine until it ground out a loud shot of ear-jarring sound.

Jax held up a calm finger to his brother. "One sec." He leaned over, still seemingly unaffected, and put one hand on her shoulder while he used the other to untwist the edge of her dress, releasing it from the console. As he helped resituate her, he made introductions. "Em, this is my brother Tag. Tag, Emmaline Amos."

Tag drove his big, square hand through the window. "Nice to meet you, ma'am."

She slid down into the driver's seat, looking straight ahead, focusing on the big oak tree, but good breeding and the threat of eternal damnation forced her to hold out her hand. "The same."

Tag took it and gave it a light squeeze before letting go and focusing on Jax. "It's Maizy. She's got a fever. I'm thinking maybe another ear infection, but I can't remember the recipe for the oil you use that she likes so much. Sorry, bro. Didn't mean to—" he cleared his throat "—interrupt."

Another face, equally as handsome, and rough in an entirely different way than Jax and Tag, appeared behind Tag. He held up a hand and waved with what was turning out to be the signature Hawthorne grin. When a smile wasn't in place, all three were gruff, hard edges, almost angry, but their smiles changed the landscape of everything. "Gage Hawthorne. You must be Emmaline."

No. Tonight she was dirty girl. Emmaline was all but ashes in a sand-doused fire. She inhaled, keeping herself from pushing the breath from her lips. "That's me. Nice to meet you."

So nice. Everything was so nice tonight. This time, she held out her hand, pushing her gaze toward Gage's—successfully meeting it—crushing the ugly impulse to pop open the passenger door, push Jax out, floor it, drive straight to her house and dive for cover under the fluffy new comforter on her bed.

Gage thumped Tag on the shoulder with a square hand that matched his brother's almost identically. "I found it, knucklehead. Told you I would if you just waited ten seconds. Leave them alone and come back in."

Jax's face was different now, too. He had on his Maizy face. Concern lined it, determination, too. "Guys, it's okay. If Maizy's sick, I want to be there."

Warmth fizzled and bubbled in her stomach. He loved Maizy the way a little girl should be loved by her daddy. Loosening her stiff lips, Em shooed him with her hand. "You should really go. Say hello to Maizy for me, okay?"

Jax's eyes searched hers, but she managed a warm smile that said all was well, and flicked her fingers again in a gesture to dismiss them all. "Go, before Maizy comes lookin' for you three out here in the cold. You don't want her to get worse."

He was so obviously trying to protect her shredded reputation by not saying anything that not saying anything was making everything worse.

Which made for the perfect escape. "G'night, Jax." She hitched her jaw toward the door, watching his fingers pop it open and his big body slide out. The gravel beneath his feet crunched in time with her tires as she began to pull away. "Nice meeting you both," she managed, before driving the window upward with a flick of her finger, blocking out any sort of response from the trio of men.

Eyes on the winding road leading back to her place, Em began the tedious process of overthinking.

Every word. Every hot caress.

Mercy.

Seven

"Dixie?"

"Yes, Emmaline?"

"Coffee, sunshine." Em handed the cup to her over the back of the couch without meeting her eyes. She stepped over Dora's—her enormous Saint Bernard's—body, stooping to give her ears a quick rub.

Dixie struggled to sit up—as gorgeous as ever, even this early in the morning and a night spent on her narrow couch. "You're a treasure."

No. I'm a dirty girl. The crass might even call me a slut. But never a treasure. "You're welcome."

Dixie's yawn made the guilty half of her jump. "Boys still asleep?"

"Uh-huh." She made her way to the small nook she'd created for the boys' school backpacks and shoes and began to straighten, fingers tight with tension.

"Can you look at me when you answer me?"

"Not a chance."

"Do you suppose hidin' in the boys' backpacks is

going to keep me from asking you probing questions about last night and where you got to until I finally passed out at one in the mornin'?"

"I was hopin' they'd act as some sort of Dixie-off." She held up the backpack over her head and danced it in the air with a bounce.

"Not likely," Dixie said from behind her, grabbing the backpack and setting it aside. She took Em's hand and walked her to the couch. "Sit. I'll make you a cup of coffee. You put together your explanation story for me while I do it. Tie up those loose ends and all." She grinned at Em before setting her mug down on the coffee table and wandering off to the kitchen.

She loved her kitchen. It was the first thing in the house she'd attacked when Clifton left. It was rustic black granite countertops and lovingly antiqued ivory cabinets, a soft-gray-and-muted-black-veined ceramic backsplash with diamond tiled patterns in cream she'd designed herself.

The shiny silver appliances were her gift to herself after Dixie hired her. The stove being her first love. A six-burner gas cooktop splayed out atop her center island and a wall oven with a digital timer set to change the temperature to cook the meals she dropped into the mouth of it before leaving for work.

The laminate flooring, a grainy dark wood, more labor and mostly love, with coils beneath to heat it, was, to date, her crowning glory. Her kitchen said, Em was here.

Like her constructional footprint was all that was necessary for her to finally be heard. Like the grout she'd mixed sang her name when she'd stirred batches and batches of it. Like the floor she'd laid, ruining saw blade after saw blade until she got it right, was her rebel cry for independence.

The peace that single room brought her, the careful choices she'd made for the colors meant to bellow, "This here be Emmaline's Kitchen—made from hours of splinters and sweat and a two-day rental on a wet saw that ended up being a weeklong four-hundred-dollar bill. See the bloodshed on the corners of the wood-grained cabinet right near the refrigerator. Look at how the wall oven glistens with the tears of the fair Emmaline as she struggled to hook it up all while she sobbed and doused everyone within earshot with some uncharacteristically foul language. Know this before ye enter!"

The kitchen was her statement. Her new beginning.

As Dixie made her way around that very kitchen, gathering up a mug for Em, she asked again, "How're those loose ends coming, Em?"

Em tucked her hands into her bathrobe, sinking as far into the couch as she could. What could she say? *I got home late because Jax Hawthorne did things to me the likes of which I can never define while I enjoyed every second of it—in a car—er,* Jeep—*like some common tart?*

Dixie held the blue mosaic mug out to her before settling into the chair opposite the couch. She tucked a rust-colored pillow to her belly and sighed. "Your couch is awful. My back will never be the same."

Neither will my vagina. Oh. Mercy. "You were sleeping so soundly, I didn't want to wake you. So I texted

Caine and told him you were spending the night. I hope that's all right."

She massaged the back of her neck and grinned. "Thank you. Now no more avoiding this. You ready?"

"With my story?"

"Yep."

"Why does there have to be a story attached to me coming home late?"

Dixie gave her the saucy "whatever" look and shrugged. "There doesn't."

Em narrowed her eyes at her friend and pursed her lips. "Oh, there does, too. Don't you try to guilt me into telling you with your pretend indifference."

"Is there any other way?"

"We went shopping."

Dixie popped her lips and tilted her head to nod. "Shopping can take hours and hours. I know. I'm a shopper. No bigger shopper 'n me. Why, sometimes, when I'm looking at paint swatches and bed linens, I make an entire weekend of it. Seventy-two hours of non-stop color wheels and Egyptian cotton." She sipped her coffee, letting her feet dangle over the arm of the chair.

"You're mocking me."

"I am."

"I can't talk about it."

"I don't want you to do anything you don't want to do. Let's just sit quietly together and enjoy the peace of this brand-new Saturday before the boys wake up. I promised to take them to the big house and let Sanjeev spoil them rotten with grilled cheese and ice-cream sundaes for lunch, then some camel time with Toe. You know, just in case you didn't make it home today after all that shopping." Dixie hunkered down into the chair, letting her head fall back and closing her eyes.

While Em squirmed. "I can't talk about it."

Dixie didn't open her eyes. "You said that. Whatever you did with Mr. Jax Hawthorne last night has left you redundant."

"I had almost sex with him!" she blurted out—the words echoing in her skull, taunting. Oh. That sounded so much worse out loud than it ever had in her head.

Dixie kept her eyes closed, but her lips twitched. "I thought we were havin' quiet time?"

"You know doggone well you'd make me tell you just by virtue of your disapproving silence."

"I did no such thing. You said you didn't want to talk about it. I was respectin' your wishes."

"With your silent condemnation—the one that makes me squirm until my skin crawls."

"I can't make you do anything you don't want to do, Em. If you squirmed, that was your guilt over not telling your best friend something you so obviously need to talk out. That's on you. Not me. Now, breakfast? I make a mean bowl of grits. Obviously, you need to re-fuel." Her straight face crumpled into a fit of laughter that had her shoulders shaking so hard, she almost spilled her coffee.

Em dropped her coffee mug on the rich-hued surface of her pine table. "This is not funny, Dixie! I've done something so unlike me, and I don't know what to do about it." Misery, be thy name.

"But does what you did feel good enough that you

might not want to take it back? 'Cuz you know, that's okay. To enjoy the company of a man."

"I didn't just enjoy the company of a man, Dixie. I enjoyed his company in a Jeep with the seat flat. I was…I was sexually festive! If word got out I was diddlin' in, of all things, a Jeep, parked right outside the man's home while his baby girl slept inside—"

"What?" Dixie sat forward with probing eyes. "What would happen, Em? People would say, that dirty Em. How dare she date a man when she's just divorced and single and well within her rights to spend time with an attractive, equally single man? Is that what they'd say? Would they call you unseemly, maybe even forward? And why is that so important to you, anyway?"

"Because of what happened with Louella when she put those pictures of him up on Founders' Day, Dixie. I wouldn't put it past Louella to be sneakin' around snoopin'. I don't want the boys to have more trouble at school, Dixie. Isn't it bad enough they're teased unmercifully about Clifton? Add me throwing myself at a man in a parked car, and they'll never recover."

Dixie's eyes flashed angry and hot. "So you're gonna let Louella dictate your life?"

"If it means the boys won't have people callin' their mother a whore on top of everything else, yes." Yes, she would.

"Because Louella's so lily-white," Dixie spat, her lips pursing in distaste. "It's your life. You should be able to live it the way you want. I understand you don't want the boys to suffer, but it isn't like you're out in the square skinnin' the seniors alive in the midday sun. You were just having some fun. As long as you're not cheatin' or hurting anyone, the notion that it's bad to have sex for the joy of it is archaic."

"But that's the PO, and you know it."

"No, here's what I know. Your life is yours until you let someone else run it. I learned that from Landon. He taught me to live, Em. Really live. I'm here to tell you, I love livin', even in this town where no one approves of how I live. There's nothing wrong with having almost sex in a car between two consenting adults." Dixie paused, her head cocked in question. "But a question. What is almost sex to you, anyway, Em?"

"Like I have to define that to the devil's playmate. You know what almost sex is."

She grinned. "I fear my definition and yours may vary."

"We hit a few bases and then some. But then we realized we didn't have a condom, so we couldn't hit a home run." Was that regret stabbing at her? Yes. She'd wanted to make love with a man she'd known less than a week.

Dixie giggled and did the wave. "Cheers from the crowd."

Still, she couldn't accept that about herself. She wasn't the kind of woman who had sex just for sex's sake. "No. Don't cheer my bad behavior."

"Why is it bad to enjoy a man, Em?"

"Because I was this close to riding him like he was Seabiscuit."

So why was that bad?

Because it was. Because her mother said so. Because it sullied her reputation to be so free with her affections.

Because it was out of wedlock. Because the rumor mill would have a field day with it. Because Jax could be hurt just by associating with her.

Em ran a hand over her hair, hoping she'd run her mother and all the other gossipmongers in town out of her head, too. "I don't know. It's not. I think." She groaned. "I have all these conflicting feelin's about it. On the one hand, I wouldn't say you were loose if you chose to do it. You did choose to do it. You chose it a lot before Caine. On the other hand, I feel like I've gone against everything I was raised to believe in. I've never had anythin' but marital relations, Dixie. I know in this day and age that's ridiculous, but it wasn't like anyone was offerin' outside of Clifton anyway."

Dixie's eyes bled sympathy. She'd been raised by a mother much like Clora. Nothing should be enjoyed, every moment of her life was a chore—a task she met with the strong hand of the divine guiding it.

"I won't pick on you for that voice in your head that tells you sex isn't for a good, upstandin' woman unless she's married, but your mother's done a real number on you, and it makes me want to shake her every time she sits across the table from me when we have Sunday dinner here. I don't want to insult you either, but as your person, I'm compelled to say something. I just don't know if you'll like it much."

Meaning, Dixie was loading up the shotgun. "But you're going to say it anyway...."

Dixie's brows crunched together, matching the angry line of her lips. "Clora Mitchell's full of horse manure. She can suck the joy out of a room with just the purse of her disapproving lips, and they're always pursed. She enjoys nothing without behaving like she just took one for Team Righteous—and it hurt—and she wants us all to know it hurt. I get the impression she's the kind of woman who endured lovemakin' rather than getting down in the dirty with it."

Em cringed. "We weren't open about…those things." Heaven forbid. She'd never had those kinds of talks with her mother. In fact, she was shocked to discover she couldn't remember talking about any of her feelings with either of her parents.

"Okay, then," Dixie pressed. "Consider this. Maybe she's slanted your views on things. If that's what *Emmaline* really believes, if you really believe you can't make love with more than one man in a lifetime without burnin' in the fiery pit of Satan's flames, and you're that worried people will talk, then okay. I'll hush. But if it's what your mama beat you over the head with and you're wafflin' about it, worried she'll cast that ugly look of disapproval every time you actually find joy in something, you need to do some soul-searchin'."

Em shook her head, overwhelmed with all the crossed wires in her brain, the confusing mixed messages—the grip her mother's lack of approval still had on her. "All that aside, Dixie, this isn't like me. To give in to impulse. But I did. I gave in to it right there in his driveway. I offered to drive because Jax doesn't know Johnsonville like I do. Now, I wonder if it wasn't some sort of subliminal premeditation on my part."

Dixie kept her face blank. "That sounds just like you, Em. Premeditated almost sex."

She hid her face in her hands. "That's exactly my point. I let myself get caught up, swept away. I'm sure I came off desperate and pathetic. None of what happened last night was like me."

Dixie sat up and dripped her mug on the table. "Oh, baloney. How do you even know what's like you? Did you know all this DIY was like you until you had time on your hands to find out? Did you know you had a stern teacher's voice in you until you used it? So here's the real question—did you like it? Was it good almost all the way?"

Good? It was gooder than good. Hot, wet, the best almost sex ever. "It was unimaginably good. I've never quite…well, you know…had so many things occur… in those parts…" She waved a hand over "those parts," her face hot and red.

But mercy, what a relief to say it was good so it didn't become a filthy secret she carried around with her like a wadded-up tissue full of snot tucked away in your sleeve. Like sloughing off dead skin.

She'd liked last night.

No, she'd loved last night. She'd like to do last night again and again, but…

Dixie clapped her hands together. "I do know, and I'm so happy for you! The two of you set a room on fire. How could it have been any other way?"

Em waved her finger in the air. "This is not an occasion to jump up and down like we just met a Backstreet Boy, Dixie." This part. The part where she confessed the last piece of the puzzle that really made her sound like a bed-hopping trollop was the hardest confession of all.

"And why not?"

Could she explain why not without sounding like she just wanted to sleep around for the sake of quenching her lust for sex? But Dixie would worm it out of her any old way.

So she just said it. "Because I don't want to get involved with anyone. Not now. Not so soon after the humiliation of Clifton leavin' me. I think I'd just like to…make the business. No flowers or fancy dinners or anything but…well, you know."

"Oh."

Em's mouth fell open. "Oh? What kind of an answer is that?"

Dixie sipped at her coffee—meaning, she was weighing her words. "I'm just wonderin' if you're cut out for sneakin' around in cars."

"Jeeps." Just the way she remembered Jax's husky voice saying it made her shiver.

Dixie's glare was impatient. "Whatever. So you're telling me you want nothing more than a sexual relationship with him?"

"Yes." The admission exploded from her throat.

She was going to do it. She was going to ask the only person she knew who understood men and their brains. Well, mostly. "I want to ask you something, but I want to do it without recrimination, especially from the devil's favorite playmate. I'm asking you a very sensitive, very private question, you being my person."

"I'm getting whiplash, honey. Why don't you just tell me what's really going on—what's really eatin' at you, and I'll try to help in the best way the devil's favorite playmate knows how."

Jax had to be the most experienced man she'd ever met, even if she hadn't met many. Or made love with many. Or even if she'd only made love with not so many. Okay, just one and a quick grope from Delroy Green at a football game.

If last night was any indication, Jax knew things she wanted to know. He did things she wanted to do again. If she could just get past the disapproval in her head, give herself permission to explore…

Em smoothed the edge of her bathrobe, licking her lips nervously. "Do you think Jax is the kind of man who'd just like to fool around? You know, without feelin' like he has to buy me dinner or take me to the movies?"

Dixie's eyes were confused for a brief moment before they gleamed. "Well, you can ask him at dinner tonight at the big house. He's coming, by the way."

"You didn't…"

"Oh, no. I didn't. I would have if Caine hadn't beaten me to it, but did I personally hand him the invitation? Innocent."

How would she ever look him in the eye after sprawling across him like a Sealy in a Jeep last night?

A Jeep.

"So are you going to call that bitch back?" Tag pressed, unlacing his work boots and kicking them off.

Jax knocked his brother in the shoulder with the heel

of his hand. "Don't call her that, Tag. Maizy's right in the other room. Jesus."

Tag's hard face turned to granite under the new recessed lighting he'd just installed in the kitchen. "Well, it's what she damn well is. I'm just callin' it like I see it. She hasn't bothered with Maizy for five years and ten months of her life. What's so damn important now?"

Jax scrubbed his jaw with his hand. He didn't know. He didn't want to know. "I don't know."

His jaw hurt from clenching it. When he hadn't been trying to sweep the message from Reece under the carpet labeled "refuse to acknowledge" today, he'd been thinking about Em and last night. Why now? On both the Reece and Em fronts? It was like the good and bad colliding at exactly the wrong moment.

Add to that, it pissed him off that he was being such a pussy about facing his biggest nightmare. Reece.

Tag, the latest owning-your-crap-out-loud convert, said it for him. "You don't want to know."

Anger, more that his brother was right than anything else, made Jax return with rapid fire. "Oh, save your AA bullshit for someone who needs it, huh? No. No, I don't want to know. Is it okay by you, preacher man, if I keep it to myself until I can process it? Or do I have to slice my gut open and throw my spleen on a table in some church where they serve you shitty coffee and tell you to take it one day at a time in order to earn my chip like you did?"

Shit. The minute he said the words, he regretted them. He was bagging on his brother for using the only device that had helped him begin to fix himself.

He regrouped, gripping the edge of his shiny new center island. "That was uncalled for. I'm sorry, but we have to face the fact that Reece does have rights—"

Tag shoved the ladder left from installing the lights out of the way. It clattered to the ground with a noisy bang. "Nah. Forget it. You have a right to still be angry with me, brother. But Reece? She has no goddamn rights, Jax. She gave all of them up when she skipped off to wherever the fu—"

"Bad word alert, Uncle Tag!" Gage yelled, flying around the freshly framed kitchen doorway, Maizy bouncing on his back.

He backed up to the center island and deposited her on the top of it while she giggled. She gave them all a solemn look, her chocolate eyes smiling. "It's okay. I know all the bad words, Uncle Gage. I hear Uncle Tag say them every day when he's working on stuff. He says the *F* word a bunch."

Jax narrowed his eyes at his brother before scooping Maizy up. "So, are you ready for the party, Cinderella?"

Maizy nodded, but her nose wrinkled. "I'm not Cinderella, Daddy. I'm Belle from *Beauty and the Beast*. Grandpa Givens says Cinderella just wanted a boyfriend, but Belle wanted a whole library. I think he said that's smarter than just wanting a boyfriend."

Jax shook his head at the conversations between Grandpa Givens and his daughter. He chuckled at her. "Grandpa Givens gives good advice. Besides, I'd never let you live in some ugly castle with a beast just so you can have a library. I'll buy you a library instead."

"And I'll help build it, squirt," Gage assured her.

"So, you go eat some fancy food for me tonight, okay? You need all the good food you can get," Tag teased, his face transforming from dark to light when centering his gaze on his niece—he and Jax's disagreement all but set back on the shelf to be taken down and fought out another time.

Jax tickled her ribs. "We gotta go or we're gonna be late."

Tag dropped a quick kiss on her forehead before grabbing the ladder. "Yeah. You don't want Daddy to miss his chance to ask that pretty Em if she'll help him with the house, do you?" He didn't wait for an answer. Instead, he dragged the ladder up over his shoulder, giving one last disgusted look at Jax before leaving the kitchen.

Jax sighed. Reece was a still-bleeding, open wound between the two of them—for all of them, but especially between he and Tag. Tag had hated her on sight, from the second she'd sat down at the table in that pub almost seven years ago. He'd driven home that dislike like it was his mission after she'd screwed Jax over.

Maizy pulled on the end of Jax's shirt, reminding him she was all that mattered. "What's fancy food, Daddy?"

"Wow. We've really slacked off in the foodie department, haven't we, kiddo? At least we taught you manners. Fancy food is food that doesn't come from a box in the freezer," Gage joked, lightly pinching her nose.

Jax looked down at his daughter, smoothing her wiry curls, and straightened her headband with the red feathers and fake rhinestones in the shape of a unicorn—her all-time favorite mythical creature.

His heart began that rapid staccato of painful beating—the one that always happened when he let his worst Reece fear surface. The one he pounded down into the ground every time it rose up like the ugly weeds out in that garden Em said he had somewhere under the brush. Jesus, he loved her. "Not icky fish sticks?"

"Are there really going to be pretty ladies there?"

His mood instantly lightened. Well, there'd be at least one. She was the only one he saw. Jax grinned down at his kid. "I sure hope so."

He damn well did. All day, while he'd pushed Reece's reasons for calling to the back of his mind, he'd devised ways to put him and Em together—a lot.

Then he'd kicked himself for hatching stupid plots to get her in the same vicinity as him.

After her reaction to last night, she was probably freaked out. She'd avoid him and he'd avoid her, and that was probably better.

Last night had been way out of her comfort zone. She'd all but said it herself. Truth be told, it was a little out of his, too. He'd never found himself so instantaneously attracted to a woman that he was willing to forgo everything just to run his tongue over her lips.

He'd gotten pushy because of it—let his lack of female companionship lately take the reins. But since Harper's death, since he'd witnessed the havoc unspoken words could wreak on your life, he'd promised himself he was going to live more honestly. For himself and as an example to Maizy. No more holding back. He was going to chalk last night up to that.

Hindsight said maybe his words were a little too honest, and he was going to pay for it tonight at Caine and Dixie's dinner party. He didn't want Em to get the wrong impression about where he stood on the single front, and she didn't come across as the kind of woman who was comfortable with a physical relationship.

There'd be awkward Em silence tonight, for sure.

Despite his firm stance on no dating, he still smiled because the awkward silence would be Em's.

He gave Maizy one last squeeze. "Let's get going, kiddo."

She held her arms out to Gage and gave him a Maizy hug, whispering in his ear, "Say good-night, Gracie."

Jax's heart shifted hard in his chest just like it always did when she used the words he'd taught her almost from birth.

Jake's words. He was why those words were so important.

Maizy was the biggest reason he had to avoid all these feelings cropping up for Em. Everything was for her. No outsiders allowed. Nothing would detract him from fixing what he'd broken and couldn't ever fix.

Gage tweaked her cheek and murmured against her hair, "Good night, Gracie."

Eight

"Clifton Junior, please don't snatch," Em corrected, placing a hand over his smaller one to prevent him from knocking over the shiny silver platter Sanjeev held in order to nab a weenie in a blanket. "We're guests in Aunt Dixie and Uncle Caine's home. They've gone to a lot of trouble to make this night fun. Please appreciate that effort and put your best manners forward."

Sanjeev, always crisp and fresh in a white kurta, his midnight-black hair stark against the backdrop of the material, held a hand up, but Em frowned his protest away. No. No more allowing Clifton to take advantage.

Ugh. A year ago, Clifton was the sweetest boy on the planet. Considerate, loving, a snuggler.

Today, at the ripe old age of eight, he was sullen, troubled and moody, nothing like the gooey dose of sunshine that had once greeted her every morning.

Clifton shot her his "every disobedient thing I do is because you're the worst mother ever" expression and rolled his wide blue eyes.

Jax's dark head was there all of a sudden, nodding his agreement. "Mom's right, you know. But I kinda get it. If weenies in a blanket are at stake, I might get grabby, too."

Enter the dreaded awkward. To-die-for awkward, no doubt. Whisper-husky-voiced awkward, check. Deliciously dressed in a navy fitted shirt and tight jeans awkward, check-check. But still awkward.

"Evenin', Emmaline. This must be Clifton Junior?" Jax stuck out his hand at Clifton, all five fingers of magic, and waited.

The slow climb of red her cheeks were growing accustomed to wearing when Jax was around began its rise. He took up all the space in the room, leaving her feeling like simply lifting her hand was an attempt to defy gravity.

She nudged Clifton, who poked his hand out like he was thrusting his chubby fingers into a pot of boiling water. "Clifton, this is Mr. Hawthorne. Please say hello."

Jax took her son's hand, swallowing it whole, and shook it briskly. "You can call me Jax if it's okay with your mom."

Clifton, ever unimpressed, looked to Em with his haughty disdain before pulling his hand away. Knowing he should acknowledge an adult, he was deciding in his little mind whether to defy her openly. It was a choice he made frequently.

Thankfully, at this moment, one where she was so fragile, if someone blew on her, she'd shatter into a million pieces, Clifton chose obedience. "Nice to meet you, Jax."

Jax's face spread into a grin. "Same here."

Clifton popped the weenie in a blanket in his mouth and took off toward the vast area in the great room where Sanjeev had set up all sorts of activities for her boys and Maizy.

"No running with food in your mouth, mister!" she called after him, for which he promptly ignored her and dived into the pool of balls in the middle of the room.

"At that stage where everything you say is a reason to roll his eyes and make gagging noises?" Jax asked, moving closer to her, sending prickly beads of awareness along her forearms.

Hypersensitive to Jax's presence and his accurate evaluation of Clifton, her sigh was forlorn. "That's me. The most disgusting person on earth."

"Totally bogus assessment. If only he could see what I see."

If only she could find a potted plant to hide behind or some fresh dirt to dig a hole for herself, maybe. He'd seen all right. Plenty. There was that thick silence he'd been talking about.

From the corner of her downcast eyes, Em saw him rock back on his feet, putting his hands in his jeans' pockets. "So here we are at awkward."

All day long, while she'd waged a full-on war of anticipation and dread about seeing him again, she'd mentally practiced her "I'll take a lover in the afternoon" theory.

So big deal. He'd done some amazing things to her

body. Plenty of people did amazing things to each other's bodies all the time, took showers, parted ways and never saw each other again.

One-night stands happened all the time. It wasn't anything new or original. So what? *But you've never had a one-night stand, Em.* Could what happened even be classified as a one-night stand when you never made it past third base?

Was it third base, anyway?

And then she'd seen him arrive at the big house. Enormous man, strutting toward the grand entryway with his long legs, and her resolve to behave as though nothing earth-shattering had happened between them melted like butter in a cast-iron pan.

Jax made her feel things she'd never felt before. He evoked words from her lips she'd never used before. Her head was spinning, and it felt good, and bad, forbidden and alluring and frightening.

She loved it, hated it, wanted it, didn't want it.

Now add in the tone of Jax's voice, amused and teasing, and it tripped her ever-sensitive trigger. That he could joke about her discomfort made her angry. This wasn't funny. Her embarrassment wasn't something to poke her through the bars of her humiliation with.

She finally looked directly up at him, fought not to get sucked in by the heart-stopping way his eyes crinkled up around the edges when he was amused. "Is this funny to you?"

Now he was looking down at her, his eyes warm and smiling. "Not at all. I'm just pointing out we're going through an awkward phase."

"You'd better not be. Making fun of me, that is."
There it was. Stern teacher's voice.

"Can I say something?"

"Can I stop you?"

"After last night, seems I have no censor. So, it isn't looking good." He'd managed to somehow maneuver her toward a corner, using his big frame as a coaxing method. The shelter that frame gave her almost stole her breath.

And that made her angry. Why should the shelter of a *man* make her feel safe? Wasn't her own shelter good enough?

But then he smiled crookedly, and Em's anger evaporated, replaced by a slight tilt upward of her lips—lips she had to clamp down on to keep from showing her cards. Her inability to control her mood swings left her little room to judge someone else's behavior. "Then fire away."

Jax stared down at her. Oh, those eyes. So expressive and intense, searching hers. "First, because I can't seem to stop myself, I like that stern teacher's voice you use. It's pretty hot. I know, I know, too much too soon. But there it is. Second, I don't like that you're uncomfortable with me after last night. Third, I don't like that we're going through an awkward phase because of last night."

"The awkward part is standin' at attention. It's a little awful." So awful she wanted to borrow her stern teacher's eraser and wipe it away.

"But you have nothing to feel awkward about, Em," he grumbled.

She stared down at her suede boots.

He put his lips to her ear, making her curl into him. "Whaddya say we start over?"

Pouty face. "And forget last night ever happened?" She leaned back and waited for his response.

He leaned into her, too, making her shivery and light-headed. "Well, I'd like to think what happened wasn't forgettable, but if it makes you feel more comfortable, we can put it on a shelf. Wipe the slate clean. Technically, we just messed around like we were still in high school."

A shelf. Like that kind of explosive reaction to him had a shelf. She had two choices where Jax was concerned. Give in to her secret fantasies or avoid him altogether.

That rush of whatever Jax did to her, the wave of plum crazy that held her brain hostage and let her lips roam free, took over again, unplanned and totally unprovoked. "I have a question."

"I hope I have the answer."

"Do you want to have sex with me?"

Jax's brow furrowed, deep lines forming on his forehead, the scent of Em in his nose. He had a brief, speechless moment filled with all the visuals her words spawned before the sweet lines of her face came back into focus. "Come again?"

In the dim corner, right beside the biggest brass planter he'd ever seen, Em's eyes flew open. Her hand went to her throat in that cute way it did when she was embarrassed. "I just said that out loud, didn't I?"

He half grinned, watching as she licked her lips—nervous, embarrassed. "Yeah. It was a little awesome."

"And not like me at all, but..."

He made sure she was hidden from prying eyes with the size of his body, but couldn't resist running his finger along her cheek. "You know, you keep saying that, but maybe it is like you and you just weren't aware of it."

She didn't look too sure about that, yet it didn't stop her from responding to his touch. Her jaw shifted an inch, the tips of her toes moving closer to his. "So you think this crude, forward half of me, the half of me that has no filter, is emergin' now because?"

"Because you like me?"

She retreated, her chin lifting, exposing her long, pretty neck. "I don't even know you, and as a by the by, I've liked plenty o' people and I've never been forward with any of them."

He leaned into her, giving him the opportunity to move even closer—smell her hair, take a quick peek at the front of her knit sweaterdress, hugging all those curves. "Well, let's face it, I do give good car."

She relaxed again. "Jeep."

Was she teasing him now? "Right. Point being, you're obviously comfortable enough with me to show me who you really are. Sometimes, it isn't just in the movies where physical connections like that happen."

"I don't want a connection." She sounded like she meant it. Jax didn't like that sound at all. He didn't want to not like it, but for the moment, he was going to concede to his curiosity.

He found himself asking, "Who doesn't want to feel connected?" Yeah. Everybody wanted to feel connected.

"Someone who just went through an ugly, very scandalous divorce no one in this gossipy town can seem to stop talking about. Someone who doesn't want to add new people to her life so the gossipy people of this town can talk about them, too. Someone who has a son that needs her and can't afford to add in the stress of a new relationship when the end of the old one is what's still tearing said son apart, and someone who isn't interested in being tied down again."

She put her boys first. He liked that about her. Even if it meant she'd just lumped him into the stressful category. He feigned offended. "Wait. Who said I'd be stressful? I'm pretty low maintenance." Said the man who had demons beating down his door right at this very moment.

The sudden shift in Em's demeanor, the way she squared her shoulders like she was preparing for battle, only made him want her more. Her quest for independence looked damn good on her.

Her life balance was just off right now. Maybe. Hopefully. Wait, why did he care?

Em smiled a smug smile. "I'm not sayin' *you'd* be stressful per se. I'm sayin' maintaining a new relationship can be stressful—especially with children. I don't want that. I don't want to worry about your happiness, or whether you're fulfilled enough, or whatever it is that keeps a relationship going. I'm more concerned with mine and the boys."

Take that, Needy. "What if I don't feel the same way you do?"

Her blue eyes sparkled up at him—teasing him—owning him. "We're due for more awkward?"

"So I have to agree to be your sex toy or it's over? Just like that?" Damn.

Now her eyes went wide as she realized she'd voiced something she wanted and what she wanted, coming from a woman, was generally frowned upon and considered too aggressive, or at least he'd lay bets in Em's mind it was.

She pushed her finger into his chest. "Yes! That's exactly what I want." Then her brows bunched together and her hand went to her throat.

She'd just asked a man to have nothing but sex with her. Right here in Dixie's house with the children playing in the background, with Caine laughing at something LaDawn had just said, and her libido squarely on her sleeve.

Where was this brash new Em coming from? Not two months ago she'd have torn her own tongue out before saying such a thing. Yet, each time she voiced another desire, it became easier. And crazier.

But just the freedom of it was an aphrodisiac. For a moment or two, she felt like her bones would burst right through her skin if she didn't say it. The words had just exploded from her mouth like a volcanic eruption.

And then she'd wanted to clamp a hand over her mouth and chew her own tongue off. Or did she? Was that notion something her mother would suggest, or was that how she really felt?

And why was every facet that made up Em all blurred lines and fuzzy outlines these days?

The space between them grew smaller, the heat of Jax's body pulsed into hers as she watched the wheels of his mind turn. He was choosing his next words carefully. Or maybe he was just choosing to opt out of her emotional roller coaster altogether.

Not that she could blame him, but the idea that Jax might, left her a little empty.

"Daddy?" Maizy was suddenly between them, pushing Em out of the way and demanding Jax's full attention.

She clung between his thighs, holding her arms upward. Jax turned her around, stooping to his haunches. "Maizy, you're interrupting a conversation. Please say excuse me."

Just as Em had suspected, the little girl attached to that angelic voice was adorable, and chubby and perfect, and a *redhead.* Her mother must have been perfection. A stab of petty jealousy poked her for this woman who'd created this child with Jax.

Speaking of, where was Maizy's mother? She'd invented all sorts of stories in her head for her whereabouts today while she'd taken extra care picking an outfit then reminding herself it was none of her business where Maizy's mother was. If you were going to ask a man to have nothing more than illicit sex with you, the rest of his life was off-limits. Those were the rules. She'd read them in a magazine a long time ago when she was still married.

Avoiding personal entanglements began with creating boundaries.

Em smiled down at her, forgetting her out-of-character behavior when Maizy muttered a petulant "Excuse me."

"Better," Jax said, smiling his approval, running a large hand over the top of her head with affection. "This is Miss Emmaline. Say hello, huh?"

"Hi," she murmured, shy, adorable in a fairy princess dress with pink sparkles on the bell-shaped skirt.

"It's nice to meet you, Maizy. I'm Em. I work with your dad."

Maizy looked to Jax. "Is this the lady you're gonna ask to help make the house nice?"

Em's eyes flew to Jax's. Had she heard that right? She'd just asked him to have sex with her, and he was going to ask her to help him renovate?

Yes. Of course that was what had just happened. Jax was keeping things aboveboard and clean, and she was rolling around in the mud.

"Yep. She's the lady I was going to ask to help us with the house."

Facepalm.

Before Jax had the chance to explain his answer, Dixie and LaDawn were there, all coy smiles and sweet, round eyes.

Dixie strolled up to them, her hands behind her back, her eyebrow raised in that playful way she had. "Y'all gonna come mingle with the rest of us, or do you just want me to drop off a platter of weenies in a blanket and a bottle of wine here in your corner and let you two talk amongst yourselves?"

A wave of dizzy embarrassment washed over Em. Had they been that obvious?

"Yes," LaDawn answered her question with a whisper in her ear, her throaty tone teasing. She glanced down at Maizy then, holding out her hand to her. "Are you Ms. Maizy? Why, as I live and breath, it's really you in the flesh, isn't it?"

Maizy, instantly drawn to LaDawn and all the shiny, colorful things she encompassed, grinned. "You know me?"

LaDawn bobbed her overly blond head. "Your daddy told me all about you over a pizza in our lunchroom. Said you were the apple of his eye. But you don't look like an apple to me. You look like a little girl with hair the color of a sunset."

Maizy giggled and took LaDawn's hand, holding it up to the light as LaDawn drew her away. "You have pretty nails. I like glitter, but Daddy says it makes too much of a mess, and it's hard to clean up."

"Well, maybe someday, if we can get your daddy's permission, we'll have a girls' day. You and me, Dixie, Miss Em, Miss Catherine and Marybell, too, and we'll paint up your nails with some glitter, okay?"

Maizy, entranced by the offer, strolled off with LaDawn, leaving the three of them standing in the corner.

Dixie latched on to Em's arm while still smiling at Jax. "Can I get you to give me a hand with a couple of things in the kitchen? I need some cookin' advice,"

Dixie prodded with the girlfriend signal in her eyes. The one that said "quit makin' an ass of yourself, Emmaline Amos."

Jax's smile was amused. "Excuse me, ladies. I'm gonna go dig up some of those cocktail shrimp. Em? It was nice talking to you." He tipped an imaginary hat with a smile and sauntered off toward the buffet table Sanjeev had arranged.

The words *nice talking to you,* as though they'd just chatted weather and the stock market, penetrated her devil-may-care lover-in-the-afternoon attitude. Slow and lazy, her blatant question began to seep in.

The second Em watched Jax's broad back retreat out of earshot, Dixie pulled her toward the kitchen. "I don't want to pry—"

Em winced. "But you will."

Dixie's eyes flashed bright, her eyes so wide her eyelashes touched her eyebrows. "Yes. Yes, I will. When the whole room hears my best friend ask a man if he wants to have sex with her, I'm pryin'."

Her bravado's bubble burst, splattering her shame all over Dixie's beautiful chrome-and-granite kitchen. "Everyone heard?"

"Okay, not everyone. Just me, and Marybell, who's now over there hidin' in a huddle like some cornered animal at the pound. I'm worried—about her and about your flappy lips."

Em's eyes scanned the room, looking for Marybell's trademark spikes of hair. She was leaning against the side of the impossibly beautiful hutch Landon had made specifically to hold his mother's china—almost as if she hoped to melt into it and disappear. She held a wine-glass of burgundy liquid in front of her face and a plate of toast points and cheese in the other.

Marybell wasn't prone to large crowds of Plum Or-chardians. They judged her like they judged no other because of her outrageous makeup and choice of hair-styles, but she dealt, and she did it often in light of her friendship with Dixie and Caine.

In the midst of her misery, it struck Em odd that Marybell, far less chatty than the rest of them, was ex-ceptionally quiet lately. Her heart tightened. Something was wrong, and she'd been so wrapped up in her dirty thoughts, she'd overlooked her friend.

Em began to pull away from Dixie, forgetting she was due a lecture on what not to say at a dinner party.

Forgetting her erratic behavior, she shrugged Dixie off and made her way toward her friend.

Tugging on Marybell's arm, she gave her a nudge with her shoulder. "What're you doin' over here hidin' like you're trying to become one with the furniture?"

Marybell's eyes instantly went to her plate and the shiny, studded leather wristband she wore. "You know how I am with crowds."

She did. She knew MB only showed up at these events because she loved Dixie, but lately, there was something…. Something else. Marybell wasn't the open book LaDawn was; they didn't know a lot about where she came from or really anything about her. But they'd all bonded over their love of Landon, so most times, it almost didn't matter.

Except for right now. "I'm gonna be a Nosy Nellie,

because the mother in me hears a faint alarm bell ringin'. Is there something bothering you, MB? Something I can help with? Because you know, I'm always here if there's something you need to get off your chest."

Marybell shook her head. "Nothing more than the usual 'I don't belong here' syndrome." Then she added on a smile to her words, one that didn't ring true to Em.

Em wrapped an arm around her shoulders. "You do so belong here. You belong here because I say you do. Got that, MB? You. Belong."

Marybell paused for a moment, her makeup-masked face making it hard to read her emotions. "You know what, Em. If ever there was a place I thought I belonged, it's here. I appreciate y'all. I don't say that much, but I mean it."

She didn't want gratitude, she wanted MB to talk to her, let her in. But for now, or until Marybell deemed otherwise, it would have to be enough. She gave her a tight squeeze. "You just remember we appreciate you, too. Got that?"

Marybell nodded and grinned, the uncertainty in her eyes gone for the moment. "Gotten."

Jax sipped at his tumbler of whiskey, looking past Caine's shoulder to watch Em as she made her way across the room toward Marybell, concern on her face.

The swish of her ass held his focus, swaying and shifting beneath the clingy red dress, her long legs making quick work of the distance between her and her friend.

He caught Caine's eyes following his, catching him watching Em. He put his focus back where it belonged.

Caine thumped him on the shoulder with a cackle. "You're showing all your cards, buddy. Every last one."

Jax eyed him, his grin sly. "Just appreciatin' a good-looking woman, is all."

"That thing over in the corner was intense. I'm just wonderin' how it happened so soon. Haven't seen you interested in anyone in a long time. Not sure if I should be glad or worried you're jumping in with both feet after such a dry spell."

"You sound like Tag and Gage."

Caine swirled the amber liquid in the glass he held, his gaze as direct as he was. "Tag and Gage are smart. How's Tag, anyway? How is he really?"

Jax flashed back to the conversation he'd had with Tag tonight and the shitty things he'd said. Fuck. He shrugged his shoulders. He didn't understand his brother anymore—or this journey he kept saying he was on. He only knew he wanted the old Tag back. Maybe that's where this would all lead—the road back to the old Tag. "Healing. That's what he says anyway."

But was he healing or merely surviving? Tag was tough as nails, but this past couple of years had been a shitpile of crap. Some of it his fault. A fault he had to live with forever. Sometimes he felt like Tag was just using all the right catch phrases, going through the motions while he tried to convince himself he was all right.

Caine's eyes were sympathetic. Jax knew he got it. Caine got loss. "Time. I know that's the cliché answer, but it's the only truth."

Time. Everyone said time would heal Tag. Ease his guilt, pacify his broken life, comfort his lost soul, but everyone wasn't living with what he was living with. "Heals all wounds, right?" he agreed.

"Tell him we're probably going to have some expansion work for him over at Call Girls, would you? See if he's interested?"

Tag could use the work. Not just for the money he refused to let Jax loan him, but for the good it would do his spirit.

Tag and rebuilding something were like mac and cheese. They went together. "I'll do that. I'm sure he'll appreciate the consideration."

"How are your parents? Are they still driving around in that motor home, lighthouse hunting?"

Jax smiled. In their retirement, his mom and dad had gone off to live the life of their dreams, traveling from state to state at their leisure, visiting historic lighthouses. They'd offered to come and help with Maizy when Harper died, but as far as he was concerned, they'd done their time raising three boys. They deserved their retirement.

"I get a postcard at least once a month with a picture of a lighthouse they've been to." His eyes strayed again to Em as she laughed and smiled with Marybell.

Caine used two fingers and pointed at his face. "Eyes on me, pal. You have stray dog all over your face."

He probably did. For the first time in a six-pack of years or so, he was having trouble focusing on anything but Em. "Sorry."

Caine laughed. "Just so you know, she's the best GM

on the face of the planet. You fuck that up, I gotta kill you or at least make a good show of it in front of Dixie. She's also Dixie's closest friend. You could make shit sticky for me. Don't do that. Plus, I like her a lot. She's a good person who's had a messed-up time of it with that jackhole of an ex of hers. I'm just gonna warn you once, then I'll shut up. No dabbling with the goods and hurting feelings. Now, if your intentions are pure, carry on."

"Understood," he said to his friend, making their circle bigger when another party attendee joined their conversation.

His intentions weren't exactly pure, because he'd thought of her naked and in a hundred different positions beneath him today, but to be fair, he'd also given equal thought to what it would be like to watch the news with her, take a walk.

Just sex? It'd been a while since he'd just been in it for the sex.

You just met her a week ago.

Yeah? Well, life's short.

Nobody knew that better than he did.

He didn't know what it was about Em that made him think about houses, and porch swings, and looking over the morning paper at her across a table littered with coffee mugs and glasses of orange juice. He didn't even know if she liked orange juice.

But he wanted to, and he didn't like that. He'd felt this kind of immediate attraction once before, and the end had sucked.

Maybe all this thinking about Em had to do with his fears Maizy would go without feminine input for the rest of her life and that was fueling this infatuation with her. Maizy was only getting older. The older she got, the more his ineptitude for nail polish and glittery lip gloss stood out like a sore thumb.

His hope she'd turn out to be a tomboy, thereby easier to relate to, had been crushed when at just two, she'd latched on to a lipstick at the grocery store and pitched a fit when he'd taken it from her.

Em was that kind of woman. Ruffles and pastel colors.

No doubt, Em was sexy as hell, but she was sexy as hell and apple pie. Warm smiles and fresh blueberry muffins on a lazy Saturday morning. Bedtime stories and reminders to brush your teeth.

And she was fighting like hell to shed that image.

So how was he going to respond to that?

Did he want to?

Jax stole another glance at her while Caine and some guy from the county courthouse talked football, their conversation growing muted as his eyes drank her in.

Her hands were moving in animated fashion until her youngest son, Gareth, stole up behind her and grabbed her leg with a chubby hand very similar to Maizy's. Em's right hand reached down to stroke his dark head, the caress light, but full of the exact sort of love he felt for Maizy.

He knew that love. The sort of love that kept you up at night, held you captive with fear, with joy, made you willing to sacrifice every solitary thing you owned in order to keep them safe—make them happy.

That was what Em's touch held.

A weird tightness bloomed in his chest, making him physically itch. His ears roared. His mouth went dry.

And all he could think was *Be her boy toy, stupid.*

Nine

Jax looked at his phone again, double-checking the number. Reece. It had to be. It was the only number he didn't recognize. No message, just the log of the phone call. After all this time, what the hell could she possibly want?

Straighten that shit out, man. Call her up and find out. Get this out of the way so you can focus on the rest of your life. You know it's what Jake would want. He said so in his will.

The resentful side of him balked at calling her back. Why the hell should he call her? If she caught him when he was available, fine. If she didn't, she could damn well have the courtesy to leave a message.

The world didn't stop because Reece Givens was calling. It didn't stop turning because she wanted something.

Old baggage, pal. You're hanging on to your resentments and your attachment to her. Those feelings have nothing to do with her connection to Maizy and parent-

*ing properly but everything to do with manipulating the
situation by allowing your crap to make the choices.*

But she left. Walked away. Didn't look back.

And now she's back.

Fuck. He scooped up the phone, ignoring the slap of
one of the operator's whips from beyond the far wall,
and dialed the unfamiliar number. Maybe it wasn't her
number? Maybe it was some telemarketer's or Maizy's
new doctor's number or anyone but—

"Hey! This is Reece—leave me a message and I'll
get back to you ASAP."

Her voice took him right back to the first time he'd
seen her, long legs, lanky, creamy skin and a riot of
red curls streaming behind her as she strode across
the street to the little luncheonette where she worked.

Bubbly, irresponsible, breathtaking Reece.

Like a moth to a flame, he'd headed straight for the
light. And he'd been burned so bad, upon reflection,
even he couldn't believe it.

Everyone had seen it but him.

More whip cracking brought him back to the present. He cleared his throat, her name stiff on his lips.
"Reece? Jax. Call me back at this number." He clicked
the phone off. There. Obligation satisfied.

Ten seconds after he hung up, the phone rang.

Em sucked in a long breath and poked her head into
Jax's office, stealing a glance of him staring at his ringing phone. "Can I borrow a minute of your time?"

She'd come with hat in hand, after a long weekend
of contemplation, wherein she'd mentally flogged her-

self and decided he deserved an apology. Had the roles been reversed, she couldn't swear she wouldn't have been offended.

Working together, asking him such a forward question, put him in an awkward position. She had to make that right. For the sake of Call Girls. She was the GM, not the femme fatale.

Jax grinned, dropping his cell phone to the surface of his desk. "If you'd said *pen,* I would have said *not on your life.* Pens are supersacred to nerds like me. But time? Got plenty of that to spare. I was hoping to see you anyway."

Who hoped to see the person that had treated them like a slab of baby back ribs? "I just wanted to..." Em licked her lips, tugging at the scarf around her neck, letting the smooth fabric soothe her hot fingertips. It was symbolic—black, the color of her unforgivable shame.

Wait. He'd been hoping to see her? "You were hoping to see me?"

When Jax rounded the corner of his desk, filling the space between them, his footsteps held determination, solid and steady. He stopped just shy of a foot or so between them, reaching over her head to close the door. "I was. So about your question at Dixie and Caine's party—"

Em's hand went up in a protective gesture—to his chest—because that's where all hands went when they were in protective mode. "That's why I'm here. I want to apologize for my behavior—"

Jax pulled her to him, wrapping a hand around her waist, and kissed her hard with delicious force.

He wasn't asking permission, either. He was demanding she kiss him, angling his mouth over hers, coaxing her lips to his will with a tongue that tasted like peppermint and sex.

Em's bones melted, became all floaty and light. She found her favorite anchor, the collar of Jax's shirt. Her fingers clutched either side of it, clinging to it to keep her legs from crumbling.

The rush of the memory of his fingers between her legs came back full throttle—and she wanted. Instantaneously, she wanted him. Wanted him naked, tight against her body, wanted all of the naked, sweaty naughty she'd played like a movie reel in her mind's eye.

His kiss got hotter, more urgent, until her back was to his office wall, his rigid thighs straining against hers. Her nipples tightened, achy, needy, crushed against his broad chest, leaving an imprint of Jax all over her. One she wanted to roll around in, inhale, devour.

Em's fingers went to his shoulders, flattening her palms against them, admiring the ripply feel of hard flesh.

Then he was pulling his mouth from hers, his breathing harsh on her face, just as she was mentally shedding her restrictive clothing and doing more un-Em-like things.

Right there in the office while phones rang and the night shift was just getting settled in.

Flirty Em, the one who seemed to take over like a possessed Linda Blair, made an appearance. "Wow." She heard her voice, an unfamiliar husky, just-been-kissed voice, and fought not to frown. How unusual.

Had she sounded like that with Clifton? Smoky and kittenish?

Jax put his hands on the wall, planting them on either side of her head, and stared down at her, his eyes with the thick fringe of lashes teasing. "Name your terms."

"My terms?"

"For this no-connection, sex-only deal. Let's negotiate."

"Negotiations never occurred to me." When a woman made an offer like this, didn't men just show up and shut up? "We have to have terms? Do we need a written contract, too?"

Jax nipped her jaw, still keeping his body from totally reconnecting with hers. "Yeah, like rules. I figure, we work together, and you probably won't want anyone here at work to know. Plus, you seem like the kind of person who likes order, so there must be rules. Name them."

Right and right, but before her thoughts landed on work, her first concern was for the boys and what more gossip would do to them. "Discretion," she blurted out, making herself look up at him. No one could ever know Emmaline Amos was having an indiscretion.

Likely, no one would believe a man as gorgeous as Jax was willing to be indiscreet with her, but she wasn't taking any chances.

"I don't want to get involved. I really don't. So discretion is a must." She didn't. She couldn't. Could she? No. She didn't want to invite more chaos. Meshing dating with children and busy lives was chaos times a million. She had to focus on her—her life—her needs—her children, especially Clifton Junior and his anger.

Jax nuzzled her jaw again, sending all sorts of new heat through her body. "Meaning?"

Her breath shuddered a little. "Meaning, we don't do it in the square? At Lucky's in aisle seven?"

Jax's head shot upward as he barked a laugh. "You're new to this, right?"

She liked his neck, solid, corded with muscle—nose-burying worthy. "I just stumbled off the turnip truck."

"I mean, my house? Your house? Or a hotel?"

She shook her head and looked him square in the eye—her lusty penchant temporarily on the back burner. "Not my house or yours. No children. That's an absolute. They can't be involved in any way. No sleepovers, no catching us in the act."

"Fair enough. Seeing as my daughter's always underfoot, I have two nosy brothers living with me and you're a single mother, hotel?"

"Not in Plum Orchard. You couldn't be seen within a hundred paces of that place without Johnson Martin blowing your cover."

"Johnson Martin?"

"He owns the Plum Orchard B and B. It's the only game in town, and if he were a woman, he'd be a Mag. That's how good he is at gossipin'."

Jax cupped her jaw, scraping his thumb over her skin. "Got it," he rumbled. "I have an idea. Don't the boys visit their father?"

Her fingers circled his wrists like they'd always been doing it. "They do...they also visit their grandparents, but I can't have your car at my house. Everyone will set to talkin' then because Plum Orchard has eyes." Everything in her cringed in panic. All she needed was just one Mag's tongue wagging.

"Is that like *The Hills* only with Southern belles and shotguns?"

"Worse."

"So am I your dirty little secret?" He moved his mouth away from hers.

"Well, you are a secret, but I don't mean for it to sound cruel. I've just had dirty little secrets on public display. I don't need to add to that by sleepin' around."

Jax relaxed again, moving his hand to the back of her neck, kneading it as he drew her closer. "But you're not sleeping around. That would imply you're sleeping with a lot of people at once. I'm only one man. Not a lot of them."

Now she pulled away, flattening her feet, her gaze direct. "If you can't understand why I wouldn't want people talking, we can end this conversation now. I don't have to explain myself or my reasons. You haven't lived in Plum Orchard all your life. You don't know what it's like when everybody knows your business. I'm not givin' those horrible women somethin' to talk about."

"Understood," he soothed, until she was straining toward him again. "So where to go?"

"My Jeep?"

Jax chuckled. "Wait. I have that big guesthouse in the back. It's not heated, but I suppose I could run an extension cord from the garage for one of those floor heaters. It's got a blow-up mattress. We meet in secret. You park your car somewhere discreet."

Em sighed, her shoulders slumping. "A blow-up mattress." A pump and some plastic had never entered her forbidden sex fantasies.

"It's all I have unless you have something better?"

She'd never done this before. Places to have sex where a Mag wouldn't find you had never occurred to her before. "I'll think on it. For now, it's the guesthouse."

"Next?" he muttered, stroking the shell of her ear with his tongue.

"No romance. You don't need to bring me flowers. I mean, I love 'em, but I don't want them from you."

"What's wrong with flowers from me?"

"Nothing's wrong with them. I'm sure they'd be beautiful. What I mean is, I don't need romance with my..."

"Sex?"

Her skin went hot and red again. "Yes. That."

He shrugged his wide shoulders, but his face said she was crazy. "Okay. No romance."

But wait. "Do I have to define what 'romance' is?"

"I think I get the meaning. No food or wine or feeding me grapes."

She giggled, maddened by the press of his lips. "How is me feeding you grapes even a little romantic?"

"Totally joking. Anything else?"

"You don't have to ask how my day was."

"You don't want to talk at all? No warming you up? Are you real?" he teased.

She was real. This bargaining was very real. And she was doing it like she'd been to the bargaining table before. "I might want you to talk, but it won't be about my day—or yours. I don't want to know about your day, either."

"What if I have a bad day and I need to talk it out?"

"Find a good therapist, but first call and cancel our date." She didn't have room for any more issues. Clifton finding himself was as much issue as she could handle in one lifetime.

"Okay, no pleasantries. None."

"We can still be pleasant."

"Pleasant without the intimacy of conversation. Got it. More rules?"

"How do you feel about experimenting?"

He backed up a little, but only enough to cock his dark head. "With?"

"Things." All the things she heard the girls talk about on the phone. Well, maybe not all of them, but a lot of them.

"I want the definition of *things* or it's a no-go. *Things* is too vague and could lead to things I'm not good with."

She couldn't possibly list all the things she wanted to try, all the things the girls talked about on the phone. His sudden acceptance had caught her off guard. "I can't define them all right now because I don't know them all right now. I only know I'd like to try some things...."

"And I can say no to these things."

"You absolutely can."

"Can I try some things?"

"Define *things*."

"How about we leave the *thing*-thing open-ended?"

"Deal."

"Is there more?"

"No hard feelings when it's over. If one of us gets tired of the other, just say the word *done*."

"Is that like our safe word?"

"Call it whatever you like, but that's the word we'll use, and no one leaves with hard feelin's. Sometimes things just run their course, and I understand that perfectly." Like marriage. Hers had run its course. She'd run Clifton's course. But wow, she was being very "lover in the afternoon," wasn't she?

"Deal. So how often are we doing this?"

"Am I allowed to call the shots?"

"Am I?"

She laughed, even as she wondered if she was a shot-caller. This bold half of her, while invigorating and exciting, was still waffling. "Let's just say, we can be free to let the other know if the mood has struck—and if it doesn't strike. We both have lives and children and responsibilities."

"Okay, so now that that's settled, I have a favor to ask you, our—" he wiggled his eyebrows "—deal aside. And you can say no, but if you do—I'm just throwing this out there—I'd be crushed."

Ripples of pleasure raised goose bumps of delight on her forearms at the contact of his hand along the curve of her hip, stroking, discovering. "Dramatic," she teased, moving her hands from his wrists to place them at his waist. Testing the waters, learning his body.

"Will you help with the house? I need serious help with everything from fixtures to paint. Top to bottom."

But that would put them together much more than just on an air mattress. Could she be his lover and his interior decorator? Did that sound too much like the ingredients for a bad romance novel?

In that moment, Jax looked a little helpless, trumping the glow of accepting her crazy offer, trumping her hot-and-bothered hormones. "Look, Em, I really need some feminine input. If I'm not careful, Maizy will grow up with a pool table and a sixty-inch flat screen for furniture. I want Maizy to love where she lives, want to come home from school to it every day like I did when I was a kid. My sister, Harper, always helped with stuff like that, but after she died, we lost our feminine influences."

His sister? She thought he only had brothers. She put a hand on his arm and squeezed it. "I had no idea, Jax. I'm so sorry."

Brief flickers of sadness played around his eyes before he erased all evidence and gave her another Hawthorne smile. "It's okay. It's been almost two years, but Harper was a terrific aunt. She loved Maizy, and Maizy loved her. She was the only female influence in her life, and even though she was only four when Harper died, she remembers her. She misses her—she misses doing girl things, which is why when you met me for the first time, I had a barrette in my hair. I try. But there are areas I suck in. All I can think is, Harper would know what color to paint the bathroom. She'd know how to situate the silverware drawer. I'm sort of drowning here. All the girls talk about is how good you are at stuff like this, how you know all the places to go for good deals. That's why I originally asked you to help in the first place."

Her heart squeezed tight in sympathy for Maizy. Maizy's mother was obviously gone, and now to find out her aunt was, too? How had so much tragedy befallen one small child of six?

She wouldn't ask. It was none of her business, but all Maizy had were three men at the helm and a house that, if Jax's description of the interior was accurate, looked like a bomb had gone off. There was little convincing needed as far as Em was concerned. "I'm in. No further explanation required."

Jax smiled then, changing the color of her world in an instant. "So when?"

"When what?"

"When do we, you know…"

"Make whoopee?"

He laughed all husky-hot. "For someone who's allegedly not very good at this, you're pretty direct."

Huh. She was. When had that happened? "It's the stern teacher in me. How's tonight—after dinner? My boys are with Clifton's parents tonight and tomorrow night. Can you sneak out after Maizy's in bed?" Anticipation welled in the pit of her belly.

"I can. You bet, I will."

"Then tonight. Nine or so, providing Maizy's in bed by then? You can text me at any time to call it off."

"Nine it is. I'll bring the heater and my body."

"One more little thing. Condoms. I can't buy them

at Brugsby's unless I want the whole world speculatin' about my private life."

"But it's okay if they speculate about mine?"

His comically astonished look made her laugh. "You're a man. You don't care what they speculate about."

"Point," he growled in her ear, rubbing his nose along the side of her neck until she almost purred. "I'll get them. Now, I've got a couple of things to clear up here if we're going to do this. So you, sexy lady, have to go or I won't get a damn thing done with you distracting me."

When was the last time someone had told her she was distracting because she was sexy? Chattering too much, maybe, but never sexy. It made her feel desired and giddy. Jax kissed her again before popping open his office door and pointing to the hall. "Hurry, or I make no promises things won't get sweaty."

She giggled then straightened, squaring her shoulders when she realized anyone in the office could see them. She smoothed her skirt and cleared her throat. "Um, thanks for the loan of the *pen,* Jax. G'night."

Jax rolled his eyes at how forced and ridiculous she sounded, but tonight, she didn't care.

She was going to have sex with the hottest man in Plum Orchard.

And the first thing she wanted to do was tell Dixie and the girls about it.

But they'd just remind her what *no strings attached* meant, and then they'd fret over her emotional state.

No. This was her secret to keep. To take out of her

fantasy box when no one was looking, and that's how it would stay.

A secret.

Ten

"What the hell are you doing, Jax?" Tag asked, scaring the shit out of him.

He scrubbed a hand over his face and palmed the condom. He forced himself to act like he hadn't just been caught stealing birth control from his brother. "Looking for the nail clippers."

"In my tackle box? Who're you kiddin', friend?"

Shit. Caught. Tag kept condoms in his tackle box. Gage kept them in the front pocket of his duffel bag, and he used to keep them in his gym bag. When they'd all lived together in a small apartment, if any one of them ever needed protection, they always knew exactly where to look. Usually, they did it more discreetly than Jax had. His secret spy skills were sorely lacking.

He'd let lust—his unbelievable, ball-clenching lust for Em—make him sloppy. But he wasn't capable of clear thought where she was concerned. She was soft curves, warm eyes, good smells. Those attributes sucked up all his clear thoughts and left him with a brain made of oatmeal.

Putting a cheesy grin on his face, Jax turned around. "My nails are a total mess."

Tag's mouth went flat. "You're a mess over Emmaline Amos."

Fair assessment. *Mess* wasn't quite accurate. *Unsettled by her* was a better way to put it. "Who?"

Tag jammed his shoulder with the heel of his hand. "Stop. She's why you're digging for condoms, buddy." He crossed the wide floor of his bedroom to the big walnut-stained armoire he'd made back in high school and opened the cabinets. "Think fast."

Jax caught the box with ease. He made a big deal out of looking at it like it was a foreign object. "What are these? I was looking for the nail clippers."

"Are you keeping your mad crush on her a secret?"

He didn't have a mad crush on Em. A mad crush he'd done. Mad crushes were off the table forever. "No. I have nails that are out of control. That's what I have." He held up his hand to show Tag.

But Tag was in one of his moods, and that mood wasn't in the mood to joke. "Okay, so nail clippers is the new code word for condoms. Question is, why's it a secret?"

"Because she doesn't want anyone to know." Damn. Cat was out of the bag. Repeat, cat's out of the bag. Their relationship used to be so easy—their communication even easier—the words slipped out of his mouth before he thought about it. These days, he still forgot to measure his words with Tag.

Tag crossed his arms over his chest, his eyes almost hidden by his black knit cap. "Because?"

Because we're just doing each other. That sounded wrong with Em's name in the mix. Dirtier than it really was. "You never heard me say that. I said nothing."

"So what I didn't just hear you say was she wants to keep you a secret. Like you're not respectable enough? I don't like the sound of that shit."

Respectability—a Tag hot button. You could never take back the press of the hot button. "It has nothing to do with respectable. It has to do with discreet. And that's how it stays. One word about her or me—if you even use our names in the same sentence together, I'll kick your ass."

Tag held his wide palms up. "First, dream on. Second, this is a no-strings-attached thing, isn't it?"

"So?"

"So you're just not that kind of dude, Jax. When you go, you go deep. Remember Reece? Which reminds me—with all the shit going down with her all of a sudden calling you, why are you adding something else that could complicate the hell out of your already-complicated life?"

Because I'm sucked in. Because there's something about her that fits me. Something I can't define, won't define because it goes no further than the bedroom. He'd thought about her proposal all weekend long after the dinner party. He'd thought about how unlike her it was. He'd thought about how she'd gone out on an unfamiliar limb to proposition him. Then he'd thought about her some more.

Still, Tag was right.

Just sex for a longer period of time than just one night wasn't like him. Even then, one-night stands weren't much like him. He'd had a few, but with Maizy in the mix, he generally avoided them. You could never be too careful when you had a child, and the world was full of nuts.

Yet, he was a big boy. He could do what he wanted. The notion he couldn't made him defensive. "It's just sex. Not a damn engagement, Tag."

"Secret sex. Got it."

Jax didn't like his sneering tone. The suggestion Em was anything other than a good human being pissed him off. "Don't make it sound so shitty and cheap. You've done it."

He thumped his chest, hardening his gaze. "And look at me now."

"Where's your comparison coming from?"

"Your life fell apart just like mine. That's the comparison. You wanna do that again?" he yelled, that hard mask he wore around everyone but Maizy firmly in place.

Jax was in front of him in a flash. "Look, I'm all grown-up. I don't have to explain anything to you. I can do what I want when I want." *Way to sound like you're ten.*

Tag's jaw went harder. "You absolutely can. I support grown-man things. Go have some sex."

"Stop damn well making it sound like I hired a hooker!" he accused, using the two inches he had on Tag to lord his intimidation over him.

But Tag was always looking for a confrontation as of late. He reared up on his toes and yelled right back, "I'm just looking out for you. Someone has to, Jax. You forget too easily."

"Or maybe it's time to finally forget? Let go? Or should I let what happened with Reece define everything I damn well do?"

"No. You should let it teach you a lesson."

Lessons he knew. He'd had plenty of lessons. "Reece is the past."

"Not if she's calling you. She's your present, and you'd be wise to remember that she's out there somewhere, lurking, looking for a way back in."

Jax clenched his jaw hard enough to make it hurt to keep from slugging his brother. "She can look all she likes. My life shouldn't stop because Reece is back." Somewhere.

"Heeeey!" Gage bellowed, pushing his way between his brothers. "What are you two morons fighting about now? Jesus Christ. I feel like a damn referee lately. Maizy's going to be back from her playdate soon. Do you want her to come home and hear you assholes going at it like you're mortal enemies? Quit this shit already. We're family. Could we start acting like it again, please?"

There'd been a time when nothing could have torn them apart. Now it took next to nothing.

"Sorry," Tag muttered. "I was just looking out for our big brother. He's having sex."

Gage gaped at them. "With what? His inflatable doll?" Then he looked down at the condoms in Jax's hand. "Whoa, whoa, whoa. A whole box worth? Hasn't it been a long time since you nailed anything other than your hand with a hammer? Maybe a whole box is wishful thinking."

Jax glared at his little brother. "Maybe you should mind your business."

Gage grinned. Easily the prettiest of the three of them, and the one who looked most like their mother, Elizabeth. "So who is she?"

"Emmaline Amos," Tag supplied smugly.

Jax was back to snarling again. "Shut your mouth, Tag. Don't damn well say her name like that."

Gage whistled. "Hold on. You're having sex with the hottie from Call Girls? The one with the dark hair and the husband who wears heels?"

Thinking about Clifton Senior made him irrationally angry, and there was no explanation for it. "Ex-husband, and I said, it's none of your business. Don't talk like that about her *ex*-husband. It's shitty."

Gage's brow furrowed. "He does wear heels. So what? That's not shitty. That's the truth. And why is it Tag's business and not mine? You two are just like you always were when we were kids. Always leaving me out of the good stuff." He held a finger up at Jax. "But wait. Hold that thought." Turning his gaze to Tag, he said, "Why are you all in an uproar over him having sex with Emmaline? Shouldn't we, as the same gender, be supporting that?"

Tag flicked his fingers in the air in a gesture that said he gave up. "Forget I ever said anything. I'll go downstairs and wait for Maizy." He stalked out of his room, the heavy thunk of his work boots clunky and loud.

Gage shook his head, driving his hands into the pockets of his hoodie. "What the hell is wrong with him lately? I know he's been through some shit, but he's always up someone's ass barking. You should have heard him bitch out that high school kid he hired to help with the framing in the spare bedroom. He made a simple mistake, but you'd think he'd blown the house up. I had to shut Tag down before the poor dude cried. He's on a serious tear these days."

Jax sighed. Tag was touchy, on edge and raw—and they were dealing, but sometimes he wanted to put him in a headlock until he just got it all out. Got everything out. Talked about it—made an effort to get to a place he could live with what he'd been through. "It takes time to get your footing after what happened." It was a feeble excuse, but what else was there to say? Everyone healed in their own way. Some maybe never did.

Gage's face twisted into a scowl. "We all miss Harper. He doesn't get to claim missing her more."

"His experience was different, Gage. You know that."

"You sound like those counselors we went to see with Maizy."

"Maybe I learned a thing or two."

Gage's pretty face went smiley. He flashed his teeth before saying, "So forget Tag. What's going on with you and the hot lady who works for a phone-sex company? Bet she knows a thing or two."

"Stop being twelve." Why did it offend him to hear her referred to in anything but the highest regard?

"Well, I'd be thirty-four, if you'd let me. But it seems I can't get out from under little-brother mode."

Jax clamped a hand on his little brother's shoulder and squeezed. "Sorry. Instinct."

"Tell me about her."

His lips lifted in a stupid smile before he could stop it. "You already know she's incredibly hot. But she's also smart, and funny, and when she's excited about something, she gets a little chatty. But it's cute." And when she said his name with that light Southern drawl of hers, it made him hard. "She's also a helluva mother."

"And she makes you smile. That's nice. So why's Tag pissed about her?"

"Reece."

Gage's head bobbed. "'Nuff said. You heard from her since she called last week?"

Gage attempted to tread lightly, but his eyes zeroed in on Jax's while he waited for an answer. "Nope. I called her back. She called me back, but didn't leave a message. Haven't heard from her since." Hope to never hear from her again.

"I'm just gonna say this and then I'll shut it. Unlike Tag, I liked Reece. I liked her a lot. I was an idiot. That said, do what you can to keep her away from Maizy. Hire some fancy attorneys with your buttloads of money. Take Maizy to Africa and hide out in a hut. Whatever. Just know, I'd cover for you."

"You're a good little brother."

"I'm the damn best. So I take it this thing with Emmaline's a secret?"

"How'd you guess?"

"The two of you screaming it at each other was a huge help in solving the newest Hawthorne mystery."

"Keep it under wraps."

"You bet. And now I'm out. There's a game and a six-pack of juice boxes waiting for me downstairs in the parlor—or whatever we're calling that half-assed room with a huge flat screen and a pathetic beanbag chair." Gage grabbed him up and bumped shoulders with him before leaving him with his thoughts and an entire box of condoms.

Wishful thinking, my eye.

Wow. It was dark. Inky blackness engulfed Em when she closed the door of her car with as much care as possible. She'd parked by a stump about five hundred feet away from Destination Dirty so prying eyes wouldn't see her car behind Jax's.

She winced when she crunched her way over a pile of dead leaves while following the sound of the creek running alongside his house.

If they were going to make his guesthouse their lair of business makin', Jax was going to have to leave her a trail of bread crumbs or something so she'd be able to find her way in. Especially if she wore heels this high and a ridiculous trench coat she'd thought was so mysterious and sexy when she'd dug it out of her closet an hour ago.

She checked her phone again, her stomach on full tilt when she reread Jax's text. Get here now.

If she didn't need her hands to feel her way around in the dark, she'd fan herself with the notebook of ideas she had for Jax's redecorating. There was an urgent tone to his words that made her feel desirable—sexy, maybe even wanton, a word that had once reminded her of soup, but now had a whole different meaning. His text made her feel as if she were the only woman in the world capable of fulfilling his need.

That's plain stupid, the voice in her head, the one that said she was headed into murky waters, blared. *Those aren't the thoughts of a woman about to embark on a no-strings-attached rendezvous. Rein it in.*

Her phone vibrated in her hand, sending her eyes to the screen.

You okay?

She smiled at Jax's text. Strangely, she really was okay. She wanted Jax. And she'd said so. In easy to understand words and with a directness she was coming to like about herself.

She'd blocked out her mother's certain disapproval, and the odd looks Dixie had given her that day when she'd confessed she didn't want to become involved, and she'd gone for it.

It felt wildly good not to overthink it, not to think about anything but the pleasure of it all.

"Em?" Jax's husky whisper cut into the dark.

Some of that pleasure she was high on rippled along her arms in the way of goose bumps. "Shhh!" was her automatic response until she realized she was as noisy as he was.

She saw his dark head in the peeling doorway of his

ramshackle guesthouse and made a beeline with his large shadow as her beacon.

He let the door shut behind him and loped down the path to greet her, holding out his hand. "Sorry," he muttered on a smile. "This might take some getting used to."

"Tell me about it. I'm about as covert as a bulldozer. I think I've crunched through every pile of leaves possible here in Forest Hawthorne." She curled her fingers into his, loving the way their skin connected.

He pulled her up tight against his back and gave the door a hard nudge with his shoulder to dislodge it. It creaked open, slamming against the wall with a heavy thud.

"Shh! The way we're going, we might as well post a sign outside the door that reads Jax and Emmaline Are Doin' It. Do Not Disturb," she chided.

Jax's chuckle rippled from his lips slow and deep. He pulled her close, his powerful chest pressing to hers. "Sorry. I've never hidden from a *whole town* before."

She batted her eyes at him, something she was getting very good at. "Now you're just bein' facetious. It's not the whole town. Just parts of it." Most of it. The big mouths of it.

Jax traced her lips with his fingertip. "It is so. You said you didn't want people in town talking about you any more than they already did. You didn't say one or two people in town. Just people."

"Are you splittin' hairs with me at a time like this?" *Now, when I have on the tiniest powder-blue confec-*

tion ever created out of a polyester blend and a matching thong to boot?

"I like the trench coat. Very discreet."

Right. Check. The trench coat had been a cliché, stupid idea. "Pathetically obvious. I never wear trench coats. I was going for mysterious and sexy."

He shrugged his shoulders and grinned when he ran the tip of his finger along the curve of her cleavage, stopping at the top of her silky negligee. "I like cliché and obvious. I think it's sexy and mysterious. What's this?" He tugged at the notebook.

"An idea book. I thought once we were done…well, I thought we could look this over and you could show me what you like and don't like. You know, for the house?"

"With you dressed like that, and me dying to see what's under that coat, the last thing I was thinking about were colors for my house," he teased.

Em forgot what she was wearing when she glanced over his shoulder. Her breath lodged in her throat. As promised, Jax had blown up the air mattress. It lay against the wall patched with old barn wood, just beside a stack of dusty pictures. He'd thrown some plaid flannel sheets across its surface along with a couple of blankets with tattered holes in them.

He'd also brought along a bottle of wine and candles. So many candles. The flames danced with the rush of the wind seeping through the double windows on each side of the guesthouse.

How beautiful.

But wait. She wasn't supposed to be feeling gooey on the inside because he'd made a romantic gesture. That was reserved for a relationship. She had to stick to the rules. "I told you no romance…no wine, no candles."

Jax gave the door his toe, closing it. He walked her backward, keeping his hands at her waist until her calves touched the back of the air mattress. "Who says this is for you, sexy lady?" He grinned.

Jax chest-bumped her in playful challenge when she didn't answer. "Well?"

She shivered, suddenly relaxing into him. "Who else could it be for?"

Cupping her face, he pulled her upward so she had to stand on tiptoe to keep her balance in heels. "For me. The booze is for me, but I'll share if you ask nice and keep being so pretty. I only brought one glass, though. I thought this party was BYOB. And the candles are just some supermarket candles with names like Party In A Pear and Green Apple Meadows. It's not like they're the really expensive ones. But I figure, seeing as there's no electricity out here, and it's as dark in this guest-house as my thoughts were about you, we might need some light."

Disappointment reared its head. Apparently, Knight In Shining Hawthorne was off the clock.

That was a grossly unfair assessment. She'd made the rules; now she had to play by them. "Do green apples grow in meadows?" she joked, wondering why she wasn't experiencing even a shred of unease. There was no hesitation when she straightened her spine and let her breasts graze his chest. None. Because it felt damn good. So good.

She looked right up at him like she'd been to this rodeo before. Like she had a T-shirt that said she had.

His eyebrow rose just as his arms snaked fully around her waist, pulling her tighter. "I think the real question is, do pears have parties?"

The flickers of light from the candles bounced off his thick hair, creating chocolate highlights she'd spent many a daydream sighing over. The angles and planes of his face were somehow sharper and even more defined with the soft glow. "You don't suppose your brothers or Maizy might wonder why the guesthouse looks like it's on fire, do you?"

Jax grazed his nose along the exposed length of her neck, making her nipples bead tight. He pulled away long enough to grab the bottle of wine and a single glass. Plopping down on the air mattress, he patted the space next to him. "Fear not, fair maiden Emmaline. Got that covered. When I'm working on a project, the beginning stages of it are always the hardest for me. I need to work things out on paper. So I requested seclusion and quiet. We have a Hawthorne family rule about space and respecting it. Because I freelance at home often, they've all learned to give me the time I need."

She watched him pour the white liquid into the glass and bring it to his lips while she settled beside him. "So you think they really believe you're out here in the cold guesthouse, working on a project instead of inside in your warm office?" Did it matter if they believed why Jax was in the guesthouse?

Maybe a little. It shouldn't, but it did. A little.

Evolution from prissy spinster to bed-hopper takes time, Emmaline.

"I don't have an office yet. It's just a room full of boxes and a cold cement floor. That's where you and all those ideas you have come in."

"I see," she said, smiling up at him, forgetting her concerns again. "Maybe you're not so bad at this after all."

Jax's fingers wound around a long strand of her hair as he offered her the glass—which she took without hesitation. "So, covert ops covered?"

She sipped at the wine and paused. Alcohol always loosened her up, but she wasn't worried about loosening up at all.

No. She was more fascinated by the idea her lips would touch the rim of the glass Jax's lips had just touched. It was a small thing, really, but intimate—sensual.

"I should be sick with nerves right now." Why wasn't she worried a man was going to see her naked—the only other man to see her naked aside from Clifton? Especially one she knew would have a body that belonged on the cover of a magazine.

Why wasn't she worried he would inevitably see the stretch marks lining her belly and hips because she'd gained fifty pounds when she was pregnant with Gareth?

Why wasn't she worried Jax would cringe at the sight of the dimpled pockmarks on the outside of her thighs or the way her left breast sagged to the right? Why? And why was she telling him she wasn't worried about not being worried about it?

"Because?"

Her fingers curled into the soft knit of the sweater at his waist and tugged him closer, gazing at him over the rim of the glass. "Because this is uncharted territory for me. I've never sailed this sea. I should be a nervous wreck."

He pulled back, the muscles lining his jaw twitching. "Not once?"

"No. Have you?"

Jax opened his mouth to answer, but Em planted a hand on his lips. "No. Don't answer. No personal information."

He nibbled at her fingers, making her toes curl. "Then I won't tell you I have sailed this sea, but the itinerary was a little different."

"So you've had a lot of cruise directors?"

Once more, he opened his mouth to speak, and she stopped him, disgusted that even at a time like this, her naturally curious nature wouldn't shut up. "Scratch that."

Jax nodded, but his eyes were amused. "Right. No sharing. Which means I won't tell you how many times I've done it."

"Have you done this a lot?"

"I can't tell you. You said I couldn't."

"Well, in the interest of diseases…"

"I assure you, I'm disease free. I've been celibate for six years, and I'm physician approved."

Her ears pricked. Jax said it like he'd taken on some

kind of celibacy challenge. Celibate for six years…she mentally did the math. That was as long as Maizy'd been alive. Maybe he'd been too busy mourning his wife? Maybe she'd died and she was so phenomenal it had taken him this long to get over her?

Should she be flattered she was the one he was breaking that vow for?

He slid his hand under her butt and moved her closer, taking the wineglass from her hand and setting it on the floor. "The celibacy wasn't intentional. I just had other things to do that were more important."

Insert pin in bubble. As always, she was overthinking her importance in this. "I haven't been celibate for six years," she blurted. Gah. Again, she was oversharing.

"That's because you only just got divorced."

"Clifton's been gone awhile now. It just wasn't official until a few months ago."

"So you've had some time on your own."

"I have. I like it." She did like it. Mostly.

His eyes said he didn't like her answer, but his response was as light as his fingertips on her bare thigh. "And you've been busy enjoying your freedom?"

She placed her palm over his, sharing his hand's easy glide over her skin. "I wouldn't use the word *freedom*. Clifton didn't keep me chained up. There are just things you don't end up doing because you're a couple. You compromise on everything from the color of your bathroom towels to where to hang a picture. I like not having to consult."

"You needed a consultation to hang a picture?"

he asked, parting the hem of her mysteriously sexy trench coat.

She shook her head. "I don't mean we had to call a press conference every time I did something. I just mean you have to include your partner in all decisions big or small. I like makin' my own decisions. I like going to bed when I want to. I like watching whatever strikes my fancy on TV." *I like having total control over the TV remote, too. I like snuggling with my body pillow instead of a real body. I like having one less egg to fry.*

That sounds suspiciously like a song, Em.

His chuckle was carefree, but his eyes were clouded. "You make marriage sound like a prison camp."

"That's not what I mean at all. You were married... you know exactly what I mean." *Hint. Hint. Weren't you married, Jax? Huh? Huh? Bet your wife didn't leave you because she wanted to.*

Ugh. She should have just winked and nudged him in the shoulder for all her subtlety.

Jax didn't confirm or deny. Instead, he said, "If there's something you want to ask me, Em, just ask."

No! "Sorry. I was born with an extranosy gene. And I'm new at this. Brand-new."

"We're doing the dreaded talking. Isn't that against the rules?"

"I made those rules, didn't I?"

"You did. But if you want to, we could adjust the setting."

She shook her head, refusing to dwell on the offer or the tone of his offer. She wasn't reading anything into anything anymore. "Nope. If there's one thing I'm absolutely certain of, it's that I don't want any complications in my life. Don't take it personally."

He smiled the Jax smile that said everything was right as rain. "Nothing personal."

Flirty Em nudged her, reminding her she was losing the point of the entire night, and it was a drag.

She curled her chin into her shoulder and smiled at him. "So, do you want to see what's under my long, mysteriously sexy, totally obvious trench coat?"

Jax cracked his knuckles like he was gearing up for the chore ahead of him. "Hit me."

Eleven

Em's fingers loosened the knot at her waist while her shoulders shrugged the coat off. She wasn't as timid as he'd expected her to be about it, either.

At first, her eyes gleamed with purpose, as though the mission was to disrobe and disrobe as fast as she could before having the chance to think about it. But then her eyes went soft when she realized she'd taken the coat off.

And there she was.

In something powder-blue with lace. Maybe ivory lace. He didn't know colors. He didn't care. It was filmy and cupping her in all the right places, accentuating her breasts, making the swell of them fuller. The hem stopped at the tops of her thighs, thighs that were as soft and silky as the rest of her was bound to be.

The material clung to her waist, dipping in to the rivet of her belly button. An innie. Em had an innie he wanted to skim with his tongue. Her hair fell around her shoulders in a dark cloud of loose curls, but it was her lips he couldn't take his eyes off.

Her lower lip trembled a little. Just a little, but it was enough to make his cock swell hard and fast with the thought of them wrapped around him. Goose bumps covered her arms and thighs.

She inhaled and Jax realized he was staring. "Do you hate it?"

His mouth was dry. So dry. So he didn't bother to use words to answer her. He didn't have a damn one anyway.

Instead, he slid off the edge of the air mattress and nudged her knees open.

Em parted her thighs without hesitation, inviting him between them. Jax spread them, reminding himself to take it slow whether his blood was boiling or not.

He kissed her then, slow and long, until she sighed a fluttery sort of noise in her throat and her fingers began to pull impatiently at the waist of his sweater. She pulled it up and over his head, and threw it on the floor. The cool air of the guesthouse hit his skin at the same time Em's flesh did, hot and cold all at once.

She pulled back when his sweater was off, her eyes skimming his chest before she put her palms on his pecs, squeezing the muscle, dragging her fingers through the hair between them.

Her eyes were wide, shiny, but she met Jax's gaze with a directness he hadn't expected—one that kept catching him off guard. "You have a great chest."

He slipped his hands under her ass and pulled her to him until her thighs went around his waist. "You have a great everything. *Mysteriously sexy, totally obvious* gets my vote."

Em's smile was shy for a quick moment. Her eyes flitted away then came back to meet his, bolder now.

His cock rubbed with painful pressure against his jeans when she tilted her hips up, settling into him, adjusting her body to his. Right there he wanted to devour her—right in the second where she fit him, where all their body parts just seemed to line up—to work, he wanted to tear the scrap of flimsy right off her, flatten her on the mattress and be inside her.

Drive into her until they came and save the exploration for round two. But that was the caveman in him talking. The primal reaction he was having would scare her.

It scared him.

Then there was the tiny piece of material between her legs, covering the sweetest part of Em. He'd caught a quick glimpse of it, dark hair pressed against the blue of the silky triangle, and it made his mouth water.

Her fingernails scraped over his nipple, hardening it, making his pulse rage. Jax clenched his teeth, wrapping his hands around her wrists. "This—" he fingered the strap on her nightgown "—has to go. *Now.*"

Her lips met his for a brief kiss before she lifted her arms up, forcing her tight nipples to press against the material. Jax skimmed his hands over her hips, taking the nightgown with him.

Shy Em's hands went to her belly, pressing her elbows into it while bold Em disappeared. She visibly sucked in her stomach, and he hated it.

"Don't do that." He placed his palms on the backs of her hands, nipping at her lips. He didn't want her to hide what she perceived were her flaws. They were what made up all the parts of Em.

And he wanted to see her.

Where was confident Em now? Where had all her "whatever" attitude run off to? "I have a small roll. Okay, maybe *small* is a generous word. But it's a roll." It was a roll, and it was an ugly roll at that—one that wouldn't go away no matter how many crunches she did. Leftover scar tissue from the removal of her appendix. After she'd had Gareth, the weight she'd gained had formed a hideous lumpy roll just beneath her incision.

Jax smoothed her hands away until they were at her sides and her ugly roll was revealed. He bent his dark head and kissed the flesh, setting off that warm, shooting vibration in her belly.

But it didn't make her forget the roll. It was that ugly. She bracketed his head with her hands, forcing him to look up at her. "It doesn't help that you're fit as a fiddle, you know." And he was. Hard, ripply-fit. "That was a catty accusation, by the way. Not just an observation."

Jax chuckled and laid his head on her breast, flicking his tongue over her tight nipple. "We'll see how perfect I am when you see my toes. They're a total turnoff. In fact, I think we should just leave my shoes on while we do this so you don't run out of here screaming."

He muttered those words before he cupped her breasts, bringing them together to circle her nipples with his tongue. She gasped and laughed at the same time.

Had she and Clifton ever laughed during sex?

But this time she really did forget about her rolls and her cellulite and comparing her sparse sexual experiences to this one because Jax was kissing her everywhere, along her arms, across her shoulders, at her rib cage, creating delicious tendrils of heat along her skin.

His mouth was hot on her flesh, his teeth nipping at her skin before soothing it with his tongue. When he circled her belly button, her stomach muscles tightened and her head fell forward.

Jax splayed his hand over her midsection; his ruddy flesh against her pale, slightly marred skin made for another sharp inhale from her.

Exquisite was the word that came to mind, an exquisite snapshot of sensuality, of possessive intent that took her breath away.

Just when she thought there was no breath left in her to steal, Jax hooked his thumbs under the straps that held her thong together and dragged them over her hips to her ankles. He held her leg up, kissing her calf with a smile when he pulled the thong over her heel and twirled it on his finger before letting it zing across the room. "These are really hot on you. You've got terrific legs, by the way, but they're probably not practical in Forest Hawthorne, huh?"

Em leaned back on her elbows and giggled again, lost in his compliments and the way his hot breath gave her chills. "Nearly broke a leg."

Jax's mouth skimmed along the muscles of her calf, working his way up until he was at her inner thigh. "And we don't want you to have to explain that to everyone in town, do we?" His eyes rose to meet hers, playful and carefree.

"No," she murmured abstractly before realizing where Jax was going with that luscious mouth. "I mean, no!" Em attempted to clamp her thighs shut. Wasn't this too intimate for their first time? Too personal?

Jax's hands went to her thighs, massaging the tops of them to relax her, and leaned back on his heels. His eyes were sweet—filled with concern. "Am I making you uncomfortable, Em?"

Her heart began to pound out a hard beat. *Uncomfortable* wasn't the word. He was doing the most inexplicable, unbelievable things to her body—every second of it was pure sensory overload. And she'd waxed for this. Really waxed for the first time in almost a year, but now the act itself seemed so personal, so much deeper than she remembered it that she was feeling like…

Like what?

It hit her like a ton of bricks. She felt like she was dirty for enjoying it. Like this particular part of making love was forbidden unless it was shared by two committed people. Clifton had once said that. Sex was sex, but blow jobs were for the girl you were going to marry.

Somehow, his view of things had become hers. But what did he know about who she really was? What did he know about what she felt? Which opinions were hers, and which were the ones either drilled into her by her mother, or formed during a marriage to a man who didn't trust her enough to reveal a life-altering experience?

Instantly, she relaxed, breathing deeply. It was time

to form her own opinion on the matter, so she called up the Em who wouldn't bat an eyelash at this deliciousness and shook her head with a smile. "I'm just a little ticklish."

Jax mumbled something before his lips were back on her thigh, traveling upward until she hissed a sigh of anticipation. He hovered there for a moment, her legs spread wide. She knew he was looking at her—seeing the most intimate part of her. She heard his breathing pick up, felt the rise and fall of his chest against her inner thigh, and Em let him look.

"You're beautiful," he said, sending a thrill of white-hot pleasure through her.

Without fear of recrimination, without an ounce of embarrassment, she stretched her arms upward, gripping the flannel sheet in preparation.

Jax moaned low before parting her, slipping his fingers between her aching, swollen folds and letting his thumb circle her clit.

Her hips responded, jutting upward at the remembered feel of his fingers, the sweet ache he created. And then Jax's lips were on her, trailing light kisses across her exposed flesh, swirling his tongue over her clit until there was no stopping the greedy way she lifted her hips to beg for more.

She was dizzy with the press of his tongue, boneless when he slipped two fingers inside her and stroked, became agonizingly hot with the sound of his mouth on her lodged in her ears.

Em's fingers tangled in his hair, clutching, clinging to anything that would keep her anchored. Her entire

focus became about Jax's mouth on her, licking, sucking until a fierce wave of heat engulfed her.

Her toes curled in her shoes, her nipples tightening
unbearably when the point of no return hit her. Jax's
pursuit was unmerciful, stroking, licking, cupping her
ass so her hips lifted off the bed and she was flush to
the hot sting of his mouth.

For a brief second, it became an unbearable pleasure,
so intense, so defined, Em's head thrashed against the
pillow. She bit her tongue to keep all of Plum Orchard
from hearing her scream an orgasm like she'd never
had before. But there was no stopping the explosion of
colors flashing behind her eyes or the sharply sweet
release of pressure when she came.

As she melted into the bed, her chest hurt from pant-
ing; her lungs felt like they'd explode as she gasped,
struggling for air.

Jax continued to run his hands over her skin, soothing, easing, kissing his way up her torso until he was
beside her, forcing her to open her eyes and look at him
when he tilted her chin. His eyes questioned her.

As the tension in her body left, she smiled at him,
smiled at the way he was waiting to be sure she was
okay with the next step. That was what he was doing.
Feeling her out, looking out for her. She knew it sure
as she knew that was the best orgasm of her life. She'd
never felt so ravished, yet at the same time, so free, so
liberated.

Rolling to her side, she let her fingers trail down his
magnificent chest, discovering the rigid planes of his

abs, dipping into the waistline of his jeans, touching the crisp hair that led from his belly button to his cock.

Jax cupped her cheek. "You're sure you're okay?"

Em leaned upward and kissed his hard jaw, now littered with rough stubble, and buried her nose against it. "I'm beyond okay, Mr. Hawthorne. Wow. For my first-time draft pick, I'd call that a win."

His mouth found her earlobe with another chuckle, nibbling it, running his fingertips along her ribs, fluttering over her hungry nipples while she busied herself with the button on his jeans.

Impatient fingers fumbled then scored by popping open the button and lowering Jax's zipper in one swift motion.

Em flattened her palm against his lower abdomen, loving the feel of his overheated skin, the ridge where his sharp hip bone gave way to the path leading to his cock. She flared her fingers, running them through the crisp hair from his belly button to his pelvis until she felt the tip of him jerk against her, and it made her smile against his lips.

Jax's reaction to the brush of her fingers reignited her curiosity, making her boldly grasp him and savor his hiss of pleasure. Her eyes fluttered open, catching a glimpse of his face in the candlelight, strong-jawed held tight in a clench of his teeth. His eyes were closed, his head falling back on his shoulders to reveal the tendons in his neck, rigid and stiff.

God. He was absolutely the most beautiful man she'd ever seen, had ever even considered seeing up close like this, and she was going to wring dry every last hot moment spent with him.

His cock pulsed beneath her grasp, giving her the courage to begin a long, slow stroke with one hand while she pushed his jeans from his hips with the other.

Jax ground against her fingers. Wrapping his hand around her wrist, he did a sort of husky growl in her ear. "Condoms. That's gotta happen soon. Swear it won't always be like this, but it's been a long time."

Pulling away, he rose, kicking his shoes off and shoving his jeans down over his thick thighs. Thighs sprinkled with dark hair and carved with muscle. Thighs she had a crazy urge to grip, run her lips across the bunched cords. For a man who spent a great deal of his time behind a computer, developing things she still wasn't quite sure she understood, he definitely didn't suffer a paunch or any of the things the girls were always complaining about.

Those thighs that led to lean calves were what carried Jax across the room to the box of condoms, while she openly admired his muscled butt and wide back. She'd missed it before, but he had a tattoo she couldn't read on his left pec.

When Jax turned around, condom in hand and an amused gleam in his eye, her eyes strayed to his erection. As perfect as the rest of him and with a slight hook to the right.

And then, this enormous, beautiful man was sliding the condom on, parting her legs, pressing the tip of himself at her entrance, making her wrap her arms around his neck and delight in the brush of his dark hair rubbing against her shoulders.

Jax brushed her hair from her eyes. "You still good?"

Each time Jax made his concern for her known, when he was offering her the time to regroup if she needed it, it did something to her heart. Something that tingled—a twinge—a warmth—a nudge of a feeling she had to blatantly ignore. His tenderness wasn't something she'd expected, and it was going to break her if she read too much into it.

Jax was a considerate lover. Just because they were only in this for the sex didn't mean they couldn't care about how the other person felt.

Still, when she nodded her consent and arched her back, and Jax drove upward inside her, rigid and hot, her throat closed up. Grew so tight from this odd emotion, she had to clench her eyes shut.

But then the world tipped sideways when Jax's hands burrowed under her, cupping her butt, driving deeper into her. Stroke after stroke he drew her closer, filling her with everything Jax, stretching her until she dug her fingernails into thick shoulders.

There was no tease to his thrusts, no flirtation with his intent, but she was right there with him, pushing harder, gulping for the same air he gasped at to fill his lungs. Her hips ground upward, seeking that delicious friction the scrape of her clit against his hair created, as she dug her heels into the edge of the bed to reach higher.

Their scents lingered in her nose, the slide of their sweat-slick bodies and the suction it created in her ears.

Em's muscles contracted around him, tightening, drawing him deeper inside her until it all became an overload of everything.

Everything incredible. Everything delicious. Everything she'd always read, heard, daydreamed about, but never dared to imagine could ever happen to her.

Jax was so much—so much pleasure—so much perfect—that when she came, her orgasm was one part wild release, and a million other parts stingingly, achingly sweet. Em slammed her eyes shut, stupidly hoping it would chase away this startling sense of connection— this sense of being right where she belonged.

Jax stiffened above her, his back muscles tightening under her palms as he settled deeper into her, taking his last long draw before he cupped her jaw and ran his thumb over her bottom lip and reared up.

And then he came, too. As strong and as powerful as the rest of him. A release of tension-filled energy before he sagged against her, breathing harsh rasps of breath.

As if it were possible, in that second, while he was above her, rigid and firm, when his chest was ripped with tight muscle, and his jaw was clenched, he was even more amazing.

Did anyone look that good when they came? But watching him from hooded eyes hadn't just turned her on, it made her heart curl, twist, beat harder as if it were begging for attention.

No.

These wispy-warm tendrils of satisfaction would not dig themselves any deeper than into a layer of her flesh. Her heart was sacred—off-limits—temporarily out to lunch.

Reason would return, and she'd look back on tonight and realize what she was feeling right now was just the afterglow of love well made. It left you vulnerable, and open to a world of hurt. It was why so many mistook love for incredible sex.

Love took time, and sometimes, even when it had time invested, it wasn't real love after all. That wouldn't fool her again.

She definitely wouldn't be fooled by this "connection" business.

They'd been connected all right. By limbs, and sweat, and mouths and tongues.

And it had been unbelievable.

The sex. Just the sex.

No overthinking it, Emmaline Amos.

Twelve

"Ms. Amos?"

Em looked up from the mound of paperwork that had been waiting for her on her desk when she stumbled into Call Girls, bleary-eyed and yawning. She and Jax had well overextended themselves last night.

After all that business makin', they'd stayed up far too late going through her idea book, choosing colors for the multiple rooms in his aunt's old farmhouse, looking on Jax's laptop at appliances, fixtures, lamps, throw rugs, outlet covers, bedding—you name it, they'd tapped it.

Every second they'd spent drinking wine and eating Jax's stash of Twizzlers, hunkered under that itchy army blanket had been pure heaven for her. A heaven she was bound to fall from if she kept thinking that way.

Em folded her hands in front of her and examined her nail polish. To look at Dixie could be likened to confession, if she was Catholic and she went to confession.

Dixie knew her better than anyone. She had a way of

making her confess things she didn't want to confess. "Yes, Ms. Davis?"

Dixie sat down in front of her desk and gave her an endearing smile. Em knew that smile. Dixie had smiled it back in high school—just before she'd talked her into prank calling the local pizzeria and ordering twenty anchovy pizzas delivered to Louella Palmer's house because Louella had made her angry at cheerleading practice. "I'm going to be bold."

Em's eyebrow rose in the way it always did when Dixie declared she was going to do something she did on a regular basis. It was the new Dixie's way of warning you she was going to stick her nose where it didn't belong. "Because you and demure are so tight?"

"You've had sex."

Oh, boy. Did I ever. I've had the best sex I've ever had, and I can't stop thinking about it. But Em cocked her head and gave Dixie the "you're crazy" look. "I have not." She had to be very careful here. If she went too far in her "I didn't have sex" defense, she'd ramble and look guilty because she was the worst sort of liar. If she remained silent, she'd look just as guilty.

This was a delicate matter she was going to have to handle with kid gloves—find the in-between and ride that fence.

"You have, too."

"No, I haven't."

Dixie bounced her hand on the desk, slapping it. "You have so, Emmaline! I know it. And if you don't want to tell me about it, that's just fine, but I know I speak the truth."

"You wouldn't know the truth if it hit you with a Louboutin."

"I call foul. You did so have sex."

"You can call whatever kind of bird you'd like. I did not have sex."

Dixie's rich laughter filled the office at Em's intentional misuse of the word. "Then where were you last night when I called you at ten sharp? I know it was ten sharp because that's when you watch the DIY channel for an hour until bedtime. Caine was in Johnsonville last night, and I thought maybe we could watch over the phone together. But you weren't home."

"I was so. I went to bed early." Sort of. Technically, she'd gone to bed.

"Oh, no. I know that's not true. Do you want to know how I know that's not true?"

"Again, we're back at the word *truth*. What does Dixie Davis know about the truth?" She gave her a saucy lift of her eyebrow and flipped through the latest Call Girl stats.

"I know it's not true because you didn't let Dora out at nine-thirty. Alder Caldwell says you let Dora out at exactly nine-thirty every night. His bedroom faces your back door off the kitchen. But last night, he didn't hear Dora whine to come in until three in the morning. Plus, you have bags under your eyes. Big, dark bags. So dark, they're like the baggage claim carousel at the airport, annnd you have a stiff neck. Suspiciously, Jax's back is sore today. Could it be that Jax and my Emmaline have similar ailments because they did similar sexually related acts?"

Damn. Most times it was nice to have neighbors who looked out for you. Especially when you were single and the sole protector of your castle.

When you were having no-strings sex like a shameless sex addict, not as nice. And they'd have to do something about that air mattress. Invest in an upgrade, find a new place to meet or something, because all these aches and pains would give them both away. "And when did Alder tell you this?"

Dixie gave her a sour look. "Well, he didn't tell me, silly. No one tells me anything, remember? Plum Orchard's favorite pariah? He was telling Louella Palmer at Madge's this morning while I was getting coffee…"

Em glanced at the clock on the wall of her office. It was almost noon—that meant all the Plum Orchardians in Plum Orchard-ville were about to eviscerate her over their grilled cheese sandwiches. But there was no proof. She'd made certain of that. So, too bad, Louella Palmer. "FYI, gossipmonger, Dora had a bit of a stomach bug last night. She woke me up, and that's why I let her out so late."

Again, not a total lie. Dora had thrown up all over the carpet, and she really had let her out at three in the morning when she'd gotten home from Jax's. Actually, it had been three-o-six when she'd caught a glimpse of her alarm clock and realized that all this illicit sex she was planning on having would have to have an egg timer set on it.

Three hours of sleep just wasn't going to keep her on her toes to fend off questions just like these.

"Oh, no," Dixie sympathized, instantly forgetting her accusations. "Is she okay? Did you call the vet?"

Em fought a yawn—one that made her mouth water. "I think it was the change in her food. The supermarket didn't have her usual brand, so I bought an in-between bag, and I think it disagreed with her touchy tummy."

Dixie nodded and made her poor baby face. "Poor Dora. Okay, now that's covered, tell me about the sex."

Em sighed, emphasis on exaggerating her impatience. "I didn't have sex."

"Who didn't have sex?" Marybell asked, strolling into Em's office, her eyes covered from lid to eyebrow in her signature smoky eyeshadow.

Dixie pointed to Em. "She didn't."

Marybell perched on the end of the desk, the spikes from the chain hanging from her leather pants scraping on the edge of the wood. "You didn't have sex? Why are we surprised by that, Dixie?"

Hold on. Was that the label prude being thrown around again? Em tapped her desk with her fingernail. "Excuse me. I've had lots and lots of sex."

"I knew it," Dixie taunted, to the tune of Marybell's soft chuckle.

"Stop misconstruing. I'm not having sex now. I meant I've had sex just like everyone else. With my clothes off."

"In the dark, with the curtains closed up tighter 'n Fort Knox. You tell 'em, honey," LaDawn teased, leaning a shoulder on the door frame. They often had talks like this just as her and Dixie's day was ending, and LaDawn's and Marybell's was just beginning.

Em loved them. She loved hearing about their crazy phone calls, or even what they had for dinner the night before. She felt included, loved, involved. But tonight? When all she wanted to do was skip back to her house, luxuriate in some bath bubbles and decide what she'd wear for her and Jax's meeting tonight, she didn't feel like touching base.

Em's cheeks sucked inward. "I have so had sex with the lights on." She had, and it had been just fine. Not like last night fine, but fine enough.

Marybell twisted one of her rings on her thumb. "Eyes open or closed? Because it doesn't count if you had the lights on but your eyes were closed, little lady."

Oh. Well, who wanted to see all of their flabby parts jiggling, and who'd made up these rules?

You did. You did last night, Em. You wanted to see all of it, and when you did, you liked it. Your eyes were wide-open.

LaDawn's eyes found Em's over Marybell's spiked head. She searched them for a moment and must have sensed Em's panic. She smiled in her direction before addressing Dixie. "Ladies? Why are we talkin' about sex when we have other, more important matters at hand? Like who, in all of heaven and hell, keeps takin' my meatball Hot Pockets from the lunchroom? I can't keep livin' like this, Dixie Davis. How can you expect me to truly perform my duties as a proper companion-ator when I don't have the right nourishment?"

"Me, I think that was me," a voice said from behind LaDawn's tall frame.

Marybell jumped, the chains on her belt loop cracking against the desk.

Em put a hand on Marybell's hand to soothe her. She understood. She'd spent all morning jumping when she heard Jax's voice every time she turned around today. A Hawthorne could do that to a woman, among the other wicked things he did to a woman. "Ladies, this is Taggart Hawthorne. He's going to be doing some work around Call Girls. I'm trustin' you to treat him nice."

Marybell slipped from the desk, head down, and nodded on her way out the door. "Nice to meet you. I have to go before my shift starts. Talk to you guys later." She wiggled some fingers over her shoulder and ducked around LaDawn and Tag.

Both Em and Dixie shared a confused glance before their attention was redirected to LaDawn—who was preparing to sharpen her claws—on an unsuspecting Tag.

LaDawn spun around, her lips in a flirty pout, her eyes playful when she widened them at Tag. "So it's you who has a hankerin' for my midnight snacks?"

Tag nodded his head, the dark wisps of his hair poking out from under his knit cap rustling on his down jacket. "My apologies. I thought the boss stocked the fridge. I didn't realize it was your personal stash."

LaDawn held her hand out and winked, letting her false eyelashes flutter outrageously. "I shoulda labeled it, but just so you know, I'll share my stash with you whenever you want."

Tag took her hand and gave it a shake, the tips of his

ears turning red. "I appreciate it, ma'am," he mumbled low, and reminiscent of Jax.

"Do you like chocolate? Come with me and I'll show you my secret Snickers hiding place." LaDawn hooked her arm through his and directed poor Tag away from Em's office.

Dixie was up in a shot from the chair. "I'd better go save him before we lose another Hawthorne to the wiles of a Call Girls woman."

Em's ears pricked—getting all hot, and her stomach plunged. "Lose another Hawthorne?"

Dixie nodded. "Well, yes. We already lost Jax to you."

Em's lips went flat. "I told you—"

"You're not having sex." She flapped a hand on her way out. "I heard all about it. I didn't believe it, but I heard it. And you are, too!"

"I am not!"

"Are, too! Are, too! Are, too!" she sang down the hallway, her husky laugh a deliberate taunt.

Disgusted with how thinly she'd veiled her lies, Em reached for her purse and noted her mother had called. She'd ignore it, but it could have to do with the boys. She pressed her mother's number and put her on speaker. "Mama? Are the boys all right?"

"Well, it's about time, young lady."

Em's chest tightened. It didn't matter if her mother was calling her to remind her to pick up a gallon of milk, she still dreaded talking to her. "What's wrong, Mama?"

"Where were you last night? I called your house phone and you weren't there."

That's because I was having sex with Jax. Her face flooded red. Oh, dear Heaven. She could never confide that to her mother. "I think I fell asleep and didn't hear it. I'm sorry, Mama."

"What kind of mother doesn't keep the phone right by her ear when her children are away?"

The bad kind. The dirty kind. She swallowed hard. "Did something happen I need to know about?"

Clora gave a grunt—one full of disapproval. "You need to know you should pay better attention when your children are in the care of someone else."

"Are you sayin' I should be worried when they're with you, Mama?" Whoa. Em looked around her office. Where had that kind of rebellion come from? She rarely defied her mother. She rarely defied anyone. What was happening to her?

But it diffused Clora's scorn. "No. I'm sayin' you should be available at all times," she blustered.

Em almost forgot about her mother when she saw her phone blinking. "I'll make sure I am, Mama. I have to go now. Talk soon." She hung up to the tune of her mother's mumbling. She could even ruin winning the lottery, and lately, it had become a heavy weight she just couldn't shake.

So instead, she read Jax's text, and her insides responded in puddly-gooey kind.

Thanks to you and your irresistible charms, my back is killing me, Jax texted with a smiley face at the end of the sentence.

Was it possible to hear his melty-warm voice in a text? That slow chuckle that made her limbs get all buttery? My neck is, too.

Wanna work out our kinks together?

A brief image of his eyebrows wiggling made her giggle to herself. We'll just end up with more if we use that air mattress again.

As if a dilapidated air mattress was going to stop her from meeting Jax. Not even a pack of wild Magnolias could keep her from reliving last night.

I bought a deluxe one today. Just for you.

She smiled a smile reserved for the smitten. Oh, your armor, it's so shiny, she teased.

So you wanna come over to Forest Hawthorne and I'll show you my armor?

Only if you promise you'll let me try it on.

Date, he texted then followed quickly with, I mean, deal.

Em's smile turned to a frown. Yes. A deal. They'd struck a deal. Not a date.

As she swept her things into her purse, she reminded herself that this was indeed a deal.

One that was made with the idea that someday it would be broken.

* * *

Jax dropped his phone into his coat pocket and turned the key in the ignition. The glimpse he caught of himself in the rearview mirror made him sit up straighter and wipe his expression clean.

You were goofy smiling.

Nope. He shook his head like Jake was in the car with him. Like they were driving off to the gym together, or going to grab a beer and some pizza. Like they used to.

Yeah, you were. Because Em makes you smile, Jake's voice said. *It's good to smile.*

Jake had said that about Reece, too. He'd said a lot of things about Reece that Jax found himself recalling lately.

He put his truck in Reverse and pulled out of Call Girls. He didn't want to think about Jake and the guilt that still pounded out a steady beat in his chest, or Reece and her smiles or anything that had to do with his life with them. It was over, and he was doing his time because of it in the way of some major regrets.

There were new things in his life now. Things he wanted to do. With Maizy.

With Em, too, Jake's voice whispered.

Jax gripped the steering wheel tighter, making a left at the huge oak tree in front of Maizy's new school.

Last night with Em was something he didn't want to define or slap a label on. It was sex. When you started to label what kind of sex it was, was when your ass was in hot water.

Nope. It wasn't just sex, friend.

He nodded while he watched the stream of kids file

out of the elementary school, looking for Maizy's bright red hair and purple bow.

Sure. Maybe it was a little more than sex. It was I-like-you-a-lot sex. Better?

That was true. Em wasn't someone you forgot overnight like you were supposed to forget a friend with benefits. You definitely shouldn't spend all damn day thinking about her unless you were just thinking about the amazing sex.

But he'd been thinking about more than just the sex. He'd been wondering what her reasons were for wanting to keep things strictly sex. She didn't act as though her divorce had been especially ugly—or even that her marriage had.

In fact, Em seemed at peace with her choice. So what made her so determined to keep her freedom, as she'd called it? What was the big deal about the color of your towels or where you hung a picture?

Those things are just symbolic, Jax. They represent her independence.

Towels and the color of them equal a woman's freedom?

You're missing the point.

Jax nodded again. Obviously, he was missing something, and it didn't matter anyway. He was going to keep right on missing anything towel/picture related. He was only going to think about the sex. Which had been mind-blowing.

All day long he'd carried the picture of Em, sprawled out beneath him, silky limbs wrapped around his, her cloud of dark hair spread out behind her on the pillow, the sweet taste of her pussy on his lips. The way she dragged her fingers through his hair when he'd sunk into her for the first time. That hot nightie she'd had on under her trench coat. That—

A knock on his car window made his head snap back into place.

A pretty blonde grinned and waved, gesturing for him to open the window. Jax flicked the button. "Remember me?"

No. He should remember a cute blonde. Remembering cute blondes was mandatory in the Man Book, but all he could think about was a sultry brunette. "Sorry. I'm terrible with names."

Her features fell for a second, but she recovered nicely. "Louella. Louella Palmer. You're Jax Hawthorne, right? We met briefly when you were here to look at your aunt's house this past summer."

He didn't remember that, but he knew the name. She was the one who'd given up Em's ex at the Founders' Day picnic. A swell of anger raged in his chest when he remembered how he'd first met Em—crying and humiliated, so raw and fragile. All because of Louella Palmer.

Why was he angry? It was a shitty thing to do. He acknowledged all things shitty. They didn't make him want to send a hit man after the person who'd done the shitty thing.

Because she hurt your woman. Guys get protective about their women.

She's damn well not my woman, Jake. And who are you to preach to me about protective and guys, right? Go the fuck away.

The pretty blonde with no heart put her hand inside the window. Covered in a tan glove, she offered it to him and smiled again, but she leaned in too close, didn't smell like pears and worked too hard. Or something like that. "Then this is the perfect time to get reacquainted, don't you think? My niece DeeDee and your daughter, Maizy, are friends in class. I thought it might be nice if we get them together for a playdate sometime."

Maizy's head, bouncing in the line of children pouring out of the school, took his attention away from Louella and her playdate. He didn't particularly care for the idea of Maizy having a playdate with anyone related to Louella, anyway.

Maizy was chatting excitedly to another little boy while she hauled the sparkly backpack that was almost the size of her over her shoulder.

Jax's heart swelled with pride every time he saw her. Every time he was able to think, "That's my kid."

He yanked the lever on the door. "Excuse me, Louella, but that's Maizy, and she's all caught up talking instead of paying attention. Kids, you know?" He didn't bother to stick around for her response.

Not when, in the swarm of parents and children gathering at the mouth of the school, there was another redhead. One just like his. But she wasn't six and she wasn't his.

Jax saw all kinds of colors flash in front of his eyes before he took off running.

Thirteen

Em grabbed Gareth's hand and squatted on her haunches when he asked, "Why are you here, Mama? Grams is coming to pick us up from school today. Grampa Amos said we can shoot cans with his BB gun if we eat all our supper."

She snuggled him closer and rubbed her nose against his cold one. "You can still go with Grandpa Amos. I just needed some Gareth hugs before I go home. That's all. You okay with that, little man?"

Gareth's willingness to still indulge her with a snuggle warmed her, and she was going to take as many snuggles as she possibly could before he took them away like Clifton Junior. She pulled him into a tight hug and inhaled the scent of Play-Doh and grape jelly before he squirmed his way out of her arms.

She tweaked his chin and rose to leave when she caught that brilliant shock of red hair swathed in a big, purple bow. "Well, if it isn't Miss Maizy Hawthorne," she said with a smile. Maizy tugged her maternal instincts in a totally different way than the boys did.

Maybe it was her sweet plea on the phone that night. Maybe it was the impish grin she used to try to hide her curiosity while her eyes devoured Gareth and Em together. Maybe it was just that she was a little girl and looked like the kind of little girl who loved all things having to do with being a girl, just like Em. But something about her drew on Em's heart, pushed it around in her chest and made it stand up and take notice.

Maizy hung back for a minute in the shadow of the maple tree—tentative and shy.

But Em gave her a warm smile of encouragement and crooked her finger at her. "I like your bow. It's the perfect color for you."

Maizy took a step closer, her light-up sneakers flashing in the coming dusk, her eyes, uninhibited by emotions adults are eventually taught to hide, were full of pleasure. "I like your gloves. They have fur on them. That's my favorite. Well, glitter's really my favorite, but I like fur almost as much." She reached a chubby hand out to touch the fluff at Em's wrist.

Em pulled it off and offered it to her. "Want to try it on?"

Maizy nodded, dropping her backpack on the ground by Gareth's feet. Em helped her put it on, and they both laughed when Maizy held it up, the fingers flopping.

A commotion off to their left had Em's instincts pulling Gareth and Maizy close, her eyes scanning the mass of children for Clifton Junior.

"Maizy!"

Jax?

"Maizy! Where are you?"

Em heard the panic in Jax's voice—it was the panic of a parent who thought they'd lost their child. She threw her hand in the air and waved it. "We're over here!"

Jax's bulk appeared in the throng of parents and children, almost lifting people off their feet to get to Maizy. His eyes zeroed in on her, and she was all he saw. Strong arms swooped down and scooped her up, hugging her tight. "I couldn't find you," he said, almost like an accusation, the words ragged and full of fear.

Maizy patted him on the cheek and gave him a toothless grin. "I was right here all the time, Daddy. With Miss Em and Gareth, waiting for you to come pick me up."

Then everything was different. The cloudy haze in Jax's eyes cleared, and his shoulders relaxed under his jacket. "I couldn't see you. When I can't see where you are, I get scared."

Em stood, Gareth's hand in hers, and she knew she wasn't imagining Jax's urgency. Not judging from the way Gareth tucked himself into her, his hand holding hers tighter. She put her hand on his arm. "Is everything okay?"

No. It surely wasn't okay. But Jax was going to tell her it was.

He nodded, most of the panic gone from his eyes, but he was forcing himself to come across unruffled. "Sorry. I didn't mean to scare you, Maizy-Lou. I just lost track of you. Everything's okay." His eyes skimmed Em's then returned to Maizy.

Had something like this happened before? Or was he telling the truth—he'd just lost sight of her?

Jax smiled now, that easygoing, everything's-all-good smile. "Really. I just panicked. You know how that is."

She did. But something about the way he was trying so hard to convince her that was how it was, wasn't convincing her. "I do know," she replied easily, while her eyes fixed on his and wouldn't let go.

Maizy held up Em's glove and put it under Jax's nose, diffusing their stare-off. "Look, Daddy. Miss Em let me try on her glove. It has fur on it. It's so soft. Can I have gloves like Miss Em's?"

"Maybe, princess. For now, whaddya say we go home and have some dinner with Uncle Tag and Uncle Gage?"

"Who's cooking?"

Em stifled a laugh when Jax rolled his eyes. "Not me, okay? I can't believe the bad rap I have for one burned fish stick."

Maizy leaned over Jax's arm and handed her back the glove, her button nose wrinkled. "It wasn't one. It was a whole box of 'em. Daddy's a really bad cook," she informed Em and Gareth.

"My mom's a really good cook. She makes really awesome macaroni and cheese, and it's not from a box. Maybe you could cook for Maizy sometime, Mommy?" Gareth's sweet, round eyes sought hers.

Innocence in all its simplicity.

Maizy nodded her head. "I love macaroni and cheese. Promise I'll eat all of it."

"I always eat all of mine," Gareth agreed.

Now she was avoiding Jax's eyes, looking anywhere but where he was. She ruffled Gareth's hair with an affectionate hand. "Maybe when things aren't so busy at work, I'll make some macaroni and cheese."

"Macaroni and cheese? We love macaroni and cheese, don't we, DeeDee?" Louella strolled along the thinning crowd, her suede boots clicking on the sidewalk, her perfectly streaked, vanilla-blond hair lifting in the chilly breeze. Hand in hand with her equally as blonde and pretty niece, she insinuated herself into their conversation.

She gave Em the once-over with critical eyes—her way of acknowledging Em and dismissing her all in one glance. "Hi, Em. How nice to see you. Still runnin' the business of somethin' that rhymes with fin?"

Hah-hah. Sin. Funny, clever Louella Palmer. Em's cheeks flushed.

Jax's eyes caught Em's over Louella's head as he let Maizy slide down his hip and to the ground, but she didn't understand the message he was sending her.

He nodded politely at Louella, giving her a brief smile before holding his arm out to Em. "She is. Like a well-oiled machine, I might add. Anyway, we were just on our way to go get some of that macaroni and cheese with the kids. Nice seeing you again, Louella."

Oh. Message received.

Was it wrong for her to smile smugly at Louella when big, handsome Jax offered his arm to her? Would she burn in the flaming fires of hell for enjoying the gasps of some of the other mothers?

Probably. But at least she'd have Dixie on the big-fat-burn-in-hell couch right beside her. Tipping her heeled foot up, she smiled wide at Louella. "As always, nice to see you, too. Bye now, Louella!"

As she let Jax whisk her away, she realized, all mom-eyes were on her, and everyone would be talking about the way she'd slighted Louella with Jax, totally defeating her "no one could ever get the slightest whiff of her relationship with him" vow.

Yet, right this second, she didn't care about propriety, or all the ugly rumors that would certainly circulate, or even that she'd one-upped Louella in public.

She only cared that the man who was directing her to her car was Jax, and her arm in his, cradled in the nook of all that power, made her feel good.

Safe. Protected. Even from the evil intentions of Louella Palmer.

"I know what you're thinking." Jax's breathing was heavy and choppy, his chest expanding and deflating with the effort.

"No. I don't think you do," Em huffed, her arms visibly shaking, the material of her long sweater stretching across her slender back. Jeans. She changed into jeans tonight when he'd talked her into checking out couches with him after they'd left Louella in their dust. A rare occurrence for her—but, Jesus, she was killing him with her long legs and that rounded ass.

He admired it from behind her back when he replied, "Sure I do. You're thinking, wow, that's huge."

"It is—" she fought for air "—huuuge," blowing the last word out with a heaving grunt as she jammed his new couch into place.

He took a step back and gave the room a critical eye. "I should have listened to you."

Em nodded with a resigned sigh, coming to stand beside him, but keeping that safe distance she always kept when other people were around. "When it comes to things like size and placement, you should always listen to me, Jax. I know huge by eye. This is what an impulse buy will get you."

He took another step back and looked at the cramped space of his home office full of nothing but this enormous couch he'd been talked into in the heat of a couch-buying moment. "Swear, I really thought it would fit."

Em gave him that you're-so-five look. "You got caught up in the moment. It was cash-and-carry. Plus, Liam Tobias is a good salesman. I tried to warn you about him before we ever hit the store. He could talk you into buyin' Brazilian butt implants. Now look. You have a couch the size of Godzilla and no room for anything else."

"You gotta admit it's a nice color." It was. A foresty-green, or something woodsy, Em had said. Manly. It was very manly—not some sort of nondescript, wishy-washy color like beige.

And it had red pillows. When Em had tried the couch on for size in the store, she'd put her pretty head on those very pillows, letting her dark hair splay out on them, and he'd had to look the other way to keep from hauling her off that couch and kissing her senseless.

Her shoulder brushed his when she chuckled, making her inch in the other direction. That was what Em always did when they were in close quarters and they had witnesses. "That's because after all that talkin' me into something I knew wouldn't fit, I was forced to at the very least choose a color that would work in the room. You want your office to be a place you want to come to every day, don't you? Somewhere that's all you?"

The more time they spent together out of their guesthouse lair, the more he liked Em. Every chance he got, he stole a glance at her. He was becoming convinced he was going to have to buy another house that needed redecorating in order to keep her around. Then he'd quash that notion. No women. Things ended badly when you let them steal your common sense.

Reece was a prime example. He'd lost all his senses when he could've sworn he'd seen her at Maizy's school. Where was she and why was she lurking around Plum Orchard?

"Are you hearin' me, Jax?"

Yeah. He heard. Stern teacher's voice got un-fucking-believably-sexier each time she used it. "Yes. But this couch feels like me." He gave her a wink and a wiggle of his eyebrow, a look she thoroughly ignored. She had on her game face while Tag and Gage roamed through the house.

He thought her game face was adorable. Her efforts to avoid any contact with him at all? Even more adorable.

For the umpteenth time in as many hours as they'd been at this, they danced the dance. If he so much as brushed against her, she was all panicked feet and bristling limbs, moving anywhere but where he was. Those very things were making her even more attractive than just a few hours ago.

He was pretty sure his intense attraction for her had nothing to do with her refusal to become involved. Maybe some subconscious protest against the fact that she'd rejected him as anything other than her boy toy. But he'd mostly tossed out the "when a woman treated you like a side of beef, the more attractive she became" theory.

At first he thought maybe it was a case of the "Gwendolyn Studebakers." Gwen being the girl he'd had the most heartfelt of crushes on in third grade. The girl who wouldn't give him the time of day while he mooned like a lovesick dog. Until she did give him the time of day and he discovered she was mean and he didn't want her time of day.

But this thing he was keeping to himself with Em wasn't like that. Em didn't make him feel like a side of beef. She did make him feel. Fuck, it was uncomfortable.

She waved a hand under his nose. "So? Now what do we do, Mr. Jeff Lewis?"

"Who?" He didn't know who that was, but he was sure he didn't have a mouth as pretty as Em's.

"He's a design guy on TV." Em shook her head like he was hopeless. "Never mind. What are we going to do about this couch, Mr. Hawthorne? It's too big—it doesn't work. It takes up the whole office. You have no room for the desk and printer stand I ordered. You should have gone with the one I showed you the other night online."

"Miss Emmaline! I'm glad you're still here," Maizy screamed her excitement, pushing her way into the newly oak-paneled room and past the couch to make a beeline for Em.

Jax smiled. He liked that, too. He liked that Maizy liked Em. He liked that while she helped him pick out carpet colors from the swatches they'd gathered tonight, she also giddily talked hair and manicures with Maizy.

He liked that she'd stopped on her way home to change and picked up chocolate chip cookies on a big flowery plate for her, claiming she had just a couple leftover after baking them for Clifton and Gareth. He really liked that she'd taught Gage and Tag how to make some crazy casserole with Tater Tots because Maizy had loved the leftovers she'd brought with the cookies.

And he loved how Maizy looked at Em. Sort of dark eyes filled with half admiration, half unsure what to do with a female presence in her life again.

Em smiled down at her, dropping a finger to her nose to run it along the tip. "If it isn't Maizy Hawthorne again. Twice in one day. How was your evenin'? Did you do what I told you to do with your hair so it wouldn't get in your eyes?"

Maizy's nod was solemn. Everything Em said was a nugget of wisdom to his daughter. She always paid close attention, almost as if she was afraid if she didn't,

Em would disappear in a puff of fruity perfume and a cloud of raven hair. "Just like you said."

"Did it work?"

"Uh-huh."

Em beamed down at her, lifting a fist in the air to celebrate the triumph of taming Maizy's hair. "Yay!"

Maizy grabbed on to her hand, tugging her out of the room. "Will you play with me? My Pop-Pop Givens sent me a new doll in the mail today."

"I'm afraid I can't, sweetie. I have to get home and let out poor Dora. But I brought you a little somethin' for a snack. I put it in the warmer in the oven."

Maizy pouted. "I like it better when you're here. You make the house smell like flowers."

"Don't you mean cookies?" Em teased, and he found himself smiling because Maizy was smiling.

Yeah. He liked it better when Em was here, too.

"I'm not sure I like this."

"Like what?" Em feigned cute from the new air mattress in the guesthouse. Totally naked, totally comfortable, totally ready for round two of Jax and Em: Sex in the Guesthouse.

"This," Jax said.

Em rose up on her elbows, the mattress sloshing and moving with her. "What's wrong with it?"

"It's threatening my manhood." He held the threat up between two fingers and dangled it over her naked belly.

"Why, Jax Hawthorne," she cooed, fighting a giggle at his look of distaste. "I didn't think anything could threaten your manhood. What kind of manhood do you have?"

He crawled up along the bed, making her laugh harder at his unsteady movements. "Something called the Annihilator doesn't sound at all threatening to your manhood?"

Em fell back, unable to hold herself up anymore due to her fit of laughter. "Never! My manhood is very secure."

Jax dropped the vibrator next to her and captured her lips, inhaling her sigh. "We've made love one time and already you're turning to devices called the Annihilator to spice things up? Is this the seven-hour itch? We could be in for trouble."

Em ran her hands over his shoulders, a shudder of breath escaping her lips when he kissed her like that. "It could have been the twelve-inch variety. Never forget, things could always be worse."

He cupped her breast, flicking a finger over her nipple, making her sigh and squirm and leaving her slick and achy. "So you've really never used a vibrator?"

"Are we here to talk about my lack of expertise or are we here to end my lack of expertise?" Jax was kissing her jaw, her neck, sweeping his tongue over her collarbone, making it increasingly hard to focus.

He worked his way back up over her shoulder until he was at her ear. "Why did Louella do something so crappy to you on Founders' Day?"

Em stiffened. He'd come to her rescue tonight at the school. She knew he had. He'd offered her his arm as a way to poke at Louella. But why? *Never you mind, Emmaline. He was just bein' gracious. Gentlemen do that.*

After all, he'd been a witness to her ultimate humiliation. Maybe he was just one of those people who took a stand on behalf of a good victim. "Louella Palmer is a sure way to throw a bucket o' cold water on this."

He nibbled at her earlobe, softening her again. "She's pretty mean. I was just wondering why all that mean is directed at you. You don't have to tell me, if you don't want to. If it's too *personal.*"

That information could definitely be considered too personal if it weren't for the fact that she'd be savin' his life. Someone had to warn Jax about that viper Louella... It might as well be her. "She's angry at me for siding with Dixie when she came back to town, swearin' she was a new woman. Again."

Jax used his free hand to stroke the curve of her hip. "Again? She's been a new woman more than once?"

Em closed her eyes and sighed when her nipples scraped his chest. "It's a long story, but it's the real reason Louella hates Dixie. I was once a black sheep Mag, aka their whipping boy. Only allowed to enter the palace when my services were needed. Until I decided my services were no longer up for the occasional grab. When Landon appointed me mediator to that crazy phone-sex contest between Dixie and Caine, I had two choices. I could be driven straight out of my mind by keepin' Louella informed of Dixie's dealings, or I could refuse to be used as a pawn. I refused the position of pawn."

For the first time in her life, she didn't care if Louella and the Mags were angry with her. Maybe it had been the first signs of her finally finding her backbone, or maybe it was just that she couldn't bear to do wrong by Landon, but she'd stuck to her guns back then, infuriating Louella.

Jax's fingers skated over her belly, making her inhale with anticipation. "So she put a pretty personal picture of your ex-husband up at a town gathering just because you wouldn't be her inside edge?"

Men would never understand the machinations of small-town life and the women who lived it. Sometimes, she didn't understand it, either. "That's not the only reason, no. Even though Louella and I were never really friends in the true sense of the word, she didn't like that I took to defending Dixie. Somehow, in her twisted head, I think she figured she was the lesser of two evils, and because she'd done less hateful things to me than Dixie, I'd choose her."

Jax frowned. "Dixie did hateful things to you? But she's your best friend."

"She was horrible to me in high school. But we've long since gotten past it. I admit, when she first came back to town, I was just tryin' to remain respectful to Landon's last wishes, and I was skeptical she'd changed. But she had. She really had."

"So Louella was jealous of your new relationship with Dixie, and she lashed out. Jesus."

"Something like that. She still hated Dixie for stealing Caine right out from under her nose. So she found a way to hurt both of us by sneakin' that picture of Clifton into the mix of the slide show on Founders' Day. She knew I'd immediately blame Dixie because of Dixie's past and all the horrible pranks she played on me. Dixie was the only person aside from Marybell I'd told about Clifton. I knew it wasn't Marybell. She almost never talks to anyone outside of us unless it's to scare them off with her infamous snarl. I didn't even consider her. I jumped to conclusions because of me and Dixie's jaded past, and well, you know the rest of the story."

"I get the impression Louella wants Call Girls gone."

"You get the right impression. She's begun a petition to rid the PO of all our sinnin', last I heard. Says it's sull-yin' our reputation and hurtin' tourism. But that night… That was dedicated to her pure jealousy over Dixie."

He ran a finger down the tip of her nose. "It was a pretty horrible night, wasn't it?"

Em shrugged as if that were no longer an open wound—as if her children weren't still fending off the horrible taunts that night had brought about.

She didn't want Jax's pity or to remember the first night she'd met him. She wanted this. Them naked. "But it's over now. I'm just givin' you some background on Louella Palmer, should you choose to take up with her." Inner Em gasped. *Did you really just say that out loud? Take up with her? That's fishin', Em.*

"I'm not taking up with anyone, remember? That's why we're doing this," he teased, pulling her closer.

Relaxing into him, she agreed, "Exactly. So let's focus on why we're here."

Jax flicked the vibrator to the on position, holding it up, the gleam in his eye wicked and full of the devil. "Your wish is my command. You want this Termina-tor on high or low?"

"The Annihilator," she corrected, giggling again just hearing him say the name. "And I don't know. I've never used one before. Have you?" The first thing she'd done when Jax had agreed to this was hunt for the vibrator Dixie and the girls had given her when she'd signed her divorce papers and declared men were dead to her forever.

She'd hidden it away in one of her old trunks in her walk-in closet and never looked back until the other night when she'd remembered a phone call Marybell had taken with a man who wanted her to pretend she was using a vibrator.

If she'd listened to her mother, all sexual paraphernalia came from the devil's personal toy box and was distributed by his filthy minions. End her curious, fifteen-year-old questions about them after she'd overheard a Magnolia talking about her vibrator back in eleventh grade chemistry class. Her mother had squashed all open conversation about sex all her life.

What she knew, or whatever misconceptions she might have about sex with anyone but your husband were from the internet or late-night TV and, these days, the conversations she heard the girls having with clients. Being as it was her mother who'd decreed all sex toys vile and sinful, made it the first thing Em wanted to discover.

"Wait. Was that too personal?" Did she want to know if Jax had used sex toys with another woman? Yes. No. Strike that from the record.

"Not too personal. And yep. I'm familiar."

When would she learn to shut up? She didn't want visuals of Jax with other women when they were in bed—even if they were remaining detached while in the bed. "Never mind. I don't want to know. I just read it heightens the sexual arousal between a man and a woman. So I thought in the interest of new adventures…"

Jax swiped his tongue over her breast all while the vibrator buzzed in her ears. "I gotta admit, it's a little hot. Not as hot as me, mind you, but it's hot to watch."

He was going to watch, and it didn't even make her blink an eye. It turned her on—gave her that achy tingle in her belly—a tingle of anticipation, making this one of the best decisions she'd ever made.

"Then let's start with low," she managed, but it wasn't easy with the way Jax hovered over her on his knees, his naked body, rippled with muscle, sharply drawn by the flicker of the candles he'd once more lit. She'd only seen small bits of him last night, but tonight, she'd seen all of him, drank him in like he was a bottle of the cheap wine she loved so much. And she hadn't looked away then, either.

She'd also finally caught a glimpse of the word tattooed just beneath his left pec and found out it was a name. Maizy's name, right beneath his heart. It was the little things about Jax that made it harder to remind herself she didn't want any part of this man's personal life.

He was a good father. His love for Maizy was undeniable. His fear today when he'd thought he'd lost her was proof of that. And now, his daughter's name just beneath his heart, tattooed there forever? It made her swoon-y, and that was the hardest piece of Jax to fend

off. The respect she had for him, her admiration of his
raising a little girl without the aid of her mother.

"Low it is," he grumbled in his scratchy-sexy voice
just before he wrapped an arm around her waist and slid
her upright, the cold of the guesthouse wall against her
back harsh at first.

Jax propped pillows behind her then kissed her long
and slow, his tongue scraping over her teeth before he
pulled away and put his hand between her thighs, pushing them apart with gentle hands.

The brush of his fingers on her inner thigh made her
shiver, the feel of his mouth as he kissed his way along
one set her on fire.

Em's fingers found the plaid flannel sheets beside
her, twisting into the fabric as Jax tongued his way
over the crease in her thigh, nudging it with his head
until she let her leg fall back on the bed, bending at the
knee. Exposed and vulnerable, her first instinct was to
clamp her legs shut, but Jax's words stopped her dead.
"You're so damn sexy, Em."

Em gulped, warring with how hot his words made
her and how forbidden this should feel. But it didn't feel
forbidden. It felt alive, and exciting, like a celebration
of her sexuality. She'd never had this kind of attention
in words as well as actions. Clifton had never told her
she was sexy anywhere, but especially not in the confines of their bedroom.

She'd weep for all that she'd apparently missed if
Jax wasn't dipping his fingers between her aching
folds, slipping them through her slickness in agonizing strokes.

Her stomach muscles tightened at the first sip of his lips around her clit. A slow draw, the flick of his tongue and then the cool night air on her flesh made her want everything all at once. His mouth made her dizzy, weak, as he teased the swollen bud.

The vibrator hummed in a distant sort of far-off way until he spread her flesh and drew it between her folds. Em moaned a sound, shuddered a breath at the suddenness of this new sensation.

Jax laid the tip of the vibrator alongside her clit, letting her adjust, moving with the stir of her hips and then his tongue moved against the swollen bud, too, and she thought she'd die of the pleasure.

Her gasp was loud and sharp with surprise, but the combination of his mouth on her and the hum of the vibrator had her silently begging for more.

Jax pulled away just as she touched the fringes of orgasm, making her open her eyes and look down at him with frustration. His head between her legs, his mouth so close to the most intimate place on her body was almost more than she thought she was capable of handling.

But she couldn't look away. She didn't want to look away, and when Jax asked, "Do you like that, Em?" she couldn't answer, her throat too tight. Was this what two people did when they were in it just for the sex? Did they create still shots just like this, and when it was over, forget it ever happened—never to call to memory something this painfully incredible?

Fear she wouldn't be able to let go of this—this amazing thing she was sharing with him—grabbed hold of her lungs. And then it subsided like the tide, it rushed back out and she found her balance again.

Her fingers threaded though his hair and she nodded. "It's pretty great," she managed in a rasp before she had to close her eyes and just succumb to the insane things he was doing to her body.

"You can always holler uncle," he muttered on a thick chuckle, licking at her, moving the vibrator up and down.

"Never," she wanted to scream, but somehow kept to a low whisper.

Jax poised at her entrance, the hum a delicious tease. "Never, huh?"

Her nipples tightened to hard points in anticipation, her hips lifted in an effort to encourage. "Never."

"Never's a long time, Em." He said that strategically, she was sure, because it was just at that moment that he slipped the vibrator inside her and clamped his mouth over her clit.

"Oh!" This time she did scream, forcing her to put her knuckles in her mouth. Oh, God. She'd never survive this. Her blood would boil over, and she'd be found lifeless, albeit sated, right here in Jax's guesthouse.

"Was that an uncle I heard from up there, Em?" Jax taunted, drawing the smooth length in and out, positioning it at a place inside her she didn't even know existed.

Her heels dug into the mattress, she clenched her teeth, beads of sweat formed on her forehead, but she wanted. Oh, heaven forgive, she wanted more. Her chest rose and fell, the winding, twisting heat between her legs grew, but she answered, "Not even close."

Jax twisted the vibrator as he plunged it into her and licked her in one long pass. He flattened his tongue out, scraping it along her swollen clit until she saw stars and colors from behind her eyelids.

She didn't have a second left in her, not another moment of this unmerciful torture left. The stretch of the vibrator inside her, buzzing and setting her on fire combined with Jax's hot, wet tongue sent her right over the edge before she had a chance to grab hold.

Her nipples went tight and painfully hard, her muscles contracted around the width of the vibrator as she thrust her hips downward onto it, driving, feeling, needing every last drop of this orgasm.

Shudders racked her body, goose bumps skittered along her arms as she came until she slumped back, boneless and weak.

Jax withdrew the vibrator and the buzzing instantly stopped. Her eyes popped open to find Jax setting the Annihilator on a plastic crate.

Instead of grabbing a condom like she thought he would, he moved her over on the bed and got in next to her, pulling up the scratchy army blanket to her chin and tucking her next to him.

His actions perplexed Em. Wasn't it his turn? "We're not done, are we?" she half joked, half really wondered. Fair was, after all, fair.

Jax's chin rested on the top of her head in a pause she didn't quite understand, but then he said, "Just for the moment."

As Em lay there, held tight in his arms, their bodies curled together, she tried not to read anything into the odd look in Jax's eyes just before he'd climbed in beside her and pulled the blanket up under her chin.

She tried not to worry he was mad about the Annihilator. She tried not to love lying here with him like this. She tried to figure out what he needed right at this moment. Then she tried to figure out how she was going to stop trying to figure everything out and try to remember she wasn't supposed to care how he felt other than in a bed.

Her insides just weren't cooperating.

But she was really, really trying.

Really.

Fourteen

Jax scrubbed his hand over his face, lobbing his pen at the desk. The chirp of the office phones had become background noise to him. The scenarios played out beyond his office walls nothing more than white noise.

He was growing used to being here at Call Girls. He liked working for Dixie and Caine. He liked the women who worked here, and he really liked knowing Em would be here every day. Avoiding the hell out of him, refusing to look at him, lifting her cute nose the other way when he came into the room, but here just the same.

Em, Em, Em.

He was never going to get a damn thing done like this.

Especially not after the other night.

Maybe he should just call it off. Maybe it was stupid to think he could keep doing this and keep her unimportant—at a distance.

Now wasn't the time to get involved with anyone.

Not with Maizy to consider. She was supposed to be his only focus, but Em was eating that promise to himself alive. At first, he'd liked that Em didn't want to ask him a million questions. That meant he didn't have to come up with answers for them. He wasn't ready to explain the parts of his life involving Maizy.

Yet, he was asking Em questions because he was interested—because he liked her—because he couldn't stop insinuating her image into the life he'd once pictured for himself.

Maizy didn't help, either. She'd informed him, after seeing her at the school, she liked Miss Em. She was pretty, and she wore red lipstick, and in Maizy's book, that equaled idol status.

The other day at the school, when he'd thought Reece was there, he'd panicked, but when he saw Maizy with Em, he knew everything was all right. That Em would look out for her—keep her from harm.

After seeing the way Maizy looked at Em, with that admiration little girls have for their older counterparts, he knew she'd be good for Maizy.

But she didn't want to be good for anyone but herself and her sons—and he thought he didn't want that, either.

He didn't. Then the other night, she'd blown him away. There was nothing special about it he could pinpoint. He thought it was cute that she'd never used a vibrator, cuter that she wanted to try one with him. That's what she was in this for, right? To experience new things.

As long as they were within his parameters, he was happy to oblige.

Until that one moment, that single second when he'd caught Em watching him between her legs. That brief flicker of a moment where her eyes darkened and she became aware of something—that *something* between them. It existed. It pulled him, touched him, made him just as aware.

He'd needed a minute to process it. Let it sit.

It was still sitting three days later. Three long days where they couldn't get together because she had the boys and he had a huge glitch in this damn security program he was convinced no one could solve but Harper.

"You forgot your lunch," Gage said from the doorway to his office. He threw a bag labeled Madge's down in front of him and pulled out a chair. "Figured I'd eat with you so you wouldn't be lonely."

He didn't want to eat. He wanted to see Em. But he didn't say that. Instead, he pulled out the deli-wrapped sandwich from the bag.

"So what's new, big brother?" Gage's eyes pinned his over a ham and cheese with onions.

"Nothing."

"How's Emmaline?" he whispered her name and batted his eyes in the worst reproduction of a woman Jax had ever seen.

Jax shrugged like it didn't matter how she was. "Dunno."

"Well, I hope you find out soon so you'll stop being such an asshole."

"I'm not being an asshole."

"Yeah, you are. Who flips out over a wet bath mat like that? You miss her, so you're cranky. No big deal."

He bit into his sandwich and considered. Okay, maybe he'd gone a little overboard by throwing the bath mat in the garbage to make a point, but it wasn't because he missed seeing Em.

It was because he was sick and tired of getting out of the shower only to find Tag had drip-dried on the damn thing without even bothering to pick it up. "It was a soggy mess on the floor. Who gets out of the shower soaking wet like that?"

Gage shrugged his shoulders. "Isn't that what a bath mat's for? To protect the floor when you get out of the shower wet?"

"I don't miss her." *Yes, you do.*

Gage dropped his sandwich on the surface of the desk and wiped his mouth with the paper napkin. "Look, whatever, okay? You keep telling yourself this is just you know what. But you'd better get some more you know what soon, or we're firing you as head of the household—because you've been an ass."

"It can't be more than you know what." Shit. Now he'd said it out loud. That meant it held meaning. It meant he was mulling.

"Why can't it, Jax? Why does everything have to be so complicated with you?"

"Because she doesn't want it to be any more than that, and neither do I."

"And you can't convince her that's a stupid decision?"

"I don't want to convince her of anything. I have too much on my plate. Reece showing up for one."

"So you really think that was her at the school?"

He'd put everyone on red alert since that day. Maizy was to leave from school with no one but a Hawthorne. Ever. "I know it was damn well her. What I don't know is why she's skulking around Plum Orchard, showing up at Maizy's school, calling my number, but not returning my calls. I'll tell you this, she better stay the hell away from Maizy."

"I agree. So what does Reece have to do with Emmaline?"

"Nothing."

Gage rumpled up his sandwich wrapper and shot it into the garbage can. He leaned forward, his face hard with anger, his words icy. "You know what, fuck you! You don't have to talk to me about it, keep it all to yourself, whatever. But I'm going to lay it on the line for you because I'm sick of you using the kid."

Jax's eyes widened. "I'm not using my kid."

Gage made a face. "Yes, you are. Maizy isn't the answer to your redemption, dumb ass. If you make her your only reason for living because you think you have to fix what happened, you're gonna be one lonely man someday. Maizy's going to run out of the house screaming the second she can, just to get away from your overprotective crap."

Jax held up a hand to shut Gage up.

But Gage didn't want to be shut up. "She's not learning about healthy relationships—she's learning how to carry grudges and isolate herself. You're a pretty good father now, Jax, but this bullshit you've been carrying around since she was born is just that. *Bullshit*. So someday, when you're a lonely asshole, and Maizy hates your guts because you smothered the shit out of her and maybe kept her from having another female in her life who loves her like you do, don't say I didn't warn you."

Jax didn't even have the time to react before Gage was shoving back his chair, tipping it over with an angry grunt and blowing out of his office.

He gripped the edge of the desk until his knuckles were white. If he let go, he'd get up, drive home and knock the shit out of Gage. He couldn't see for the anger—a red, ugly haze where he was smashing Gage's face against the wall.

"Jax?"

Em put her hand on his, soft, questioning—everything Em. "Is everything all right?"

Jax snatched his hand away, driving back his chair with a shove so hard it hit the wall. He came around the desk and dragged her to him, simultaneously closing and locking the door to his office. "I am now." He hauled her against him, lifting her off her feet until she wrapped her legs around his waist.

"Tell me to stop and I will," he ground out, his cock so hard, all he could think about was being inside her.

Her eyes were wide, but they stared straight at him—blue—full of questions—but perfect, so fucking perfect. "Don't stop," she whispered, like she didn't know what she was getting herself into, but was willing to take the ride anyway.

Jax yanked her skirt up over her hips, grateful for her wispy panties—they made it easier to rip them and drop them on the floor. He walked backward until she was up against the wall, until his hand was in her wet-hot pussy, touching, sliding, thumbing her clit.

Her gasp, that little sound she made that was a hitch of breath and a shudder, drove him crazy.

Em's arms went around his neck, her lips, soft and full, crashed against his, her chest pumped hard, pushing her breasts against his shirt. "Condom?"

"Wallet," he rasped, letting her wiggle her fingers into his back pocket and pull it out. She dropped it between them and he fumbled for it, managing to locate it while Em busied herself with his belt buckle and zipper.

She pushed his pants down over his hips, taking his boxer-briefs with it, and then her fingers were circling his length, grasping it and twisting her hand up and down until he had to make her stop before he came right there.

No. He wanted to be in her wet pussy, drive into her hard, so he'd drive her out of his head. *"Enough,"* he demanded, shoving her hands away and replacing them with the condom while she clung to his shoulders and waist.

"Hold on to me," was all he could manage from his tightly clenched jaw with the tip of his cock so close to all that heat.

Em did as instructed, putting her arms around his neck, still looking him square in the eye. But she wasn't asking questions now. Now she had the same look in her eyes he imagined he had in his—like they were going into battle and the first one to come won.

Christ, she was so damn sexy, Jax didn't think anymore, he reacted by driving upward, jarring her slender body with the force of his first stroke. He tightened his stance, planting his feet firmly on the floor and drove into her hard again.

So damn tight, Em was tight and wet and she fit his cock like a hot glove, surrounding him with her slickness.

Jax cupped her ass with one hand and slammed a palm against the wall with the other in order to get the proper leverage. Em responded by tightening her legs around his waist, squeezing him so tight, he'd come in a split second if he wasn't getting better at keeping his focus.

Which was to fuck her ruthless, remind himself this was just some sex with a hot woman. Her soft whimper meant she was close—he knew it now—craved the sound slipping from her throat.

Upward again, a tighter thrust into all that silken pussy he just wanted to lose himself in. Over and over until Em hissed in his ear, circled her hips one last time before she gasped and stiffened.

Her eyes were closed now, her head falling back against the wall, her creamy white throat a long column he pressed his lips against when he came, too. The sting of it, the sharpness of it tightened his chest, made his muscles curve and flex like an archer's bow.

Jax sagged against Em while he came to terms with what he'd just done, cradling her, smoothing his hands over her back, striving to catch his breath.

Damn. He'd been rough. He'd taken his crap out on her.

"Did we just have angry sex?" she asked, her lips against his neck.

Jax's head popped up to see her smiling. "Yeah, but I wasn't angry with you. I shouldn't have—"

Em's fingers went to his lips and she shook her head. "No. Don't explain, *please*. Now I can check another thing off my list."

"Your list?"

"Uh-huh. I've never had angry sex before. *That* was incredible."

Now he shook his head. This woman. He'd just taken his bad day out on her and she was checking things off her sexual to-do list? "I was wrong to—"

Her fingers were back on his lips. "No. Not another word. I don't know why you were angry, but it doesn't matter. And it's not like you forced me, Jax. You did ask. I said yes," she said, her grin smug and impish at the same time.

"You've never had angry sex?"

Her eyes squinted while she thought about his question. Jesus, she was adorable. "I don't think so. I mean, I've been angry, yes. But it wasn't in the heat of the moment. The argument was usually long done and I was just holding a secret grudge. So, no. I've never had angry sex like that. That was passionate, and spontaneous, and awesome."

He wanted to tell her he'd have angry sex with her anytime she wanted. He wanted to tell her how much he'd missed her. Instead, he smoothed the back of her hair down. "So that means you've never had makeup sex, either."

"Nope."

"Well, then. Wanna fight?" he joked, kissing her ir-resistible lips

Realization hit her as the voices of the other women and the sounds of the office began to filter back between them, and Em was all business. "What have you made me do?"

He gave her his best guilty look, reaching behind her to pick a paint chip from her hair. "But you just said I didn't make you."

She slapped at his chest, pushing at him to let her down. "You know what I mean, Jax Hawthorne. We're at work! How am I ever going to get out of here with an office full of people out there? Oh, gravy. What if they *heard* us, you sex maniac?"

He loved when she went all bossy and professional on him. He kissed the tip of her nose while pulling up his pants. "You're right. I'm a disgusting heathen. I'll create a distraction, you slip out, okay?"

Despite the fact that she was clearly annoyed with him, she giggled, smoothing her skirt back down over her thighs. She waved a finger under his nose, her eyes glittering and playful. "It better be good, Mr. Hawthorne. If someone's out there, you'd better give the best, red-carpet-worthy performance of your life. Now go. And hurry up—I have a Skype meeting with our accountant."

Jax grabbed her finger and brought it to his lips. "So, tonight?"

She rolled her eyes while she slipped her lost shoe on. "Tonight, what?"

"Makeup sex. You're angry with me now. We have to make up, right? Isn't that on your list?"

She stood on tiptoe and planted a kiss on his lips. "Fine, fine. Tonight. Now hurry!"

He chuckled to himself when he popped the door open. Mostly because he'd gotten his way. A quick scan of the hall said it was all good. Turning back to her, he said, "Coast is clear."

She gave him one last warning glance that said it better be, and slipped past him out into the hall, leaving the scent of pears in his nose.

Jax chuckled again at the sight of her cute ass sashaying down the hall to her own office.

He didn't have the heart to tell her the zipper on the back of her skirt was still unzipped.

Em sipped her coffee, pushing her grilled chicken around on her plate with disinterest.

"So, what's new?" Dixie asked.

"Not much."

Dixie grabbed the fork in Em's hand and stilled her motion. "Are we having dinner, or are you, me and Jax's lingering memory having dinner?"

Em's eyes met Dixie's. Almost. It was sort of eye contact but not a total immersion gaze. She was getting so good at it. "I don't know what you mean." She studied her plate.

"You do know what I mean. I mean, accordin' to those who gossip, Jax was taking you and the kids out for macaroni and cheese right after you spit in Louella Palmer's eye in the school yard."

"I didn't spit in her eye." She'd wanted to when she'd seen him talking to her through the window of his car at the school. She'd wanted to pull her hair out, knock her on the ground, steal her shoes. But she hadn't because it was none of her beeswax who he talked to.

"You might as well have, according to all Plum Orchard reports."

Em dropped her fork and threw her napkin on the plate. "You know, for someone who was a victim of all the cruel gossip this town dishes up, you certainly hear a lot of it, don't you?"

Dixie gave her a wide-eyed innocent look. "I don't do it on purpose. I do it so I can keep track of you, seein' as you don't want anyone to know what you're doing. I have to look out for you somehow. Even if it's through the gossip mill. Besides, who can ignore Louella Palmer and her Southern henchwomen? The woman has a voice like a bullfrog."

Em laughed, loosening up a little. Her guilt for not sharing her "Em and Jax Exploits" with Dixie was making her tense and nervous. Dixie was her best friend. She'd probably know how to deal with all these feelings Jax was making her feel. Feelings she neither wanted nor had asked for.

But she knew what Dixie's answer would be. Em wasn't the fling type. She was the keeper type. She'd end up hurt.

With all of these new feelings cropping up for Jax, she was beginning to wonder if the speech she'd get from Dixie and the girls was accurate.

"So, did you spit in Louella's eye?"

"I didn't spit in Louella's eye. Not literally. But you'd be so proud to know, I did kick up a heel when he escorted me off that curb."

Dixie's hands went to her chest. "Look at my little girl all grown-up. Now answer the question."

"I just played along with Jax. He obviously doesn't like Louella, though I don't know why. He was trying to get away from her. I was his getaway car. Nothing more."

"Because she did something horrible to you, and he saw it unfold before his very eyes. That's why he doesn't like her."

"That's silly. He hardly knows me. Why would he take up for me?" Mostly true. He knew her body. He knew how to make her come longer and louder than she ever had before. But he didn't know her.

Dixie let her head fall to the Formica table in a dramatic drop. "How long do you suppose you're going to keep skirtin' the truth with half-truths, Em? Because I'm exhausted from the subterfuge," she said, resting a cheek on the table.

Em stroked Dixie's hair and totally ignored her question. "I have to go."

Dixie's head snapped up. "Where?"

"Home."

"So soon?"

"I know. I'm sorry." *I'm sorry I'm ditching you so I can have amazing sex, but I don't know how long that's going to last. I can't miss this boat.*

"But it's date night."

"Dora's sick. I have to go check on her, and Clifton

Junior forgot his science project on the counter. I have to drop it off to him at Idalee's." *And I have to hurry if I hope to shower and find something sexy to wear.*

Dixie hauled her purse from the corner of the booth. "Then I'll go with."

"No!"

Dixie's eyes narrowed. "Why?"

Look away from the light of Dixie, Em! Do it now or you're sunk. She'll wring your slutty right outta you. "Because…"

"Because *why*, Emmaline?"

"Because she's sneakin' off to see her boyfriend she doesn't want anyone to know about, just like her mama did," Louella Palmer said, loud enough to be heard by the entire diner.

Em stiffened. Like her mother did? "My mother?"

Louella winked. "So, what do the boys have to say about their replacement daddy?"

Em's head whirled—as she tried to figure out how much Louella knew about Jax. Surely she couldn't know the truth? It was all just speculation on Louella's part after the school incident. Wasn't it? Louella was just baiting her—testing to see if she'd crack and spill the torrid details. She was no good at the kinds of games Louella played. You never knew if she had something on you she was going to share in the most humiliating manner possible, or if she was just bluffing.

Em slid out of the booth, towering over petite Louella. "I guess sneakin' off to see any kind of boyfriend is better than having none at all, isn't it?" Then she smiled—pretty—innocent, just like Dixie had taught her.

Dixie shoved her way out of the booth and stepped in front of Em. "Go home to your spinster apartment and do spinster things, Louella. Don't you have a shawl to knit? You'll need it for all those pendin' nights, rocking on a porch while all your cats snuggle at your feet."

"I see I've hit a nerve." Louella responded in kind with a smile.

"Hah! Silly Louella. You mistake me for one of your amateur prey. Lest you forget," Dixie warned, "I'm the queen of this cat-and-mouse chase, and if you don't take your insinuations and stop sticking your nose where it doesn't belong, that plastic surgeon you saw for your rhinoplasty won't be the last surgeon on your dance card."

Louella budged first. It was a small twitch, but noticeable enough to concede she'd lost this round. "Are you suggesting violence?"

Dixie cracked her knuckles. "You bet I am. And another thing, if you don't hush your mouth and stop fuelin' the talk about Clifton Senior, if I hear one more time one of Em's boys has gotten into a fistfight because you really don't care who you hurt in your pathetic attempt to pay me back for stealin' your man—even small children—I'm comin' for you."

As always, when Louella and Dixie were in the same room, and there were witnesses, a buzz began. An uncomfortable one. One Em didn't want. It put an ugly spotlight on her and her recent situation she'd rather not have.

But Louella was apparently feeling sassy tonight. "Will you teach me the ways of the reformed, Dixie? Learn me how to be a good person, maybe? Make me see Jesus?"

Dixie gasped—loud and long for dramatic effect. "Did you just use the Lord's name and yours in the same sentence? Louella Palmer, you should know better than to use *His* name in vain—especially when associated with you."

Em grabbed Dixie's arm. "Let's go. Right this minute. Everyone is staring." And remembering the picture of Clifton as Trixie. And the shock on her face when she saw it. And it was like reliving that night over and over.

Dixie shrugged her off and faced the scattered tables, her face angry and red. Dixie was hard to ruffle, and much harder to anger these days, but Louella had gone for the throat. Dixie never stood by and watched that. "No, Em! If you haven't had enough, I surely have. This stops now. *Right now.*"

Dixie moved around her, spry in her pumpkin-colored heels, and grabbed a glass from a nearby table, clanging a spoon against it.

"Listen up, people of Plum Orchard! That means you, too, Nanette Pruitt." She pointed an accusatory finger toward the older woman. "Y'all better hear me loud and clear when I say, mind your business, you bunch of gossiping know-it-alls! You've involved the well-being of children. Children I love, with your hushed whispers and gutter minds. Your cruel chatter has trickled down to your children who're passin' it on. Shame on all of you for perpetuatin' that kind of behavior, for teaching your children to be mean little monsters just like the lot of you! If you wanna talk, talk about me. Talk about how I'll take my dirty little business right on out of this town and you'll rue the day you didn't heed my words. Because you know what goes with me when I go? Landon's money! Who's going to pay for your fancy exit off the highway then? Will it be you, Louella Palmer? Do you get paid for all the shootin' off your mouth you do? Because it's the only way you'd come close to making the kind of money I pour into this godforsaken town!"

"Dixie!" Em whisper-yelled. She hated confrontation. She hated that there had to be a confrontation at all. She hated that she wanted the floor to open up and swallow her whole.

She hated even more that in the middle of Dixie's rant, while everyone was staring at her, Jax had slipped inside Madge's.

Fifteen

Em's cheeks were hot, her blood was boiling and if she put her hand to her brow, she'd probably find beads of sweat on it. "Dixie Davis, if you don't stop now, I'll never speak to you again." Pivoting on her heel, she lifted her chin, avoided Jax's eyes and walked out of Madge's to the tune of the harsh clack of her shoes, echoing in the astonished silence.

The cold air rushed at her, cooling her cheeks or the tears that stung the corners of her eyes. They were hot and seeping out with a will of their own.

Why couldn't Dixie just let her sweep this under the carpet? The more attention she gave it, the more it grew out of control. Clifton Senior had been gone plenty long by now, but because nothing more exciting than finding out he was a cross-dresser had happened in Plum Orchard since then, she was the latest target.

Worse, why hadn't she been the one to have the angry outburst? Why was she always quieting the part of her that was outraged by the horrible things they were saying about her? Because she hated to make a scene. She'd been taught not to make a scene. At all costs, stay out of the fray.

She'd been in the middle of plenty of humiliating situations since high school, and she hated that she'd never found a voice big enough to tell everyone what Dixie had just told them for her. Hated that she was even too yellow to stand up for, at the very least, her children.

A hand came to rest at her back. A large one. Warm and wide, it spanned part of her waist and made her want things she didn't want to want right now.

Jax.

Exactly what she didn't need. "Please don't." *Please, please, please don't pity me.*

"Can I help?"

"You coming after me in front of everyone doesn't help." She glared up at the twinkling lights in the tree of the square and prayed no one was looking.

"I was just grabbing some burgers." He held up a bag.

"Then take your burgers and go home."

"I didn't know things were that bad for the boys— or even for you."

She looked down at her feet. No way would she let him see her cry. "I'm fine. The boys are fine. Go before your burgers get cold."

"You know, just because we have this…thing going on, it doesn't mean we can't be friends. Friends talk." He said the words in her ear, which meant he was too close.

She took a step away. She didn't want to. There was nothing she wanted to do more right now than lean back into him. Pull his arms around her and just close her eyes—lose herself in the security of having someone else around to help shoulder the burden.

Instead, she kept her body language unapproachable. "I don't need any more friends. As you just saw, Dixie has that covered."

He tucked the burgers under his arm, watching her. Always observing. Always seeing something she didn't want him to see. "She loves your boys, Em. So do Caine and Sanjeev. Caine said as much. I think it hurts her that all of this was brought about because Louella used your situation to hurt her. She feels responsible. She wants to make it right."

Em stuffed her hands inside her jacket pockets. "Look how right she's made it. If she would just let it lie, it will eventually go away." Of course, it would only happen if another big scandal came along. But she could wait.

Jax allowed her the space between them, but it didn't stop him from pursuing the subject. "Do you think it's going to just go away if you don't address it?"

"Do you think it's going to get better when Dixie is screaming and threatening everyone in the PO with her bags o' money in the middle of the diner?"

"I hate to say it, but I'm sort of on Dixie's side here. She's defending you because she cares about you. It hurts her to see you hurt. That's not a bad thing in a best friend, Em. If I was your best friend, and I had to listen to the people in this town always talking about your ex-husband or what led him to stray from your marriage, I'd get fed up with all the crap, too."

The speculation, the intimate details people thought

they knew about why Clifton hadn't come out to her, were still rampant. After three months, they still talked like it had happened yesterday. Sometimes, she wanted to scream the truth at them. But what would that accomplish? "Then it's a good thing you're not my best friend," she said, thin lips and all.

He grinned. "Nope. Just your boy toy."

"Go home, Jax." *Before I beg you to hold me and make this all go away. Before I lean on you when I need to learn to stand on my own two feet.*

"Because that's where all good boy toys go when they're dismissed?"

"Because that's where I'm going."

"To lick your wounds?"

"What are you tryin' to accomplish with this pep talk, coach?"

"I'm trying to get you to stand up for yourself. I saw the way you reacted when Louella showed up at the school. That woman's a piranha. I can smell her desperation from a mile away. Add in the fact that she's pretty horrible, and not a chance in hell I'm going to stand by and let her behave as though you're not standing right in front of her. Why don't you do the same?"

"Chivalry really isn't dead. And I do stick up for myself." She did. Maybe not in a screaming fit filled with blackmail and rage, but she took jabs at Louella. Small ones. But they were jabs. They counted.

Jax called her on that. "You poke at her. But I'd bet you've never let her really have it. Sometimes, you have to teach people how to treat you."

"Then here's your first lesson. Leave me alone before everyone's stickin' their noses to the window in Madge's to see what we're doing out here."

"Why would it be such a bad thing if people saw us together, Em? Am I ugly? Do I have a hunchback?"

Did he ask that because of his ego, or because he really wanted to be seen with her? "Because people will talk about you and Maizy just by association. I won't have it. I won't have you and Maizy dragged through the mud because I'm everyone's target right now. You don't know the people in this town. They can make a life miserable."

"Only if you let 'em. And if you're going to live your life the way you think other people decide you should, it's better I'm only your boy toy."

Because a man like Jax would only want a strong woman who took no guff. Ouch. "Thanks, life coach. Now that I'm all pumped up and ready to go huntin' bear, you can go."

"I'll do that. And glad I caught you. I sent you a text. Maizy has a fever. Can't make tonight. But call me if you want to talk. 'Night, Em." He reached behind him and brushed her fingers with his before strolling off into the shadows of the square, his long legs eating up the pavement until she heard a car door open and shut, an engine start, and he was gone.

Just like that.

Then she was alone, standing outside of Madge's, the cold air biting at her cheeks, Jax's words pounding in her ears.

"So as if it's not bad enough my daughter runs a company where fornicatin' with your words outside of marriage is accepted, today, while I'm mindin' my own business at Brugsby's, Blanche Carter tells me she saw you drivin' around late at night with that new man in town. Jack, is it?" Her mother's continual state of disapproval glared at her over the island in her kitchen.

Dressed in a gray sweater buttoned to her neck, sensible shoes on her feet, Clora worked with purpose, wiping down the messy counter after breakfast.

Em sucked in a breath of air and reached for Gareth's lunch box. "*Jax,* Mama. His name is Jax Hawthorne. He's Miss Jessalyn's nephew."

Clora sucked in her cheeks and grunted. "I don't give a hoot if he's Pontius Pilate's nephew. You shouldn't be driving around with him late at night alone in a car."

"Jeep. It was my Jeep."

"That matters how, Emmaline? Is the make of the car necessary when the deed's been done?"

The pressure of her recent uncharacteristic behavior, coupled with the idea that she'd have to face Jax this morning at work, that she'd see every shade of disgust on his face when she apologized to him for shunning his advice like it was no more valuable than day-old bread, forced her to clamp her lips shut.

"Are you hearin' me, Emmaline?" her mother prodded, handing her a juice box to load into Gareth's lunch pail.

Heard. But it was vague. She'd tuned out after her mother said she'd been minding her own business. That was ludicrous. Clora minded everyone's business like she was in charge of the righteous stick. "I heard you, Mama."

Clora's lips formed a flat line. Scolding complete. Reminder number one million, Em would never do anything right accomplished. "Good. So no more runnin' around town like you don't have a reputation to protect. I can't have people talking about you and the boys any more than they already do these days."

Em jammed Clifton's cheese sandwich into a Ziploc bag to prevent hurling it against the wall. Lately, her mother's disapproval didn't just make her sad it infuriated her—suffocated her. Drove her almost to the point of violence.

Used to be, she took her licks from her mother rather than suffer the tight knot of fear a confrontation with her brought. She'd spent most of her childhood either looking for ways to please her, or hiding from Clora's stifling anger. She didn't know why her mother was always so angry. She didn't know why she took pleasure from almost nothing.

Maybe it had something to do with whatever Louella was insinuating last night. She'd been very specific. She'd said Em was sneakin' off to see her boyfriend just like her mother.

That made no sense. Her mother never had a boyfriend. She'd had a husband who'd left when Em was an infant. Boyfriends implied fun and dates at Madge's, ice-cream sundaes and secretive giggling. None of which applied to her mother.

Growing up, there were far more chores and lectures than there were kisses and hugs or cookies and milk. There was also little laughter. Em had vowed, when she had children, things would be different. She'd give them all the things she'd craved and lacked in her childhood.

But lately, she noticed the boys had begun to adopt some of her old habits around their grandmother, and it wasn't sitting well with her. In fact, at one Sunday dinner, she'd come close to telling her mother what a horrible downer she was—how oppressive and depressing her very presence was. But the words wouldn't come.

The knot of Clora fear tied itself tight in Em's belly, and instead of defending her sons and their silly dinnertime banter, she'd hushed them with a stern frown. These days, she wondered if the help her mother offered her with the boys was worth exposing them to her negativity.

"Did you hear what I said, Emmaline? I can't have people talkin' about you and the boys."

Crack. A little crack in her emotional dam fractured. "Of course not. People talkin' about me and the boys is the worst thing that could ever happen to *you,* Mama."

Clora didn't even look up at her. She didn't have to. Her dissatisfaction dripped off her in invisible drops. "Is that sarcasm I hear comin' from your lips?"

"From our Em's lips?" Dixie chimed from her front doorway, breezing in with two foam cups of coffee. She handed one to Em and teased, "Never, Clora."

Em breathed a sigh of grateful relief, wrapping her hands around the base of the cup, letting the warmth seep into her frozen fingers. Dixie—ever her savior. Dixie understood better than anyone what it was like to live under the constant scrutiny and censure of your mother.

Dixie smiled over the rim of her cup at Em. "Still your person?" she mouthed.

Em nodded and smiled back at Dixie. "Always," she returned. After a sleepless night of contemplation, she'd decided Jax was right. Dixie loved her and the boys, and she felt responsible for the pain they were suffering. She'd done what she did best. Put people in their place.

It wasn't Dixie's fault Em was too much of a coward to do it for herself.

Em turned her back on the flare of Clora's nostrils and her sour eyes. Clora didn't like Dixie, but Em was never sure if it was that she didn't like Dixie, or if it had more to do with Dixie's mother, who'd once ruled Plum Orchard like a queen and had dubbed Clora unworthy as one of the Magnolias' subjects.

Like mother like daughter.

Dixie flung an arm around Em's shoulders and aimed her mischievous smile at Clora. "So what are we talking about, ladies?"

Clora's lips thinned again. "Emmaline's disreputable behavior and how it affects her and the boys."

Dixie widened her eyes to the point of exaggeration. "You? Are you sure we're talkin' Emmaline Amos here? The Em I know, my best friend Em, would never behave badly. Surely you're mistaken, Clora? My Em is amazing and smart and has impeccable manners. So many good things about her, I've lost count."

Em bit back a snort, zipping up Clifton's lunch box and wincing while she waited for Clora to react.

"Your best friend was in a car with a man."

Dixie gasped, propping a hand on her hip. "Oh, that's

dreadful. Deplorable. I mean, with all the murderers running loose these days, how could she?"

Clora bristled, narrowing her gaze in Dixie's direction, her finger raised. "You'd do well to watch your tone, Dixie Davis. You're just not happy unless your smart tongue is waggin' and causin' nothin' but trouble. I heard all about your screamin' fit in the diner last night. Haven't you tainted Emmaline's name enough by association?"

Confrontation. That's where this was heading. Divert, avoid, redirect.

Em plunked the boys' backpacks on the counter in front of her mother, giving Dixie the warning sign with her desperate eyes. "Mama, Dixie didn't taint me. I tainted me. Me. Nobody else. By choosin' to run a place that promotes fornicatin' with your words and marryin' a man who likes to wear lipstick. Now, I have to get to work. Are you sure you'll be all right droppin' the boys at school?"

Clora yanked the kitchen towel from her shoulder and slapped it on the counter with a snap. "We'll be fine."

Disaster averted. "Thank you, Mama. Boys!" she bellowed. "Time for school. Grandma Clora's waitin'."

Dixie turned her back on Clora, opening her arms to Clifton and Gareth, who ran into them willingly, like anyone who wasn't female did. She plopped kisses on their dark heads, and the picture of the three of them together in a huddle struck Em as ironic that her best friend showed more affection to them than their own grandmother.

So many things were wrong with that picture. When her children received more outward love from her friends than they did from their own flesh and blood, it might be time to reevaluate.

Clora gathered the keys, the jingle of them rousing Dora from her dog bed on the far side of the kitchen. "I'll warm the car," she said, gathering her coat, frowning again at Dora's bulk, filling up the kitchen, leaving clumps of hair all over the place.

Dora nudged Em's hip with her big, wet nose. She'd never been allowed to have a pet when she was a child. Dora had been an act of passive-aggressive payback to her mother, a silent eff you.

She recognized it for what it was now, though, over the past three years, she'd no sooner part with Dora than she would one of her children. The act of adopting her was a ridiculous way to show her mother she was going to give her children all the things she'd lacked as a child.

The boys had been so taken with her, sticking their fingers in her cage, giggling and cooing at her, it made Em smile wide. She loved to see them happy.

She'd adopted her at an adoption fair right in front of Clora while the boys looked on—defiantly holding up the squirming brown-and-white puppy like some trophy, as if to say, "Look at me not taking your advice. Hah!"

Clora had griped that Dora would only add to her workload, already pushed to its limits with a full-time job and a husband who wasn't always present, even when he was in the same room. The more Clora protested her decision, the more Em was determined to pay the adoption fee.

Dora whined. She didn't like Clora, hid from her every chance she got. Half St. Bernard and half something no vet from here to Johnsonville could identify, her big body harbored a total chicken.

Em ran a hand over her vast head and smiled. Dora was a good decision, clumps of hair, swamp breath and all. "How would you like to gnaw on some grandma for breakfast? I hear disapproval and cranky taste good in the mornin'."

Dixie blew out a breath of air, shooting her a look of apology. "Sorry. She gets under my skin. I hate the way she talks to you, Em. Sometimes I forget my manners when I'm around her, but she makes me so mad."

"Who makes you mad, Aunt Dixie?" Clifton asked, his blue coat still unbuttoned and half hanging off his shoulders.

"Button up, please, Clifton. You'll catch your death. And I was talkin' adult things with Dixie. Never you mind," Em scolded, watching his face change from a half smile to put upon the moment she began to speak.

Sunlight streamed in from the trio of arched windows in her breakfast nook, glinting off Clifton's hair, dark and thick, making her want to ruffle it. But that would only make him mad. Everything made him mad, just like her mother.

With that in mind, Em latched on to his chin and planted kisses on his rounded cheeks until he tried to pull out of her embrace, but he'd lingered for a moment. It was only a moment, but it was. "Now, go to school and learn something you can teach me when you get home tonight."

"I hate school. It's stupid."

Em's heart wrenched. She didn't blame him for hating school. Clifton endured painful taunts because of what Louella had done. Her hope that the incident would die down was proving futile.

"So stupid!" Dixie agreed. "I say we skip stupid school forever, stay home and watch lots of TV until the cable man comes and turns it off. Because he will, you know. They do that when you don't have a good job that pays you enough money for your bills. If you don't go to school, that's what happens. But I'm game to see how long we can last. You get the chips, I'll get the beer."

Clifton warred with a smile, but he managed to wrangle it in and scowl instead. "That's so lame, Aunt Dixie. I'm not old enough to drink beer."

"Or quit school—so get a move on, mister!" Dixie's sympathetic eyes met Em's over Clifton's head.

Dixie understood the kind of torture the boys were experiencing at the hands of Louella's quest for revenge. After last night, now Em understood, too.

"To the car, young man." Em pointed to the door, blowing him a kiss.

He made a face at her and did what he was told, blissfully without protest.

Dixie clapped her hand on the counter the moment Clifton was out of earshot. "And that's why I said what I did last night, Em. You can be as mad as a hornet at me, but someone's got to speak up. Because I won't have Clifton Junior hate goin' to school. Does this happen every day? Still?"

"Not every day, but often enough. I've talked to the principal and the teachers until I'm blue in the face, and they keep a close eye out. I've watched Clifton like a hawk for all the signs his therapist said to watch for when a child is teased the way he's been teased. But you know what children are like. Somehow, they still find a way to niggle you." It was as much torture for Em as it was Clifton. Once the object of Dixie's cruel taunts throughout high school, she understood how much it hurt to be singled out.

"I'm sorry I made you the center of attention. I know you hate it, but I'm not standin' by and watching Louella take her licks out on you anymore. So if you want to keep bein' friends, you'd better get ready for some fireworks. No more, Em. She will not get away with this. If you'd just let me, I'd gladly wring her neck for you. We could have a party. Invite all the Mags—maybe make some pink punch?"

The similarities between the problems the boys were having and the issues she and Dixie had back in the day were too close.

Dixie was a different person now, kind and generous, but she'd never understand what it was to be taunted every day of her life. "Isn't it ironic, that you, once the meanest girl in all the land, now want to beat up your predecessor for startin' the same kind of trouble you once did?"

"Can I just tell you how sick I feel every time I realize what's happening to the boys was what I specialized in?"

Instantly, Em was remorseful. She loved Dixie. She'd

forgiven her. "I'm sorry. That was wrong of me. But it hurts like I can't tell you watchin' them go through the same kind of torture I did."

"Don't apologize. The truth is the truth. I was horrible back then. Now I have to watch my best friend's boys, boys I'd give an organ to, suffer because Louella Palmer wanted to hurt me. I hate that, Em. If you'd just let me, I could make it stop, you know I'd do it."

"By takin' your buckets o' money on outta Plum Orchard? And what would that accomplish? The girls would be out of a job, and you'd have nothing to throw in everyone's face."

Dixie straightened her scarf. "But you can bet your stash o' wine, I'll do it."

"It'll die down, Dixie." *Please, let it die down.*

"Or I'll kill Louella."

Em chuckled—the uncomfortable moment where present met past over. She hugged Dixie. "No killin'. It makes for messy cleanup, and you know how I hate to work a shovel."

Dixie sipped her coffee, aimlessly flipping the pages of a stray magazine. "So, on today's agenda—have sex with Jax in front of an entire office?"

Em sank into the bar stool, her legs shaky, but she gave good face. "I have no idea what you're talking about."

"Oh, I know you don't. Know what else I know?"

Em gave her a guarded glance. "What else do you know?"

"I know that Sanjeev cleaned Jax's office this morning and he sent me a text."

"So?"

"So, Sanjeev said there's a three for twenty-five sale going on at Victoria's Secret. He saw it in their catalog. He asked me to pass that on to you."

"Why would he say somethin' like that?" she squeaked. Yes. That was definitely the squeak of the guilty.

"He thought you'd be interested in replacing the underwear you left in Jax's office yesterday."

She'd forgotten to scoop up her underwear after Jax had torn them off. A flush of red landed on her cheeks. She wasn't sure if it was because she'd been caught or because the memory was so hot. Mortification washed over her. She was so bad at this. "Dixie—"

Dixie batted an eye at her. "No. Don't deny it. It'll just make you look guiltier. Don't say anything. You seem to want to keep this all to yourself, and that's fine by me. Sometimes you don't want to share, even with your person. I understand. But let me just say this and then I'll leave it alone for as long as you want me to keep my nose out of it. Deal?"

"Deal."

"I know you don't want anyone to know what's going on with you and Jax. I know you're afraid to add another element to the boys' lives for the worry you'll upset their tender hearts. I also know you don't want to drag Jax into your life because you think he and Maizy will suffer the tongues waggin' if he does. That's just who you are, Em. Always putting someone else before you."

Em shook her head, but Dixie put a finger to her lips. "Hush. Let me finish. If you're doin' what I think you're doin', which is doin' the do with no regrets and no strings, don't do it because you think it's the only way you can do it."

Her throat was dry, her tongue thick. "What exactly are you saying?"

"I'm saying you don't have to be someone's fling because you don't think you're good enough for anything more. You don't have to be Jax's fling because you think he wouldn't want a woman like you for a serious relationship. You are good enough, Em, and I don't want to see you hurt by the notion you can just walk away from this and remember it fondly somewhere down the road."

Here it came. Because she wasn't the type of woman who could love 'em and leave 'em. It made her sound clingy and obsessive, and she hated that. "Because I'm not that kind of girl."

"Hey. Don't you get defensive with me, Ms. Amos. You're *not* that kind of girl. You're just not, honey. You can kid yourself into believing you are, you can want to be, but you're not. There's nothin' wrong with those kinds of girls, Em. Make no mistake about what I'm saying. It's healthy and perfectly acceptable to enjoy the company of a man and not want to wash his underwear the next day. But I want you to really think about why you've ventured into this territory with Jax and not some stranger you don't have to see every day."

Em shrugged, her chin lifting. "Maybe I don't want to think about it. Maybe he's just amazing to look at and that's all I need for right now." *Maybe he's also amazing in bed. Maybe he's an amazing father.* Maybe Dixie was right and she was too chicken to hope for more with Jax because she really didn't think she was good enough. She didn't want to hear him say she wasn't good enough. And the best way to do that was avoid it altogether.

"Good. You go on and be defiant. Be angry with me for speakin' my mind. Be whatever. Just don't be hurt. I can't bear to see you hurt." Dixie dug her keys out of her jacket pocket and gave her a return defiant gaze.

Em broke first, latching on to her friend's arm, because she was solid, and she made sense right now and she had to find a way to make light of this so Dixie wouldn't harp on the fact that she could end up hurt. "Something very unsettling is happening to me, Dixie. One minute I recognize the skin I'm wearing, the next I'm outside myself, looking at a total stranger."

Tense moment diverted. "The evolution of an independent woman. It's invigorating to watch. Maybe not as invigorating to be the subject of."

"I will not evolve if it means Sanjeev finds my underwear in one of the offices at work."

Dixie stopped short and eyed Em, scanning her face, searching for an answer Em probably didn't have. "So you really are just having sex? That's it?"

After these past couple of weeks, she didn't want to think about what she wanted. She wanted to feel more like there was solid ground beneath her feet. She wanted her son to accept Clifton Senior's absence, and not hate her for it. She wanted a lot of things.

Em avoided the question with more diversion. "He wants me to help him redecorate his house."

"So he wants a decorator and a sex kitten?"

Being referred to as a sex kitten made her laugh out

loud. "Take me to work, Dixie. I have underwear to leave lyin' about."

And a heart. She had one of those lying about, too. She only hoped it wasn't lying on her sleeve.

Sixteen

Em stretched her arms upward and rolled her shoulders. This air mattress would be the death of them, but what a lovely way to go.

Jax plucked the hooks on her garter belt and grabbed her leg, pulling her down the length of the bed for a kiss. "Roll over, I'll give you the once-over." He held up his hands and wiggled his fingers.

She gratefully did as she was told, so relieved to find Jax harbored no hard feelings when she'd approached him today at work. She'd rudely lashed out at him due to her own insecure inadequacies. But he'd just smiled and said it was none of his business and he shouldn't have intruded. Later in the afternoon, he'd texted her to see if she could meet him tonight like nothing had ever happened.

Back to business as usual, and she tried not to let any hurt creep in because of it. He was sticking to the rules she'd set forth. How could she blame him for that?

Jax nibbled at the small of her back, making her sigh with pleasure. "Did I mention this outfit is megahot?"

Em had decided to go vixen tonight, a total non-Em outfit. Corsets and garters and stockings and shiny black leather pumps. "I think you showed your appreciation." Her stockings and garters were all she had left on because he'd shown his appreciation so well. So well that when Jax was done licking her to orgasm, she decided if everything ended now, she'd be happy she decided to do this.

Em heard him rub his hands together with the slick massage oil and smiled when his hands rolled over her back, so strong and wide, he soothed her aching muscles.

"Why so tense?"

"Just a long day." Her mother and their conversation this morning, and what Louella had said to her last night. She couldn't stop thinking about her mother and the mention of a boyfriend.

Jax weaved a pattern along her shoulders, slippery and delicious. "Anything in particular?"

Well, there was Clifton Senior, too. "Clifton wants to meet to talk when he picks up the boys next week."

"Why's that a problem?"

"Because Clifton never wants to talk to me. He wants to pick the boys up halfway to Atlanta and not have to look me in the eye when he does it. So he must want something." What that was, she couldn't imagine. And once more, she was sharing personal details Jax could probably do without.

"How does he feel about you working at Call Girls?"

"Probably the same way I feel about him not telling me he liked to wear skirts."

"Touché."

There was no reason to explain Clifton's displeasure about her working at Call Girls. Yet, she had trouble stopping herself. "Clifton has no right to judge me. I don't take the calls, I manage them. I keep the boys from ever entering that building without putting everyone on notice. There's no naughty when I bring them in."

Jax rolled her over, planting his hands on either side of her head, and straddled her. "Hey, no judgment from me. I'm writing their security software, remember?"

She softened her gaze. She was touchy about her work when it came to the boys. Everyone always had something to say about it, mostly her mother and Clifton, and neither had any right to judge her. "Sorry. I'm touchy about Clifton. He doesn't like that I left my job as Hank Cotton's secretary for Call Girls. He said it's not respectable work. But he's not a single mother with an ex-husband who likes fancy dresses more than he likes to pay his child support, is he?"

Jax grinned. "Fair enough. So the boys…"

Her ears pricked. "What about them?"

"They take a real beating for this thing with Clifton and Call Girls, huh?"

And it was killing her. She had to make a living. What Hank had paid her had barely paid the bills, and with Clifton giving her so little for the boys, there really wasn't any choice at all. Taking the job with Dixie had been the smartest financial move she'd ever made, but it was taking its toll on Clifton and Gareth.

Obviously, Jax was fishing around for something more than he'd heard at the diner. "How'd you hear that?"

"Well, there was the diner last night, but Maizy mentioned it to me the other night when we were reading her bedtime story."

That made her sit up on her elbows with worry. "She did?"

Jax nodded, his eyes cautious. "She said that Gareth got into an argument because some other kid in their class was saying he had two moms."

Her heart sank. Would this never end? She swallowed hard. "I had no idea. He didn't say a word." That Gareth wasn't saying anything to her led her to believe he was giving her some of his stiff upper lip. Taking one for the team.

Jax cupped her face. "No worries. My Maizy told the kid to shut up and if he didn't quit picking on Gareth, she'd punch him in the nose."

Em laughed then covered her mouth. "You did tell her putting her hands on another person is unacceptable, didn't you?"

"Nope. I told her to knock the little shit out cold."

"You did not!"

"No, I didn't. I gave her the no-hands-rule speech. But I really wanted to tell her to coldcock him."

Somewhere deep inside, the notion Jax was standing up for Gareth, even if it was because his daughter was involved, made her warm inside. "I'm sorry she got involved in this. That's part of the reason I didn't want anyone to have even a hint about us. So you and Maizy wouldn't suffer."

"Hey, the kids would have become friends whether we had any involvement or not, Em. They go to school together. They don't know thing one about us, and look, they're hanging out at recess together. This has nothing to do with you and everything to do with my remarkable kid and your equally remarkable kid. Remarkable attracts remarkable."

"She's pretty remarkable." Just like her dad.

Damn.

Jax stretched out next to her, stroking her bare belly. "So is Gareth, and so are you."

Jax's voice had taken that turn. The gravelly, smoky turn it took when he was turned on. "I'm nothin' of the sort. You on the other hand," she said, reaching between them to slip her fingers around his cock, "are a little remarkable."

He grazed her knuckles over his chin and hissed his approval. "I'm all ears."

Em slid down along his chest, running her tongue along his abs, caressing his chest as she went. She loved the taste of his skin, loved to rest her cheek on every rigid line along the way to his lower belly.

She teased him with her mouth, flitting her tongue across his belly button, letting her fingers curl into his crisp pubic hair. His moans, thick and low, gave her that sharp-hot pull in her belly.

Jax's hands drove into her hair when her breath grazed his cock, urgent and impatient, but she took her time, touching him, learning what made his hips grind upward, discovering what made his breathing speed up.

He definitely liked when she pressed her breasts against his chest. He also liked when she let her hair drag over his skin. He really liked when she licked the spot just beneath the head of his hard length.

Em snaked her tongue over the pleasure point, satisfied when he tightened his grip on her hair. "You'll kill me with that one of these days," he husked out from above, his stomach muscles tightening.

Rising to her knees, she planted her hands on his thighs, kneading the planes and ridges, letting her body slip into position between his legs. "Death? So dramatic," she teased, massaging the thick muscles before dipping down and taking her first taste of him.

Jax groaned, closing his eyes, his head falling back against the pillow when she wrapped her mouth around him and drew him between her lips, twisting her tongue along his shaft. She loved the feel of his reaction to her touch, loved that she was in charge—his moans always left her wet and aching.

Em's hand followed her mouth, matching it stroke for stroke until Jax latched on to her shoulders and dragged her upward. Chest heaving, he drew her lips to his, kissing her long and hungry before easing a condom on and setting her atop his cock.

Em slid down on him, savoring every inch until he was rooted deep within her. A long sigh escaped her lips as he stretched her and she responded by tightening around him.

With his hands on her hips, Jax began to move inside

her and her hips began to circle, her fingernails running through the hair on his belly, her nipples tight and hard.

Em's eyes fell to Jax's when he thumbed her clit, spreading her wide while thrusting into her. Their pace picked up, the shadows of their limbs and bodies entwined, dancing on the wall in the flicker of candlelight. She loved the power he exuded, the control he took when he made love to her. It was as if he was claiming her, demanding, for that moment, she be only his.

He pulled her down to him, cupping her breasts, bringing them together and licking at her nipples, tweaking them until that white-hot sizzle of hunger sliced through her and she came with a whimper.

Jax's palms flattened on her butt, squeezing her flesh until he stiffened beneath her and came, too.

Boneless and shaky, Em fell into him, burying her face in his neck, inhaling his scent, the scent of their lovemaking.

When Jax caught his breath, he rolled her on her back, still inside her, nuzzling her jaw and making her squirm with the rough scratch of his five o'clock shadow.

"Thirsty?" he asked, pulling out of her and rolling to a sitting position.

"Are you sharing?"

He rose and reached for the bottle in the ice bucket, popping the cork. "Depends on what you have to barter with?" Jax wiggled his eyebrows suggestively at her.

She loved to watch him move, loved to see the way his muscles flexed, tightened and released beneath his skin. While Jax poured, she sat up and stretched, reaching for the glass when he handed it to her.

"So what are you going to do with all this space? Wouldn't it make an amazing playhouse for Maizy?" She'd had all sorts of ideas about how to renovate the guesthouse with its shabby walls and rotting barn wood.

"We still have to finish my house, and if we turn this into a playhouse for Maizy, we have nowhere to do all the wicked things we've been doing. We'd have to relocate."

It wasn't like they could renovate it overnight. He said those words like they'd be doing these wicked things for a long time to come.

She pulled her thoughts up short and called her daydreaming to an immediate halt. There would be no placing meaning on any of Jax's words. She shrugged, keeping her response light and her smile warm. "I guess we'd just have to figure it out."

"Besides, where would I put all this stuff?" He nodded toward the boxes stacked as high as the ceiling, taking the glass from her and sipping.

The wheels of Em's mind began to turn as she took in the possibilities of the space, unable to keep herself from making suggestions. She wrapped the itchy army blanket around her and wandered toward the first pile by the door. "Built-ins, maybe? Some tall whitewashed ones? You know, the size of wardrobes? You could make a desk for Maizy right next to it."

Her fingers went to the box as she thought out loud, startled when Jax yelled, "Be careful!"

Boxes came tumbling down around her head just

as Jax lunged for her, dangly bits exposed and all. He pushed her out of the way as glasses and picture frames came spilling from the mouth of the top box, crashing at her feet. "Oh, Jax! I'm so sorry. I hope it wasn't anything expensive." She muttered another apology, tightening the blanket under her arms and stooping to begin cleaning up.

A black frame, worn around the edges, with a vivid streak of red caught her eye. She grabbed it just as Jax was pulling his pants on to help her.

Her breath lodged in her throat as she plucked the frame up and eyed it. At first she'd thought it was a picture of Maizy, but a closer look revealed a warehouse-type building behind them as the setting and Jax with his arm around two people. The first a man, blond and athletic looking, with the same hard jaw as Jax, but smiling, playful blue eyes, and the other...

Maizy's mother. There was no doubt in her mind. She had the same amazing shock of vibrant red hair, the same beautiful skin, the same eyes. Gorgeous, this woman was absolutely breathtaking. Em couldn't even summon up an ounce of jealousy for her—she was that beautiful. The gorgeous woman's gaze was on Jax's face, and her eyes screamed head over heels for him.

"Maizy's mother?" She knew she should hush, but her curiosity, her mother had always said, would be the death of her. Looking up at Jax and the hard line of his mouth, she definitely should have just hushed.

His nod was curt. "Reece."

This was a no-no subject, but did that stop her? "Where is she?"

"Gone," he said, and then he was silent. So silent, she heard him purposely being silent.

Em hopped up, cursing her shredded nylons. Danger, Will Robinson. Stop. Do not trespass. "I'm sorry. I didn't mean to intrude. Here." She held out the frame to him, putting a hand on his arm, but he turned away, brushing her off.

"Just throw it in the pile."

Em frowned. This was his child's mother. She spoke before she thought. "But it's a picture of Maizy's mother. Won't she want it?"

"It's also a picture of my dead best friend, Jake. Throw it in the pile, Em." His voice had risen just enough to warn her she should back off.

Suddenly, he was all angry vibes and tense gestures, the light mood between them gone. Time to go home and glue her lips shut. "I'm sorry about the mess. I'll help—"

"I got it," Jax said, running a hand over his jaw.

She waved a hand like it was no big deal he was angry for some unknown reason he didn't care to divulge. "I have to go anyway. Six o'clock comes really early."

Without another word, she gathered her clothes, pulling on her silly trench coat and heels and gathering up her purse.

He seemed to remember she was going out into the cold, dark night without him. "Let me get dressed and I'll walk you to your car."

But Em just smiled and dismissed him like she made

all her lovers in the afternoon angry. "No need. I'm fine. The car's not that far, and I have to be up early to take the boys to meet their father anyway. It's Clifton's weekend. See you Monday. Thanks for a great night. Sweet dreams, Jax." Then she was yanking open the door and moving as fast as her incredibly high heels would allow her.

When she finally made it to the car, she turned the heat on full blast and sat, staring at the guesthouse, watching the flicker of candles from the small arched window, and wondered what had set Jax off.

Reece. Where was Reece? Was she dead like Em had first assumed? Jax's glance at that picture didn't scream a lingering affection—for either of the people in the photo. So where was Maizy's mother if she wasn't dead?

Why did Jax look like he'd sooner cut off her head than keep a picture of her, and why would he keep a picture of Maizy's mother from his daughter?

What had happened to his best friend Jake?

Why was whatever happened a sore subject?

Stop now, Em. Go home. Take a hot bath. Go to bed.

Or look them up on Google…

Jax threw the picture of him and Reece and Jake in the pile of glass and damned himself for overreacting to Em's innocent question. The look on her face when he'd shut her down was like a kidney punch.

But how could he explain the sordid mess that was Reece and Jake? How could he explain the guilt Jake's name drove through the core of him? How did he explain the kind of sorrow the subject of the two of them dredged up?

He pulled his shirt over his head and grabbed the bottle of wine, slugging some back before digging out a broom and sweeping the chunks of glass along with the picture into a pile.

He didn't hide Reece from Maizy. He just didn't talk about her a lot. That time would come, if Maizy kept being as intuitive as she was, but it wasn't a conversation he was looking forward to.

A conversation he was forced to have because of Reece. Because she was an irresponsible, fucked-up mess. She'd interfered enough in his life; now she wasn't even here and she was still pushing her way into a place he'd come to think of as sacred. The place where he felt more alive than he had in a very long time.

Here, in this shitty, crumbling guesthouse. With Em.

And now he'd hurt Em because of the meddling bitch.

Nope. You hurt Em all alone, pal. Reece didn't have anything to do with this. You could have just told her all about Reece.

That was against the rules.

And very convenient.

Jax fingered the frame and tried for the millionth time to understand where it had all gone so wrong.

But he was tired of dissecting what happened. He was tired of living in the past. He was tired of keeping secrets. He was tired of worrying his world would explode at any second and there'd be no way for him to prevent it.

* * *

Em dropped the limp French fry on her tray, taking in the face of the man she once thought she'd spend the rest of her life with.

He was so little like the man she thought she knew. He was so little like Jax….

With trembling fingers, she forced her bad parting with Jax out of her mind and focused on this task. Finding out what Clifton wanted.

Clifton sat across from her at the restaurant they'd chosen as a drop-off/pickup point for the boys. The halfway point between the beginning of their separate lives. A greasy burger joint the boys loved and Em tolerated for the sake of amicability.

"I'm thinking of filing for full custody of the boys, Em." He wiped his mouth with the paper napkin, crumpling it up and dropping it on the table much the way he'd discarded their marriage.

A prickly shot of anger whispered along her spine as his handsome face stared back at hers. How dare he sit there cool and collected like he'd just told her he was takin' the boys fishin'? "You can barely manage regular visitation with them. How do you expect to have full-time custody, Clifton? It's plenty more involved than just a meeting place and twenty dollars for some hamburgers and a milk shake."

He'd changed so much in the year since their divorce. Gone were the days of red-checked flannel, Wrangler jeans and a John Deere cap. Now he wore boldly colored shirts with collars that tipped upward under his salon-styled hair and square glasses that enhanced his cheekbones and made his eyes a brighter blue.

Those eyes were hard as they looked at her from across the table. Icy and hard. "I'd see them more often if I didn't live in Atlanta. It's a long ride from there to Plum Orchard."

She tightened her grip on her purse, trying to keep her voice low. "Is the ride ever too long when your children are involved? And it was your choice to move to Atlanta, Clifton. You could have stayed in the PO and been divorced just as easily."

His mouth, the mouth that had lied so many lies, thinned. "Right. That would have worked out great."

"You can't wear women's clothes in Plum Orchard? Only Atlanta allows that?"

He fisted his hand, clenched it, unclenched it. She knew that gesture. He was fighting the urge to yell. "I can't live in Plum Orchard anymore, and you know why, Emmaline."

"Because your girlfriend's in Atlanta and she doesn't like us hillbillies?"

"Leave her out of this. You know why. Because I'm a laughingstock there. What would that be like for the boys?"

"Don't you mean what it *is* like for the boys?" Clifton loved them. She knew that. But while he'd gone off to try to understand what was happening to him, when he'd left on this journey to find acceptance with who he really was, he'd left everything up to her.

All the mess was hers to clean up. All the tears and nightmares were hers to soothe. And it wasn't fair. He didn't get to have everything he wanted when he'd made the mess.

His eyes grew softer, almost like the old Clifton. "I didn't do this to hurt them. I never wanted to hurt them."

"But it did, Clifton!" she whisper-yelled, leaning into the table. "If you'd spent less time sneakin' off to find yourself, and more time thinking about what could happen to them if someone found out, none of this would have happened. No good comes from secrecy and lies. Yet, it isn't you who's paying the price. It's the boys, and me. Me who has to stand by and watch them suffer because of what you did. It was selfish and cruel to think you could get away with it without any repercussions—especially comin' from the small town we come from. Do you have any idea the things the children at school say to them about you? How they're constantly teased?"

His spine went straight. "I won't apologize for my lifestyle."

"Don't you wave that PC stick at me! Don't you even consider accusing me of asking that of you. You don't get to be a self-righteous jerk in the name of your lifestyle. You're missing the whole point here. I'm not askin' you to apologize for bein' who you really are, Clifton. But could you have at least given us the chance to accept this side of you before you decided for us? Before you lied and cheated on not just me, but them? In the process of finding out you liked to wear women's clothes, you were selfish. This is what happens when you think only of yourself. You get divorced and sacrifices have to be made. We've all made sacrifices lately. Why shouldn't you?"

He looked down at his hands. "Clifton called me the other night."

Em reached for a napkin to cool her flushed face. "Good. He should call his daddy."

"No, you don't understand. He called me and told me he wanted to come and live with me. He was crying, and there was nothing I could do about it."

Em felt like she'd been slugged in the gut. Clifton was calling his father, reaching out when he was hurting and it wasn't to her? "There was somethin' you could have done about it. You could have gotten in your car and come to see him. But you won't do that because you're a coward. As yellow as they come. Doesn't all this living honestly mean you face all the people you lied to when you left Plum Orchard? If you've made peace with who you are, who cares what everyone else thinks? It's not like they're waitin' to burn you at the stake, Clifton. So folks in town will stare at you. Is being comfortable worth not answering Clifton's call?"

But he ignored the part where he was at fault. "Clifton Junior is miserable. He hates school. He wants to come live with me." There was almost a quiet resignation to his voice.

She didn't know this man anymore. This man dressed like he'd shopped with his twenty-year-old girlfriend. This man with gel in his hair, and the residual stain of red polish still on his pinky finger.

Em couldn't believe she was hearing this. "You'll take those boys over my dead body, Clifton. I have primary custody, and that's how it'll stay. There's no way they're better off with you than they are with me."

Clifton paused for a moment before he said, "Do you think a judge will say that when he finds out you work for a *phone-sex* company?"

Fear rippled up and down her spine, her tongue grew thick just like it used to when they were married. "I'm the general manager, Clifton, and I make good money. Money the boys need because their father conveniently forgets they need to eat! I don't talk to the clients unless there's an office problem, and you know it."

"But you consort with those who do. How is that a good environment for the boys? Being around a bunch of women who talk to perfect strangers."

Em popped up from the chair, the angry scrape of its legs screeching on the tile flooring. "And who do you do all your consortin' with? Members of Mensa? I hate to remind you, Trixie LeMieux, but while I'm earnin' a livin', you're moochin' off your fancy girlfriend and entering beauty contests! This is ridiculous, you slingin' arrows at me. You've taken enough from me, Clifton Amos. You won't take my boys. My employment at Call Girls is honest work and it pays me well. If it weren't for Dixie and Caine, your boys would have lost their home while you *found* yourself. I'm going to leave now, but if you aren't right back here on Tuesday evenin' at exactly six sharp with my sons, I'll hunt you down with old man Coon's shotgun myself. I'm not the old Emmaline With No Spine, Clifton. You'd do well to remember that!"

He was bluffing. There wasn't a chance in the fiery depths of hell Clifton could take on the boys. He might have the power of his rich girlfriend's money backing him, but Clifton was all hot air.

She prayed he was all hot air.

Seventeen

"Miss Emmaline?"

Em nearly jumped out of her office chair. Guilty. Oh, God. She was so guilty. Two deep breaths later and she smiled up at Sanjeev.

"Am I disturbing you?"

Yes. I was just getting to the good part where I find out what happened to Jax's best friend Jake Landry. Good gravy. Was there no privacy when you were being a nosy biddy? She clicked the computer screen off and smiled at him. "Of course not, Sanjeev. How are you?"

Sanjeev bowed his head, his serene smile in place, his deeply bronzed skin glowing. "I am well. You?"

Em massaged the back of her neck. Sore. She was sore from sitting in the same spot for three hours hunting down information about Jax, and Jake, and the infamous Reece. She was mostly coming up with nothing more than aches and pains to show for it, but it wasn't for lack of looking.

Jake and Jax had a software security development

company they'd started right out of college along with Jax's sister, Harper, who joined the company after Jake was killed in a car accident six years ago.

But there wasn't much else to find. The company dissolved when Jax's sister, Harper, was also killed in a mugging four years later. According to a couple of articles, their company had been very successful, but no mention of Reece.

Jax had suffered so much loss in such a small amount of time, her heart ached for him and little Maizy. Maybe his reaction to Reece's picture played a part in that. Or maybe he was just angry she'd crossed the no-personal-information line? She hadn't heard from him for two days, and it stung.

It more than stung. It hurt. It ached. She'd picked up her phone a hundred times to text him an apology, but thought better of it. She'd touched a nerve with the picture of Reece. Gone too far, or something.

She didn't know how to approach this with him. "Hey, sorry I brought up a sore subject. Want to try that new vibrator I've been eyeing online?"

So what will it be like when it's really over? Will it hurt less, Em?

"Emmaline?" Sanjeev peered over the top of her computer at her, his eyes full of concern. "Shall I make you a poultice for the cramps in your neck?"

Not a chance would she allow Sanjeev to heal her when she was doin' the work of the devil by snooping on Jax. She shook her head then winced at the shooting pain on the left side of her neck. "No, Sanjeev. But thank you. What brings you here today? More of my undergarments lying about?"

His inky eyebrow rose, but his eyes laughed. "Not today. Though, I confess, I'm happy to see you're moving forward and enjoying your…womanhood."

Em's head tipped back and she laughed. "I'm sorry I embarrassed you."

"I'm not. I'm pleased to see you taking time for yourself. You are a selfless woman. Sometimes, in all that selflessness comes a draining of the spirit."

"Do you really see me like that, Sanjeev? I'm not asking because I'm fishin', mind you. I'm just not sure why everyone thinks that." She was definitely being selfish right now.

"I do. Landon saw you that way, too. That's why he left you in charge. You had to be selfless in order to handle his Dixie-Cup. She requires a great deal of selflessness—or she did."

Em's heart warmed. Whenever she felt alone, she thought of Landon, of his last days with her. Of the lessons he'd taught her about this thing called life. *"Live,"* he'd said. *"Live hard."*

He knew what she'd been going through with Clifton. He'd offered his help. Help she'd refused. She hadn't wanted anything more from Landon than his friendship, and she'd gotten that in spades.

"I miss him so much. It's funny, I didn't know him very well till the end of his life. Us livin' in the same town and all, we shoulda been better friends. But those last weeks with him are some of my most treasured memories."

"I assure you, he reciprocated those feelings. And to answer your question, I miss him every single day." He held out a hand to her and Em took it, giving it a squeeze.

"So what brings you to this neck of the woods, Sanjeev? You bringin' Dixie lunch?"

He shook his head. "This came for you today." He held out two manila envelopes with her name scrawled across them and the company's address beneath.

She shrugged. "Must've gotten mixed up in the big house mail. Thanks, Sanjeev." She dropped it on her desk and motioned to the chair for Sanjeev to sit.

"Oh, I mustn't. There's work to be done at the big house. Are we still on for our Dora the Explorer, Mona and Lisa playdate later this week? I promised those heathens of Dixie's a meal fit for a queen."

Em grinned. Dora loved Sanjeev and she loved playing with Dixie's dogs Mona and Lisa in that enormous football field they called a backyard. "Absolutely. But promise me, no filet for Dora. She's got a touchy tummy and the vet says we have to watch her weight."

Sanjeev bowed again. "I promise, no filet. I cannot promise there won't be gravy. Surely you can't expect me to allow Mona and Lisa to dine on steak as Dora looks on with only her pitiful dry kibble? It's unkind."

Em laughed. "Fine. Gravy it is. Just a little." For the umpteenth time in as many days, Em found herself counting her blessings. This motley crew of friends might not be what Plum Orchard or her mother titled respectable, but she didn't care.

She was loved. Her boys were loved. Even Dora was

loved. Nothing else mattered. Clifton could, in the immortal words of Landon, "suck it."

These people gave more to her children than their own father did. She would not allow Clifton to sully it with his sudden bid for morality.

"Then I bid you good afternoon, and, Emmaline?"

"Uh-huh?"

"About your womanhood?"

Her cheeks went bright red.

Sanjeev's eyes twinkled. "You go, girl!" He glided out of the door as softly as he'd entered, making her smile again.

With a sigh, she turned her attention to the flowery scrawl on the first envelope and slit it open. Probably more hate mail. Usually, it was easy to identify which member in town had sent it.

Jared Tompkins had a penchant for forgetting to cross his *T*'s just like in high school, and Charla Sue Lawson's letters smelled like Chanel No. 5.

But this one didn't smell like perfume, and the *T*'s were definitely crossed. Em's eyes flew over the official piece of paper with the raised seal.

It was a birth certificate.

Hers.

Her heart began to crash in her ears while the rest of the world crumbled around her. This was a lie. It had to be a lie. Who would do something so awful?

Her fingers shook, her stomach sloshed with the weight of her lunch. She took several deep breaths and forced herself to read again the line designated for Name of Father.

Well, that was wrong. Of course it was wrong. Someone was playing a cruel joke on her.

Her father was Edward Mitchell. He'd left when she was just an infant then died three years later of lung cancer. He'd been an outsider from Texas. Not from Plum Orchard, and according to her mother, he'd never been happy living here.

He was an accountant. He liked numbers. He'd run off to Texas when he'd left Clora. She remembered very clearly the open-and-shut discussion she'd had with Clora about him. She had one picture of him—a picture of him with her mother on their wedding day. Neither of them looked wildly in love, but then, Clora wasn't wild about anything.

It was the only picture Em had, old and faded; she'd clung to it when her mother had banished all talk of him.

But he was absolutely not Ethan *Davis,* husband to Pearl, father to her best friend in the whole world— Dixie Davis.

The phone rang and rang, just like it always did when he called the number on his phone that was supposed to be Reece's. This time, he wasn't hanging up. This time he was going to leave her a message and find out what the hell she wanted because he had other things he wanted to do, and Reece was standing in the way of it all.

He knew she was here—somewhere. He knew he'd seen her at the school and he knew she was trying to get a glimpse of Maizy.

What scared the shit out of him was why. Why did

she want to see her after all this time? Was she hatching some crazy plan to snatch her? Was Reece really selfless enough to care that much about another human being?

His lips thinned when he got her voice mail. "Reece? It's Jax. Let's stop the bullshit. Meet me down by the bridge off Lambert *tomorrow*. Five o'clock. If you don't show up, I'm calling the cops."

Clicking the phone off, he dropped it on the kitchen table like it was hot.

Time to face your demons, Jackson Hawthorne.

Face them so you can move on to something better. Something in the here and now. Something like Em.

He'd behaved like an ass with her. A total ass, and he didn't know how to fix it. He'd wanted to stop in her office a hundred times today—smell her perfume, see her smile—apologize for being such a dick, but she'd left work early, and he had things to handle first. He wanted to go to her with a clear head. Reece was muddying those waters right now.

Em played a huge part in his calling Reece. If he could figure out what she wanted, then he'd know what to do next. But if he didn't clear it all up, see her one last time and let it go for good, he couldn't move forward with Em.

To Em.

He wanted to move forward. The hell with her protests and her nothing-personal mantra. She wanted him, too. He felt it in his gut—now he just had to convince her to get on board.

A chair scraped, startling him.

"Why you here in the dark, big brother?"

Jax spun the phone around, not looking at Tag. "Just thinking."

"About?"

He sighed. "Look, I don't want to fight with you tonight, Tag. I'm tired and it's been a shitty couple of days."

"So you're thinking about Reece?"

He remained silent, trying to gauge his brother's mood by watching his face in the light from above the stove. "Yep."

"I've been really hard on you about her."

"No harder than I've been on myself."

"She doesn't deserve Maizy."

"And it'll be over my dead body before she gets her. But I can't just keep ignoring her existence, Tag. If I'm going to move forward, I have to find out what she wants. I'd like your support in that."

"She pisses me off."

"Yeah. I got that."

"But I've been a real asshole about it."

"You won't hear me protest."

"I'm trying to work that all out. I just get so pissed off. I keep hearing it's because of my guilt about Harper."

Guilt and regrets. They had plenty of that going around these days.

Tag based every reaction he had for every situation on his pain over Harper's death. But it had to stop. "Listen, don't think I don't get a thing or two about how you're feeling, Tag. Remember Jake?"

Tag shook his head. "Totally different."

"Maybe the reasons for our regrets are different, but it's the same damn guilt. Harper knew you loved her. But I can't say that to you anymore, Tag. I've only said it a hundred times. Harper knew what you were going through before she died. She understood. She really did, better than all of us, and her death was tragic and it hurt us all like hell, but I can't keep going over the same shit with you. I also can't let you take it out on all of us, either. I just can't stay stuck here in the past with you anymore."

"So seeing Reece is your way of finding the closure everyone says is so healthy?"

"It's gotta beat yelling and fighting with everyone all the time. Guilt can eat you alive. I'm done being guilt's midnight snack. I wish you were, too."

"What brought this on?"

"A chance at some real happiness and the need for a clean slate."

"Em?"

He smiled. In the midst of all the misery they'd endured as a family, in the height of Tag's agonizing trek back from the darkest point in his life, Em still made him smile. Feel. Want. Look forward. "I think so."

Tag smiled back. It wasn't the smug upward turn of his lips that had become his standard—it was real, and it was warm. Like the old Tag. "Good on you, man. You need me to come with you when you meet Reece? Somebody to be there for you when you open up all those old wounds?"

He smiled again. The best thing about choosing

to move forward was the freedom from all those old wounds. They didn't feel like wounds as much anymore. They felt like a scar from a lesson learned. "Nah. I'm good. Just keep a close eye on Maizy, okay?"

"Always." He pushed his chair back and slapped Jax on the back before heading out of the kitchen.

"Oh, and hey, Tag?"

He paused in the doorway, his clothes covered in Sheetrock dust, his knit cap planted on his head, his face open and relaxed. "Yep?"

"Thanks for having my back."

Tag's Adam's apple worked when he swallowed hard. "Always, brother. Always."

"Maizy said she don't got a mommy."

"Doesn't have," Em corrected Gareth, planting a kiss on the top of his head and flipping to the next page in their book. Maizy brought to mind Jax, and Jax brought to mind the empty ache she hoped to ignore. "When did she say that, honey?"

"When we was talkin' about mommies at lunch. She said she has no mommy. She had an aunt Harper, but she died. All she has is her dad and her uncles and her grandparents."

So Jax didn't acknowledge the woman who'd given birth to Maizy? It was almost as if Maizy were hatched. Like she'd cropped up out of the ground after a seed was planted. No wonder he'd been so angry about her picture.

Why? And how did Maizy feel about that? She was at the age when asking questions was second only to breathing. And what had happened to her mother? Maybe she'd left them? That made Em's chest hurt. Never. Not as long as she had life in her would she leave the boys. Or let Clifton take them.

After getting caught looking Jax up on Google, she'd closed the computer and refused to pry further. He was keeping Reece close to his chest for a reason—one he didn't want her to know because it was personal and they had Nothing Personal stamped on their relationship.

Yet, it hurt.

But you have no right to hurt. We've gone over this. You have no claims to Jax other than the right to say you made him your boy toy.

Gareth tightened his hold on her arm, letting his head graze her shoulder. "I'm glad I have you for my mommy. I don't want to be like Maizy."

Em's heart shifted in her chest. "You do know daddies can be good mommies, too, right? I think Jax is a pretty good daddy." A pretty good everything. Especially good at not texting her when she was desperate to hear from him.

"Nuh-uh. He's nowhere near as good as you. He makes dee-sgusting fish sticks."

But amazing conversation… Em wrinkled her nose and giggled with him. "How do you know?"

"Maizy said so."

"You and Maizy are becoming real friends, huh?"

"She's funny."

Clifton Junior stomping down the stairs interrupted their conversation. When the light from the stairway hit his face, Em's eyes flew open. "Clifton! What happened to your face?"

"Nothing," he replied, ducking his head and heading for the kitchen.

Em set Gareth aside and ran after him, grabbing him by the arm to spin him around. "Oh, honey! How did this happen?" How had she missed a lump the size of Ukraine on his forehead? His hat. He'd worn his ballcap all through dinner and right up until he'd gone to take a shower.

"Get off! It's no big deal." He pulled away from her, hard enough to make tears sting her eyes.

"Clifton, this is a big deal. What happened? You have to tell me so I can decide whether we need to see a doctor."

"It's just a bump. No big deal."

Gareth wrapped his arms around her thigh. "Jared Carpenter beated him up today. After school. Because Clifton called him a bad word after he called Daddy a girl."

Clifton whipped around, his face red, his eyes bulging at Gareth. "Shut up, Gareth! I told you not to tell anyone!"

Em pushed Gareth behind her. "Do not speak to your brother like that, Clifton. I won't have it. He's only telling me to protect you. Now tell me what happened. This instant!"

"Or what?" His eyes grew round with defiance, his small body rigid with more anger than she'd ever witnessed from him.

"Or I'm going to take away all of your privileges. TV,

Xbox, all of it, and we're going straight to the school tomorrow to have a chat with Principal Crawford—that's what!"

"Good. Then I'll be a snitch, too!"

Em softened. She remembered this rock and a hard place well. If you tattled on the person who'd picked on you, you were labeled a snitch. If you didn't, you were subject to more torture. She wouldn't have this for her boys. "Clifton, I know how hard this has been. I know what it feels like to be teased and picked on. I want to help if you'll just let me. Please, let me help you."

Violence was in the mix now. It was one thing to call names, but it was quite another to use your fists. This would end. She'd see to it.

"Just leave me alone! This is all your fault anyway!" he screamed, making Gareth cling to her leg and cry. "If you were a good wife, Daddy wouldn't have left to live with Gina! I heard Grandma Clora say it!"

The wind soared right out of Em's lungs and left her with a stinging pain, so sharp, so real, it was like someone had jammed a flaming knife into her back.

Clifton raced up the stairs, and she let him. She was too hot with anger—too incensed with her mother to speak to him.

Gareth tugged on her skirt with a sob. Em scooped him up in her arms and rocked him. "I hate Clifton!"

Tears stung the corner of her eyes. "Never, ever say that, Gareth. Not ever. Clifton's having a bad time of it right now, but he loves you. He's saying things out of anger."

"I shouldn't have told you what happened."

Em sat him on her hip, thumbing away his tears. "Yes. Yes, you should have, Gareth. You were right to tell Mommy. No one is ever to lay their hands on either of you, understand? You must always tell an adult."

He snuggled down on her shoulder and closed his eyes, his sobs easing to soft hiccups then to a light snore.

But she couldn't let him go just yet. She had to hold on to something to keep her from getting in her car, driving to her mother's and screaming her rage like she was off her rocker. It was enough that she'd dealt with her mother's anger all her life, but she wouldn't have it infiltrating her children.

Settling into the couch, she held Gareth close and eyed the ugly envelope with the fake birth certificate. It had to be a fake.

She hadn't given it much thought after opening it and getting past the initial shock of just how far people would go to get rid of them. Obviously, shame the head Call Girl in charge was the latest tactic.

But she knew the Mags and just how far they'd go to get what they wanted. They wanted to embarrass her—humiliate her into leaving her job at Call Girls because it would surely stir trouble between her and Dixie if something like that were true.

It was creative; she'd give 'em that. Instead of paying it much mind, Em had made several copies of it to keep on hand for Call Girls' prank files and kept the original.

It was clearly someone's idea of yet another cruel joke. It wasn't the first, and it wouldn't be the last. This one was more thought out than the typical, "Dear Emmaline, The devil is saving you a seat next to him" or "You've paved the road to Perdition for Plum Orchard" letters she got as GM, but it was also ridiculous. Fun, easygoing Ethan Davis and her staid, purse-lipped, disapproving mother?

Never.

She and Dixie would laugh about it just like they laughed about all the crazy letters and angry email they got from all sorts of people in town and from all over the world, in fact. What they should have done was change the name of her mother. That she might have fallen for. She was nothing like Clora, and when she got her hands on her…

Em took a deep breath and reached for the second envelope. It was thicker and much heavier than her fake birth certificate.

Tucking Gareth next to her and covering him with a throw, she sat back and ripped open the envelope.

The first thing she saw was the legal header—something she was familiar with as Hank's former secretary.

And then she saw Clifton Senior's signature.

The breath left her lungs.

She'd thought he'd just been spitting in the wind. Throwing threats around because that's what Clifton did when he was frustrated and angry.

But this sealed the deal.

Clifton really was suing her for custody of the boys.

Eighteen

"Hey!" Caine yelled to Jax, running to catch up to him as he left Madge's. "Where you off to, brother?"

To meet the woman who could potentially ruin my life. "Nowhere special. How's things?"

Caine smiled, clapping him on the back. "How's anything where Dixie's involved? Crazy, as always."

Now Jax smiled. He liked seeing his friend so damn happy. It gave him hope. "But you love it, and you know it."

He threw up his hands with a bark of laughter. "Fine. I love the chaos. She makes mayhem like no other, but I love it. So listen, been meaning to talk to you since yesterday, just wasn't sure how to approach it."

Instantly, his mind went to the software he was developing. "Everything okay with the security program? It's got glitches, but it's early yet. I'll work 'em out."

"Everything's cool with that. It's something else. Wasn't sure if I should tell you or not. Haven't told anyone in fact because at first I thought I was seeing things."

His gut tightened. "Sounds ominous. So, shoot."

"That woman you dated back after college. You know, the one who worked in the coffee shop under Jay? Reece, was it?"

Fuck. Now what? How long had she been skulking around? "What about her?"

Caine was measuring his words. Jax heard it in his pause, saw it in his eyes. "I saw her the other day. I'd swear my left arm on it. Can't miss that red hair, you know? Just wondered what she'd be doing here in Plum Orchard. I thought…well, you know, with all the shit that went down with Jake…I dunno. I'm just looking out for you."

All the shit that had gone down with Jake. Yeah. There'd been plenty of that. "Where'd you see her?"

"Right here in the square. I think." He scrubbed his jaw. "Shit, I could be wrong."

Jax's jaw tightened. "You're not wrong."

Caine tried to hide his surprise, but it was pointless. Of course he'd be surprised Reece was here. They'd kept in loose touch since their college years. Caine knew what had gone down with Jake and Reece. "Why the hell would she be *here* after…"

"After she ditched me and got knocked up by Jake?" Damn, hearing himself say that was like a punch in the kidney. It sounded goddamn ugly. "Sorry. That was shitty. Jake was your friend, too."

Caine shook his head in understanding. "Hold on. You're saying Jake knocked up Reece? *Jake?*"

"Jake."

"Well, it's not like I was that tight with him, but he was like your brother. I had no idea. Does that mean…"

"Maizy is Jake's. Jake and Reece's."

"Clifton?"

"Go away."

"No. I will not go away. I'm your mother whether you like it or not and I will not be spoken to in that tone. Now, sit up on your bed and you give me your full attention. Understand?" Em pushed his door open, crossing the room to perch on the edge of his bed.

He scooted to the other side like she had the plague, and that was just fine. He could be as angry as he liked, but he would hear her. "Why didn't you tell me about this fight?"

"Because it's no big deal."

"It absolutely is a big deal when you come home with an egg the size of the ones Miss Prissy's prized chicken lays."

Stony silence.

"I won't allow anyone to lay their hands on you, Clifton. It's unacceptable, you hear me? You could have been seriously hurt, and nothing—*nothing* about that is okay with me. What kind of mother would I be if I let someone hurt you just because you don't want to be a snitch? I'm going to Principal Crawford this morning, and we'll see to makin' sure no one puts another hand on you."

He pressed himself against the wall and shrugged a shoulder. "I said it's no big deal, Mom."

Em tugged on the leg of his jeans. "If it's not such a big deal, why did you call your daddy and tell him you wanted to come live with him?"

"I don't know."

"Clifton, I want you to know something, and I want you to really hear me when I tell you, I love you and your brother more than I've ever loved anythin' else. If you're really unhappy with me, then we'll talk about where you should live. Maybe we can find a way for you to see your dad more. I don't ever want you to be unhappy, son. I surely don't want you beat up. I know what happened with… Your dad is—"

"He wears girls' clothes."

Em nodded, her expression grim. "He does, but I'll defend his right to do so with my last breath. Know why?"

"Why?"

"Because hidin' who you are inside hurts. Your dad wasn't happy pretending to be someone he wasn't. But he pretended because that's what everyone said he should do. Because that's what all his friends said he should do—it's what society says you should do. I don't want your dad to hurt. But I don't want you to hurt, either, and if living with your father makes you hurt less, then…" She fought the hitch in her words. She needed to stay strong when she did this. "Then we'll talk about it. I don't want to, but I will. We'll figure something out. Work out some new rules for more visitation."

His silence sat in her heart like a heavy stone. Em rose to leave, pausing for a moment. She couldn't bear how conflicted Clifton was. Couldn't bear this lost, angry boy, a mere ghost of the child he'd been just a few months ago. That was when she knew what she had to do. "Clifton?"

"What?"

"I need you to remember something for me, okay?"

"What?"

"No matter where you live. No matter how near or far you are from me, no matter how angry you are with me, I'll always be here. There'll never be a day your mama won't be here. And I love you. So, so much."

She padded silently out of his room, heading down the stairs to devise the beginnings of the plan that had kept her up all night. She was going to put her life back on track and focus on what was next. Keeping the boys with her. If that meant rearranging her entire life to do it—then that's what she'd do.

Part of that began with Jax. Em picked up her cell phone, her throat tight, her eyes stinging with tears, and she texted him.

"Done."

Jax sat in his truck on the bridge, waiting for Reece to arrive with his stomach on full tilt, his fingers like ice. He'd been texting Em all day with no luck. She didn't answer her office phone, and he didn't want to rouse suspicion by calling Dixie and asking her about it.

But he had to see her. He needed her to know that this was no longer a fun, sexy game for him. This was real. They could be real. Damn the people who'd talk—he'd handle it. Damn everything but him, and Em, and their kids. Together.

Somehow, he had to make her see that it didn't have to be like it was with her ex. She didn't have to give up anything for him. She could have whatever color she damn well pleased on the walls, for some towels, wherever. The only thing she had to give him was her heart. Her trust that he wouldn't discard it…dismiss it.

He just had to do this one thing, and he wanted to do it right.

Checking his phone again, he scowled. Where was she? He lobbed the phone on the passenger seat, running a hand over his jaw when he glanced at the digital clock on his dash.

Where was the one thing he had to take care of? Leave it to Reece to be late. When had she ever cared about inconveniencing anyone? Reece lived by her own rules—her own timetable. She was whimsical and flighty, and he'd known it from the moment he'd fallen in love with her.

Thinking about Reece never failed to bring up Jake. His face, his laughter, his determination to be something. Memories of his dead best friend crowded Jax's head, shoving their way in after keeping them out for so long, making it throb.

Jake Landry had been his best friend since eighth grade. They'd bonded over Cheez Doodles at lunch on Jake's first day of school, and it stayed that way right up until Reece.

The Jays—that's what everyone called them back then. Wherever there was a Jax, there was a Jake, was the joke. He'd loved Jake—considered him a Hawthorne through and through. A brother. That's what Jake had been. No different than Tag or Gage in his mind.

They'd played football together in high school, chased cheerleaders, drank their first illegal six-pack together. Jake had worked his ass off to get a scholarship to the same college as Jax just so they could keep Team Jay alive.

He was Jake's lifeline—his link to healthy, normal relationships when his home life was so shitty. Raised by an alcoholic father, Jake was a welfare check—a six-pack of beer and cable TV for his dad after his mother left when he was just five.

It was a miracle none of it rubbed off on Jake. He attributed that to Jax and his family—pushing him to keep his grades up, inviting him into their tight circle, supporting him the way they'd supported their own sons.

First chance Jake got after he graduated, he got the hell out and never looked back, and Jax helped him, throwing his shoddy duffel bag in the back of the used truck they'd both worked to buy.

After college, they'd begun their own software development company. *Jay*. He wrote the code; Jake, and all his varied charms, marketed and designed it.

After four years of struggling to pay their rent, their big break came in the way of a top-secret defense contract with the government. After five years, they met Reece, who worked in the coffee shop just below their newly purchased warehouse space for Jay.

Jax fell in love with her, and then Jake slept with her. Stole her right out from under his nose, and when Jax found out—he never spoke to Jake again. He'd never forget the second he realized Reece and Jake had betrayed him. Sitting across from them at the pub they frequented, offering up their bullshit, cliché excuses about how them falling into bed with one another had "just happened."

He'd never forget how he couldn't catch his breath. He'd never forget how in five minutes, everything he'd loved, his company, Jake, Reece, was all just gone. Done. Over.

He'd never forget how losing Jake was like losing a limb. There was the phantom pain of it—Jake, so much a part of his life, suddenly gone, but still there every time he did something they used to do. Yet, it was only Jake's memory there, and that hurt like hell. There was the physical pain of it—every time he saw Jake pick Reece up from his office window. Every time he ran into him at the gym. Every time, it felt like his guts were being ripped from his stomach.

When Jax cut him off, refused to speak to him, wouldn't take calls from him, shunned him like he'd never existed, Jake finally offered to sell his shares in Jay to Jax, and they cut all ties.

He'd run off to live happily ever after with Reece, and the next time Jax saw him was in his coffin.

He'd fed off his anger for a long time after that, letting it rule every decision he made, holding on to it, always with the skewed thought, somewhere far in the back of his mind, that someday, he'd have Jake back in his life again. Maybe it would just be to tell him to go the fuck to hell, maybe it would be when he and Reece broke up, but Jake would always be "around."

Until he wasn't. Until he damn well got himself killed in a car accident, and there was no Jake. There was no Jake to persecute. To slaughter him with his words, to rage at how soul crushing his betrayal had been, to get it all out. There was no physical Jake to yell his anger at. There was just a shell of Jake, pale and still in a suit he'd never have worn, in a coffin Jax wanted to haul him out of and hold him close until he breathed again.

Until Jax could tell him that no matter how much he'd hurt him with Reece—Jake was still his brother.

And now, he was about to meet with the woman who'd helped take everything he'd loved away—only to throw it all away.

I helped her, Jax. She didn't do it alone.

A knock on his window startled him. Reece gazed into his truck, just as beautiful as she'd always been. He turned the ignition off and popped open the door, tucking his chin into the collar of his jacket and nodding in her direction. "Reece."

Her hair flew around her in familiar shocks of red. Hair she claimed she hated, but he'd once loved. "So we finally meet."

Though he regretted like hell not speaking to Jake, lived with the guilt of that every day, he'd never regret cutting Reece out of his life. "What's your game here, Reece? You've been hanging around here for a month, not returning my calls, yanking my chain, showing up at Maizy's school. Cut to the chase."

If she was offended by his harsh tone, she didn't react. Reece was clearly on a mission and when that happened, she was unshakable. "I was sorry to hear about Harper. There's been so much death in the past few years, hasn't there? So many important people in our lives gone."

Jax's lips went flat. Harper had been the only one who'd liked Reece when he'd dated her. He didn't want to remember that. She didn't deserve that. "Look, let's cut to the chase. Why are you here and what the hell do you want?"

She let her eyes fall to the ground, but it wasn't that coy, innocent gaze she'd always used when she wanted something. It was almost haunted. "I just had to see her. She's perfect. So perfect."

Alarm bells began their distant ringing. She wanted Maizy. Goddamn it, it wasn't bad enough she'd taken Jake, but she wanted Maizy after all this time? Never gonna happen.

He checked himself. Forced himself to remain calm. "So what is it? Do you want to meet her, Reece? Talk to her, get to know her?"

Reece paused for a long moment, staring off into the distance, and he wasn't sure if he saw regret or relief when she answered. "I know this will make you hate me even more than you already do, but no. I don't want to get to know her. She's better off not knowing me."

Fuck. He had to hope she wasn't going to play the martyr here. That wasn't gonna fly. *Jake wouldn't want this, buddy. Do the right thing. He made you promise in his will you'd let Maizy see her.* Damn it. "Look, aside from everything's that's happened between us, she's your daughter. Yours and Jake's. Jake loved you, Reece. He loved Maizy. He wanted her to know you. He said as much in his will. I had to promise I'd let you see her before I was granted custody of her."

She shook her head, her mouth a grim line. "I never wanted her, Jax. Didn't Jake tell you?"

"He didn't tell me anything, remember? We weren't speaking."

Her finger shot up in the air. "Right. Because of me. Well, here's the cold, hard truth. I was going to abort Maizy."

He clenched his teeth together, clamped so hard, it was a miracle he didn't crush his jaw. "Don't. Don't talk about her that way." *Or I won't be responsible for what I do to you.*

The cold wind whipped her hair against her creamy cheeks, rather sunken, something he hadn't noticed when he'd first laid eyes on her today. "It's the truth, Jax. Jake never would have known if I hadn't been stupid enough to leave that damn EPT stick in the trash. I would have aborted her before he ever even knew she existed. Just before I dumped him, that is."

"Stop."

But Reece wasn't stopping. She plodded forward, her eyes distant as though she was reliving her conversations with Jake. "He talked me out of it. You know what Jake was like—he could talk anyone into anything. Against my better judgment, I fell for the whole white-picket-fence dream. Turns out, it was his dream. Not mine. I just got his dream confused with mine for a little while." She gripped the steel railing along the bridge, her pale skin reddened from the harsh wind.

Jax couldn't move. He wanted to wrap his hands around her creamy throat and choke her right out of her red coat for almost taking Maizy from him by aborting her.

The picture she made, standing against the backdrop of the purple-and-blue-streaked sky, stopped him, though. She was frail. Reece looked frail and vulnerable. "The second I had her, I knew. I knew I didn't want to be a parent, Jax. Jake knew, too. He just wouldn't admit it. So I left him a note and I ran away and hid for all these years. I knew Jake was dead, and still, I hid. Because I was afraid, if anyone knew I was alive, they'd make me take her."

The breath he'd been holding escaped his lungs. "Where? Where the hell did you go?" *How? How could you have gone?* "Jake looked day and night for you before he died, hired private investigators, according to his lawyers. Your father was worried sick. Did he need more grief after your mother?"

"Abroad," she said flatly, as though Jake's fears, her parents' fears, never even occurred to her. As though the word *abroad* cleared it all the fuck up because it had helped her get what she wanted.

"That's it?" He had to fight not to yell. "Just abroad? Do you have any idea what your parents went through? What Jake went through before he was killed?"

She cocked her head in his direction, her eyes still flat and dull. "How do you know what Jake went through? You two weren't speaking before he died, Jax."

Boom. Reece's jab at the status of his and Jake's relationship was like a sonic boom in his ears. "Yeah. We damn well weren't." And he'd been making it up to him ever since. Taking care of the one last thing he had in his life that kept him close to Jake.

"Thanks to me."

"Yep."

Now he wanted to hurt her. For taking pieces of people she had no right to take. Because her whims, her flights of fancy were all that mattered to her. "Did you know just a few weeks after you left your mother was diagnosed with Alzheimer's? Do you have any idea how hard that was on your father? You missing, his wife diagnosed with a disease that would eventually eat her brain and a granddaughter with a new father who was half out of his mind with worry about you?"

Jax had seen it all. All the tears, the agonizing mourning Reece's parents had suffered while they searched for their little girl. "They thought something happened to you, Reece. They spent thousands of dollars looking for you in those first months. They just wouldn't believe Jake when he told them you just left."

He'd heard it all after Jake died, and he was as convinced as Jake that Reece wasn't taken by force or whatever story her parents had concocted in their heads to ease the selfishness that made up Reece.

Reece curled her hands around the bars on the bridge, her cheeks red from the harsh wind. "I didn't know Mom was so sick until it was too late."

"That's what happens when you go *abroad*, Reece.

People die. Babies live without their mothers." Jax wanted to hurt her the way she'd hurt her parents, Maizy—Jake. He wanted to see her suffer the way everyone she'd left in her abroad wake had.

Still, she didn't bite. No angry words, no defensive reactions, just straight ahead on a path he couldn't figure. "But Dad says he still sees Maizy. Thank you for that."

She'd talked to her father? Why hadn't Lorne mentioned it? "I make it a point to bring her to see him twice a year, and she calls him once a week. She loves Pop-Pop Givens, and he spoils her senseless."

Reece smiled then, that dazzling smile—the one that held the secret to everything. The answer to any man's ills. Except his. Looking down at her now, he couldn't even remember what she'd been like before today. Couldn't remember a single thing he'd been drawn to.

All he could see, all he could hear, was how Maizy had been an afterthought to her. How she'd run away and left everyone to pick up the pieces of her broken life.

"I'm glad my dad knows her. What about Jake's dad? Has he seen her?"

"Jake's dad has no interest in anything but a case of beer and his misery. He was happy to walk away and never look back." *Just like you.*

"Just like me, right?" She mirrored his thoughts.

"So let me get something straight here—even after you knew about your mother's illness, when you knew Jake was dead, and you knew your dad couldn't help with Maizy because your mother was so ill, you still stayed *abroad?* Not knowing what would happen to her? Jesus Christ, Reece! How the fuck could you be so damn selfish? She was two months old."

"Because I knew."

"*Knew?* Knew what?"

"That Jake would take care of everything. I knew he'd make sure his father never got anywhere near her, and I knew he'd take measures to ensure her safety after I left."

Jax crossed his arms over his chest and glared at her. "Well, look at you. Always so sure everyone would handle your shit for you. Do you have any idea what could have happened to Maizy if Jake hadn't made sure that will was airtight? If there'd been a single screwup in the language, she could have ended up in the foster-care system."

But Reece didn't take his angry bait. Instead, she shook her head, the mass of her red curls whipping in the wind. "Nope. I knew Jake. I knew that would never happen because Jake didn't make mistakes, except for getting involved with me, and I knew, if my parents couldn't take her, or if anything ever happened to them, he'd leave her to you. You were everything to him, Jax. He loved you like a brother."

No. No, he wouldn't allow that to hurt him anymore. He would pull that damn arrow out of his gut and drop it at her feet. "Until I wasn't like a brother." Jake had broken that pact, and it still killed him. "Last time I checked, there was some unspoken rule about sleeping with your brother's girlfriend."

She put her hand on his arm then, squeezed it before releasing. "Don't hate Jake. Please don't hate him. If there's one thing I wish you wouldn't do—it's hate Jake. He was sick over the loss of your friendship. Sat up late at night trying to figure out ways to win you back and still keep me. Forgive yourself for not making up with him before he died. Don't use Maizy as your way to make everything right with Jake. Because you can't. You shouldn't."

Jax swallowed hard. He'd seen all sorts of red when he'd found out about Reece and Jake sleeping together. He'd walked away, and he'd never looked back.

And when Jake's team of lawyers had contacted him about Maizy, when he'd seen her for the first time, realized that his former best friend since eighth grade had left in his care the most precious thing he had, Jax swore nothing, *no one* would ever take away his chance to make things right. "How could you not want to meet her?"

The shrug of her slender shoulders made him angrier. It was dismissive. As though this life she'd created with Jake was something she'd picked up at the grocery store on her way home from work. "I don't know how to explain it, Jax. I don't want to try to justify it to you. I just know that all through my pregnancy, all while Jake planned and prepared, bought books, signed us up for Lamaze classes, I kept waiting to feel attached. I kept waiting for that magical moment when I'd fall in love with this thing growing in my belly. Waiting to feel something other than ugly and bloated. I wanted to. I tried to. I prayed for it. I wanted to be as excited as Jake. I wanted to want to paint a room for her, buy blankets and strollers and cribs."

He was offended—offended that this amazing kid she and Jake had created stirred nothing in her. So he kept his mouth shut. For the moment, she didn't want to see Maizy. He wanted to keep it that way. Never, ever would he allow Maizy to know her mother felt like this about her.

"That pisses you off, doesn't it? That after everything that happened between you and me and Jake, I couldn't love Maizy. The least I could do for all the trouble I caused is love my own flesh and blood."

"You're goddamn right it pisses me off."

"That's good. It should piss you off. You know why it pisses you off?"

"Because you're heartless and Maizy is amazing?"

"No. Because you're her *father,* Jax. You love her because, aside from biology, Jake *was* your brother. In your mind, she's as much your flesh and blood as Jake was. Only someone who loves Maizy as much as you do would hate me for not loving her the way you do. That's why I'm here. To tell you she's all yours. That I wouldn't dream of taking her from you, and I've signed papers to that effect—because you can give her the kind of love I'll never be capable of. I don't want to lay any claims to her. I don't want visitation or weekends or anything. I just want you to stop worrying I'll crop up someday and try to take her from you. Because I won't."

He should walk away right now, let her go while she

was handing off her kid like a football pass, but he had to know. "Why? Why *now,* Reece?"

"Because my life fell apart, Jax. It didn't fall apart when it should have. It didn't fall apart when society dictates it should have fallen apart, but when it fell, it fell hard. And there was no one there to *fix* it but me. So, that's what I'm doing. I'm fixing it. I'm fixing all the things I should've fixed a long time ago, and I'm letting go of the guilt for not feeling guilty about leaving Maizy with Jake. For instinctively knowing I never wanted children, and letting Jake and his brand of charm talk me into it anyway."

"Is this some kind of weird redemption?" He'd seen a lot of that lately—in all forms.

Reece rolled her shoulders. "Just an admission. I'm admitting the truth I ran away from six years ago. I would have been a crappy mother, Jax. Maizy deserved so much more. At least I wasn't too selfish to recognize that—even if Jake wouldn't. Isn't it better to admit to it than to have let her suffer my inadequacies?"

"So when Maizy asks about you, and she has, what do I say?"

Reece's eyes met his, but this time they weren't dull and lifeless. They held a raw honesty he couldn't say he'd ever seen from her. "Tell her I left to make room for the woman who was better at this than I'll ever be. Tell her sometimes, when the parent picking happens, every now and then, the stork makes a huge mistake. Tell her I left so the right mother, the one who knows all of the important lessons it takes to be a good person, could step in and teach her."

Emmaline.

Jax didn't have to say her name. Reece already knew. "She's so good with Maizy, Jax. With her boys, too. I hope you'll let them get to know one another. I hope you won't let what happened with me and Jake keep you from loving someone who'll love you back just as hard."

That caught him off guard. "You've seen them together?"

She finally smiled again—easier this time. "I'm not so heartless I didn't want the best for her, Jax. Of course I've seen Maizy with her. I know all about Emmaline Amos. I did some poking around before I made the decision to come here and see you. I watched her after I did. I think your friend Caine saw me. Either way, she's amazing, and patient, and beautiful, and so in love with you, she's up to her stinkin' eyeballs in it."

His jaw got so tight from his clenching, it began to ache. "She claims she isn't."

Reece grinned. "She lies."

They stood for a little while, the sounds of the park beneath the bridge filtering between them. The wind blowing, the sun setting. Jax absorbing, Reece letting go.

"I have to go now, Jax."

Letting Reece go, letting her leave without looking back, was like letting the last piece of Jake go. The last person who'd been with Jake before he died was shrugging off her old life, walking away from it and taking Jake with her. "I don't know what to say."

"Why don't we say what Jake always said?"

He closed his eyes, hearing the phrase Jake always used on the whistle of the wind. "Say good night, Gracie."

Reece's laughter was soft, echoing along the bridge. "G'night."

When Jax opened his eyes again, Reece was a small dot on the horizon, bleeding into the vivid colors of the purple-and-blue night.

An engine started, a door slammed and she was gone.

Jax climbed back in the truck and shuddered a sigh, letting his head fall to the steering wheel in relief. He sat like that for a little while—catching his breath, grateful. Grateful that the tie that once bound him to Jake with guilt and anger was no longer cutting off his circulation. That he could think about Jake and remember the good times.

Pulling his wallet out, Jax dug deep into it to find a smaller version of the picture Em had found. In a fit of anger, he'd torn the half with Reece in it off, but he'd kept this tucked away, pulling it out only from time to time, staring at it and trying to figure out how everything had gone so damn sideways.

He tapped Jake's smiling face with a finger and smiled to himself. "I miss you, brother, but I gotta go now. I have a woman to win, and it isn't going to be easy, but never give up the fight, right?"

The sound of his phone buzzing on the passenger seat made him drop the picture of Jake on the dash and grab up his phone, hoping it was Em.

He read the single word she'd sent him.

The one word he knew he was going to regret the minute he'd agreed to it.

Done.

Fuck.

Nineteen

Em stared at her phone, ignoring the texts Jax had been sending over for the past two days now. He wanted to talk when she couldn't speak. There was nothing left to talk about anyway. Continuing with Jax would only bring more misery to him and Maizy.

But heavens, she wanted to. She wanted to burrow against his wide chest and catch her breath against this storm of fury raging in her. Hear his heartbeat beneath her ear.

He'd been angry with her when they'd last parted. It was better she just cut him off, even if seeing his texts, at first funny, then urgent, were breaking bits of her heart off piece by piece.

She'd taken some personal days, telling Dixie she had the flu, sent the boys to Idalee's, parked her car in the garage, locked up and hidden away.

All the crying and raging she'd been doing over what her mother had said to Clifton Junior and ending it with Jax had lent to her fake cold story when Dixie showed up with chicken soup. From behind a wad of tissues, her eyes red and runny, Em had told her to stay away so she wouldn't catch it. But that wouldn't hold water for long.

If Dixie and the girls knew what she was about to do, chaos would surely ensue. She hated scenes, even if they were out of love.

They'd try to talk her out of it. They'd somehow manage to convince her that Emmaline With No Spine could fight Clifton and the big bad meanies of Plum Orchard. Dixie would wave her money around and threaten to sue the pants off someone in her outrageously dramatic way in Em's defense.

LaDawn would offer to sock the gossips in the mouth and Marybell would growl at Louella a little extra the next time she encountered her.

But would that keep Clifton from trying to take the boys to Atlanta? Would that keep his rich girlfriend from using her money to help him fight fire with fire? Would any of that money keep her son from being teased in school day after day?

She couldn't risk a custody battle. How could she possibly win when she worked for a phone-sex company? Add in all the grief the boys suffered at school, and it left her too afraid to take a chance she'd lose them forever.

Appease Clifton were the first words that came to mind. *Make a deal with him. Negotiate. Do whatever you need to in order to keep the boys close.*

Her fingers tightened on the papers Clifton had sent. She'd tried calling him, tried to find a way to work this out, but he wasn't taking her calls.

Now that he'd lobbed the arrow, and she was considering rearranging her whole life, moving to Atlanta to allow him to see the boys more often, he was hiding. The same way he had when she'd found out he was cheating on her.

Her phone buzzed, turning her red, puffy eyes to note a voice mail message from Hank Cotton, her former boss.

Grabbing a tissue, she put the phone to her ear. "Emmaline, Hank Cotton here. I think I might have found you an opening at my brother's firm. He's willing to interview you Friday morning, if you can make the trip. On one last note, Plum Orchard is losin' one of its finest. Best to you always, Emmaline."

Em grabbed a pen and took down the information and tucked it into her purse, relief flooding her.

Now she just had to get out of her pajamas and pack a bag and speak to her mother.

And find the courage to let go.

Two deep breaths later and she was on her feet when the pounding on her door began.

"Emmaline, damn it, open this door!" Jax yelled, giving little to no shit that Em's neighbor Arlo was peeking out of his window.

The hell with the busybodies of this town. He didn't care if they saw him at her house. He didn't care if they talked. Let 'em. Let 'em come for Em while he was around.

No one had seen Em for two days due to her alleged flu, but something wasn't sitting right with him.

Couldn't put his finger on it, but something wasn't right. She'd ignored every text, every phone call he'd made, and if Em was nothing else, she was polite.

Completely ignoring him didn't fit her character.

If it was really over between them, he wanted her to say it to his face. He wanted to hear the words, see her when she spoke them.

Fuck, he just wanted to see her.

Because it wasn't over for him. He had apologizing to do—explaining to do. He had to tell her he was falling in love with her. Even if she rejected him, he was going to say it anyway. Because he didn't want to miss the chance to do what was right for him and Maizy. For his heart.

Fueled by that thought, Jax fisted his hand and banged harder. "Em, I know you're in there—talk to me, Em. Just talk to me."

Nothing. Nothing but the stares of the neighborhood people he'd acquired with the racket he was making, nothing but the sounds of the coming night.

He had to clench his fist to keep from driving it through the cold metal of the door. "This isn't over, Em. Not by a long shot. I'll keep coming back until you see me. Until you hear what I have to say."

He pressed his ear to the door and waited, as though after all that banging, she'd suddenly pop open the door and welcome him with that warm Em smile.

More silence.

Damn it.

If he had to come back with a backhoe, he was going to get her to open her door.

* * *

Em let her cheek rest against the door, distantly watching tears roll off her face and onto the hardwood entryway. The sound of Jax's truck revving its engine and driving away left her empty and cold.

She wanted to fling open the door and launch herself at him. To tell him it was all her. This had nothing to do with him. But she couldn't. Seeing him would only make everything that much harder in light of their sex-only relationship.

Why did he want to talk anyway? Did you talk about ending a sexual relationship, or didn't you just end it? Wasn't that what they'd agreed on?

Did he need to see her to end it? Admittedly, texts were bad form when breaking up, but they weren't breaking up, breaking up. They were quitting the sex games.

This was the no harm, no foul part.

But she'd realized something today. Dixie was right. She wasn't a fling kind of girl. She wasn't the kind of girl who could take a lover in the afternoon.

Because she was in love with Jax Hawthorne.

"Daddy?"

"Maizy?"

She hopped up on the couch next to him, the feathers of her boa shedding on the new couch he'd been talked into, and pressed her nose to his. "Do you feel sick?"

"Nope. Why do you ask?"

She used the back of her hand to feel his forehead,

knocking him in the eye with the charms from the bracelet Em had given her. "Because you look sick."

"What makes you say that?"

"Your face is all pouty like Uncle Tag's."

Jax rubbed his nose against hers. "I'll try not to be so pouty."

"If you're sad, it's okay to be pouty. Em said so."

Em. She'd only been in their lives for a little while, and already she'd left an impact on Maizy. "Em's smart."

Maizy giggled, that light giggle dipped in fairy wings. "She's nice. Can she be your girlfriend? You're not so cranky when she's around."

His smile was wry. His girlfriend. What had started this all, Maizy's call to Em. "I don't think she wants a boyfriend right now, Maizy."

"Can you make her want to be your girlfriend?" she asked, putting her hands on either side of his face and pressing their noses together so when she twisted her head, their eyes made funny shapes.

"You can't make someone do something they don't want to do."

"You make me eat vegetables and I don't want to."

"That's a little different, honey." Vegetables and girlfriends. Totally different.

"You said I had to eat vegetables because they're good for me."

"What does that have to do with Em?"

"I heard Uncle Gage tell Uncle Tag Em's good for you."

The way she connected dots in her head never failed

to amaze him. "Still kind of different, and very grown-up stuff you shouldn't worry about. But vegetables are good for you—that's why we make you try everything first."

"Then maybe you should try to make Em your girl-friend. Maybe she doesn't know she's good for you, either? Like I didn't know I liked vegetables."

Yeah. He'd just make her want to be his girlfriend instead of his lover. It was easy. Yet, a new fire burned in his gut. Why couldn't it be that simple?

He wanted Em. He wasn't giving up until she told him to. And even then, he might still not give up.

"Know what, Maizy?"

"What, Daddy?"

"You're A-Maizy." He dropped a kiss on her nose, scooped her up and ran her up the stairs quarterback style.

Tomorrow, Em better get ready, because he was going to make her be his girlfriend if it was the last thing he did.

The next day, he stormed Call Girls take-no-prisoners style. He'd texted her to a deafening silence. Left her voice mail message after voice mail message with no response.

The hell she was sick.

"Em!" Jax headed for Emmaline's office, ignoring the startled looks on the girls' faces as he flew past them.

"Jax?" Dixie called, almost running into him in the hall leading to Em's office.

"Dixie. Jesus, have you seen Em today? I've been calling and texting her and haven't heard a damn thing."

Dixie's face collapsed. "Thank God, you're here. I can't find her anywhere, either. I'm worried sick. We all are. Especially after she left me this on my desk."

He plucked the piece of paper from Dixie's hand and skimmed it. "She's resigning from Call Girls?" Now he knew something was wrong. Really, really wrong.

"She had to have been in here bright and early. I'm always here by seven, but this was waiting on my desk for me when I got here, and now, none of us can find her anywhere. The boys are with Idalee getting ready for the Winter Solstice fair in the square, but even Idalee doesn't know where she is. Em told her she needed to leave the boys with her because she had some things to take care of, and it was the last she saw of her. That was two days ago. She's not sick, Jax. She was covering for something else."

Why would Em resign from Call Girls? She loved her job. She loved Dixie and the girls.

Marybell and LaDawn were right behind Dixie, faces full of worry. "Did we find her?" LaDawn asked.

Dixie shook her head but her eyes were full of determination. "Not yet. But we will. Okay, girls—Jax, you, too. Let's spread out and find Em. Marybell, you all right with goin' to Madge's and askin' around?"

Marybell was half out the door. "Couldn't stop me even if Nanette Pruitt was waitin' for me with Holy Water."

Dixie raised a fist in the air and laughed. "Go get 'em! LaDawn—"

"I got it. I'll hit the coffee shop and Lucky's. Maybe she's got her head buried in a pile of wood and she just forgot to turn her phone on."

Dixie gave LaDawn a quick hug before grabbing Jax's hand. "You come with me. We'll start at her place and work from there."

Jax went willingly, first, because these women were a force to be reckoned with, and if anyone could find Em, it'd be them.

Second, because these women were a force to be reckoned with.

Twenty

"Mama! You open this door right now!" Em pounded on her mother's front door, shooting a toxic glare at the people staring at her from the front porches lining her mother's street.

Good. Let 'em stare. The lot of them were bitter, mean, ugly spirits who had no right to judge. It wasn't enough to talk about her and Clifton. She was an adult—she could take her licks, but Clifton Junior? He'd been physically assaulted because Louella's bid to hurt anyone in her path had spiraled out of control.

In fact, maybe she'd just tell them that. Em marched down the neat pathway of her childhood home, with its cobblestone pavers and its perfectly aligned boxwoods, the breath coming from her lungs in cloudy huffs.

She planted herself just at the edge of the lawn and raised a fist in the air. "Y'all listen up, you nosy bunch o' biddies, and yes, that means you, too, Kitty Palmer!" She shot an accusatory finger in Kitty's direction. "You leave me and my children alone—you understand? One more foul word from your daughter's forked tongue, and I'll punch her in the nose even harder than Dixie did! While y'all are talkin', why don't you talk about *that!*"

She wiped the spit from the side of her mouth and stomped back along the path to the steps of her mother's wide front porch, prepared to knock Clora's door down with just her rage alone.

She'd had two days to figure out how to handle this, but the longer she'd thought about it, the angrier she became. Maybe it was because she'd dropped her resignation off today like some kind o' thief in the night. Maybe it was because she resented feeling forced to leave a place she loved, despite the cruelty that abounded in Plum Orchard.

Or maybe it was just the very idea that her own mother didn't have her back. And as she got past the tears and began to focus on what hurt the most, it all came down to her mother and what she'd said to Clifton Junior.

"Mama!" she bellowed. "Open this door!"

The front door popped open and Clora stuck her head out—the first thing she did was scan the street to see if anyone was watching her daughter's bad behavior.

In that second, Em realized something. Her entire life had been based on Clora's fear everyone was talking about them. Why was that?

"Emmaline Amos! You get in here right now!" she demanded, her lips tight. "Do you want the whole neighborhood to hear you?"

You bet your tail she did. And she said as much. "You bet I do, Mama! I want them all to hear the horrible things you've been saying about me to my son." Em leaned over the porch railing and yelled out into the street. "I want them to hear it from me so they don't have to talk about it behind my back like the yellow-bellied cowards they are!"

Clora stamped her foot and pointed inside the door. "Get in here this instant, Emmaline!"

"Or you'll what, Mama?" She heard the whispers now, out in the dim vestiges of the oncoming night. Everyone talkin' about Emmaline Amos gone crazy.

"Emmaline!" her mother hissed.

Em decided to take her mother's advice; pushing past her, she flew into the living room. It was as cold as it had always been. As cold as her mother had always been.

"What on earth has gotten into you, Emmaline? How dare you come to my door in a fit!"

"Oh, I dare, Mama. I dare because you involved my children! I don't know why you are the way you are, Mama. I don't know why you can't enjoy anything, not even your grandsons, but I will not tolerate you speakin' ill of me to them. You hear me?" she bellowed loud enough to make the lone picture of Jesus on the wall shake from her fury.

Clora paled, but only a little before she rallied and railed at the idea Em would speak so disrespectfully to her elder. "I don't know what you're talkin' about, Emmaline, but you will not speak to me like that."

Em hiked her purse over her shoulder, her emotions seesawing in wide, crazy-ish arcs. "Oh, yes I will! When it comes to my boys, I most certainly will. You're

always so concerned about everyone talkin' about me—
about Clifton—about you—why is it you're not concerned when you're talking out of turn and telling my
boys their father left because of me? How dare you say
something like that to them? How dare you plant one
of your bitter seeds? Isn't it bad enough that you made
my entire life miserable with your Bible thumping and
your bitterness, but you want to do it again with my
sons? Not. In. This. Lifetime!"

Clora's hard mask of a face cracked for a moment before she turned on her heel and headed into her equally
cold kitchen. "I spoke nothing but the truth."

Em raced after her, cutting her off at the pass, spilling the contents of her purse all over the yellowing linoleum. *"What?"*

Clora's eyes flashed as she stooped to pick up Em's
purse. "I said, I spoke nothing but the truth. If you'd
been a better wife, Clifton wouldn't need to wear wom-
en's clothes."

Em couldn't breathe from the accusation. She
reached blindly behind her for something to hold on
to. "Have you plum lost your mind? How does my being
a better wife have anything to do with Clifton wearing high heels?"

"If you'd been a better wife, he wouldn't have
strayed."

"So what's your excuse, Mama? Why did my father
leave? Because *you w*eren't a better wife?"

But Clora wasn't hearing Em, she was staring at
the ridiculous birth certificate she'd gotten in the mail,
sprawled across the kitchen floor in a heap of makeup

and loose change. "Where did this come from, Emmaline?"

Em was genuinely taken aback. She'd just insulted her mother's wifely skills and she was more concerned with a piece of paper.

Em snatched it from her hand. "Someone thought it would be funny to scratch off my father's name and put in Ethan Davis. It's just another one of the many pieces of hate mail I get because I work where women fornicate with their words, Mother."

But Clora wasn't responding to her snipe. Her hand was shaking as she slumped down on the floor against the wall. "Who sent it?"

She peered at her mother, confused by the look of terror in her eyes. "Mama, are you hearin' anything I said? I don't know who sent it. People who send things like that don't leave a return address."

"Someone knows."

The ominous tone to Clora's voice startled Em. "Should we cue the spooky music? Someone knows what?"

"That Ethan Davis is your father."

Dixie opened the door to Em's with her spare key to dead silence. Nothing but Dora greeted them. Dixie cupped Dora's muzzle in her hands and cooed, "Where's your mama, Dora?"

Jax reached down and scratched Dora's head, taking in Em's house. It was just like her—everything about it said Emmaline Amos lived here. From the warmth of all those crazy pillows she was so big on to the wall of pictures of the boys—it said Em. It smelled like her, it felt like her—if he could wrap himself up in it, he would.

Dixie began digging through a pile of papers on the counter.

"Maybe we shouldn't go through—"

Dixie's hand with the bangle bracelets on her wrist flew upward, her eyes fixed on the manila envelopes amongst the sale circulars. "Emmaline and I know everythin' there is to know about each other, Jax Hawthorne. We have no secrets. There is no privacy when my best friend is missing. I know your arrangements are different, but I'm not above snoopin' through her things if she's in some kind of trouble. So you just hush with your concerns."

Jax could see why Caine had chosen Dixie. She was a leader, a strong personality, strong and smart. So he nodded and kept his mouth shut. But he couldn't stand still. Pacing in front of the wall of pictures of Em and the boys, he stopped at one in particular.

Em with Clifton Junior in a pile of autumn leaves, his chubby hands bracketing her face, his toothless grin wide, his eyes gleaming with adoration for his mother.

And Em, happy, free, beautiful.

His gut tightened when he reached for his phone again to see if maybe he'd missed a text. It was pointless because it hadn't vibrated in hours, but he looked anyway.

Nothing. *Damn it, Em, where the hell are you?*

Dixie's gasp pulled him from fruitlessly scrolling his phone. "You okay?"

She slid onto the breakfast bar stool and took deep breaths.

Jax crossed the room with Dora in tow and put his hand on her shoulder. "Hey, you feel okay?"

She held up a finger this time. "Give me just a second to process."

Jax looked over her shoulder at the papers she'd been rifling through then he leaned in closer to be sure he was reading correctly. His eyes narrowed. "That son of a bitch is suing her for custody?"

Dixie's nod was slow. "That's not all." She held up another piece of paper that looked official. "I know where Em is, and we have to go before a murder occurs right here in Plum Orchard!"

Em felt the life whoosh out of her then return in a rush of flashing lights and her blood pulsing through her veins. *"What?"* she whispered, her voice cracking.

Clora crumbled, right in front of her eyes. Like someone had stuck a pin in her and she'd deflated. "Ethan Davis is your father."

Her breathing picked back up. "No. Thomas Mitchell is my father."

"Emmaline, we need to sit down—"

Em shook her head, horror spreading throughout her body. "No! I will not listen to you tell me you slept with Ethan Davis! I will not listen to you tell me my whole life was a lie!"

Clora reached for her hand. Physically put her hand out and sought to touch Em's. Who was this woman?

Em cringed, pushing herself away from her mother across the smooth linoleum. "Don't."

Clora pulled her hand back and shook her head, using the towel on her shoulder to wipe her eyes. "Then will you at least listen?"

Em fought for breath. Tears? Her mother was shedding real, live tears? "I will not listen to something so despicable. All my life you've lied to me. All of it. You've been hateful and angry and now I'm supposed to listen?"

"That's why I lied to you, Emmaline! To protect you from the people of this town!"

"I don't understand. How did this happen? How could you have done this?" To hear that her mother was anything but all the things she'd preached to Em—chastity, faithfulness—left her unable to process anything else.

"I loved Ethan first. Long before Pearl even knew he was alive, but my father, your grandpa, didn't like Ethan. Back then, it was just different. Marryin' the right person was important. Your parents' approval was more important than it is today. They thought Ethan was irresponsible, and I suppose, at that time, he was. But I loved him." Her voice cracked and her shoulders shuddered.

Em shook her head. This was all wrong. This wasn't her mother, talking about love like she was some teenager. This wasn't her disapproving, purse-lipped mother. This was someone who needed medication.

"So I broke it off with Ethan, and I met Thomas

shortly thereafter. I cared about Thomas. I won't have anyone thinkin' otherwise."

Finally, she summoned up some words, words she wanted to use to hurt Clora. Make her hurt like she was hurting. "Because Lord forgive if someone thought otherwise, right, Mama? Never create any scandal, Emmaline. Be a good girl, Emmaline," she mocked.

Clora trembled under the weak light of the stovetop range. "I never wanted you to suffer for my misdeeds, Emmaline. I didn't want people to talk about you the way they talked about me. If I kept you on the Lord's path—"

"The Lord's path? Have you lost your gourd, Mama? How is infidelity the Lord's path?" All of the sermons, all of the beating her over the head about being a good girl were because her mother had done something despicable? She'd paid the price for her mother's sin?

But her mother was lost in her memory, hell-bent on purging herself. "I know what we did was wrong. I don't know how it happened. It just happened. I knew I deserved every last bit o' the scorn Pearl set out to shower on me."

Em clutched her purse, her hands shaking. "Pearl knew? How?"

"She caught us together." Her mother sobbed a ragged whimper.

Em began to gag, forcing her to press her fingers to her lips.

"But she's the only person who knows aside from Thomas. Not even Ethan knew. He went to his grave never knowin' he had two daughters. Pearl'd never tell a soul. It would only bring her humiliation and shame, and she'd never allow that. But it's what she used to cut me out of the Mags. It's how she kept me rooted here in my misery. How she kept me in line. I never wanted that to fall at your feet, Emmaline. So I kept quiet."

"Thomas knew?"

Clora nodded, her eyes filled with tears. "He left me because of it."

"Why didn't you tell Mr. Davis about me?" Oh, sweet heaven. He was no longer Mr. Davis.

Her mother looked like she'd just asked her if pigs flew, but her eyes sank to the floor. "How would that have been for you, Emmaline? The illegitimate child of a powerful man like Ethan Davis, livin' in a town like this with a teenager like Dixie Davis was? She was horrible to you all your life, Emmaline. I never liked the idea of you two bein' friends, and I like it even less now."

Everything clicked for Em then. She heard the pieces of it snap into place. All the lessons in decorum. All the anger. All the reminders of bitter retribution were because her mother was making up for her past mistakes. She was punishing herself for sinning, for doing one of the very things she preached was wrong.

It explained her mother's aversion to Dixie.

As though it was Dixie's fault she'd grown up with everything and Clora had struggled all her life to provide. "Don't you mean half sisters, Mama? You leave Dixie alone! She surely had nothin' to do with you beddin' her father!"

Dixie… What would this do to Dixie? She'd been

Daddy's little girl, the apple of his eye. Looking back, she remembered seeing them together. He came to all of Dixie's games when she was a cheerleader, and he'd adored her. She'd adored him.

How would she ever face Dixie again?

Twenty-One

In the aftermath of her mother's confession, Em looked at Clora and felt nothing but empty, a wind tunnel of nothing. Not angry or even resentful, just empty. "You will never, ever breathe a word of this to Dixie—do you understand me, Mama? If you so much as speak her name with ill regard, I'll never see you again, you hear? You keep your secrets close to your chest the way you have for well over thirty years, but you will not hurt my friend with your angry recriminations."

In direct opposition to Em's dry eyes and wooden words, Clora sobbed openly. "I'm sorry, Emmaline. I'm so sorry. I never wanted you to know. I never wanted you to pay for what I'd done."

Em sighed, brushing her skirt to smooth the wrinkles in it. "But I did pay. You kept a leash on me so tight, all I wanted to do was get away. You smothered me with your words from the divine and this righteous path you claim we should all be walkin'. All because *you* did wrong. You veered off the path, Mama. You were cold and disapproving, and while I want to hate you for all of it right now, I don't. I just don't know you. I don't know anything."

Clora's face, puffy from tears, a startling contrast to her stern facade, made Em sad. "I didn't want you to make the same mistakes I made."

Em looked down at her mother—she looked so small now. Small and afraid. "And I didn't, did I? You sure taught me. But while you were teachin' me, you stole my joy. You made me afraid. You kept me from making the same mistakes you made, but at the same time, you made me resent you, and I won't allow you to do that to my boys. Hear me now, Mama—you will never bring your negativity around them again, or you'll never see them again. I will not have you taint them with your bitter regret the way you tainted me. Life is meant for livin', enjoying the people you love, laughter, friends and the freedom to do all those things. Maybe you should try it." Then she held her hand out to her mother and waited.

Clora reached up and let Em pull her from the floor. When they were eye to eye, she felt like she was seeing her mother for the first time. Really seeing this person who no longer had to live with a painful secret—who'd let the cat out of the bag after so long and had nothing else to keep her warm. "I have to go now, Mama, but I need you to think about what I said. Really think about it, and know I meant it."

Clora gave her a brief nod, a small indication she was going to reevaluate.

Em gave her a quick hug, feeling the tremble of her mother's shoulders. "Bye, Mama."

She took a long breath before making her way out of the kitchen and out the front door, leaving behind the place where she'd earned her own angry resentments. She clung to the railing along the front porch, keeping her head high for all the eyes of Plum Orchard to see.

A car came to an almost screaming halt at the curb. "Dixie?"

The passenger door opened and a long leg attached to a cowboy boot touched the curb.

Em froze. Jax. At her mother's house? Why was he here?

She didn't have time to think about it before he was pulling her into his arms in front of everyone peeking out of their windows. "Don't ever do that to me again," he muttered against her hair, tightening his hold on her.

Jax's words, his gentle admonishment, made her crumble. Tears began falling down her face as she clung to him—right there on her mother's front porch.

Huge, gulping sobs of relief escaped her throat. "Don't cry, honey. Jesus. Please don't cry. I know everything. I swear to you, I won't let Clifton take the boys. I know a lot of people. They'll help. But don't leave, Em. Don't run away from this. Stay here and fight with me."

Em sniffed against the soft leather of his jacket, resting her cheek on his chest, letting go of the tight rein she'd kept her emotions in check with. "This is certainly crossing the line between nothing personal and personal, Sir Hawthorne," she teased.

The best part about that was she didn't care. She didn't care if everyone saw her with Jax. She didn't care if they disapproved. She was going to do what she'd told her mother to do. Live.

He rested his chin on top of her head. "I see your personal and raise you a possible monogamous commitment."

"High stakes indeed," she said on a happy giggle. "This coming from a man who didn't want any personal entanglements, either."

"That was stupid. I was stupid. I apologize for my stupid. Can you ever forgive all that stupid?"

"Can you forgive mine?"

"We could have a round of forgiveness sex. That might help. Is that on your list?"

"Isn't that the same as makeup sex?"

"It's very similar, in that sex is involved. It's just sex with the promise of maybe a movie with our kids? Dinner?"

All her doubts disappeared at the mention of their children. "What are you suggesting, Jax Hawthorne?"

"I'm suggesting you let me tell you all my dark secrets."

"Like?"

"Like, Maizy isn't my biological child and while Reece is her biological mother, she had Maizy with my best friend Jake when she left me for him. Jake died just after Reece ran away and named me her guardian."

Em wrapped her arms around his waist and burrowed her nose in his chest. Jax was just a little more amazing than she'd given him credit for. And she didn't care who Maizy belonged to. She didn't care how she'd come to be Jax's. She only cared that Jax was the kind of man—a wonderful one—who'd raise someone else's child. "So that makes her less yours? What is it you're trying to say here, Hawthorne?"

"You're not surprised she isn't mine?"

Her heart ached, tightened, released. "I don't care that she isn't from your man parts. Does it really matter how she got here? She's beautiful and full of life and she offered to beat someone up for Gareth. That you'd raise your best friend's little girl under such hurtful circumstances, and wear barrettes, says something about you. So get to the point, would you?"

"I acted like a total ass when you found Reece's picture the other night because for a long time now, I was angry with her. I was angry with Jake for stealing her right out from under my damn nose. I didn't just lose a girlfriend—I lost my best friend of twenty-two years when they ran off together. He was like my brother. He was my brother. I never spoke to Jake again when he left with Reece. And then he died."

And left Jax his most precious possession. She felt Jax's ache—the grief that kept him rooted in one spot. "So you never had the chance to make amends then."

"No, and every day since he died, I've been trying to make it right. Come to terms with it."

Suddenly, she understood. He was apologizing over and over to Jake though Maizy. "With Maizy."

Jax sighed a ragged breath. "I know it sounds crazy, but I thought if I could just focus on her, put all my energy into giving her everything Jake would have, somehow, I'd make it up to him for kicking him out of my life."

"And Reece?"

"I was angry that she just up and left Maizy only a couple of weeks after she was born. She hasn't seen her in almost six years."

Em's heart twisted into a tight knot. She didn't want to judge Reece. She didn't know what her demons were, but to leave without ever knowing what it felt like to have that tiny head nuzzled under your chin as you rocked. To never know what it felt like to hear Maizy sigh with contentment in her ear as she drifted off to sleep. To miss her first steps, to miss everything? Her life would never have been the same. "And now?"

"I saw her today. I spent the past month hiding from her because I didn't know what she wanted. She popped up out of nowhere after six years and I panicked. Now I know, and I've made my peace with her—with Jake."

"Your peace?"

The rumble in his chest, the pause in his words, was a signal to Em, the meeting with Reece had been painful. "She never wanted Maizy. I won't claim to understand it. I won't even try, because I can't go there. She wanted me to know she's not interested in seeing Maizy, and she'd sign papers to that effect."

Em pulled away from him. "I don't know that I know how to respond to that without usin' the Lord's name in an inappropriate way."

Jax pulled her back into his embrace, resting his chin atop her head. "That's why you're the girl for me, and Reece never was."

"I'm sorry, Jax. I'm sorry for Maizy, too."

She felt his smile against her hair. "I'm not. Maizy and I have other plans."

"And what exactly are those plans?"

"Well, first up, I plan to make you fall madly in love with me."

Em fanned herself and giggled. "My goodness. I don't know that I've ever been courted quite this way."

"You were only courted once."

She flicked the collar of his jacket. "Is this the part where you make me fall madly in love with you? Because if so, we have work to do."

His low chuckle rippled in her ears. "Touchy, touchy. Then, you know, after you fall madly in love with me, I plan to sweep you off your feet."

"The children…"

"Already know each other. Now they'll just get to know each other *with* us."

This man. This man who made her heart pound and her soul full wanted her. Her. "So that madly in love part?"

"Uh-huh."

"Could be working."

Jax tipped her chin up and kissed her thoroughly, reminded her why he was so hard to resist since they'd set out to keep things impersonal.

"Ahem."

Em's head shot up. Dixie? "What are you doing here?"

Dixie's red head popped out from behind Jax. "I was the driver of the escape car."

"Escape car?"

"After what I just saw sitting on your kitchen counter, I thought surely you'd come to murder Clora, *sister*."

Em began to protest, to apologize, but Dixie stopped her, her eyes warm. "Don't, Em. Don't you dare blame yourself for our parents' bad behavior. And everyone wonders why I was such a hellion. Hah! Just look at my genes."

Em reached for Dixie's hand. "Dixie. Oh, my God, Dixie. I never wanted you to find out. I would never want to hurt you."

Dixie grinned. "How could it possibly hurt me that you're my sister?"

"Technically, I'm your half sister. The good half, anyway."

"Half schmalf. We're blood now, Emmaline Amos, and don't you forget it. The question here is, are *you* okay, honey? Clora?"

Em looked past Dixie toward her mother's house. "I have a lot to think about. Everything's changed. Yet, it all just makes sense now. As for Mama, only time will tell."

"We'll have a good sit-down once we get everything else settled, okay?"

"You're not mad about this? You loved your daddy, Dixie. You talked about him like he was your knight in shining armor."

Dixie sighed; the breath she released held resignation. "He was, or at least that's what I let everyone believe. I knew my daddy was a philanderer. Mama never let me forget it. She stayed married to him for a reason,

Em. Surely you know that reason was the prestige of the Davis name and all that money. But while she held on, she never let him forget he was a cheat. I loved him regardless. Because he was the only person at home who showed me any kind of approval."

Em fought hard not to share her disbelief, her disappointment, that the Ethan Davis she'd admired from afar was, after all, only human. "I didn't know, Dixie. I don't think anyone knew."

Dixie nodded, her expression sad. "That's because it was a Davis family secret. I won't say I'm not shocked by how close to home he played, or that your mama kept this from all of us for so long. I wouldn't be surprised if my mama had somethin' to do with makin' her keep that secret, and if she did, I'm sorry, Em. You were entitled to as much as me."

Em stayed silent. Dixie had more than her share of disappointment with her mother. She wouldn't add to it.

Dixie peered at her. "My mama knew, didn't she, Em?"

Her mouth went dry, her next words thick. "Accordin' to my mother, yes."

Dixie nodded. "Looks like Pearl and I have some talkin' to do." She shook off her visible disappointment and put a smile on her face. "Let's forget about how I feel for the moment. The question is, are *you* mad? This is huge, Em. A huge part of your life kept from you. It has to hurt."

Em closed her eyes, still shaky. "I'm not mad, no. Maybe I haven't processed it all yet? Or maybe it's because it explains everything about my mama? It's funny, but the part about your father bein' mine isn't what sticks out in my mind right now. It's the part about us bein' half sisters. It's plum crazy after our history."

Dixie gave her a tight hug. "I dunno. I feel like it's the icing on the cake of our friendship. We've come full circle. I am a little sad, though. Sad that I was so awful to my own flesh and blood."

Em grinned. "Sadder than when you thought I wasn't your flesh and blood? Because that would cut me so deep, Dixie. After all your apologizin' and everything."

Dixie laughed. "I'm sad that I treated you that way, relation or not. My point is, if my father had to have a child from a torrid affair, I couldn't have picked better than if I'd picked you myself."

She knew Dixie was just joking, but the word *affair* brought up a new crop of issues. "I'm illegitimate."

"No. You're Emmaline Amos. My best friend, and now, my sister. Who uses the term *illegitimate* anymore, anyway?"

Dread began to fill her stomach. This meant more gossip. "Everyone in Plum Orchard."

Dixie made a face at her, dismissing the notion. "Everyone doesn't count, Em. Only the people who love you count."

"What do we do now, Dixie? How do we explain all of it?"

"Well," she drawled, a twinkle in her eye. "First we call up Pearl and tell her the Davis family will has some fixin' to be had. Then we go find the person who sent you that birth certificate and we end this once and for all."

She'd never explored past the idea that it was all a joke. "Who do you think it was?"

Dixie planted her hands on her hips. "Who do you know that has more time on their hands than a clock, not a single request on her dance card and loves to make trouble?"

The comment Louella had made about her mother and a boyfriend. Now everything made sense. It hit her like a ton of bricks. "Louella?"

"Who else, Em? Now, I don't know about you, but this crazy grudge of hers has gone too far. Her bid to get rid of Call Girls by pickin' us off one by one won't work. I won't let it. I'm not going to let her run you out of town with her gossip. I won't allow her sordid wish to make me miserable affect the boys anymore, and I certainly will not allow you to resign as my GM, leave all the people you love and who love you while you sit back and take it. So, person, what do you say we go handle this—*together?*"

Em and Jax strolled the town square hand in hand with Dixie and Caine in tow. The Winter Solstice festival was in full swing, lights swayed from the trees and the gazebo was aglow with dozens of battery-operated candles.

Booths were set up along the street, the scent of hot buttered popcorn and plum wine mingled with the chilly breeze.

Maizy was waiting with Gage and Tag by the cotton candy booth. She waved when she saw Jax and bounced up and down. "Cotton candy, Daddy!"

"Sugar rush, huh, kiddo?"

Maizy cocked her head. "Hey! Why are you holding Miss Em's hand?"

Jax plucked a piece of her cotton candy from the cone and squeezed Em's hand. "Because I like her. That okay with you?"

Maizy grinned. "Uh-huh. Does holding hands mean she's your *girrlfriend?* Because Cooter James said it does."

Jax looked at Em and winked. "I dunno. Does this mean you're my *girrrlfriend,* Em?"

Em laughed, her heart lighter than it had been in weeks. "Well, if Cooter James says so, how do we dispute that? I guess I'm your *girrrlfriend.*"

"Can I go play in the bouncy house, Daddy?"

Jax nodded, tweaking a curl of her hair. "As long as you stay where Uncle Tag can see you, okay?"

"Okay," she yelled over her shoulder. "Bye, Miss Em. I'm glad you're my daddy's girlfriend!"

Jax dropped a kiss on her lips. "Daddy's glad, too."

Gage slapped his brother on the back and smiled at Em, his handsome face open and welcoming. "Emmaline, welcome to the Hawthorne family madness."

Em chuckled, her cheeks flushing. "Thank you kindly."

Tag grabbed hold of his brother and hugged him. "I'm proud of you. Good to see you again, Emmaline." He nodded to her before chasing after Maizy.

"Mommy!"

Gareth grabbed her legs from behind and squeezed.

Em turned to gather him up in a hug when, over his head, she met Clifton Senior's eyes.

"Can we talk?" he asked as he approached.

Jax tucked her next to him, making Gareth give her an odd look.

Clifton offered his hand to Jax. "Clifton Amos."

Jax assessed him before taking it. "Jax Hawthorne."

"I'd like a moment with you, Em, if I could."

She didn't know what to say. Here stood the man who wanted to take her children from her, who'd had her so afraid, she'd resigned from Call Girls and was going to begin hunting for a job he would consider more respectable.

Yet, here also stood the man she'd accused of being a coward for not showing more interest in his children by coming back to Plum Orchard to see them. Right in the middle of the town square.

Jax pulled her tight to him. "Will you be all right?"

Just knowing he was on her side was all she needed. She grazed his cheek with her finger. "I'll be just fine. Gareth, can you wait here with Jax while Mommy talks to Daddy for a minute?"

Gareth looked unsure until Jax said, "Bet my brother Gage has a ball. You wanna toss it around a little bit while we wait?" Jax held out his hand to him.

Gareth took it and nodded with a shy smile, sliding down Em's hip. "Okay."

Em turned to face Clifton, a man she'd once thought she would love forever, but now couldn't feel anything for. "What do you want, Clifton? The house? My car? Dora?"

Clifton held up his hands as a gesture of peace. "I want to apologize."

Her eyes pierced his. "For?"

He put his hands in his pockets, his face grim. "For everything. For leaving you and the boys while I tried to figure out what was happening to me. For hurting you, for lying to you. For threatening to take the kids. They need you, Em, and I overreacted."

"What brought on this sudden change of heart?"

"The realization that I was teaching Clifton to do the same thing I did. Run away. Look, Em, I don't want to see him beat up because of me, but I don't want to teach him to run away from it, either. I don't want anyone to ever keep him from being where he wants to be, and that's with you and Gareth. Here in Plum Orchard."

Her knees felt weak. "But he told you he wanted to live with you and Gina in Atlanta."

Clifton's chest expanded with a sigh. "He told me that when he was scared, when he was angry and hurt, Em. I used that to my advantage because I couldn't stand that I was the reason everyone was picking on him. I set him straight today, about why I left and about how it had nothing to do with you."

Clifton's hurt compelled her to reach out, put her hand on his arm and squeeze. "They need you, Clifton. They need you to be their father. If you're going to live your life with this truth you keep telling me about, then the truth is, you have to show up. You have to teach them how to live truthfully."

As people milled about them, the occasional few curious, pausing to stare at the town cross-dresser, Clifton nodded. "And stop hiding from everyone."

Em stayed quiet, keeping her eyes fixed on Clifton's jacket. When she'd first found out about Clifton's secret life, she'd ached for him, his infidelity aside. It had to be almost unbearable to watch all of your lifelong friends desert you just because you liked to wear a dress. Because they couldn't understand what it felt like to want to be someone else.

"I made this really hard on you, didn't I?"

Her spine stiffened in response to his hushed question. "If you want me to say this has been easy so you can ease your guilt, that won't happen. You left me to do it all while you had your crisis. But the rumors and the cruel treatment of the boys isn't entirely your fault."

"About that, I spoke to Principal Crawford today."

Her head shot up. "You did?" Clifton had taken an active part in his son's life? Maybe, just maybe, this was a start.

"I did. I made him very aware of just how ugly I can make things for him with the kind of connections Gina has."

"You threatened him? Oh, Clifton, is that really the way to handle it?"

"Sometimes you gotta get down in the mud, Em. I won't stand by and let Clifton get hurt. The boy who hit him will be punished, and a better eye will be kept on Clifton. I won't have my boy end up like one of those kids on the internet with a Facebook page dedicated to him because he did the unthinkable."

Em had to close her eyes at the thought. Close them

and squeeze. But he was right about running away. She'd been planning to do the same. Quit her job, take the boys and leave Plum Orchard. Move closer to Clifton in the hope that he'd drop the custody suit if he saw the boys more outside of Plum Orchard. "What about Call Girls?"

He scuffed his feet, looking away from her. "I was being a jackass. I know you keep the boys away from the sex talk, and I know Dixie and the girls love them. I just wanted to protect them, but I didn't think it through very well. Just like I haven't thought a lot of my life through very well. I'm still trying to figure this all out, Em. Me. Gina. How to deal with the boys, the people who turned their back on me. You got caught in the cross fire."

Relief washed over her, so much relief, her legs felt weak. "So where do we go from here, Clifton?"

He finally smiled at her under the twinkling lights of the tree. "Well, you go finish up your date with your new beau, and I spend some long-overdue time with my boys. Boys I promise to be there for, and we move forward and try to work this parenting thing out."

"Thank you, Clifton."

Clifton pulled her in and dropped a quick kiss on her cheek. "I hope Jax makes you really happy, Em. You deserve it."

He left her with those words and for the second time in a day, she felt like everything made perfect sense.

Twenty-Two

Which lasted all of ten seconds. "How sweet, you and Clifton makin' nice. Did he ask to borrow your nail polish?"

"Louella Palmer, I have a bone to pick with you!" Dixie hollered from across the square. The clack of her heels as she stormed over to them was matched only by the silencing of the crowd and the turn of heads.

And here they went again. Another loud, public display wherein Dixie would take up for poor, can't-stick-up-for-herself Emmaline Without A Spine.

No. More.

Marybell and LaDawn were right behind Dixie, ready to help her protect their friend.

And she loved them for it. She just didn't want it anymore. It was time to take a new tack with Louella. One she'd thought over while driving to the festival.

Em stepped in front of Dixie and smiled. "This one's on me."

Dixie's eyebrow rose in silent question, but she

backed right off, rolling her hand and giving Em the floor.

"Louella? Walk with me, won't you?" Em said, sticking her arm through Louella's. "And keep smiling or I'll tell everyone what you did in the corner of that hayfield with that summer worker Coon Ryder hired. In detail. While your mother listens."

Louella's body language said she hated Em's guts, but she strolled alongside her, smiling as they made their way through the surprised crowd. Em stopped at the benches, located just outside the perimeter of the square, and pointed. "Sit."

"How dare you tell me what to do?"

Em pointed to the bench. "Sit, Louella. Sit now. The summer of '93 hayfield hijinks are callin'."

Louella dropped down on the bench, crossing her legging-clad thighs and folding her hands in her lap. "So?"

Em sat next to her. Right up close. "I don't like you, Louella. You're mean and ugly and bitter about things you no longer have control over. Has all this, all that you've done, gotten you anything but some lonely satisfaction? Who do you celebrate your wicked victories with? Who pops the champagne and pours the bubbly with you?"

Louella glared at her.

"That's what I thought. No one. Who wants to celebrate little boys bein' beat up at school? Isn't that like pickin' the wings off moths?"

"That wasn't my fault, Em."

Em leaned into her, nudging her shoulder. "But it

is your fault. If you hadn't wanted to exact revenge on Dixie through me and something very private, none of this would have happened."

"Dixie deserves every rotten thing that happens to her."

"Because she stole a man who would have never been yours anyway?"

Louella's lips tightened.

"That's the truth, isn't it? Caine never loved you, and he never will. You'll always be second fiddle to Dixie Davis."

"Dixie Davis doesn't deserve Caine."

"Whether she deserves him or not isn't the point. She has him, you don't, Louella."

Louella's lips thinned to a cruel line. "You women are destroying the purity of Plum Orchard. This town's reputation was built on family and good Southern values. Phone sex is hardly a family value. How will we ever hope to drum up more tourism with a phone-sex company harbored in the middle of everything? Who wants to visit in a bed-and-breakfast that sits right in front of a company that sells sex, Emmaline? Who wants to have a cup of coffee right beside a woman that looks like she just stepped off the stage at some heavy-metal concert and scares children to boot?"

"Suddenly this is about the purity of Plum Orchard? You'd better look past the end of your stuck-up nose before you start lobbin' insults. And if you're referring to Marybell, when was the last time you went to the library and read to the children, Louella? Made balloon animals for the sick babies in the waiting room to ease their fears? When was the last time Louella Palmer did anything—anything other than stick her broken nose in where it didn't belong?"

Louella sat very still, her lips clamped tight.

Em shook a finger at her. "So, don't you talk purity and values to me. And don't you dare insult my friend with your fake values and your fake Southern nonsense. You don't care about whether the coffee shop thrives or how many guests stay at the bed-and-breakfast. Your jealousy fuels this grudge, Louella. Don't tell yourself anythin' other than that when you put your pretty head on your pillow."

When Louella didn't respond, Em went in for the kill. "Now, I've let you slander my good name. I've sat back and allowed you to gossip about me, watched my boys hurt by your narrow-minded thoughts, and it's about to end."

"I can't stop people from talkin', Em. People will do what they do."

"Will they do what they do when they find out how you got your dirty little hands on my birth certificate? The real one? That's a legal document, stolen from the State of Georgia's records."

Louella bristled, but she didn't crack. "You can't prove it was me."

"I can't, but that poor man who works down at Johnsonville Emergency surely can. The one you talked into doin' your dirty work for you. The one who helped you steal that birth certificate? The one that's married?"

Louella's eyes shifted. "What does that prove?"

Em folded her hands primly in her lap. "It proves

you were the one who sent me the birth certificate because when that poor, misguided man you lied to finds out you were only using him, he'll be angry enough to dust it for fingerprints for me. Now, while you're a smart girl, you're not that smart, but I am. I watched *Dexter*. All seven seasons."

Now she cracked—wide-open. "Spit it out, Em!"

"If you don't stop diggin' up things you have no right unearthing, if you don't make your puppets dance to a different tune, I will go to a lawyer. I'll show him the birth certificate and tell him you stole it from me. That nice lab man will back me up, too, because if he won't, I'll tell that nice forensic lab man's wife all about you. I wouldn't like it, but I'd do it to protect my children. These are some pretty serious offences, Louella. Isn't that identity theft? Some even require jail time if you're prosecuted. Won't that be somethin' here in lil' Plum Orchard? A trial. Maybe you might even end up on *truTV*. Imagine the tagline. Bitter, older Southern socialite seeks revenge and finds herself in hot water after the man she loves jilted her for prettier rival."

Louella's eyes, always so hard and cruel, hardened. "You'd never be able to prove a thing. It'd be your word against mine."

Em smiled and patted Louella on the arm. "Well, sure it would. But it'll make your life miserable for a little while—maybe even a long while. You know, the courts bein' so slow these days. And while we waited, all eyes would be on you, Louella Palmer, taking the heat off me. So let me say this loud and clear, you will never, ever say another word about Dixie, or my boys or me again. If my sons are harmed as a result of this spiraling any further out of control, if I hear people talkin' about me at Madge's, or anywhere, I'm holding you personally responsible, and I'm going to pick up my phone and call an attorney and drag the Palmer name through the mud. I'll make YouTube videos with cute captions and music. I'll start an online petition. I'll devote an entire Facebook page to you and your heinous Plum Orchard crimes. In short, I'll make you wish you'd gone off to your otherwordly resting place. Do we understand each other?"

Louella didn't answer; in fact, she sat very still, but it was all the understanding Em needed.

She slipped from her place on the bench and looked down at Louella and almost felt sorry for her. What drove her to be so cruel? "You're an awful person, Louella. I don't know why you do what you do. I don't know why you take such pleasure from hurtin' people by publicly humiliating them. I don't know why you don't put all that evil to better use. But I do know this— you'll die alone with the title Head Magnolia as your only purpose in this world if you keep goin' the way you're goin'. I hope you'll think about that before you hatch another hateful scheme, and before it's too late."

For the second time today, she held out her hand to someone who'd created a great deal of pain in her life. "Now, we're gonna walk back on over to the festival— *together*—and you're going to put a fake smile on your pretty face and we're gonna show everyone what a big girl Louella Palmer really is, or I'm going to find that microphone in the gazebo you're so fond of and use it."

Her lips tightened in an ugly purse, but she put her hand in Em's.

Together, they walked back to the square where Dixie and the girls and Jax waited for them. Astonished gazes flitted past them as they walked. There was even a surprised gasp or two.

But Em paid them no mind. Nothing was ever going to keep her from living her life again. Not all the cruel gossip, not the stares, not her mother and certainly not Louella Palmer.

Dixie and the girls stood wide-eyed, mouths open, a reflection that mirrored every other Plum Orchardian. "What happened?" Dixie was the first to ask.

Em winked. "Never you mind, Dixie Davis. That's between me and Louella Palmer. All you need to know is, no one's going to keep me from stayin' here in Plum Orchard."

Dixie gathered her up into a hug and squeezed. "I'm so proud of you."

Em squeezed back, catching a glimpse of Marybell, standing in the shadow of the tree by herself. Something was still off with her these days, despite her protests otherwise. She'd been so wrapped up in her own personal crisis, she'd let her concern fall to the wayside.

LaDawn tugged on a length of Em's hair and dropped a kiss on the top of her head. "Now that the most recent Louella Palmer crisis has passed, I'm gonna go find Gareth and see if I can talk him into winnin' me one of those teddy bears. You—" she tweaked Em's cheek "—have yourself a *good* night."

Em blew her a kiss before turning to Dixie. "Have you noticed Marybell's been actin' strange these days?"

Dixie's face was full of immediate concern. "What do you mean?"

"I mean, somethin's just not right with her. Can't put my finger on it, but it's been buggin' me since the party at your house. I'm gonna go check on her. You go see who you can slaughter at the apple-dunking booth, huh?"

Dixie's eyes widened, the thrill of a possible victory in her eyes. "There's an apple-dunking booth? How did I miss that?"

Em laughed. "Your competitive spirit's gettin' soft, Dixie Davis."

Dixie gave her one last look—searching her eyes. "So, we'll talk tomorrow? You know, about you bein' my sister and all?"

Em nodded and grinned, giving Dixie's arm a squeeze, and made her way to Marybell.

"Mama?"

She found Clifton Junior not far from Marybell's spot under the tree. "Hi, honey. How was your day?"

Clifton surprised her by hurling himself at her and giving her a hug. "I'm sorry I was so mean to you," he said, muffled against her arm, hiding his face.

Em reached down and cupped the back of his head, almost afraid to move for fear this would all disappear. "Oh, Clifton, I know you didn't mean it, but you know, no matter what, I love you, right?"

Clifton nodded. "As big as the whole wide world, right?"

Her heart tightened and twisted in her chest at the familiar phrase. "Bigger," she confirmed. "Now you go find your daddy and spend some time with him. Maybe you can see if he wants to give Aunt Dixie a run for her money at the apple-dunking booth?"

Clifton leaned back and smiled up at her. "Nobody can beat Aunt Dixie at anything."

Em laughed, sharing the first easy moment with her son in ages. "She's unstoppable." Grazing a thumb over his cheek, she sent him off to find his father.

Marybell, her spiked hair glowing under the twinkling lights of the tree, her shiny bracelets and eyebrow piercings all in place, smiled at her. "You go, Em. I'm so proud of you for going after what you want."

Em plucked at her arm. "Hey, can we talk?"

"You can always talk to me. Everything okay?"

Em gazed into her face, at her Kiss-like makeup and her purple lipstick, and knew she was right. "Is everything okay with you? I'm not buyin' what you were sellin' at Dixie's party, and I've been too wrapped up in my own misery to stop and tell you. But I wanted to remind you that I'm always here if you need to talk."

Marybell took a step back. Whether it was subconscious or not, she was letting Em know she was in her space. "That's so sweet, Em. But everything is fine. Why wouldn't it be?"

"I'm just checkin' on you. I didn't want you to think I'd forgotten you."

She smiled then, a warm tip upward of her lips beneath all that makeup. "I'm fine, Em, and I'm really happy for you and Jax."

Jax came up behind her, wrapping his arms around her waist and pulling her to his chest. "I hear my name. Evenin', Marybell."

Marybell's head dipped low again, her eyes skipping along the ground. "Evenin', Jax."

Em leaned back into his chest, sank into the warmth of him and sighed.

Tag's laughter rang out from behind Marybell, Maizy on his shoulders, her chubby fingers gripping his head. "Hey, you two—Maizy's all cotton-candied out. We're gonna head home and get our princess sleeps. I'm assuming you'll be late tonight, Jax?"

Em answered for him with a cheesy grin. "Assume correctly."

Tag chuckled, his eyes amused. "Well, all right then. You two have a good evenin'."

At the sound of Tag's voice, Marybell was suddenly all motion. She gave Em a quick pat on the arm and said, "I have to get going. G'night, lovebirds." She made a polite break for it, garnering more concern from Em.

"'Night, Daddy," Maizy crowed from her perch, distracting Em from her worry.

Jax pulled her down from Tag's shoulders for a kiss. "'Night, A-Maizy. Sweet dreams."

"Good night, Miss Em."

Em gave her a little wave and winked. "G'night, Miss Maizy."

As Tag trailed off with Maizy in tow, Em and Jax watched, leaning into one another.

She spun around. "So, Mr. Hawthorne, how do you

feel about givin' all these nosy busybodies somethin' to talk about?"

Jax chuckled low and husky. "Right here in the square? I'm all for loud and proud, but there are small children involved."

Em laughed. "Right here in the square," she said, and pulled him down for a kiss.

A very long, public display of all the incredible things he did to her kiss.

"I can't believe we're officially a couple and we're still holed up in this dive," Jax said, teasing her nipple with his tongue, trailing his hand over her hip and making her shiver.

Em sighed a happy, girlish sigh. "This was the place where it all began. It has sentimental value." She murmured her protest, threading her fingers through his hair and wrapping her leg around his waist.

He groaned in her ear. "It's cold and damp."

Em reached between them and grasped his cock, hard and hot. "This does not feel cold and damp."

Jax worked his way back up along her shoulder to her lips, slipping his hand between her thighs. "Neither does this."

Em squirmed when he spread her flesh and thumbed the swollen nub of her clit. "I think you should turn this into our sex palace."

Jax pulled her beneath him, settling between her thighs. "Thinking long-term already? I like it."

Em lifted her hips, and ran a finger along the strong lines of his jaw. When he thrust into her, she gasped, shuddering at the instant heat he always evoked in her. "I don't want to be presumptuous," she teased, nibbling at his ear, running her fingers through his hair.

Jax hiked her thigh higher over his hip and plunged deeper then withdrew almost all the way. "Towels," he huffed, raspy and tight in her ear. "We'll need towels."

"Towels?" Em gasped in return, meeting his thrusts, roaming her hands over Jax's strong back, reveling in this man she now called hers.

He slowed again, frustrating her and exciting her in the same movement. "You have to pick the color. You know…that freedom thing?" he said, watching her, tracing her lips with his finger.

Em wrapped her arms around his neck and pulled him tighter, moving with him, feeling the rise of heat in her belly, between her legs, until she cried out right along with Jax, luxuriating in the connection their skin made, finally free.

She clung to his neck while she collected herself, nestling against this man who wanted the real Em. "You know that madly-in-love thing?"

Jax lifted his head and grinned, rubbing his nose against hers. "Yeah. I do."

"You're gettin' closer," she whispered up at him. "So much closer."

* * * * *

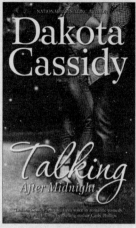

$7.99 U.S./$8.99 CAN.

Limited time offer!

$1.⁰⁰ OFF

From
national bestselling author

Dakota Cassidy

When Marybell's past comes calling, the
Call Girls prove no one handles scandal
like a Southern girl!

*Available June 24, 2014,
wherever books are sold!*

HARLEQUIN® MIRA®
www.Harlequin.com

$1.⁰⁰ OFF

the purchase price of
TALKING AFTER MIDNIGHT by Dakota Cassidy

Offer valid from June 24, 2014, to July 24, 2014. Redeemable at
participating retail outlets. Limit one coupon per purchase. Valid in the
U.S.A. and Canada only.

52611546

5 65373 00076 2   (8100)0 11930

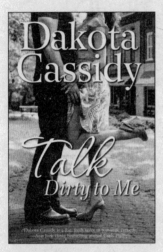

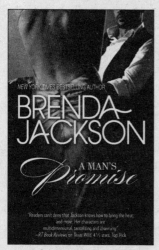

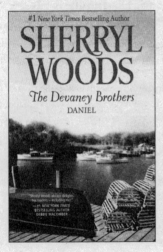

REQUEST YOUR FREE BOOKS!

2 FREE NOVELS
FROM THE ROMANCE COLLECTION
PLUS 2 FREE GIFTS!

YES! Please send me 2 FREE novels from the Romance Collection and my 2 FREE gifts (gifts are worth about $10). After receiving them, if I don't wish to receive any more books, I can return the shipping statement marked "cancel." If I don't cancel, I will receive 4 brand-new novels every month and be billed just $6.24 per book in the U.S. or $6.74 per book in Canada. That's a savings of at least 22% off the cover price. It's quite a bargain! Shipping and handling is just 50¢ per book in the U.S. and 75¢ per book in Canada.* I understand that accepting the 2 free books and gifts places me under no obligation to buy anything. I can always return a shipment and cancel at any time. Even if I never buy another book, the two free books and gifts are mine to keep forever.

194/394 MDN F4XY

Name	(PLEASE PRINT)
Address	Apt. #
City	State/Prov.	Zip/Postal Code

Signature (if under 18, a parent or guardian must sign)

Mail to the **Harlequin®** Reader Service:
IN U.S.A.: P.O. Box 1867, Buffalo, NY 14240-1867
IN CANADA: P.O. Box 609, Fort Erie, Ontario L2A 5X3

Want to try two free books from another line?
Call 1-800-873-8635 or visit www.ReaderService.com.

* Terms and prices subject to change without notice. Prices do not include applicable taxes. Sales tax applicable in N.Y. Canadian residents will be charged applicable taxes. Offer not valid in Quebec. This offer is limited to one order per household. Not valid for current subscribers to the Romance Collection or the Romance/Suspense Collection. All orders subject to credit approval. Credit or debit balances in a customer's account(s) may be offset by any other outstanding balance owed by or to the customer. Please allow 4 to 6 weeks for delivery. Offer available while quantities last.

ROM13R

#1 *New York Times* Bestselling Author

DEBBIE MACOMBER

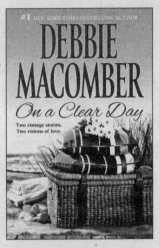

Two vintage stories.
Two visions of love.

A Man's Future…

Rand Prescott believes his chances
for happiness are limited because
he's going blind. When he meets
Karen McAlister, he begins to
imagine a different future—one
filled with love. Karen already
knows she wants to be with him for
the rest of her life, but Rand refuses
to bind her to a man who can't see.
Brokenhearted, she's prepared to
walk away. Can he really let her go?

A Woman's Resolve…

Joy Nielsen's latest patient, businessman Sloan Whittaker, is confined
to a wheelchair after a serious accident—and he's lost the will to walk.
Joy is determined to make sure he recovers, and once he does, she's
prepared to move on to her next patient, no matter how strongly she
feels about Sloan. There's only one problem. She doesn't think she can
get over him….

Available now, wherever books are sold.